Miss Julia Paints the Town

Miss Julia
Paints the Town

ANN B. ROSS

Doubleday Large Print
Home Library Edition

VIKING

This Large Print Edition, prepared especially for Doubleday Large Print Home Library, contains the complete, unabridged text of the original Publisher's Edition.

VIKING
Published by the Penguin Group
Penguin Group (USA) Inc., 375 Hudson Street,
New York, New York 10014, U.S.A.
Penguin Group (Canada),
90 Eglinton Avenue East, Suite 700,
Toronto, Ontario, Canada M4P 2Y3
(a division of Pearson Penguin Canada Inc.)
Penguin Books Ltd, 80 Strand,
London WC2R 0RL, England
Penguin Ireland, 25 St. Stephen's Green, Dublin 2, Ireland
(a division of Penguin Books Ltd)
Penguin Books Australia Ltd, 250 Camberwell Road,
Camberwell, Victoria 3124, Australia
(a division of Pearson Australia Group Pty Ltd)
Penguin Books India Pvt Ltd, 11 Community Centre,
Panchsheel Park, New Delhi - 110 017, India
Penguin Group (NZ), 67 Apollo Drive, Rosedale, North
Shore 0632, New Zealand
(a division of Pearson New Zealand Ltd)
Penguin Books (South Africa) (Pty) Ltd,
24 Sturdee Avenue, Rosebank,
Johannesburg 2196, South Africa

Penguin Books Ltd, Registered Offices:
80 Strand, London WC2R 0RL, England
First published in 2008 by Viking Penguin,
a member of Penguin Group (USA) Inc.

**This Large Print Book carries the
Seal of Approval of N.A.V.H.**

This is for Clare Ferraro, Carolyn Carlson and Ann Day, my guardian angels. Thank you.

Miss Julia Paints the Town

Chapter 1

Running my hand down the placket of my dress to make sure I hadn't missed a button, I walked down the hall, through the living room and, at the sight of Sam, came to an abrupt stop in the dining room archway.

"What are you doing?"

Sam lowered the *Abbotsville Times* and looked at me over his glasses. "Having breakfast, and good morning to you, Mrs. Murdoch."

My eyes swept the table where another place was set and the sideboard where chafing dishes steamed from the sterno flames under them. "Yes," I said with a distracted wave of my hand, "and good morning to you, too. Why are we eating in here?"

"I don't know, Julia. Lillian told me to sit in here, so here I am." He gave the paper a quick snap and turned a page. "I always do as I'm told." I rolled my eyes.

"Sausage and eggs're over there," he said with a nod toward the sideboard. "It's clear and sunny, about fifty-eight degrees. No rain expected." He looked up and smiled. "And my day just started when you walked in."

"Oh, you," I said, but I patted his shoulder as I went over to pick up a plate, giving thanks again for such a husband. Maybe some of his good nature would rub off on me.

Lillian pushed through the swinging door from the kitchen. "Thought I heard you in here," she said, setting a basket of hot biscuits on the table. "Y'all mighty late this mornin'. I already got Lloyd fed and off to school an' Miss Hazel Marie, too. She helpin' with some little chil'ren's readin' lessons."

"I guess I am late, what with the whole

household being rearranged in my absence," I said, somewhat crabbily since I'd not yet had my coffee. I put a spoonful of eggs on my plate and turned as Lillian started back to the kitchen. "Wait a minute, Lillian. What's gotten into you to serve breakfast in here? We've been eating in the kitchen for ever so long, and putting us in the dining room only means that many more steps for you."

"No'm, it don't. It jus' mean I have my kitchen to myself like I like it, without nobody comin' over to get coffee or help theyselves, or help me out when I don't need no help. Ever'body keep gettin' in my way when I'm tryin' to cook. And 'sides, that little boy ought to be learnin' what a dinin' room is for, which is for dinin', even though you don't hardly ever use it no more."

Well, that set me back on my heels, because she was right. A good part of my agenda for Hazel Marie's boy consisted of instructing him, by word and by example, in the finer things of life. Gracious living, along with observance of social and moral proprieties and conventions, was high on my list. And, assuredly, sitting down to a properly laid table in a restful environment would be considered an important part of anybody's idea of the decorous conduct of one's life. And, I conceded, it would be a welcome change from the usual hectic kitchen scene with everybody eating on the run, jumping up and down from the table and talking over each other.

"Well," I said, "well, I expect you're right. Thank you, Lillian, this is certainly pleasant and quite proper, too."

"Yessum," she said, pushing through the door, "that's what I mean."

As I took my place at the table, Sam gave me a sweet smile. He said, "Lillian keeps us on the straight and narrow, doesn't she?"

"Yes, she does." I picked up my napkin, noting that it was one of my good linen ones. "I'm not sure I like it, though, since I should've thought of it myself. Is the coffee hot?"

"Hot as hell and black as night," he said, lifting the silver pot from its trivet and filling my cup.

I had to laugh, although I'm not usually in a jocular mood so early in the day.

He refilled his own cup, then said, "Have you seen the paper this morning?"

"Why, no, Sam. You have it."

"Well, so I do," he said, as if he'd just noticed it in his hands. "Anyway, looks like our new mayor has taken the bit in his teeth. In spite of having run as a home-town boy, he's coming down clearly on the side of big-time developers. Listen to this, 'I'm doing what I think is best for Abbots-ville.' How do you like that?"

"What's he talking about?"

"Tearing down the old courthouse so some New Jersey developers can build on the site."

"New Jersey! What're they doing in Ab-botsville? I declare, Sam, I can't believe the mayor would be so foolish. He ought to know better." Stirring cream into my cof-fee, I sighed and went on. "What do they want to build?"

"Condominiums. Eight floors of them."

I nearly choked. "A *high-rise?* Why, Sam, there's not a building on Main Street taller than two stories. That thing would stick up like a sore thumb. The mayor is getting above himself. Nobody'll stand for it."

"Well, I don't know." Sam studied the article intently. "Says here that several Main Street merchants are all for it. They're

figuring that condominium residents trans-
late into downtown shoppers."

"Yes," I said, getting riled just thinking
about changes to our town, "and where
are they going to park? And what're they
going to shop for? There's nothing on Main
Street but antique shops and craft stores,
and when you've seen one, you've seen
them all. We have to do something, Sam.
They'll destroy all that gorgeous landscaping the garden club put in, and the gazebo,
Sam! We worked hard to make the grounds
a showplace, put up all those plaques and
markers and planted about a hundred azaleas. I can't tell you how many fund-raisers
we had to have to get all that done. And
now all those New Jersey people'll come
in here and bulldoze everything, tearing
down a historic landmark and throwing up
something that'll look nice for about two
years. Then they'll be gone with their profit
and we'll be left to live with an eyesore and
a blot on the landscape from then on."

Envisioning what our small town with its
three stoplights on Main Street could become, I said, "Why, Sam, they can't possibly consider tearing down the courthouse.
We may have a new one a few streets

over, but the old one ought to stay where it is. It's a stately building, and wasn't it built around the turn of the century? The twentieth century, I mean, which would make it about a hundred years old. So it's an antique and ought to be preserved and put to good use."

Sam looked over his glasses at me. "I'm not sure it's quite that old, Julia. But what good use?"

"Well, I don't know," I said, thinking about it for the first time. "I'd have to give it some thought. But there's plenty of space for meeting rooms. The garden clubs could use it and Scout groups and all kinds of civic and service clubs."

Still intent on the newspaper, Sam mumbled, "They like to meet where they can get lunch."

"Oh, I know," I said, fired up with a new thought. "Archives, Sam! It's perfect as a place to keep historical records and, if you ever finish your legal history of the county, that could be in there, too. Wouldn't that work?"

"It might. Why don't you propose it?"

"Well, I just might."

"Before you get too carried away," Sam

said, turning a page of the paper, "remember that the building's had problems for years. Every time the wind blows, the whole place begins to creak, and I always used to check the weather along with the docket. That's why the county built a new one, you know, too expensive to repair the old one. Uh-oh," Sam said, sitting up straight. "Listen to this, Julia. Assured Estate Planners may be in trouble."

"Who're they?" I asked, but I was barely interested, for my mind was still on the arrogance of our new mayor and how he might be brought down a notch or two.

Instead of answering, Sam turned a page and kept on reading. "Says here that the office has been closed for over a week and nobody's answering the phone. Investors haven't received their interest checks and can't find anybody to tell them why. That doesn't sound good."

"It certainly doesn't. People ought to be more careful where they put their money." I helped myself to another biscuit. "Pass the butter, please, Sam. But when you invest in a fly-by-night outfit, you have to take your chances."

Sam was so wrapped up in what he

was reading that he forgot the butter. "Not so fly-by-night, Julia, or at least it didn't seem so, considering who owns it. It's a fairly new corporation, but it's done well. Listen to this. One investor says he gave the company his entire life's savings, and he's not the only one. Looks like millions of dollars may be missing, and they're filing a complaint with the North Carolina Secretary of State's office, alleging fraud. That'll get some action, if they can find the owner."

That got my attention. "You mean the owner's missing? Who is it?"

Sam looked over the paper at me. "Richard Stroud."

I felt the bottom drop out. "Richard Stroud? You mean, *Helen's* Richard?" No wonder the name, Assured Estate Planners, had sounded familiar.

Sam nodded. "It's too bad, Julia. I know how much you think of Helen, and she'll surely suffer from this, even if there's a good explanation."

"Oh, Sam, she'll not only suffer, she'll be tarred with the same brush. I can't believe this." Then realizing what he'd said, I asked, "What kind of good explanation?"

"He could be sick or away at a business meeting," Sam said, but not with conviction.

"And his office help also sick at the same time or away at the same meeting? No, Sam, this is bad news for Helen." As I swallowed hard, struggling to regain my composure, another thought occurred to me. "She's not missing, too, is she?"

"Doesn't say. Just that no one answers at the Stroud home. She's not mentioned at all."

That was a relief, because a respectable woman like Helen wouldn't want her name to appear in a newspaper unless she'd been elected to an office, or won a blue ribbon at a flower show or been recognized for some honor. Or died.

But my relief didn't last long, as I thought of the consequences of Richard Stroud's sudden and unexplained absence. I rose from the table. "I'm going over to Helen's. She needs friends at a time like this."

I stumbled away from my chair, anxiety flooding my soul, determined, though, to get to the bottom of whatever was going on. Helen was one of the most admired women in town and a dear friend of mine.

I wanted to offer her what comfort and support I could, which under the circumstances might not be much. I didn't intend to mention it to her, because it would shame her beyond words, but if Richard Stroud had truly flown the coop, he'd taken some of my money with him.

Chapter 2

⌘

Sam was going to kill me. Well, not really, but it was all I could think of as I hurried to our bedroom. He would be disappointed and hurt if he found out that I, too, had invested a fairly decent amount with Assured Estate Planners.

I hadn't wanted any estate planning when I did it, since Binkie Enloe Bates, the young lawyer who took over Sam's practice when he retired, was doing an excellent job for me. But a certificate of deposit had matured a few months back, and I'd made the decision to put the proceeds into Richard Stroud's hands—as a courtesy to a friend's husband, you know. It had been a purely personal gesture on my part, and I had paid no attention to his company or its name. More's the pity now.

Still, I recalled that, at the time, he'd hinted heavily that he could do better with my assets than Binkie was doing, which had come close to offending me. He'd gone on to say that he could get a higher rate of return on my investments and save me on taxes as well. All I would have to do was sign on the dotted line, and he'd relieve me of any and all financial worries.

I'd ignored his sales talk, since I'd gone in for one transaction and one transaction only and had no intention of signing over my half of Wesley Lloyd Springer's estate to anybody. If something sounds too good to be true, nine times out of ten, it is. Besides, I hadn't liked the way he'd implied that Binkie didn't know what she was doing.

Because Binkie did. She looked after my assets like they were her own, and if she ever needed financial advice, she consulted Sam, who most certainly knew what he was doing. Besides, Sam was the trustee for the other half of Wesley Lloyd's estate which would come to Lloyd, my late and unmourned first husband's illegitimate child, so Sam had a finger in my half of the estate's pie as well. That gave me the benefit of two financially knowledgeable heads for the price of one.

So why had I invested even a minimal amount with Richard Stroud? Well, for one thing, he'd spent most of his working life in real estate, buying and selling and seemingly coming out ahead every time. And I liked real estate. I liked it much more than pieces of fluctuating corporations in the form of stocks, when the CEOs made off with millions while the corporations failed.

They're not making any more land, you know. Richard said he was putting together a real estate venture, and my contribution would give me a voice in how it was structured and developed. Saying what, how and where something was to be built had appealed to me, because there'd been too many architecturally challenged buildings already thrown up in our area of the state. I couldn't help but believe that any such venture would benefit from my input.

And, as I've said, the other reason I'd

invested with him was Helen. You couldn't ask for a nicer, more willing person. Helen had been an officer in every civic, social and religious organization I knew of. Why, she'd been president of the garden club for three terms running, and we only elected somebody else when she broke her hip last winter and had to be in a full-body cast for weeks on end. Every once in a while, Helen had implied to me that she'd like to just attend a meeting sometime without having to chair it, but she was generally amenable to whatever anybody wanted her to do. She was the most capable and trust-worthy woman I knew. I had thought it an act of friendship to put a little money into her husband's hands and, in the doing, lend my support to a local business.

I stood in the middle of the bedroom with all these thoughts running through my mind, wondering what I should do. If Richard was really guilty of fraudulent behavior with other people's money, and mine, it would be a scandal of monumental pro-portions. How would Helen bear up under it? Or had she known what he was doing all along? Was she now off somewhere on a South Sea island with him?

Lord, I couldn't believe it. Not of her, of all people. Still, you never know.

I had a sudden pang in my breast, remembering another office that Helen held. She was the treasurer this year of the Lila Mae Harding Sunday School class and had our weekly collections in her keeping.

Giving myself a mental shake, I recalled that our Sunday school offerings couldn't amount to enough to finance a flight from fraud, much less a trip to the South Seas.

"What you doin' jus' standin' there?"

"Oh, Lillian," I gasped, spinning around. "You scared me to death. My mind was a million miles away."

"You ought to be settin' down. You as white as a sheet. You want me to call Mr. Sam?"

"No. No, don't do that. I'm all right. I've just had some disturbing news. Lillian, you know Helen Stroud, don't you?"

"Yessum, she that little lady what always look so put-together. Her husband in the real estate bus'ness, I think."

"Well, not anymore, apparently. It's in the paper this morning. It looks like he's absconded with all his investors' money."

"He what?"

"Left. Gone. They can't find him, and his office is locked up tight. Nobody knows where their money is, if he's lost it or stolen it or what."

Lillian frowned. "How'd he get they money in the first place?"

"Well, they gave it to him. To invest and make more money. You know, like when you put money in a bank and it makes interest."

She laughed. "My money don't stay in long enough to make anything."

I nodded. "You're more right than you know." The way interest rates were these days, you were more likely to lose money than gain it. I decided, then and there, to make arrangements with Binkie to look after what I'd provided for Lillian when I passed on, even though I didn't intend to do so anytime soon.

It was just such innocent and trusting people like Lillian who got hurt in this current scandal. Well, Lord, and like me, too.

"Anyway, I'm going over to Helen's. She'll be prostrate with shame, if I know her. And worried, too, if Richard's taken off without her." I took a sweater out of the dresser drawer. "It's still a little nippy out there, isn't it?"

"Yessum, you'll need that, but it s'posed to warm up later on." Lillian's face was knotted with concern. "I might know some people what give they money to Mr. Stroud. I hope I don't, but I maybe do. What you think he do with it, if he not in bus'ness no more?"

"I don't know, Lillian. I can't imagine that he started out deliberately to steal from his investors. He is a Presbyterian after all. More likely, he made some poor investments and then couldn't meet his obligations." I thought about the frantic efforts Richard Stroud must've made to prevent exactly what had apparently happened. "On the other hand," I went on, "there's such a thing as a pyramid scheme, where you pay your first investor with money from your second one and on and on down the line. The problem comes when you stop getting new investors."

"Law, that sound like robbin' Peter to pay Paul."

"Exactly. Maybe that's what happened, but anyway, I've got to go see Helen and reassure her that whatever Richard did, or is still doing, won't reflect on her." Of course it would, but I'd pretend otherwise.

After slipping on my sweater and finding my purse and car keys, I went through the dining room to let Sam know that I'd be back soon.

Finding the room empty, I called to Lillian, "Has Sam already gone?"

"Yessum, he make a telephone call, then say he got to make steps."

"Well, that's odd," I said, but it was more than that. As far as I could remember, this was the first time that Sam had left the house without a by-your-leave, much less a good-bye kiss. Since my first husband had held in contempt any demonstrations of fondness, I had thought I'd never get used to being married to a man of Sam's affectionate nature. But the bereft feeling that swept over me made me realize that I was not only well accustomed to it by now, I missed it when it wasn't there.

"He say to tell you," Lillian went on, "to tell Miz Stroud if she need help to let him know."

"I'll do that," I said, picking up my pocketbook and heading for the door. I left, wondering what had been so important that Sam would leave without saying a word to me.

Driving the few blocks to Helen's neatly landscaped Cape Cod house, I commiserated with her situation by reflecting on my own fairly recent past. If anybody knew what it was like to bear the brunt of a husband's missteps, errors in judgment or actual crimes, I did. Whatever Richard had done would indeed reflect on Helen, her longtime reputation for good deeds notwithstanding. They would all be for naught if he'd actually defrauded his clients. She would be linked to his misdeeds from now on, regardless of her innocence. Unfortunately, that's what for better or for worse meant, although none of us thought of that when we made our marital vows.

Well, I thought as I eased through a four-way stop, I could certainly speak from experience, which might be of some help to Helen. I still carried some of the scars left over from my first marriage. So, if Helen listened to anyone, she would do well to listen to me. My advice would be to hold her head up and plow right on, leading her life as she'd always done, in spite of what people might say. One thing was for certain, I didn't intend to urge her to *stand by her man* without regard for whatever mischief he was up to.

I smiled grimly, remembering Hazel Marie humming that tune while she straightened her closet just the other day. She'd stopped in the middle of the chorus and looked at me as if a light had suddenly turned on.

"That's Tammy Wynette's signature song, Miss Julia, but I just thought of something. That woman had five husbands in all and didn't stand by a one of them. Where does she get off, telling other people to do what she didn't do herself?"

At the time, I hadn't been interested in the romantic antics of the country singers who entranced Hazel Marie. But as I pulled into the Strouds' driveway, I realized that Miss Wynette's advice would surely be urged on Helen. Presbyterians believe in standing by your man, too. Except not this Presbyterian, for it was to my everlasting regret that Wesley Lloyd Springer had passed before I'd known enough to cut my losses for all and sundry to see. Every time I thought of what he'd done, which wasn't all that often these days, I had to deliberately remind myself of how all things work together for good—the good, in this case, being Hazel Marie and Lloyd in my life, and Sam in my bed.

I stepped out of the car and started toward the brick walk to Helen's door. The grass in the neatly mown lawn and the azalea bushes on each side of the entrance looked fresh and new from the showers we'd had during the night. Except for some birds flitting around in an oak tree, nothing stirred. The garage doors were closed, and the curtains in every window were drawn tight. That wasn't like Helen. Ordinarily, her house would be open and immaculate, which was the way she kept it. By this time of the morning, she would have been planning her next meeting or making calls or checking her calendar. But everything was still and quiet.

I sidestepped a puddle on the brick walkway, admiring the herringbone pattern as I walked up onto the front stoop. I rang the doorbell, not once but three times. Then I used the lion's head knocker, which I usually hesitate to do at any house because the thundering noise it makes shatters my nerves. But there was no movement or sound from inside. So I removed a calling card from my purse and jotted a note to Helen on the back. Then I slipped it into the mail slot, hoping it wouldn't slide across her highly polished floor and lie hidden under her Williamsburg block-front chest.

Feeling more concerned than ever after my futile attempt to comfort a friend, I walked back to the car. Just as I opened the door and started to slide in, I felt the presence of someone right behind me.

Whirling around, I almost bumped into a slender man who was hanging onto my door, looking avidly at me.

"Who are you?" I demanded, clutching my pocketbook.

"Andy Jordan, ma'am. *Abbotsville Times.* Would you care to make a statement?"

Chapter 3

"About what?"

"About your husband. Where is he? What do you think of the fraud charges filed against him? Is he willing to be interviewed so he can tell his side of the story?"

I looked the young man up and down, sweeping my eyes up from his muddy sneakers to the Panthers ball cap on his head, taking note of his pleated khakis and his overly large windbreaker and the stenographer's pad in his hand. His other hand held a poised Bic.

"Young man," I said, drawing myself up

sharply, "I don't know how long you've been in this line of work, but you have accosted the wrong person. I am not Mrs. Stroud, but I am a friend of hers and you may quote me on that."

I couldn't believe it. He immediately started scribbling on his pad. "And your name and address? I'll need your age, too."

"You'll need a lot more than that before I'm through." I slid into the car and slammed the door. The idea, wanting to know my age. What is it with people who think they can ask the most personal questions and expect an answer?

I cranked the car and backed out, hoping but not especially caring if he was out of the way.

"Sam!" I called as I came through the back door at home. "Where is he, Lillian?"

She turned from the sink, water dripping from her hands. "At his house, I reckon. That's where he go every morning of the week."

"Oh, well, I was hoping he'd be back by now."

Other than his strange omission earlier

that morning, Sam was usually fairly regular in his routine. Every weekday he went to the office at his house to work on a legal history of the county, something that kept him occupied and out from underfoot. He said he'd been doing paperwork all his working life, and retirement just meant more of it.

"What's the matter with you anyway?" Lillian said, looking closely at me. "You all out of breath."

"I'm all right. At least I think I am." Just as I started across the kitchen, I changed my mind and collapsed onto a chair by the table. "Oh, Lillian, the newspaper is already after Helen. They're going to smear her all across the front page. I know they will."

"Why they do that?" Lillian asked, frowning at the thought. "She don't take nobody's money. What she say, anyway?"

"Nobody answered the door, and everything was closed up. Oh, Lillian, what if she took off with Richard?" I slumped over the table, then with a renewed spurt of anxiety, said, "A newspaper reporter jumped out of the bushes and wanted to interview *me*. At first, he thought I was Helen, then he wanted *my* name and address. And my *age*!"

Lillian smiled. "What you tell him?"

"That it was none of his business," I said. "Or words to that effect." I leaned my head on my hand. "Oh, Lillian, this is so upsetting. I don't know whether to be mad at Richard for stealing or worried about him for being falsely accused. And I don't know if Helen has aided and abetted him or if she's as crushed by this as we are."

"If I was you," Lillian counseled, "I wouldn't judge neither one of 'em, 'less I be judged likewise. You ought to wait 'fore you do anything till you know who done what. But, I tell you one thing, Miz Stroud ought to be gettin' herself a good lawyer." Lillian punctuated that statement with a firm nod of her head. "Though I try not to ever need one."

"Maybe that's what Sam meant when he offered to help. I know he'd give her good advice. Except he's retired, and may not be able to. But if they're coming after her, she does need a good lawyer."

"Maybe she talk to Miss Binkie."

I shook my head. "I don't think so. Binkie doesn't do criminal law, and Helen may need one who does. Richard certainly will."

I started to moan again, but the sound of the front doorbell stopped me. "Maybe that's Helen now." I rose from the chair to answer it, then said, "But probably not. If she wouldn't answer her own door, why would she be at mine?"

Hurrying through the living room, I hoped my visitor would be Helen or at least someone with news of her. As soon as I opened the door, though, it was LuAnne Conover who breezed past me and headed for my Victorian sofa.

"Julia, I am so mad I could spit," she declared, her mouth so tight she could barely get the words out. My closest friend for many years plopped down and glared at me as if I were the object of her anger.

"I expect a lot of people're upset," I said, as I sat down beside her, glad to have someone to talk with. "I am, too, but we don't know that anything really wrong has happened. Sam says there may be a perfectly reasonable explanation."

She glanced up at me through narrowed

eyes. "Perfectly reasonable . . . ? How can you say that?"

"Well, he could be sick, or just needing to get away for a while. This could all be the fault of his office help. You know, the mice will play when the cat's away."

She jerked upright and stared at me as if I were crazy. "He doesn't *have* office help! Why would he?"

"Well, I don't know, LuAnne, I just assumed. Anyway, I guess you invested with him . . ."

"Of *course* I invested in him. What do you think I've been doing for forty-one years!"

"Uh, LuAnne, are we talking about the Strouds?"

"Helen?" A shocked look passed over her face. "You think it's Helen?"

"Well, no. Actually, I think it's Richard."

Shock turned to horror as she gaped at me. "Richard? No, oh, no." She suddenly leaned over and put her head between her knees. "I'm going to be sick."

"Let's get you to the bathroom," I said, standing and trying to pull her up.

She resisted me, and finally straightened up. "Quit pulling on me, Julia, I'm all

right. But my nerves are shot. Just look."
She held out a trembling hand for me to
see, then used it to push back her hair.
"This is where faith comes in, Julia, when
you need strength to bear up. But it's such
a shock to even consider . . . what you
said."

"What did I say?"

She waved her hand and turned away.
"He said he wanted to get away for a while
and think about things. Why would he want
to do that? He's never needed to think
about things before."

I sat down again. "You've been in touch
with him? Has Helen? Is she with him?"

LuAnne sprang to her feet. "It *is* Helen,
isn't it? How long have you known? Why
didn't you *tell* me, Julia?"

"Tell you what? All I know is what was in
the paper."

I thought LuAnne was going to keel over.
"The paper? It was in the newspaper?
How did the state of my marriage become
a news item? Who told them?"

"Your marriage? I thought you were talking about Richard and Helen."

"I didn't start off talking about them,"
she screeched, shaking her finger at me,

"but if you know something, you owe it to me to tell me. I can't believe it's Helen. I thought she was a friend, a close friend, but if she's done this . . . Oh, that sly, deceitful woman! Butter wouldn't melt in her mouth, while all along they've been sneaking around behind my back."

"Wait a minute, LuAnne, I'm lost here. I don't know a thing about Helen. All I know is that Richard has apparently defrauded his clients and skipped town. That's what was in the paper. Not a word about Helen or you or your marriage. Now, start at the beginning and tell me what's wrong."

She balled up her fists and stood before me, trembling with the effort to control herself. "You're sure it's not Helen? *Or* Richard? Because if it is, believe you me, I am going to take steps."

"I'm pretty sure it's not either one. Now, what's going on with your marriage?"

LuAnne sat back down, then she leaned her head against the sofa back and gazed at the ceiling. "I think Leonard's lost his mind. I truly question his sanity. He's moved out, Julia, can you believe that? So he can have some space, of all things. What does he need with space, I ask you? I'm the one who needs space, but you don't see me moving out and breaking up a perfectly good marriage." Color bloomed on her face and her eyes took on a fiery glint. "He *says* there's nobody else, but I'll tell you this, there has to be. Leonard can't cook, he can't do laundry and he can't pick up after himself. He can't even find the remote when he's the one who punches it all the time. What's he going to do in all this *space* he wants?"

If I'd been shocked at Richard Stroud's alleged misdeeds, it was nothing compared to what I felt at hearing of Leonard Conover's sudden about-face. The man was a nonentity in our circle of friends. He had few social skills and little interest in anybody or anything. He simply existed, following meekly on the heels of his wife's bright chatter and avid concern about everything in town. And now, suddenly, he needed space? Room to find himself?

What would he find when he looked?

I couldn't help but lower my voice, in awe if nothing else. "You really think there's another woman?"

LuAnne's eyes narrowed. "There's *always* another woman, Julia. Especially for a man like him—you just don't know. But I'll tell you one thing. When I find out who she is, I'm going to pull out every hair on her head."

Chapter 4

"Now, LuAnne," I cautioned, "you don't know that there's anybody else. I can't imagine there would be. Leonard's not the flighty kind, and I've never seen him give any woman a second look." Barely a first one, if the truth be known.

"You're not hearing me, Julia," LuAnne said, smacking her knee with a fist. "Leonard has *needs.* He may be looking for space, but he'll fill it as soon as he can." Her whole body began to shake.

"Oh, LuAnne, I'm so sorry. But if I were you, I'd just let him go and let him find out how much he needs you." I took her hand in mine and pressed on. "I hate to see you torn up like this. Leonard can't get along without you, and it's not going to take any time for him to find that out."

"Julia," she said, taking a deep breath, "I'm going to tell you something I've never told a living soul. And if you repeat it, I'll never speak to you again."

"Of course I won't repeat it," I said, drawing back in offense. Between the two of us, *I* was not the gossip.

"Well, you better not." LuAnne bit her lip as her flinty eyes probed the room. "This is just between you and me. And Leonard, of course, but he won't know that you know." She glanced at me, then looked down at her hands. "Leonard wants to . . . you know, all the time, and I mean almost every night. He nearly wears me out, but I know that some men have stronger needs than others, and Leonard's one of them."

"*Every* night?" I whispered, almost struck dumb by the thought.

"Well, it's gotten worse since he retired and started taking that medicine. He doesn't have enough to occupy him, you know, so it weighs on his mind."

I glanced across the room at the hall

door that led to our bedroom, wondering if Sam's behavior would change when he finished his legal history. Lord, I'd have to think of something else he could research.

"My word, LuAnne, I don't know what to say." Except, if it were me, I'd be glad he'd moved out.

"Wait a minute," I said, recalling a similar scene from the past. "Didn't you have the opposite trouble with him a couple of years ago? I mean, when he had no interest at all in, well, in what we're talking about?" I clearly remembered LuAnne sitting on this very sofa lamenting Leonard's total lack of what she called *needs*. At the time, not long after Wesley Lloyd's passing and my discovery of his secret life in which he'd pursued needs that I'd never known he had, I'd not been all that sympathetic with LuAnne's loss of marital comforts. As far as I'd been concerned, she would've been better off without a husband at all, since my own husband had betrayed and abandoned me.

But now that I had Sam, my views on marriage and the comforts therein had undergone a change, and the thought of how I'd feel if he suddenly wanted some space made me ache for LuAnne. Of course, Leonard was no Sam, so it was hard to see why she'd want to hold on to him.

"You're right," LuAnne said, nodding. "He did go through a little spell when I would've done anything for a little affection. I mean, there was nothing, nothing at all for the longest time. But when he went on that medicine, well, it's just been constant." She looked at me to see how I was taking this intimate information. "It's been either feast or famine."

"Well, it seems to me that his doctor could regulate that medication. You should be able to reach a happy medium somewhere. Or just take his medicine away from him. I bet he'd settle down then."

She shook her head. "He'd just get more of it. That doctor he sees over in Asheville thinks he's a real success story. But I'll tell you this, Julia, I think Leonard's sick, I mean, really sick. No man in his right mind would be trying to find himself at his age. Why, he's pushing seventy, which is just asking for a stroke or a heart attack."

"That's a dangerous age," I said, almost to myself. Everybody thought that the forties was the age that men started to stray, but from what I'd seen, the older they were the closer you had to watch them. And add a little medication to the mix, and you'd have a man with more than a gleam of recaptured youth in his eye.

"I know it is." LuAnne blew her nose. "You wouldn't believe all the old men who have come on to me."

"Who?"

She waved her hand in dismissal. "I think Leonard's going through the change, like a lot of them do. And he can just suffer through it like I did. He might have his eye on some other woman, but by the time I get through telling all I know, she won't have hers on him."

"Now that's the way to think," I said, wanting to encourage her. "Just keep your wits about you and look at it rationally. And think of this, LuAnne, half of his retirement money is yours. Let him try to manage two households on his pension and see how he likes it. I'll be surprised if he lasts a week without you."

She was silent for a few minutes, thinking over what I'd said. Then in a quiet voice, she said, "I'm not sure I'd want him back, if he came just because he couldn't afford another place."

"I wouldn't, either."

"But, oh, what am I going to do without him?" And she dissolved into tears, rocking back and forth and moaning.

Well, Lord, I didn't know, except I'd done fairly well in the same circumstances. And not just fairly well—I'd done better than I'd ever done in my life. But she wasn't ready to hear that.

"How am I going to hold my head up, Julia?" LuAnne said, as she pressed the wet remnants of a Kleenex to her mouth. "Everybody'll know that he left me for somebody else. They'll think something's wrong with me. Nobody'll know how I've tried to please and satisfy him. All they'll see is him off with somebody else while I'm sitting home alone—an abandoned wife is what I'll be. I can't stand the thought of it."

I was about to lose any sympathy at all for her. I'd gone through much worse, and I'd never cried and moaned on anybody's shoulder. I'd made sure that nobody knew the trouble in my soul. I'd handled the pain and shame on my own and had never let anybody see how much it had hurt. So I wanted to shake LuAnne and tell her to dredge up some dignity from somewhere. Why try to hang on to somebody who wanted to be gone? Say good-bye and good riddance, and get on with your life.

But LuAnne wasn't the kind of person you could say that to. The appearance of a good marriage was more important to her than whatever went on inside it.

Hearing the swish of the swinging door from the kitchen, I looked up to see Hazel Marie walking through the dining room. When she saw LuAnne with her face buried in her hands, Hazel Marie stopped, her mouth dropping open. She gave me a questioning look, then turned and tiptoed back out.

LuAnne lifted her head and straightened her shoulders. "I'll tell you one thing, though," she said with sudden resolve as she dried her face. "I'm not going to take it lying down. Leonard Conover is not going to play me for a fool. I'll make sure that everybody in town knows what a randy old goat he is. He won't be able to hold his head up by the time I get through." Her fist came down on the sofa this time. "And I'm going to start with the pastor. We'll just see how Leonard likes being drummed off the diaconate for adultery!"

She stood up, preparing to go immediately across the street to the First Presbyterian Church where Pastor Ledbetter reigned supreme.

"But you don't know that, LuAnne," I said. "I can't believe that Leonard's taken up with anybody. But," I hurried on as she turned an angry gaze on me, "talking to the pastor is a good idea." I wasn't sure that it was, though, because getting the pastor on Leonard's case could backfire on her. If the pastor laid a load of guilt on Leonard and pushed him back into a marriage he no longer wanted, what good would that do LuAnne?

Well, probably a lot, given LuAnne's concern with simply having a husband of any kind at her side. I felt a deep tug of pity for her since I now knew what a real marriage could be.

As LuAnne stood before my Chippendale mirror and began to repair some of the damage to her face, I heard the telephone ring in the kitchen. Since both Hazel

Marie and Lillian were nearby, I ignored it and went on trying to encourage LuAnne.

"I'm sure things will work out," I said, patting her back. "Leonard will realize how much you mean to him, and he'll be back. Why, LuAnne, he may even be thrilled to come home. This little episode may be just the thing to rejuvenate your marriage."

She gave me a withering look. "It's not just a little episode, Julia, and I resent you calling it that. My whole life is being torn apart and here you are, acting like it's nothing at all."

"Well, I'm sorry," I said, taken aback. "I didn't mean to downplay it, you know I didn't. I'm just trying to find a bright side to all of this."

"There *is* no bright side." She snapped her pocketbook closed and stomped toward the door. "The pastor will know what to do, even if nobody else does. The only good thing about having troubles: You learn who your *real* friends are."

And out she went, leaving me stunned, though I shouldn't have been. I always seemed to say the wrong thing to her, even with the best will in the world. As I closed the door behind her, I leaned my head against the wall, wishing I'd been able to find the right words to say. Lord knows, I knew what it was to have an errant husband. And I'm certainly not referring to Sam.

"Miss Julia?" Lillian came into the living room. "Telephone for you. She don't say who it is, but I think it that Miz Stroud."

Chapter 5

❧

"Helen?" I said, as I pressed the phone to my ear, anxious to hear her voice.

"Who?"

"Is this Helen?"

"No, Julia, it's Mildred, your neighbor. Remember me?"

"Oh, Mildred," I said, trying to cover the disappointment I felt. I'd lived next door to Mildred Allen for years and should've recognized her voice. "I'm sorry. I was hoping it was Helen, not that I'm not glad to hear from you, but, well, you know."

She sighed. "I do know, and that's why I'm calling. I was having breakfast in bed and reading the paper when I came across the article about Richard. And it has just floored me. Who would've thought he was a thief? I mean, he was so nice, always a gentleman and, if anybody could be such a thing in Abbotsville, suave, wouldn't you say?"

"Yes, I guess I would." But I had to think about it. *Suave* was not a word I'd normally associate with anybody in Abbotsville. But Richard Stroud had always appeared to be the most thoughtful of men, treating Helen with the utmost courtesy. A lot of men make an effort to be thoughtful of women in general, but ignore their wives. Not Richard. He treated Helen as if she were a queen, and many of her friends threw Richard up to their own husbands as a model to be emulated. Which didn't make him all that well liked by the men in our circle. But maybe that's too strong. It wasn't that they didn't like him—he was, after all, successful in his business and that's always admired. His real estate business, I mean, not his estate planning business, as we had all just learned.

"Julia," Mildred went on, "I'm going to tell you something that I don't want you to repeat. If you tell anybody, I'll never speak to you again."

"I'm not in the habit of breaking a confidence, Mildred. You know me better than that."

"Yes, well, that's why I called you. I have to tell somebody, because it's just eating me up." She paused, took a breath, then as if she could hold it no longer, went on in a rush. "I invested with him."

"You did? Oh, Mildred, how much? No, wait, I didn't mean to ask that. I mean, was it a little or a lot?"

"Well, it depends on how you look at it," she said. "To some people it might seem a lot. For me, I'd say it was maybe a medium amount."

"Oh, my," I murmured, for Mildred Allen was one of the wealthiest women in town. She had inherited old money, which was much more respectable than the new money that had come to me, although when it comes down to it, money is money, regardless of its age. But, knowing her financial status, I knew that a medium amount to her would choke your average horse. "Well, since we're having true confessions here, I'll admit that I did, too."

"You did? You don't know how much better that makes me feel, Julia. Everybody knows how good Sam is with money, so if he recommended Richard, I don't feel so foolish."

"You might as well go ahead and feel foolish, because I did it on my own. Although I'd call my investment a small amount, certainly compared to yours. Still and all, I don't want to lose it. Now, Mildred, Sam doesn't know a thing about it, and I want to keep it that way. So don't you tell him."

"I won't say a word. But do you think they'll put investors' names in the paper?"

"I hadn't thought of that." I pictured a list of the names of prominent people on the front page and cringed. "Surely they won't. Wouldn't they have to have our permission?"

"I don't know, but I'm about ready to sue somebody and if Richard can't be found, why, I'll just sue whoever's left."

I let the silence lengthen as I thought about that. Then as her meaning became clear, I said, "You can't mean Helen? Mildred, I can't believe she had anything to do with whatever he's done."

"Maybe not, but they own property and that house of theirs would go a long way toward returning what he's stolen from me."

"Oh, Mildred, you wouldn't sell Helen's house out from under her, would you?"

"If that's what it takes, then that's what it takes. Besides, I only invested with Richard because of her. I think the world of Helen and wanted to show it by supporting him. She has to take the bad along with the good, like we all do when it comes to husbands."

"Not necessarily," I said with some asperity. "What if Helen didn't know what he was doing? What if he's fooled her, too? It's not right to punish her, just because Richard's gone and she's not."

"It's just business, Julia. I would expect the same treatment if Horace did something like that and, believe me, people would be after me in a shot if he did. That's why I don't let him get within a mile of my assets."

It was a well-known fact in town that Horace Allen hadn't cracked a lick at a snake ever since he'd married Mildred years ago. Oh, he'd piddled with first one thing and another, but never in a forceful way. Mainly because Mildred kept him on a short financial leash, and he seemed content enough to be her consort rather than her partner. Over the years, Mildred had intimated to me that she doled out clothes money and spending money to him, along with just enough to allow him to dabble in flipping a run-down house or two every now and then. Actually, though, the only real job Horace had ever had was being Mildred's husband, but his pay could hardly be commensurate with the demands of the job.

I drummed my fingers on the countertop after hanging up the phone, distressed by Mildred's threat to sue Helen. If that was the first thought Mildred had had, wouldn't the other investors soon come up with the same idea?

Lord, I couldn't bear the thought of Helen being stripped of everything she owned. Then I realized, as I mused about it, that I didn't know if Helen owned anything. Some men put all their assets in their names alone, and Richard may have been one of them. It might have made it easier when he was buying and selling property not to have to run home every time to get her signature.

So if Helen got sued, the suers would still end up with nothing. Of course, Helen would, too, which might be exactly what she had now. Except she'd end up with an added load of shame for being taken to court.

I could've wrung Richard's neck. Well, and Helen's too, if she'd taken off with him.

"You want some coffee?" Lillian held the pot over a cup, ready to pour. "You look like you need some."

"Yes, I do, Lillian. Thank you. I declare," I said, sitting at the kitchen table, "this started out as a perfectly normal day and look what all has happened. Richard Stroud has apparently taken off with other people's money and his wife is nowhere to be found. And Mildred Allen is up in arms and ready to sue Helen, and Leonard Conover has left LuAnne to find himself and she's . . . Oh, my goodness," I said, clamping my hand over my mouth, "I wasn't supposed to tell that. You have to keep it to yourself, Lillian. Don't tell a soul."

"No'm," she said, as she sat across the table from me and reached for the sugar bowl. "I don't never tell anything I hear in this house."

"Well, good." I picked up my cup and brought it to my mouth, then set it back down. "You know I don't normally tell everything I know, but knowing LuAnne, it'll be all over town by nightfall. Which doesn't excuse me, but it makes me feel a little better."

"Uh-huh." Lillian nodded, her attention on the sugar she was stirring in her coffee. She knew my friends and was interested in what happened to them, but she was rarely personally affected by whatever they did. So she was a good person to talk to, even though I'd promised not to talk to anybody. That didn't include Sam, though. I took it as a given that anything anybody told me would be shared with him. And here I'd told someone else.

Well, in for a penny . . .

"Lillian, can you believe that Leonard Conover had the gumption to just up and move out? As concerned as I am about Helen, that has just floored me. And LuAnne is a wreck. She's over at the church right now telling the pastor, but what he can do about it, I don't know."

"Where he move out to?"

"I forgot to ask. But, Lillian, you won't believe what she told me about him." I leaned across the table and whispered to her what LuAnne had said about Leonard's *needs.*

"No!" she said, rearing back. "Mr. Conover? Why, he seem like a shy kinda man. I guess still water do run deep."

"Well, something does. But don't you tell that, Lillian. LuAnne would have my neck if word got out. Of course," I went on, looking off at the ceiling, thinking it through, "if he starts showing up with another woman, people'll know it wasn't himself he was trying to find."

"Law, law," Lillian said, shaking her head, "people do the foolishest things sometimes. But I don't know what you can do to help 'em, they start leavin' they wives an' stealin' folkses' money an' suin' they best friends."

"I don't know, either, Lillian, but," I said, rising from the table, "I'm going to try to get Helen again. Seems to me that she's the one who needs help the most. But I want to talk to Sam first."

I went to the phone and dialed Sam's number. It rang and rang without an answer. "Where is he?" I mumbled. "James ought to be there, even if he's not."

Shrugging it off, I dialed Helen's number, getting nothing but a busy signal. I hung up and turned to Lillian. "It's busy. Either she's left the phone off the hook, or her message machine is full. I don't know what to do, Lillian. I really want to talk to her and let her know I care about her."

"Yessum, and you want to get yo' money back."

I nodded. "That, too."

Chapter 6

"Here you are," Hazel Marie said, as she pushed through the kitchen door the next morning, a cheery smile on her face. "I just dropped Lloyd off at the tennis courts, where he'll probably be all day. Any coffee left?"

"Yessum," Lillian said, pushing herself up from her chair. "I get you some."

"You stay right there," Hazel Marie told her. "I'll get it. Listen, y'all, this town is buzzing with talk. I mean, even at school yesterday morning all the teachers were talking about Richard Stroud. I hadn't seen the paper, so I didn't know a thing about it until I heard what they said." She pulled out a chair at the table and joined us. "And what about the mayor? From what they were saying, people're ready to impeach him or recall him or something. Nobody wants to tear down the old courthouse." She grinned. "But nobody wants to put up money to fix it, either."

"We've been talking about the same things," I said. "I don't know what this town is coming to. It just beats anything I've ever seen, what with New Jersey developers coming in with bulldozers and the mayor having no sense of history. To say nothing of what's going on with the Strouds and the Conovers."

Hazel Marie's head jerked up. "What's going on with the Conovers?"

Lillian said, "Uh-oh."

"Oh, me." I leaned my head against my hand. "Looks like I can't keep anything to myself. I don't know what's the matter with me. Hazel Marie, you can't tell a soul, but Leonard has moved out and LuAnne is just beside herself."

"Moved out?" Hazel Marie whispered, her eyes wide with shock. "Where to?"

"I don't know. I forgot to ask."

Hazel Marie frowned. "I wouldn't think he had it in him."

"Well, me, either," I said. "And I'm sure it won't last long. I mean, what will he do all by himself? Of course, LuAnne's convinced he has another woman somewhere." I smiled wryly at the thought. "I can just imagine who."

"Who?" Hazel Marie asked.

"Who what?"

"Who does she think the other woman is?"

"Oh," I said, waving my hand dismissively, "her first thought was Helen Stroud . . ."

"Helen!" Hazel Marie levitated from her chair.

"No, no, wait. I said it was her first thought, but of course it's not Helen. She wouldn't have him on a silver platter." Concern for Helen swept over me again. "Hazel Marie, I am just worried sick over that woman. I've called her and gone over there and I can't get in touch with her. Everybody's trying to find her to see what she knows, including a newspaper reporter who was hiding in that privet hedge I wish she'd get rid of. I don't know what to do."

"Oh, it's just awful about Richard," Hazel Marie said. "I hope . . ."

"Knock, knock, anybody home?" James, who'd worked for Sam for years, opened the back door and stuck his head inside. "Oh, 'scuse me, Miss Julia, I didn't know you in here. How you do? Hey, Miss Hazel Marie, Miss Lillian."

Lillian's eyes rolled up in her head at the sound of his voice. A grim look settled on her face, as she lowered her head and heaved an exasperated sigh. She rarely had the time of day for James, but he popped in at our house often enough to make me wonder about his intentions, as well as her reception of them.

"Come in, James," I said. "It's nice to see you. If you came to visit Lillian, we can leave you two alone."

As I picked up my cup and motioned to Hazel Marie, Lillian gave me an imploring look just as James said, "No'm, I don't mean to in'errupt yo' coffee-drinkin', I jus' hear something that make my blood run cold an' Mr. Sam not home, so I stopped off here to tell somebody about it."

"Isn't Sam at his house?" I asked. "That's

where he said he'd be, though why he's working on a Saturday, I don't know."

"Well, yessum, he come this mornin', but he say he have to go downtown an' he went. An' I went to the sto' to get him some snacks he like . . ."

"Snacks!" I said. "He's not supposed to be snacking, he's supposed to be working. James, he'll ruin his dinner if you feed him all day."

"No'm, I don't all day, jus' ever' now and then to keep his stren'th up."

But Hazel Marie wasn't interested in Sam's eating habits. "What made your blood run cold, James?"

"It all over the grocery sto'," he said, his eyes getting wide with the thought of what he'd heard. "Folks all talkin' in the aisles an' at the meat counter, an' somebody say it'll be in the paper in the morning. So I'm not tellin' anything don't nobody else know." He paused, perhaps to be sure he had our full attention. "They talkin' about one of them sheriff's deputies findin' a car what'd run off Blake Mountain Road up where it twist an' turn 'fore it run into the interstate, an' that car ended up 'way down the side of the mountain in a gully, like. Nobody know how long it been there, it bein' all smashed up and wrecked and stuck down in a creek with bushes all around it. But wasn't nobody in it or nowhere around it, and nobody seen what happen or when it happen."

"That's a treacherous stretch," I said. "I expect the driver just lost control. Probably somebody from out of state who didn't know how steep the grade is."

"No'm," James said, shaking his head from side to side. "They got all them 'mergency workers an' rescue people an' sheriff's deputies an' police dogs out there, an' they all lookin' ever'where for a *body.*" James stopped and looked around, again making sure he had our attention. "They sayin' likely it been th'owed out, maybe a long ways away. An' what scare me so bad is them sayin' that mashed up car b'long to Mr. Horace Allen, an' the body he left behind ain't nowhere to be found."

"Oh, no," I said, grasping the edge of the table. "That has to be wrong. I spoke to Mildred just yesterday, and she didn't say a word about Horace being missing and nothing about a car wreck. Hazel Marie, we ought to go over there. She may not know a thing about it."

"Yessum," James said solemnly, "she do now. Ida Lee, she be in the sto' an' she hear it, too. She take off for home soon as I tell her 'bout poor Mr. Horace. That girl won't have much to do with me, but she purely grateful to me this mornin'."

"Uh-huh," Lillian mumbled, as her face twisted with derision.

Hazel Marie picked up my cup and saucer along with her own and took them to the sink. "We better go right on over, Miss Julia. Mildred'll be out of her mind with worry. We should be there when somebody comes to notify her, which they'll do when they're sure it's his car."

"They sure," James said, nodding his head up and down. "Least ever'body at the Winn-Dixie say it his."

Lillian was up and bustling around, turning on the oven to preheat and getting out the mixing bowls. "That po' Miz Allen, she be hurtin' now, but I'm gonna fix her my carrot cake 'cause I know she like it." She opened the refrigerator door and took out the egg carton. "You can go on home now,

James. You already done all the damage
you can do, an' I don't have no more time
for you."

Leaving them to it, I followed Hazel Marie out of the kitchen, reminding her to put
on a sweater while I hurried to the bedroom for mine. I knew that as soon as the
word got out, women all over town would
be doing exactly what Lillian was doing—
baking, cooking, mixing casseroles and
covering one dish after another. That's what
we did whenever there was grief in the
family of someone we knew. There would
be many who didn't know the Allens well,
but just a slight acquaintance would send
them to the kitchen and then to Mildred's
with dish in hand. Every inch of her long
dining-room table and kitchen counters
would be filled with platters and cake plates
and Pyrex bowls full of first one thing and
another. Some women I knew had a favor-
ite recipe for condolence calls and kept all
the ingredients on hand just for those unexpected moments. Emma Sue Ledbetter,
for one, always took the same thing, and
I heartily wished she'd come up with a different recipe.

I met Hazel Marie as she came back

downstairs and both of us, our faces creased with concern for Mildred—and for Horace, too—hurried out to the car.

"You drive, Hazel Marie," I said, veering toward her car. "I'm too jittery. I'll tell you, when death comes calling practically next door, it is too close for comfort."

Hazel Marie turned on the ignition and backed the car down the drive. Then she had to wait for several cars to pass. She glanced at me. "You know, we could've walked. We'd probably be there by now."

"I didn't even think of it, that's how upset I am. Oh, well, Mildred might need something and it'll be more convenient if we have a car with us."

The last car went by, and Hazel Marie got us out on the street. Just as Mildred's large, Federal-style house came into view, a sheriff's car pulled out of her driveway, passed us and headed on toward town.

"Why, that looks like Lieutenant Peavey," I said, craning my neck to look at the patrol car.

"Oh, my," Hazel Marie said. "I guess that means it's official. Wonder where they found the body."

"This is just terrible, Hazel Marie. Who

would've imagined Horace Allen dead on a mountainside? He was the least likely person I know to be an outdoorsman."

Hazel Marie shook her head, murmuring, "It all sounds so crazy." Then she pulled over to the curb hardly half a block from our house. "I'll park here," she said. "I don't want to get blocked in when everybody else comes calling."

I nodded, as we continued to sit there in front of Mildred's stately home, neither of us all that eager to go inside. Mildred was a woman of intense feelings, and she was never reluctant to make them known. I felt for her and wanted to be of help, but at the same time I dreaded the lamentations I knew were coming.

"Wonder what he was doing up on that mountain road," Hazel Marie said, tapping her fingers on the steering wheel.

"I wonder, myself. It had to've happened last night or early this morning, don't you think? I mean, if Horace had been gone any length of time, we would've heard about it before now. Mildred wouldn't stand for it, for one thing, and Horace knows to toe the line. *Knew,* I mean he knew to toe the line."

At the sound of a car turning into the drive behind us, I turned to see who it was. "Oh, my goodness, Hazel Marie, there's LuAnne already and she hasn't had time to cook anything and probably wouldn't feel like it if she did. We better go on in, but listen now, don't say a word about Leonard. Nobody's supposed to know that he's gone, too. Though not in the same way as Horace, as far as I know. But don't even ask her how he is or anything. It'll just set her off, and Mildred doesn't need any more stress. We're going to have our hands full as it is."

Chapter 7

Ida Lee, neat and trim in her black nylon uniform, opened the door as soon as we rang the bell. Her usually serene face was knotted with anxiety, but relief washed over it when she saw us.

"How are you, Ida Lee?" I asked, stepping inside and putting my pocketbook on the demilune table in the foyer. "And how's Mrs. Allen?"

"It's bad around here, Miss Julia," Ida Lee said in her soft voice. "Miz Allen's up in her room and I can't get her out of bed. She's so upset that she even received the sheriff's deputy in her nightgown. Mrs. Conover's up there with her now."

"And Tonya, too?"

"No'm, Miss Tony, he . . ." Ida Lee's face crumpled as she realized how badly she'd misspoken. Tonya Allen had been born Anthony, or Tony, Allen, but years of working up north had made a monumental impression on him and he'd come home as Tonya, complete with bosoms. Or, as Mildred called them, ta-tas. Mildred was barely over the shock of losing her boy to 36-D cups, and here she was suffering another loss.

"It's all right, Ida Lee," I said. "I still get mixed up, too, even though I admire Tonya much more than I ever admired Tony. Anyway," I went on, trying to put things back on course, "where is he? I mean, *she.*"

"She gone to New York to visit old friends."

"She needs to be here for her mother. Do you have a phone number?"

"Miz Allen tell me to call already, an' Miss Tonya on her way," she said, her small body trembling. "Miss Tonya the only one can do anything with her mama."

Hazel Marie put her arm around Ida Lee

and said, "Well, we're here to help you." And Hazel Marie went right to work organizing things. She was awfully good in times like these.

"I'll answer the door for you," Hazel Marie said, leading Ida Lee toward the kitchen. "And we'll put a pad by the phone to take down any messages. And we need to keep a list of who all brings food or sends flowers. Mildred will need that. Miss Julia, you go on up and see her. I'll stay down here and help Ida Lee."

I stood in the foyer, looking up at the graceful stairs and dreading going up them. Glancing toward the living room on one side and into the dining room on the other, I was reassured by their impeccable condition. Mildred might have stayed in bed all day, but Ida Lee was still on the job, running the house like a general. Ida Lee was one of the most refined and capable people I knew, and I had often wondered why she wasn't heading up a business somewhere. Of course, Mildred knew a good thing when she saw it and was more than generous with salary and benefits. On top of that, she gave Ida Lee complete oversight of the house, hiring day workers for the laundry, the yard and the heavy cleaning, with Ida Lee supervising all of it. So I guess she was already running a business right here.

I sighed then and commenced the climb toward Mildred's bedroom, dreading the dramatic scenes to come. Mildred was an emotional woman who loved drama in her life, but she was ill prepared to handle a situation like this. Recalling my own bereavement after Wesley Lloyd Springer keeled over in his car and before I'd known what he'd been up to, I felt a surge of sympathy for her and resolved to comfort her in any way I could.

Instead of the expected hysterics, though, I found Mildred languishing on several pillows in her bed, the Porthault linens overflowing with lace. Mildred's arms were flung out to the side, while LuAnne leaned over her, bathing her ashen face with a cloth.

I tiptoed over to the canopied bed, marveling at the quiet grief that she was suffering. The room was dim with the curtains still drawn and only one lamp burning, and it took a minute for my eyes to adjust. Mildred had the bed covers pushed down to her waist, with her arms and legs spraddled out across the bed. She wore a celadon satin bedjacket over a matching gown, and I was relieved that she'd apparently covered herself to some extent when she received Lieutenant Peavey. Mildred was a full-bodied woman who could've shocked the lieutenant beyond recovery if she'd not made some effort to cover herself. But then, Ida Lee had probably seen to it.

I put my hand on LuAnne's back and leaned over the bed. "Mildred, Hazel Marie and I have come to help. What can we do? Is there any word on Horace?"

"Oh, Julia," Mildred said with a monumental sigh. Without opening her eyes, she waved her hand around and finally seized mine. "My heart is broken. My dear, sweet Horace could be out there suffering somewhere and nobody knows where."

I looked with surprise at LuAnne. "They haven't found him? We saw Lieutenant Peavey leaving, and I thought there'd been some word."

LuAnne shook her head. "He just came to tell her about the car and the accident. And to ask where Horace might be."

"Oh," I said, "then I guess that's good

news. At least, it could be. Maybe Horace will come walking in any minute."

Mildred suddenly came to life, her eyes popping open as she shoved herself upright in the bed. "He better not come walking in after putting me through all this. LuAnne, quit wiping my face. Sit down, both of you, I'm tired of being treated like an invalid."

"Well quit acting like one," LuAnne snapped, backing away from the bed. I frowned at her and shook my head, cautioning her to overlook Mildred's outburst. Grieving people are allowed to be short and discourteous within reason, but LuAnne's feelings were close to the surface because of her own situation. She was in no mood to be tolerant of anybody.

But we both pulled chairs up close to the bed and sat down, waiting for Mildred like a queen's attendants. Mildred plumped the pillows behind her back and scooted farther up in the bed. She seemed to be her old self, except for her hair which was mashed down in the back and standing out from the sides. But her face now had some color in it, and her eyes had gained some sparkle.

"I want to know where he is," she said. "Believe me, the longer he's gone, the worse trouble he's going to be in."

"Now, Mildred," I said, concerned at her sudden mood swing, "you have to keep your spirits up until you hear something definite. He could still be wandering around up in the mountains, hurt or maimed, maybe with amnesia or something. People get lost up there all the time, even without a car accident."

"I know that, Julia," she said, flapping her hand. "But that doesn't answer the question of what he was doing up there in the first place."

LuAnne leaned forward. "How long has he been gone?"

"I don't know!" And Mildred slung her head back and wailed. Exactly the way I'd been expecting. But then, she seemed to gather herself, took a deep breath and continued in a normal voice. "We have separate bedrooms," she said, cutting her eyes at LuAnne, then at me. "I don't expect either of you to understand, knowing how your marriages are." I heard LuAnne make a mewing noise at the reference to her marriage.

Mildred didn't notice, just went right on. "A lot of people have separate bedrooms, you know. They just don't advertise the fact. So," she said, reaching for a Kleenex, "I assumed he went to bed last night same as always, but apparently he didn't." Tears flowed down her face. "So I don't know how long he's been gone, and that stern-faced lieutenant acted like he didn't believe me."

"Oh, I'm sure he did, Mildred," I said, reaching over and patting her hand. "He can't believe you had anything to do with it. I wouldn't worry about that at all."

LuAnne sat beside me, her mouth twisting to one side and her eyes narrowing. "You don't sleep together? How do you keep your marriage going?"

"My marriage is just fine," Mildred said, pursing her mouth at her. "And just because we don't find it necessary to be up against each other all the time doesn't mean we don't on occasion." Mildred threw up her hands. "Our sleeping arrangements are beside the point and nobody's business. Besides, Horace snores."

"I think we should try to figure out what has happened," I said, wanting to turn the

conversation away from the tender subject
of marriage. "When was the last time you
saw him, Mildred?"

"That's what the lieutenant asked, and it
was yesterday at lunch. Horace wanted an
advance on his allowance, and I gave it to
him, although not as much as he wanted.
All right, don't look at me like that." Mildred
glared at us. "You both know that Horace
has never made a nickel in his life, but he
hasn't needed to. We have our own arrangements which have worked for us all
our married life, and if it's not what most
people are accustomed to, it doesn't matter. I married Horace because he was
such a gentleman, cosmopolitan and, well,
worldly. He has always been available to
me and devoted to me. That's what I
wanted and I was willing to support him to
get it. So if that doesn't meet your middle-
class ideas, then I'm sorry."

Mildred tightened her mouth and stared
us down. Of course, I'd known pretty much
all of what she'd just told us, simply from
observing the two of them over the years.
Mildred had been raised with unlimited
wealth, and it's a settled fact that people
like that are different from you and me,

whether in their money management or their sleeping arrangements. None of it mattered to me, but I knew Hazel Marie would be fascinated and I couldn't wait to tell her.

"Well, I just think it's strange," LuAnne said. LuAnne only liked it when people did exactly what they were supposed to do with no variation from what she considered normal.

"LuAnne," I said, in an attempt to get us back on track, "none of that has anything to do with the current problem, which is where Horace is now. Mildred," I went on, turning to her, "didn't Horace have a cell phone with him? Looks to me like he'd call somebody if he was lost."

"Well, I know he would've," Mildred said, "if he'd been able to or if it survived the wreck. It just goes to show that something's not right with any of this." She suddenly rose from the bed, flinging back the covers to reveal more than I wanted to see. "I'm getting up from here and getting dressed. Julia, you and LuAnne go on downstairs and ask Ida Lee to come help me. That doorbell has about rung off the hook, and I need to be down there."

"Good," I said, glad to see Mildred stirring herself. "Come on, LuAnne, let's go see if the coffee's made."

She and I closed the door behind us as Mildred lumbered toward the bathroom. We lingered a minute in the upstairs hall, still slightly in shock at all that had happened that morning.

"Julia," LuAnne said, so quietly I could barely hear her. "If things were fair, that should've been me."

I stared at her. "You mean, married to Horace?"

"No! I mean, it should've been me grieving for Leonard after he'd been thrown out of a car wreck with his body nowhere to be found."

"Now, LuAnne, you don't mean that."

"I certainly do. Everybody will sympathize with Mildred, but they'll all laugh at me. It would be so much easier if Leonard had died instead of leaving me."

Having no adequate response to that, I just rolled my eyes and took her arm as we proceeded down the stairs. "I think you're jumping the gun, LuAnne. We have to remember to keep reminding Mildred that Horace is not dead until his body is found. There's no need to envy her, Lu-Anne, because you're both in the same situation. Both of your husbands are gone, and nobody knows where they are."

Chapter 8

Like Mildred, I had heard the doorbell ring off and on during our stay in her bedroom, and upon reaching the foyer, I saw several people sitting in the living room and others trolling the table in the dining room.

There was a low rumble of voices rising from the visitors, expressing shock and curiosity over what had happened to Horace. They had come with the best of intentions, wanting to offer help and condolences to Mildred, as well as to hear the latest news as it happened.

"People do show up when there's a tragedy, don't they?" LuAnne commented, her eyes narrowing as they swept the gathering. I detected a trace of sarcasm in her voice, but didn't comment on it. I was still stunned at her wishing Horace's fate upon Leonard.

"Julia! LuAnne!" Emma Sue Ledbetter, our pastor's wife, said in a loud whisper as soon as she saw us. She put down a tray of sliced ham and cheese on the table and hurried over to us. Leaning close, she asked, "How is she?"

"Better, I think," I said, keeping my voice low since others were looking toward us, anxious for the latest word of how Mildred was taking it. "She'll be down in a few minutes. How are you, Emma Sue?"

"Oh," she said, pushing back the hair that had fallen on her forehead. "Just frazzled. I had a full morning already planned, then when I heard about Horace, I had to drop everything and make my dump cake. It's on the sideboard, so do have some."

LuAnne began to edge toward the dining room. "I love your dump cake."

I didn't, so I stayed where I was.

As soon as LuAnne moved away, Emma Sue clamped a hand on my arm and edged closer. "How is Mildred really? I heard they haven't found Horace yet, is that true?"

I nodded. "That's what they told her. She doesn't know any more than we do. Is the pastor here? She'll need him if they ever find Horace." I paused. "Or if they don't."

Emma Sue glanced toward the front door. "He's on his way. He had some business to take care of, so I just came on. Listen, Julia." She took my arm again and eased us under the curve of the staircase, out of the way of people headed for the table. "I need to talk to you. I'm so worried and upset, and I have to talk to somebody. When can we get together?"

"What about now?"

"No, I don't want anybody to get an inkling of this. It has to stay a secret until . . . well, until it's announced. If it's announced."

"About Horace?"

"Julia, I don't know a thing about Horace. Why would I? No, it's about something else entirely. How long are you going to be here?"

"I don't know. I'll stay as long as Mildred needs me, I guess."

"That won't be long. Just look around, she has all the help she needs. We could leave now and she'd never miss us."

"I don't know, Emma Sue. She doesn't even know you're here, although she would expect it, I'm sure. I'd like to stay until we get some word on Horace, wouldn't you?"

"I guess," she sighed. "Well, then don't forget. When you decide to leave, let me know. In fact," she said, her eyes lighting up, "I'll leave as soon as Larry gets here and Hazel Marie can stay in your place. Then I'll follow you to your house and we can talk there."

So that's what we did, although no word of Horace had come before we left. I felt badly about leaving Mildred in her time of trouble, but I knew that Emma Sue wouldn't be satisfied until I did. And, in fact, Mildred had finally come downstairs to greet the well-wishers and the curiosity-seekers, taking her place in the middle of her living room by the fireplace. By that time, the pastor had shown up and he was sitting by her side with his Bible open. I wasn't sure how much comfort Mildred could accept from him, since she'd still not completely gotten over that sermon he'd preached on the sins of the flesh. In that sermon, he'd covered not only what we usually think of as fleshly sins, but he'd also included cigarette smoking, liquor drinking, card playing, too much clothes buying, overeating and obesity. At that point, Mildred had gotten up from her pew and sailed down the aisle and out the door, with every eye in the church on her. She was outraged, as she'd told me, that the pastor hadn't taken into account her thyroid condition, and he'd had to practically grovel to get back into her good graces.

As Emma Sue and I slipped out the door, I glanced back at the people flocking around Mildred's chair, offering food and drink of various kinds, eager to be called upon to aid the assumed widow. I couldn't help but recall the dazed state I'd been in after Wesley Lloyd Springer's sudden demise. I had hardly known if I'd been coming or going, but at least I'd had no doubt as to Wesley Lloyd's whereabouts—which was the Good Shepherd Funeral Home— while Mildred didn't know whether Horace was among the living or the dead.

I could imagine the turmoil in her mind,

swinging back and forth from being a widow grieving over a dead husband to a wife angered over a missing one. But Mildred handled her inner conflict well, dabbing a handkerchief to her eyes and accepting the plates of food offered to her. She had chosen to wear a deep purple crepe in which to receive her guests. I thought it a felicitous choice, given the fact that it was close to black, but not quite, reflecting what was known of Horace's location and condition.

I hurried into the house after parking Hazel Marie's car and told Lillian that Emma Sue was on her way.

"They found Mr. Horace yet?" she asked.

"Not yet. I declare, Lillian, it's a mystery to everybody, including Mildred. I hated to leave until we'd heard something definite, but Emma Sue insisted on speaking to me privately. I don't know what could be so important on a day like this."

As the front doorbell sounded and I started out of the kitchen, I asked, "Has Sam called?"

"No'm, but I 'spect he be in for supper here in a minute."

I hurried out to answer the door, telling

Lillian as I left the kitchen that I wouldn't be long.

"Don't worry about serving anything," I said. "Emma Sue's not in the mood to be entertained. But if that carrot cake's ready when she leaves, I'll take it back to Mildred's."

I let Emma Sue in, noting the anxiety that lined her face and the wad of Kleenex clutched in her hand. She'd been crying on her way over, which was no surprise since Emma Sue's tears flowed at the least concern she had, and she had a lot of them.

"Have a seat, Emma Sue," I said, trying to ignore her red eyes and streaked face. I'd hear soon enough what her immediate problem was and hoped to put off hearing about it as long as I could. "What in the world do you think has happened to Horace?"

"Oh, Julia, I know we're supposed to comfort the grieving and feed the hungry and clothe the naked, and I try, you know I try. But today, I am just so nerve-racked I can't put my heart into it."

"What is it, Emma Sue?" I switched on the lamp next to my Duncan Phyfe sofa and sat down beside her.

Clasping my hand, she blinked back tears. "It's Larry. I don't know what I'll do if he does it, and I know that a wife has to submit to her husband, but, Julia, I just don't want to. And, and," she said, a sob catching in her throat, "and Larry says that's what submission means."

"What does that mean, 'that's what submission means'?"

"He says it can only be submission when you do something you don't want to because your husband wants you to. It doesn't count when you do something you want to do."

"All right," I said, frowning. "I'm not sure I agree with that, but okay."

"Well, we don't have to *agree* with it," she said, somewhat forcefully. Emma Sue thought of herself as a student of the Bible and a teacher thereof to anybody who would listen and to some who wouldn't. "We just have to follow it, but, oh, it's so hard."

"What are we talking about, Emma Sue? What does he want you to submit to?"

"Well, see," she said, as she blew her nose into a Kleenex that could hardly take any more. "There's this group of people over in Raleigh? And they've pulled out of their church. I hate to call it a split, but that's what it is." She looked up at me to be sure I was following. "You know how bad some of our Presbyterian churches have gotten—so liberal and all, so I don't blame them. Anyway, this group is forming a new church, kind of based on the Presbyterian order but they won't be affiliated with any denomination. They'll be independent, see, and they've already bought property to build on and everything. Larry says he doesn't know what will happen to their old church, because its most generous contributors are the ones who have left. But he thinks they're doing the right thing." She began shredding the Kleenex, strewing bits of tissue on her lap. "Well, of course he would, since he can get so exercised over some of the things the General Assembly does."

"Yes, I know," I murmured. I wasn't surprised that our pastor would sympathize with the church splitters, since he'd tried off and on for years to get our members to do the same thing.

"Well, anyway," Emma Sue went on, as she blinked back another gathering of tears. "They contacted him, this group, I mean, and asked him to recommend a sound, Bible-based man to pastor them. They know Larry's as conservative as they come and is in touch with other ministers who're of the same mind, and they thought he could help them find the right man to call."

"He'd be a good one to ask," I said, nodding. "He must know any number of ministers who'd jump at the chance to start a new church, especially a well-financed one."

"That's just it! *He's* jumping at the chance, or at least thinking of it." Emma Sue's face crumpled and tears spurted out again.

"Thinking of what?"

"Accepting their call, Julia. That's what I'm talking about. He said," she hicupped, "he said that it was in-incumbent on him to recommend the right one, and he thinks he's it."

A jolt of joy shot through me. Pastor Ledbetter was leaving—something I'd hoped for and occasionally prayed for more times than I cared to admit. Visions of a new pastor danced in my head, someone who would lead us along a middle way, somewhere in between the wild-eyed radicals on the right and the fuzzy-minded do-gooders on the left. I couldn't wait to see a pastor-seeking committee formed. I would tell them exactly the kind of preacher we wanted.

But for Emma Sue's sake, I had to stifle my hopes for better things to come.

"They may not want him," I said, trying to offer a little encouragement. "They didn't specifically call him, did they?"

"No, but they asked him to find the best man for the job, and . . ." Emma Sue could hardly speak for the sobs in her throat, "and he's going to recommend *himself,* Julia."

"Oh, dear," I said, taken aback by such overweening self-confidence. Or was it arrogance? "Well, Emma Sue, if he does, they may surprise you and not take him."

"Oh, they will, I know they will when they find out he's interested. Everybody knows he's a leader in the conservative movement, so they'd take him in a minute."

"Then I guess you have to look on the

bright side. Maybe it would be a good thing. Of course, we'd hate to lose him, but nobody would stand in the way of a better opportunity for both of you."

"But I don't want to move! He promised me that we'd stay in Abbotsville until he retired, and this is my home now. It's not fair for him to suddenly pull up stakes and move all the way across the state and start something new. Why, Julia, do you know what starting a new church involves?"

"Well, no. Our church has been here for over a hundred years, so we're pretty well settled in."

"Well, just listen to this. In their letter, they told Larry they want to call someone with a wife who'll work right by his side, organizing the Sunday school and the Women of the Church and vacation Bible school and helping out in the office until they can afford a secretary. And do they offer a salary for all that? No, they don't. And Larry thinks that's perfectly all right. He says most churches figure they'll get two for the price of one anytime they call a pastor. That's why congregations always want a married man." Emma Sue straightened her back and made one last swipe at her eyes. "And I'm tired of it. I've done my part right here in Abbotsville, and I don't want to start over in another place. But don't tell anybody I said that."

"Well, I don't blame you." And I didn't. Emma Sue had never stinted herself when it came to contributing time and effort to church activities. She had always been part and parcel of every mission—home or foreign—that the church supported, so much so that many of us backed away and let her take over.

"So, will you talk to him?" she went on. "You can talk him out of it, Julia. You and Sam, both. He'll listen to you, I know he will. Point out to him that he's too close to retirement to start something new. Tell him it's not fair to me to lose my home. And, and, Julia, I hate to even think of this, much less say it, because you know I'm not mercenary. But if Larry leaves the denomination, he'll lose his retirement pension."

"He will? Oh, my, that would be bad. Surely he'll think twice before risking that."

"No, he won't. He says the Lord has always provided in the past and he'll keep on providing. And I know I'm not showing any faith, but, Julia, all I can see being provided is Social Security, and since I've never worked, it'll be a pittance. Just a pittance!"

Yes, and if the politicians she and Larry so avidly supported had their way, there wouldn't be even that.

Chapter 9

❦

I promised Emma Sue that I would do what I could to deter Pastor Ledbetter from answering a call he hadn't yet received, but frankly I was of two minds about it. There had been times when I would've rejoiced to see the last of him. Here lately, though, he had seemed somewhat resigned to doing things our way. Although he did change the order of worship, as well as the starting time of the Sunday service, just to prove he still had some authority.

So I had also become resigned to keeping him on, especially since his retirement wasn't that far off. And, I reminded myself, getting a new preacher in his place would surely create a new set of problems, which I didn't want to deal with. A new preacher would undoubtedly be young and untried. He'd be full of modern ideas he'd want to try out on us, like coming up with new names for every activity and adding new committees when we had a Lord's plenty already. It would take years to calm him down and get him settled into the routine we were accustomed to.

So as much as I would've willingly contributed to a going-away present for Pastor Larry Ledbetter, I came down on the side of sticking with what we knew, rather than risking what could be outrageous fortune.

"I'll talk to Sam," I told Emma Sue, when she finally seemed to have cried herself out. "He's much better at dealing with the pastor than I am. He's so sensible, you know, and people listen to him."

"But you need to talk to him, too, Julia. I know you and Larry have had your ups and downs, but he respects you. Really, he does."

So I promised, though not believing for a minute that I could have any influence over the pastor, since I'd never had any in the past.

"I'll see you over at Mildred's," I said, as she prepared to leave. "Lillian's carrot cake should be done by now, and I'm hoping there'll be news about Horace."

"Oh, me, too," Emma Sue said. "It's just so awful, not knowing what's happened to him. But listen, Julia, have you heard from Helen? I couldn't believe what was in the paper and I've tried and tried to get her on the phone, but nobody answers. But can you believe Richard, of all people, being accused of fraud?" She stopped for a minute as her face took on an awed expression. "And they can't find him, either! You reckon there's a connection?"

"Between Richard and Horace? Oh, I wouldn't think so. They've never been particularly close, as far as I know. Besides, Horace is not what you'd call financially experienced, since he's never had any finances of his own. Still," I mused aloud, "it is strange that they're both missing at the same time."

"Mark my words, Julia, something weird is going on, but," she said, heaving a great sigh, "I have enough to worry about. I don't need to take on anything more." She stepped out onto the porch, then turned back to me. "I guess I'll see you at Mildred's. Just because Larry's ready to abandon his flock doesn't mean I have to."

After seeing Emma Sue off, I went back into the kitchen where Lillian had her carrot cake ready for delivery.

"Lloyd call and say to tell his mama he keep on playin' tennis till suppertime," Lillian said. "Then he be home. An' tell Miz Allen I be prayin' for her."

"I will, and I know she'll appreciate it." I walked over to the counter to pick up the cake. "You haven't heard from Sam?"

"No'm."

"Well, James said he went downtown, so maybe he ate lunch there. But if he comes in, tell him to call me at Mildred's. I need to talk to him, and I can't understand why he's always gone every time I need him."

"He pretty much around when you do," Lillian said, always quick to defend Sam, or anybody for whom I had the least tinge of criticism. "An' you be careful with that cake, and don't squash down on that tinfoil. I put yo' name on the bottom of the plate, so we get it back."

"Good, there's so much food coming in over there that it'll be a wonder if any plate makes it home again."

I hurried out to Hazel Marie's car and set the cake plate down carefully on the floorboard of the back seat. Just as I straightened up and prepared to get behind the wheel, Lillian stuck her head out and called to me.

"Miss Julia! You got a telephone call, an' I think it's that sweet Miz Stroud."

"Oh, my goodness." I hurried back into the house, hoping Lillian had gotten it right this time. Picking up the phone, I said, "Helen? Is that you? I've been trying to get you all day."

"Yes, and so has everybody else," Helen said, her voice low and subdued. "I'm not answering the door or the phone, Julia, and I hope all my friends will understand. I just can't face the questions, especially since I don't have any answers. I just heard about Horace on the radio and wanted to know how Mildred is doing."

"She's doing as well as can be expected, under the circumstances. When I left about thirty minutes ago, there'd still been no news. They've not been able to find him, and I tell you, Helen, she doesn't know which way to turn."

"I know how she feels. Tell her I'm thinking of her, and would love to be there, but, well, I just can't right now."

"I will, but, Helen, you need support, too. Let me come over just as soon as I drop a cake off at Mildred's. In fact, I'll ask Lillian to start another one for you."

"No," she said with some firmness. "Thank you anyway, but I can't see anybody right now. I have to go. Tell Mildred she's in my prayers."

"But . . ." But she'd hung up. "Lillian," I said, turning to her, "I didn't get to ask her where Richard is. My goodness, I didn't even ask her where *she* is. I'll tell you, I've never seen so many strange things happening in one day."

"It be that way sometimes," Lillian said, nodding her head as if she'd predicted it all. "I don't know I b'lieve this, but my granny used to say when the stars line up just right an' you hear hoot owls at midnight an' dogs crawl under the house an' stay there, why, you jus' better look out for trouble, an' they's a owl been flyin in an' outta that ole barn down next to Mr. Willet Bennett's house."

I started to laugh off her dire predictions, but I didn't have time for it. "You may be right," I said and headed out to the car again.

Cars filled Mildred's driveway and more were parked up and down the street. Since I couldn't get near, I went around the block and parked in my own driveway. Then carefully bearing the cake, I walked in the lengthening shadows to Mildred's house, which was what I should've done in the first place.

I went around the house and in the back door, hoping to avoid the crowd I knew would be in the front rooms. The first person I saw was Hazel Marie, who was slicing a pie before putting it out in the dining room.

"Oh, Miss Julia," she said, looking up with a smile on her face. "Just put that down wherever you can. Would you believe all this food? We could feed two armies with it. Ida Lee's going to freeze everything that'll freeze, so they'll have it for a while."

I made room on a counter, shoving two casseroles closer together, and put down the cake. "Where is she, anyway?"

"Upstairs, straightening Mildred's room," Hazel Marie said, pointing the pie server at the ceiling. "She is really upset over all this, and I tried to get her to lie down for a while. But she won't do it."

"Well, Ida Lee's very close to the family. She's been with them for so long. What about Tonya? Any word on when she'll get in? And I guess I should ask if there's been any word on Horace, though I expect you would've told me if you'd heard anything."

"No, to both questions," Hazel Marie said, as she ran her hands under water from the faucet. "As far as I know, Tonya's still in the air somewhere, and Mildred's heard nothing about or from Horace." Hazel Marie turned off the water and began drying her hands. "Miss Julia, do you think I ought to suggest that she hire J.D. to look for Horace? I don't want her to think I'm drumming up business for him, but you know how good he is at finding people."

"That might not be a bad idea, Hazel Marie," I said, mulling over her suggestion of putting Mr. Pickens on the case. "And she won't think you're drumming up business for him. She probably just hasn't thought of engaging a private investigator.

But, I tell you, if the sheriff hasn't found Horace by tonight, I would certainly be looking elsewhere. If it were me."

"Me, too. Okay, as soon as some of these people clear out, I'll ask her to think about calling J.D." She picked up a plate and handed it to me. "Here, fill this up. You haven't had a bite all day, have you?"

"I haven't had time to think about it. Hazel Marie, you wouldn't believe all that's happened today. Every time I've turned around, somebody else is telling me their problems."

"Really? Let's both fix a plate and go out to the gazebo. Nobody's out there, and you can tell me everything."

Chapter 10

❦

As warm as the early afternoon had been, it had now turned a bit chilly and I wished for a sweater. Still, it was a fine, cloud-free late spring day. Balancing our plates and glasses, we walked across the side lawn to the gazebo that faced Mildred's rose garden. Taking seats inside the latticed structure, we had a clear view not only of the formal plantings but also of the array of blooming azaleas that lined the edge of the yard.

"Okay," Hazel Marie said as she speared a forkful of asparagus casserole. "Let's hear it. What else is going on? I mean, besides Horace missing and Richard missing and Leonard walking out and the mayor going off half-cocked."

"Well," I said, somewhat hesitantly since I couldn't remember how strongly Emma Sue had sealed my lips. "You can't breathe a word of this, Hazel Marie . . ."

"Wait," she said, looking past my shoulder, "here comes Ida Lee." And indeed she was hurrying across the lawn toward the gazebo.

"Miss Julia," Ida Lee panted, "Miss Mildred needs you. She's going up to the upstairs sitting room and wants you to come, too."

"Well, of course," I said, rising with plate in hand. Hazel Marie took it from me, saying she would take care of it. "Has she heard anything?"

"Not yet," Ida Lee said worriedly, "but the sheriff's office called to tell her that the lieutenant is on his way to talk to her again."

"Oh, my goodness," I said, stepping out of the gazebo. "That means he has news of some kind. Hazel Marie, I'll see you in a little while."

I followed Ida Lee across the lawn and

into the house, where we threaded our way between the knots of people gathered in the public rooms. Hurrying up the stairs, we gained the landing where Ida Lee led me to Mildred's sitting room. I tapped on the door, then entered to find Mildred sitting in a bergere beside the Adams mantel of the fireplace. The room was an oasis of quiet tones of blue, from the grasscloth that covered the walls to the silk fabric on the sofa and chairs. The Venetian glass chandelier provided bits of color, along with the gilt frames of the mirrors and pictures.

"Mildred?" I whispered, hesitant to disturb her as she sat immobile, staring at the wall. "You wanted me?"

"Oh," she said, turning with glazed eyes to look at me. "Julia. Yes, thank you. The sheriff is sending somebody over to bring me up-to-date, and I need somebody with a level head to hear what they have to say."

"Of course," I said, taking a seat beside her. "They didn't give you a hint of what they've found?"

"Not at all, which means it's too tragic to tell me over the phone. I've just been sit-

ting here, trying to come to terms with widowhood."

"Oh, now, Mildred, you mustn't jump to
conclusions. I doubt they tell anybody anything over the phone." Besides, I thought
to myself, widowhood, in my experience,
hadn't been all that bad. Of course, mine
had been a special case and no comparison to the present one.

There was a tap on the door and Ida
Lee stuck her head in. "Lieutenant Peavey
to see you, ma'am." She opened the door
wide to allow the large navy-uniformed
man to enter. Then she stepped out, closing the door behind her.

Lieutenant Peavey stood there in all his
muscular glory, hat in hand, looking out of
place in the silken room. It didn't seem to
bother him, though, as I recalled his supreme and distant professionalism in previous encounters. "Mrs. Allen, ma'am, sorry
to bother you, but I need to go over a few
more things with you."

Mildred had bestirred herself, leaning
forward in the chair, anxious for news.
"Have you found him?"

"No, ma'am, we've not. At least, not at
the accident site."

"Have a seat, Lieutenant," I said, standing to vacate the chair nearest Mildred. He glanced at me, then his eyes flickered just the least little bit. Lieutenant Peavey, I remembered, had a mile-wide streak of suspicion in his nature. But he nodded and proceeded to the chair, leather appendages creaking with every movement.

"That's why I need to speak with you again," he went on, as he rested his hat on his knee and removed a pad and pen from a pocket. "We've searched every inch of the mountainside, and we're confident that Mr. Allen is not there."

"That's good news, Mildred," I said, patting her shoulder.

Lieutenant Peavey glanced at me. "Maybe. And maybe not. The question is, where is he? Which is what we're dealing with now. So," he said, turning his full attention to Mildred, "you told us that the last time you saw him was yesterday around noon. That's a little over twenty-four hours ago. What I'm trying to do is track his movements from that point on. Do you have any idea where he might've gone or who he might've seen immediately after he left here?"

Mildred closed her eyes in thought, or so it seemed, then said, "He might've gone to the bank, Lieutenant, the Mountain Trust, which is where he has an account."

"Good," Lieutenant Peavey said, jotting down the information. "That's something we can follow up on. Do you know if he intended to make a withdrawal?"

"I wouldn't think so. I assume he would be making a deposit. At least, I hope he was, since he left here with a check for a few thousand dollars."

Lieutenant Peavey's eyebrows shot up. "A few thousand? How many, exactly?"

"Six, I believe," Mildred said, as if she wrote so many checks of that size that she couldn't quite remember. "I can confirm that by my checkbook." She took her lower lip in her teeth for a second. Then releasing it, she went on. "I suppose it might be relevant to tell you that that was the third check I'd advanced him in the past week."

Lieutenant Peavey blinked at this news. "How much in all, would you say?"

Mildred waved a languid hand. "Close to twenty thousand or a little more. But I told him that was the last check I was giving him until next month. He was already into me for much more than that, always needing an advance on his allowance, always complaining about his creditors." Mildred looked down at her hands in her lap. "He's never been good with his finances, and even worse here lately. I have to say that I reminded him of that rather forcefully."

Lieutenant Peavey wiggled his pen in his fingers, letting the silence build in the room. I expect he'd never come across anything like the relationship between Mildred and Horace, and hardly knew what to ask next.

"So," he finally said, "can we say that Mr. Allen had a greater than usual need for money in the last several days?"

"Over the past month, I would say," Mildred said. "And I don't mind telling you that I had had enough. I told him yesterday that there'd be no more." A tear trickled down Mildred's face. "We argued, Lieutenant Peavey, on what might've been the last day of his life, we argued. And he left the table, angry and upset with me. Called me selfish and miserly. And I . . . well, sharp words were spoken, and now my poor Horace is gone forever." She reached up and took my hand where it rested on her shoulder. "Julia, take a lesson from me, don't let the sun go down on your wrath. Value Sam and let him have whatever he wants. Within reason, of course."

I nodded, while Lieutenant Peavey looked exceedingly uncomfortable at Mildred's sudden gush of tears. I gave her a handful of Kleenex from the box on a side table and patted her again.

Attempting to bring the interview under control, Lieutenant Peavey asked, "Instead of depositing that check, do you think he would've cashed it? Do you know if he was in the habit of carrying large amounts of cash?"

"Well," Mildred said, wiping her eyes, "it's possible. Horace liked to be prepared for emergencies, but I don't know what you mean by a large amount."

"I mean," Lieutenant Peavey said as he jotted a note on his pad, "well, we can get that information from the bank."

Mildred gasped as she understood the implication. "He could've been robbed! Somebody could've run him off the road and hidden his body. Oh, what am I going to do without him?"

"Mrs. Allen," Lieutenant Peavey said in

what I took as an attempt to comfort, "he may be gone, but we're not convinced that he's gone for good. What we do know is that he's not near that accident site. We've searched every inch of the mountainside and combed the road for a mile in each direction, and there's nothing to indicate what happened when his car went off the road. Of course, it rained last night, which washed away any footprints or tire marks that might've been there." Lieutenant Peavey leaned forward in an intimidating manner and hardened his voice. "We've come to the conclusion that he walked away from the accident, so I repeat, where could he be now?"

I could keep silent no longer. "Well, she certainly can't tell you. Don't you know that a wife is always the last to know anytime a husband gets in trouble? I'm surprised at you, Lieutenant Peavey. You seem to think that his own wife is hiding him away somewhere. This is not a criminal case, you know. If indeed you haven't found Horace's body, then it's simply a missing persons case and he hasn't been missing for forty-eight hours yet, so what's the purpose of all these questions?"

The lieutenant gave me a freezing glance, frowned and addressed Mildred as if he'd just decided to share something with her. "It's like this. We found a sheet of paper wadded up under the passenger seat, a sheet that indicates some connection to Assured Estate Planners. Which, as you may know, we are investigating and whose owner is also missing."

I thought Mildred was going to faint dead away. If there was one thing she could not abide it was fraudulent dealings where money was concerned. Her financial reputation, as well as her family's, had always been impeccable, and now to have her husband associated, all unbeknowst to her, with a company accused of defrauding her friends and neighbors was almost more than she could bear. She began to cry in earnest, hyperventilating and emitting with each gasp little cries of anguish. She sprawled back in her chair, making me wonder if she'd slide right off that silk chair onto the floor, where I'd never get her up again.

"I better get Ida Lee," I said, my futile efforts to fan Mildred's face going for naught. "This session is probably over, Lieutenant.

I've seen her like this before when her son came home in a dress and high heels. You can't get any more information here anyway. She's told you all she knows, and I think that you can see she knew nothing whatsoever of any dealings that Horace may have had with Richard Stroud."

On hearing Richard's name, Mildred's cries reached a piercing crescendo, and Lieutenant Peavey came to his feet in a hurry. Backing away, he said, "Should I call for an ambulance?"

"No, just Ida Lee." As I hurried to the door, Ida Lee herself opened it and ran to Mildred. I heaved a sigh of relief since help had heard and answered the call. So I went out into the hall, with Lieutenant Peavey close behind.

Closing the door on Mildred's pitiful cries, I looked up at him. "I can't believe that Horace Allen and Richard Stroud could be connected in any way, Lieutenant. Except I think they both like to play bridge and maybe in the same bridge club. And they both belong to the country club, but so does most everybody else in town. What kind of paper did you find, Lieutenant? And how does it connect those two?"

Lieutenant Peavey stared down from his great height and said, "That's evidence and not for public dissemination. But people who've lost money are up in arms, and we're going to get to the bottom of it sooner or later. And if not us, the FBI."

He turned and headed for the stairs, leaving me stunned at the unsettling knowledge of all the underhanded dealing by and with and to my friends and neighbors that I had known nothing about.

Chapter 11

Then as another thought came to mind, I took myself in hand and trotted after Lieutenant Peavey. He was well ahead of me, his long legs making strides down the staircase and through the crowd in the foyer. No one dared delay him with questions, but they all stopped and watched as he went out the front door. I was right behind him.

"Lieutenant Peavey," I called, as I hurried to catch up to him before he reached his squad car. He'd parked on Mildred's lawn, which was the only clear space, but

I knew she'd have a fit when she saw tire tracks on her grass.

He stopped and barely turned to see who had called him. At the sight of me, I do believe he would've continued on if I hadn't moved in front of him and stood there on the walk beside the corner of the sunroom, next to a camellia bush.

"Lieutenant Peavey," I said, all in a rush since he wasn't what you'd call the conversational type. "Mildred Allen is a good friend of mine, and I would be remiss if I didn't bring to your attention something you seem to have overlooked."

His eyes narrowed and he looked down at me from his great height. "If you know something germane to this case, let's hear it."

"I don't know if it's germane or not, but you seem to have only two possibilities in mind—either Horace was killed in that wreck, which is unlikely since you can't find his body, or he's involved with Assured Estate Planners and is running from the law. I'd like to remind you that there is another possibility." I stopped to take a breath, then hurried on before he could dismiss me, which he had a way of doing whenever he thought somebody was interfering with the way he enforced the law. "Think about this: What if Horace was a victim of a carjacking? What if somebody bashed him over the head, far from that accident site, left him dazed and injured, then drove the car up that mountain and crashed it? Then that thief walked away, leaving everybody to think that Horace had been driving it, when in fact Horace is on the other side of the county or in Asheville or who-knows-where, all unaware of what he's being accused of. And furthermore," I went on hastily, since Lieutenant Peavey didn't seem too impressed with what I was saying, "that driver, whoever he was, could be the one who left that paper in the car. He, not Horace Allen, could be connected to Assured Estate Planners. Don't you see?"

I didn't think the lieutenant's eyes could get any narrower, but they did. Then they lifted from their gaze of me to look over my head as he slipped on his dark aviator glasses, in spite of the fact that the sun had almost set. "It's possible," he said.

"Of course it's possible, and . . . oh, my

heavens!" I almost reached out to support myself on his arm, but decided against it.

"Are you all right?" The touch of concern in his voice moved me since I'd never known him to be all that sensitive to human feelings. "You look a little peaked. Maybe you better go inside and rest."

"I don't need to rest," I snapped. "I just thought of something else." I swayed just a little, trying to think of something else I'd just thought of. "I'm supposed to send somebody to meet Mrs. Allen's daughter at the airport, and I forgot all about it. She'll be punching that cell phone all afternoon, unable to get through. There's been so many calls here, you know. Excuse me, Lieutenant, I'd better see about that right away. That poor girl will think we've abandoned her."

I sidled around him, hoping to get away from those piercing eyes before he saw what a tale I'd told.

He stopped me cold. "Mrs. Murdoch. Don't let your imagination run away with you. I can assure you that we have not overlooked any possibility. That's why we're tracking Mr. Allen's movements since yesterday, although I didn't want to distress Mrs. Allen any more than necessary by laying any of this out. And I'd caution you against making it harder on her by telling her."

"Oh, I wouldn't dream of it," I said, but he'd already sidestepped me and was heading for his car.

"Hazel Marie," I said, drawing her into a corner of the dining room and keeping my voice low. "I think it's time to call Mr. Pickens."

"Oh, good," she said, turning to leave. "I hope he can get right on it. I'll call him from the kitchen."

"Wait, Hazel Marie. We'd better talk to Mildred first."

Hazel Marie's eyes widened. "Oh, I thought . . . well, yes, I guess we better."

We met Ida Lee on the stairs as we were going up and she was coming down.

"Is Mildred still in the sitting room?" I asked.

"No'm, she say that lieutenant give her a migraine, so she laying down now. I'm going to fix her something to drink."

"Oh, dear. What do you think, Hazel Marie? Should we disturb her?"

Hazel Marie said to Ida Lee, "Is it a bad one?"

"Yes, ma'am, she say she about blind with it."

Hazel Marie made the decision. "Then let's wait till Tonya gets here and talk to her. Ida Lee, I bet you haven't had a bite to eat. Why don't you fix a plate and take it upstairs where you can eat in peace and rest a little? You need to stay close to Mrs. Allen, anyway. There're enough people to see to anything that needs doing down here."

"That's good advice, Ida Lee," I said. "And I hope you take it. We can't have you giving out. Have you heard from Tonya?"

"Yessum, the only flight she could get was to Charlotte, and she called from there a minute ago. She's driving a rental car on home, so she ought to be here in a couple of hours."

"Then let's go on home, Hazel Marie, and see about things there. Ida Lee, please ask Tonya to call us as soon as she can. It's extremely urgent that we talk with her. We may have a way to find her daddy."

"Lillian," Hazel Marie said as soon as we walked into the house. "Is Lloyd home yet?"

"Yessum, he upstairs workin' on something. He say he got a big report due on Monday, an' he don't wanta mess up his whole weekend with it."

"I thought he'd finished that," Hazel Marie said, as she started for the back stairs. "I'll run up and speak to him."

"Don't be long," I said. "We need to talk things over before Tonya gets here. I've come up with something that's worrying me to death."

As she ran up the stairs, Lillian looked at me from under lowering brows. "What you cookin' up to do now?"

"Not one thing, except to talk Mildred into hiring Mr. Pickens. I tell you, Lillian, I don't have much confidence in Lieutenant Peavey. You remember him, don't you?"

"Yessum, and you better leave that man alone. He chew you up and spit you out 'thout thinkin' twicet."

"Well, I can't just stand around and let him ignore clearly marked leads and evidence, as he seems to be doing. He has one thing on his mind and one thing only, and can't see the forest for the trees."

"Well, I'm jus' sayin'. You want some ice tea? I got some in the Frigidaire."

"No, I'm too nervous to think about anything right now. Has Sam come in?"

"No'm, he stayin' scarce today."

I strode across the kitchen to the telephone, mumbling to myself, "What has that man been doing all day?"

"James?" I said, when he answered the phone. "Let me speak to Mr. Sam, please."

"Who I say's callin'?"

"*James!* You *know* who's calling. Now put him on the phone."

"Yessum, I would if I could, but I can't. He come in a while ago and get a call on the telephone. Then he go back out, so I'm fixin' to go on home myself. 'Less you need me for something."

"You don't know where he went?"

"No'm, he don't say."

I hung up after telling James he might as well go on home, then turned to Lillian. "I don't understand it. Sam's been in and out all day and, come to think of it, he was doing the same thing yesterday. It's not like him to be out of touch so long."

"He prob'ly got things to do, an' jus' let the time get away from him."

"Well, he's never let time get away from him before. If he doesn't show up soon, I may have to set Lieutenant Peavey on his trail."

I smiled when I said it, but there was a niggling worry in the back of my mind. With all the husbands that had gone missing in this town, I certainly didn't want mine numbered among them.

I waited in the living room for Hazel Marie to come down, which she did before long. "My goodness," she said, "Lloyd's really working on that end-of-term paper, which I thought he'd already finished. But it'll be half his semester grade, so he wants to get it right. In spite of playing tennis all day. He said he wasn't even hungry."

"Hazel Marie, I don't want to have to worry about that boy, but don't you think he ought to be putting on some weight? He's tired all the time, and it's not like him to wait till the last minute to get a major paper done."

"I know, but he had a checkup last fall, and the doctor said he was fine."

"Well, I'm wondering if he could be wormy. Children get those things you know, and he might need a few doses of a laxative to clean him out."

"Oh, don't say that!" Hazel Marie was

aghast at the thought, and I felt pretty much the same way. "I'll make another appointment for him this week."

She shuddered and sat down beside me on the sofa. "I don't know if I can concentrate on Mildred after that. But tell me what you think is going on."

"Well, it's like this. I almost told Lieutenant Peavey, but I knew he'd discount anything coming from me, so I didn't. But what I've come up with is all the more reason to get Mr. Pickens on the case, and I hope Tonya will talk her mother into doing it." I straightened my shoulders and began to bring Hazel Marie up to date in my thinking. "Lieutenant Peavey conceded that it was possible that Horace's car could've been stolen. You know, carjacked? Leaving him injured on the side of the road somewhere. Maybe even with amnesia, but I didn't mention that because I didn't think of it at the time. And he seemed to allow that it was possible that whoever stole the car was the one who ran it off the road and wrecked it, and could've been the one who left that wadded-up paper about Assured Estate Planners in the car. You didn't hear about that, did you?

Anyway, that was as far as I got, because another thought came to me that I couldn't bring myself to share with him."

I squirmed in my seat, hesitant now to put into words what I was thinking. "Hazel Marie, what if the person who was driving Horace's car and wrecked it and left that paper in it was none other than Richard Stroud? What if Richard was the carjacker and the thief? You know, if a person would steal money, he'd do most anything else." I paused to see how Hazel Marie was taking it, then my thoughts jumped ahead of even me.

"Oh," I said, grasping Hazel Marie's arm, "what if Richard didn't just leave Horace on the side of the road? What if he kidnapped him and has him tied up somewhere? What if Horace is a victim, while all this time he's being accused of fraudulent intent and leaving the scene of an accident?"

"Oh, my," Hazel Marie said, "you reckon? I can't believe Mr. Stroud would do something like that. But maybe you're right. Maybe it's not that Mr. Allen doesn't *want* to come home, but that he can't. Of course," she mused, tapping her fingers on the armrest, "we're not considering Mildred. He might not want to face her, regardless of what's happened to him."

"Well," I said, recalling the flashes of anger Mildred had occasionally displayed toward Horace, "taking her temperament into account, I wouldn't, either."

Chapter 12

Idly twisting the charm bracelet on her arm, Hazel Marie said, "I wish I could talk to J.D. about it."

"I don't see why you can't. I certainly intend to tell Sam. If he ever gets home. But, Hazel Marie, you can't hire Mr. Pickens. Only Mildred, or maybe Tonya, can do that."

"Oh, I know, but he may have some ideas without being officially on the case. If you think it's all right, I'll call him now."

As she got up, the doorbell rang and she veered to answer it. LuAnne came swishing in past her, saying, "Hey, Hazel

Marie, I need to talk to Julia. You don't mind, do you?"

"Not at all," Hazel Marie said, unperturbed by LuAnne's rudeness. "I was just going upstairs anyway."

LuAnne plopped down on the sofa beside me, her eyes following Hazel Marie as she left the room. Twisting her mouth, she said, "You think she's been enhanced?"

"What're you talking about?"

"Well, she's got such big . . ." LuAnne's hands made a rounded motion in front of her own ample bosom. "And she's so skinny everywhere else. Just all out of proportion."

"No, LuAnne, there's nothing artificial about Hazel Marie. She's been like that ever since I've known her. Some people are born that way, you know. With the potential, I mean." Then, because I was offended by her comments, I said, "How's Leonard?"

"I don't know how he is, and it's hateful of you to ask when you know how upset I am. Besides, you have your own problems, which is why I dropped by. Do you know where Sam is?"

"Not at this exact minute, no. But he'll be coming in any time now."

"Well, good. I hope so." She stood up, clasping her purse under her arm. "I've got to be going. It's almost suppertime."

"Wait a minute," I said, standing, too. "What do you mean, saying I have problems of my own? What's going on, LuAnne?"

"Well, I thought you'd be worried about Sam, so I just came by to put your mind at rest." She sniffed. "But I see you're not at all concerned. It must be nice to have a husband you can trust, no matter where he is."

"LuAnne, stop this. I know you aren't happy with me, but you don't need to take it out in innuendos. If you want to tell me something, then tell it."

"All right, I will. Your husband is over at Helen Stroud's, and he's been there all afternoon."

That rocked me back on my heels. I stared at her as a white haze blurred my vision. "How do you know?"

"Because I've been driving by to see if Leonard's car is there. And it's not," she said triumphantly, "but Sam's car is. I told you, Julia, I told you that woman is up to no good."

Not wanting to give her the satisfaction of being right, I made an effort to appear unruffled. "I'm sorry, LuAnne, but I just can't get bent out of shape over that. I'm sure there's a good explanation, and Sam'll tell me all about it. Just as soon as he gets home."

"For your sake, Julia, I hope so. Now I've got to go."

And go she did, leaving me feeling as bereft as an orphaned child. Sam had been with Helen all afternoon? Maybe all day? With no time to call, no time for lunch, no thought of me? My heart felt as if a huge hand was squeezing it, and I almost had to sit down.

But at the thought of Helen, whom I'd been defending every time I turned around, I took myself in hand and marched out to the kitchen.

"Lillian, I have to run out for a minute. I won't be gone long." I grabbed my car keys and headed out the door.

Lillian stopped pouring beans into a bowl and called after me. "This supper 'bout ready. What I gonna do with it?"

"Dip it up," I called back. "I'll be back."

As I drove the few blocks to Helen's, I

felt myself trembling inside. I knew that checking up on Sam was beneath me, but I had to see for myself. LuAnne could've been mistaken, especially since she was in a state herself. Maybe it was somebody else's car, maybe she just wanted to shake me up, maybe any number of things, but I had to find out for sure.

Lord, I nearly drove into a mailbox. Sam's car was parked in Helen's drive, right up against the garage, as big as you please, with no effort made to conceal it. I knew it was his, and not one like it, because there was the Tarheel sticker on the rear bumper.

The next thing I knew I was speeding away, fearful that Helen or Sam would see me. Pulling to the side of the street a few blocks away to gather myself, I wondered why I was the one feeling guilty. I held the wheel with shaking hands, my head bowed and my chest aching with a pain I'd never before felt. There *was* a good explanation; there had to be.

I kept telling myself that until I was blue in the face. And I almost believed it. Sam would tell me all about it when he came home, then I'd laugh at myself for ever doubting him. For that reason, I would just die if he found out that I had been checking up on him, sneaking around trying to catch him in a compromising position. And with Helen, of all people!

Gradually, I began to calm myself down. Sam had never before given me a moment's worry, even though he'd been halfway around the world and back without me. He'd always been open and aboveboard even when he was practicing law, which was a marvel in and of itself. He was a faithful husband, I assured myself, and I would not, absolutely would not, turn on him with suspicions and accusations.

So I determined to keep my own counsel unless and until I became convinced that he was doing something he shouldn't. Then I would be as suspicious as I needed to be. For now, though, I had talked myself into believing that Sam was worthy of trust, and so was Helen. LuAnne had only been trying to make trouble. Misery loves company, you know.

I drove home slowly and carefully, still shaken but determined to bide my time until Sam told me the full story. Jealousy is a terrible emotion, twisting everything you know to be true into half and semi and partial truths. I simply was not going to fall prey to it, regardless of Sam's car being in another woman's driveway.

But why hadn't he returned my calls? Why had he been out of touch all day?

"No," I said aloud as I pulled into our drive, "I will not ask him. I will not demand answers. I will not let him know that anything's amiss. But I will give him full opportunity to explain himself."

Then as I removed the key from the ignition, I smiled, thinking, *This is a test.* If he voluntarily tells me of his day, leaving nothing out, then that's one thing. But if he doesn't, then that's certainly another. My mouth turned from smiling to a tight line of determination, and I went inside.

Lillian started grumbling as soon as I stepped into the kitchen. "Everybody runnin' 'round like chickens with they head cut off. I got my supper ready and jus' look. Nobody here to eat it."

"Where're Hazel Marie and Lloyd?"

"They upstairs. I already call 'em, but they slow comin' down. An' Mr. Sam not here, an' you go runnin' off, an' I had to put my beans back on the stove to keep 'em warm."

Just then, Hazel Marie stuck her head in and said, "Sorry, Lillian, but Lloyd only had a closing paragraph to do. We're at the table now."

I followed her into the dining room and took my place at the table, patting Lloyd's head as I passed him. When Hazel Marie seated herself, Sam's empty place screamed for attention.

"Where's Mr. Sam?" Lloyd asked.

"I'm sure I don't know," I said, complacently, as if his absence was nothing to me. I nodded to Lillian as she brought in dishes and set them on the table. "Will you return thanks, Lloyd?"

We bowed our heads in prayer, but my mind wasn't on the giving of thanks, but rather on the pleading of a wounded heart.

Then we heard a car door slam and soon after, Sam came through the back door. My heart lifted. At least he wasn't spending the night at Helen's.

"Hello, everybody," he said, looking as normal as he always did, giving no indication that he'd been engaged in any wickedness whatsoever. Some people are like that. They can do the most under-handed things imaginable and still appear as innocent as a newborn. He took his place at the head of the table, giving me a wink as he smiled at us all. "Sorry I'm late. I got held up longer than I expected. How was your day, Lloyd?"

The boy passed Sam the mashed pota-toes. "Pretty good, now. One more week of school and I just finished my last paper. At least I hope I have. I was playing tennis this afternoon, and it just hit me that I'd done the bibliography wrong. So I had to go through it again and fix it."

"That's what you call an epiphany," Sam said, nodding in approval. "Glad you had one before you turned in your paper. Ha-zel Marie, what's going on with you?"

Hazel Marie was looking a little bewil-dered, what with all the unfamiliar words being tossed around. But she perked up at Sam's question. "Oh, this has been a day and a half for us," she said. "Miss Julia and I have been at Mildred's most of the day, and they still haven't found Horace. It's the strangest thing I've ever heard. I didn't know that somebody could just disappear."

"Everybody's talking about it downtown, too," Sam said. "I had lunch at the Bluebird Cafe, and if it wasn't Horace they were talking about, it was Assured Estate Planners." Sam shook his head. "Maybe it's a good thing Stroud isn't around. Some people're mad enough to string him up."

Hearing the Stroud name, I lifted my head in anticipation of what he might say about Helen. But he made no mention of her, which was suspicious to me, in and of itself. He went right on talking and mostly listening to Hazel Marie, who was telling him about wanting Mildred to hire Mr. Pickens and about Tonya on her way home and about Mildred's migraine and on and on.

I continued to pick at the food on my plate, more and more anguished at Sam's seeming inattention to me. He hadn't asked about my day. He hadn't directed one word to me. My spirits dropped lower and lower. Ignoring me could be the first sign of his interest in somebody else.

"Julia?" Sam said, and I couldn't help but look up expectantly, in spite of wanting to appear serene and composed. "I saw a couple of city commissioners at the Bluebird today, and you'll be happy to know that your idea of using the old courthouse for archives was well received. Tom Tinsley wanted to know if you'd be interested in heading a study committee to come up with a plan to pay for the restoration it needs. That would give them an alternative to the mayor's push to sell it to developers." Sam picked up his glass of tea. "I told him you'd be happy to do it."

I blinked, unable to respond. My first thought was that he wanted to keep me busy so I wouldn't find out what he was doing. Finally, I managed to say that I'd think about it, and the conversation went on without me.

The evening wore down to bedtime with everything seeming as normal as usual. Except my nerves, which were strung so tight that I thought I'd jump out of my skin. Tonya called about nine o'clock, letting us know she was home and there was still no word of her father. Mildred, she said, was inconsolable and had been given a sedative. I passed the phone to Hazel Marie, who talked at length with her about the advantages of hiring J. D. Pickens, P.I.

I left her to it and went into the living

room to sit with Sam. *Now,* I thought, *we're alone and he'll tell me about Helen.*

"Julia," he said, "this is bad business about Horace. Did you pick up any hint of what might have happened?"

Ah, I thought, *he's ready to talk and is just leading up to Helen.*

So I told him some of the possibilities I'd come up with and how Lieutenant Peavey had dismissed them out of hand. "But, Sam, it makes sense. That piece of paper they found in Horace's car links him to Richard in some way. Or at least, links whoever was driving the car to Richard. And it's entirely possible that Richard had something to do with Horace's disappearance. Don't you think?"

Tell me, I thought, *tell me what Helen thinks.*

"I don't know," he said, shaking his head. "It's a long shot any way you look at it. I've not heard of them having any dealings with each other, although," he stopped and smiled, "the way Mildred treats Horace, I can see how he'd want to do something on his own. Maybe he just took off for Las Vegas or somewhere. Thousands of people disappear every year, you know, and it's usually because the home situation is intolerable."

"Well, speaking of that," I said, hoping that as I confided in him, he would in me. "Have you heard about Leonard Conover and Pastor Ledbetter?"

Sam laughed. "Don't tell me they're in cahoots."

But his eyebrows went up when I told him of Pastor Ledbetter's potential call to another church, and he was as shocked as I was when I told him of Leonard's absence from hearth and home.

"Leonard Conover," he said, shaking his head in disbelief, "who would've thought it."

"That's not all," I said, daring to bring up the name. "LuAnne thinks he's been lured away by Helen." I watched him carefully to see if he would betray himself.

All he did was laugh again. "Leonard and Helen? That would be one for the books, wouldn't it? LuAnne must really be distraught to come up with that." He stood up and yawned. "It's time for bed, Julia. I'm about wiped out."

I would think so, I thought, *after the day you've put in.*

As Sam checked the doors and turned off lights, I prepared for bed, trying to overcome the despair I felt. My hands shook and my chest tightened with anxiety, but my will, which had been sorely tested before, was gaining strength. I was now all but convinced that Sam was following the same road that Wesley Lloyd Springer had taken.

We got into bed, and Sam gave me a perfunctory good-night kiss before switching off the lamp. Then he turned over and told me he hoped I slept well. His breathing soon eased into a rhythm that should have lulled me into thinking that he had nothing on his conscience, but I lay there wondering how he could live, much less sleep, with such deception on his mind. I stared into the darkness, shoring up my determination to bide my time, say nothing, do nothing, until I had them both dead to rights. *Then* they'd see that they'd misjudged Julia Springer Murdoch. I would not be so easily fooled this time.

I turned over in the bed, wrapped the covers over my shoulders and determined anew to play my cards close to my chest, even though I was not a card-playing woman.

As the house settled into the stillness of night and Sam breathed softly beside me, I lay there, staring into the dark. Images of what Sam might have done or might still be doing flashed in my mind, as feelings of pain and betrayal and, yes, flat-out anger blazed through my heart.

Unable to stand it any longer, I flung off the covers and sprang up in bed. *"Sam Murdoch,"* I yelled, backhanding his shoulder, *"what were you doing at Helen's all day!"*

Chapter 13

⚜

Sam bolted straight up in the bed. "What? What is it?"

"I *said*," I said, "how can you lie there sleeping like a baby, when I know what you've been doing? Did you think you could hide it? Don't you know that everybody in town saw your car? And ran as fast as they could to tell me? And did you think I'd just take it lying down? Well, think again, because I won't and I'm not."

Sam reached over and switched on the lamp. "Julia, what in the world are you talking about?"

"Don't play innocent with me! You know

what I'm talking about. I'm talking about *Helen* and what you were doing holed up with her all afternoon." I took a deep breath that came out almost as a sob, making me even madder. It did me in that I couldn't control myself, especially when he put his arm around my shoulders.

"Is that what's bothering you?" he asked, in the most calming and understanding way, although his eyes were still heavy and unfocused. "You should know me better than that."

"Well, I don't," I said, shrugging off his arm. "And you can unhand me. I don't need patronizing, and I don't need a pat on the head. What I need is for you to explain yourself, and I needed it without having to drag it out of you."

Sam yawned, then rubbed his hands across his face. "It's a long story. Can it wait till morning?"

Rearing back in disbelief, I threw back the covers and sprang out of bed, my long gown flowing. With my hands on my hips, I glared at him. "Oh, it certainly *can* wait till morning. In fact, it can wait forever as far as I'm concerned. I'm leaving!"

I turned and headed for the door, then

stopped. "What am I doing? This is my house, so *you* can leave. Get up from there and go back to Helen's. I expect she's over there waiting for you, now that Richard's gone. Very conveniently, too, I might add."

"Julia, my goodness, honey. What's gotten into you? Come on back to bed. I'm not interested in Helen, and she's not interested in me. Now come on over here and keep me warm."

"I'm not about to. If you think I'm going to put up with another stunt like Wesley Lloyd pulled, you are dead wrong. I've had my fill of tom-catting husbands."

Sam pushed back the covers and swung his feet to the floor. "I know you have, and you don't have one now." He walked toward me as I eased backward. "Come tell me what's wrong."

"What's *wrong*? Everything's wrong, and you know it."

"No, I don't. Now, what's Helen done to upset you?" He reached my side as I turned and opened the door to the hall.

"You stay away from me, Sam Murdoch. I am not playing around. I'm serious about this. And it's not Helen who's done anything, it's you."

Sam stood there, his hands spread and his face drawn with concern. "Tell me what I've done, and let me put it right."

I thought I'd cry because he was so good and decent and honest. Still, he should've known what he'd done, and he should've known how badly I'd been burned once before.

My eyes filled with tears at the unfairness of it, as I stumbled out into the hall with Sam right behind me. I didn't know where I was going, but on my way I bumped into the Sheraton chair by the door. It fell over with a clatter, probably waking the whole house.

As I stood waiting to see if anybody had heard it, a door opened upstairs and Hazel Marie called out, "What's going on down there?"

Sam's arms wrapped around me from behind, and I leaned against him, wanting so badly to regain my trust in him. We stood there for a minute, hoping she'd go back to bed. "It's all right, Hazel Marie," I called. "We just knocked over a chair."

There was a second of silence, then she gave a little laugh. "Well, I'd keep it in the bedroom if I were you." Then her door closed.

"Good idea," Sam whispered. "Come on now. Lloyd'll be the next one if you keep this up."

"All right," I conceded, not wanting the boy to be disturbed. "But this is not over and I'm not changing my mind."

"I know, but come on."

I let Sam lead me back to the bedroom, where I meekly crawled into bed. My feet were freezing.

"Now," he said, getting in beside me and scrooching up close, "listen to me. If it's Helen you're concerned about, I am not interested in her or any other woman. I've got more than I can handle right here." He turned my face so I had to look at him, then whispered in the most loving manner, "Don't you know that?"

I pulled back and pushed him away. "I don't know anything that I thought I knew. You spent the day with her when she wouldn't see anybody else. And you've been out of touch all day, eating at the Bluebird and volunteering me to the com- missioners and visiting Helen. And what's worse, you told about everything but her when you got home." I lifted my head and glared at him. "How long were you going to keep me in the dark? Did you think I'd put up with it like I did with Wesley Lloyd? Well, I'll tell you this, Sam Murdoch, if you want to go after Helen Stroud, then you can just keep going. You can move in with Leonard Conover, for all I care, and chase all the women you want."

I thought he was going to laugh, but he pulled himself together and said, "My chasing days are over since I've caught the only woman I want. But here's the story: I went to Helen's because she called and asked me to come over. She wanted some legal advice without going down-town to an attorney where everybody would know about it. She's very upset and rightly so, since she doesn't know where Richard is or what he's done. She called me as a friend who could advise her, hope-fully without stirring up more gossip."

My mouth tightened. "Uh-huh, and don't you know that's the oldest ploy in the book? A distressed woman, leaning on an old friend. I would never have thought it of Helen, much less that you would fall for it."

Sam put his hand on my cheek. "Sweetheart, where did all this come from? Don't you know you can trust me? I'm married to the only woman I care about. Why would I risk losing you?"

"I don't know, but you've certainly run that risk today."

Sam smiled and kissed my hair. "Yeah, I guess I have, but you don't have to worry about me. I am as true to you as the day is long, because I love you. It's as simple as that."

"Well," I said, picking at the sheet as my anger began to melt away, "well, why didn't you tell me what you were doing? All I could think of was that you were keeping it from me because you had something to hide."

"I should've told you, even though Helen didn't want anybody to think she needed a lawyer. She thought it might damage Richard, if he's ever located. Of course, I'm not bound by the rules of confidentiality now that I'm not practicing, but I was trying to respect her wishes."

"You didn't count on LuAnne Conover, did you?"

"Is that who told you?" Sam laughed again and pulled me close. "I'm surprised she was the only one. See, honey, that ought to prove I wasn't trying to hide any-thing—parking my car in plain view of any-body who came by. Now listen, my advice to Helen was to get a good lawyer, maybe in Asheville where no one knows her." Sam rubbed his hand along my arm, making me feel warm and comforted. "You still mad at me?"

I turned my face into his chest. "I'm not really mad at you," I mumbled, then re-sorted to the most guilt-inducing justifica-tion I could think of. "I'm just hurt."

"I'm sorry," he said, leaning his face on my head. "I'm really sorry to put you through all this, but I just didn't think it was all that important. I get asked for legal advice all the time—on the street, over the telephone, at parties and you name it. I don't tell you about them because they're mostly petty or sordid little problems that take care of themselves. And if they don't, I give them the same advice I gave Helen: Go see a lawyer.

"So I want you to forget all this and trust me. I'm not doing anything I shouldn't be doing, and I'm certainly not tomcatting around."

"Well, I can't help it if I thought you were. Anybody would. Ever since LuAnne told me about seeing your car over there, I have been torn apart. Then when you didn't say a word about it, I thought it was Wesley Lloyd all over again."

"Let me tell you something," Sam said, pulling me up to look in my face. "I am not Wesley Lloyd, never have been and never will be. Do you believe that?"

I leaned against him with infinite relief. "Yes, and I thank the Lord for it."

Then he began whispering a few sweet words that, after a while, warmed and comforted my sore heart.

So I slept the sleep of the pacified, at least for a few hours. The next morning, though, it was a different story for the seeds of doubt had been sown. Oh, I was nine-tenths convinced that Sam was as faithful as any man can be, which is probably not saying much for any of them. It was that leftover one-tenth that continued to niggle away at me. Because, tell me this: Did it take all afternoon to advise Helen to go see a practicing attorney?

Chapter 14

❦

"Miss Julia? This is Tonya."

"Oh, Tonya, any news?" I quickly prepared myself to hear the worst. Why else would she be calling at seven-thirty in the morning while we were getting ready for Sunday school and church?

"Not one word," Tonya said, sighing. "We don't know what to think, although I've told Mother that as long as his body's not found, we have reason to hope."

"How is Mildred?" I asked. "I can come over after church if you need me."

"Oh, do come over any time you can. Visitors are a distraction for her. They keep her from dwelling on all the terrible possibilities. Actually, that's why I'm calling. I am just torn in two, because weeks ago I promised a friend to help him set up a shop he's opening in Charleston. He wants me to arrange the displays and the windows and so on, since I've had some experience doing that. In fact, I was in New York on a buying trip for him and had planned to fly from there to Charleston to help him. Of course, I had to cut it short, and now Kevin's pulling his hair out, just frantic because he's already advertised the opening date which is the day after tomorrow. But Mother needs me here, and I hate to leave without knowing what's happened to Daddy. I'm just in agony over what to do."

"That is a problem," I said, thinking that Kevin could just go on pulling his hair out if I'd had to make the decision. "But Charleston's not all that far. You could be back in a few hours if there's any news. And Ida Lee will be there with your mother."

"Well, that's just it. We had to take Ida Lee to the hospital about four o'clock this morning."

"My word, what happened?"

"She was sitting with Mother last night, but when she got up to get her something, she fainted dead away. We called the doctor and he put her right in the hospital. They'll be doing some tests today. So if I leave, Mother will be all by herself, and to tell the truth, I'm worried about her state of mind. So I wanted to ask you . . ."

Oh my, I thought, knowing what was coming.

"Would you mind coming over and spending the night with her? There's so much to do here today that I can't leave until late this afternoon. But I'll be back tomorrow night."

"Well, my goodness," I said, not particularly wanting to, but unable to think of a good excuse for refusing. I couldn't possibly admit that I didn't want to leave Sam on his own. "Well, I guess I could since it's just one night."

"Oh, thank you. That is such a relief. I know I should stay here with her. She's really upset with me, but Kevin is losing his mind and begging me to come. And I ought to be at the hospital for Ida Lee, too. I feel pulled in a dozen different directions, but when it rains, it pours, doesn't it?"

"That's true. Now, when do you want me, Tonya?"

"Why don't you plan to come for dinner? There's plenty of food, so don't worry about that. And I'll leave then so we can get an early start at the shop in the morning. I told Kevin I'd give him eight hours, no more, then I had to get back here." Tonya stopped, then said, "Of course, if there's word from Daddy today—good or bad, I guess—I won't go at all. Kevin will have to manage on his own."

At church, Pastor Ledbetter led the congregation in prayer for Horace and Mildred, even though neither was there to hear it. He didn't mention Helen or Richard except in a roundabout way, asking the Lord's attention to the weak, the fallen and the heavy-laden, but we knew who he was talking about.

Even so, there was no word from or about Horace, or about Richard for that matter, all that day. After lunch, Hazel Marie and I visited with Mildred in the early afternoon, but we didn't stay long. Since I'd be spending the night, I saw no need to hang around all day, too. There were still people in and out of Mildred's house, but with no news coming in, the number of visitors had slacked off considerably. Abbotsvillians were very good about offering immediate help, but when the need began to drag on for days, why, they had other matters to tend to.

"Hazel Marie," I said as we walked home, "if it keeps on the way it's going, Mildred will soon be agonizing over Horace's fate all by herself."

"I know, and don't think she hasn't noticed, either. She's keeping a list of who's visiting today. I saw it when you went out to the kitchen with Tonya."

"Well, if that's the case, I'm glad we went over, even though I'd think my staying all night would count for several daytime visits. Mildred has to realize that people have short attention spans, especially when nothing's happening. When they find Horace, in whatever condition he's in, they'll come swarming back."

"Speaking of spending the night," Hazel Marie said as we turned into our yard, "why don't I go with you? I'm not sure I want you and Mildred in that big house by yourselves."

"Well, speaking of that, I've already made arrangements, or had them made for me. Lillian hit the roof when she heard I'd be spending the night, and she put her foot down. She says she's going with me, especially since Ida Lee won't be there. And it's probably a good idea with all that food that's going to waste. Lillian will know what to throw out and what will last a few more days."

"What about Latisha? She's not going, is she?"

I stopped as we reached the back door and smiled. "Lord, no. Can't you just imagine Mildred and Latisha together? But, as a matter of fact, I sort of volunteered you and Sam to look after her. So she'll be spending the night here, if that's all right with you."

"Of course it is."

"I know I should've asked you first, but nothing was going to deter Lillian so I had to work something out in a hurry. Now, listen, Hazel Marie, I want you to have something to do after dinner tonight so that Sam will have to help Latisha with her numbers. That's what she's studying now, and he'll be good help."

Hazel Marie grinned. "Are you saying he'd be better than me?"

"No, no, Latisha's only learning her 'teens, according to Lillian, so you'd be fine with that. It's just that Sam needs something to occupy his mind." And his time, I might've added but didn't.

Late that afternoon, Lillian and I headed out for Mildred's house, carrying our overnight bags. Or rather, I was carrying mine, while Lillian had her things in a paper sack from the grocery store.

"I hope Miss Hazel Marie don't burn nothin'," Lillian said, as we walked along the sidewalk. "She get to talkin' an' forget about what's on the stove. I wish we coulda waited till I had supper ready for Mr. Sam an' Lloyd."

"You did have it ready, which you didn't have to do on a Sunday. All Hazel Marie has to do is heat it up."

"Yessum, that's what worryin' me."

I stopped as we came to Mildred's long driveway. "Would you look at that."

"What? I don't see nothin'."

"That's just it. Nobody's here. There's Tonya's car and nobody else's. I thought there'd be a few people still around to help us through the evening."

"I 'spect they got they own fam'lies to tend to."

We began the long walk up the drive-way, as I began to dread the interminable night ahead of us. There would be several hours of entertaining Mildred—providing distraction, as Tonya had called it—then the night in a strange bed, if not in a chair at Mildred's bedside.

"I just thought of something," I said, coming to a stop as we reached the cor-ner of the house. "Tonya didn't mention this, but I guess we're in for all day tomor-row as well as tonight."

"Why you say that? She jus' say spend the night."

"Yes, but she won't be back till late to-morrow, so unless I can find us some sub-stitutes, I think we're here for the duration."

Mildred answered the door, for what was probably the first time in her life. For a woman who, even temporarily, had lost her husband, she looked remarkably com-posed and put together.

"Oh, Julia," she said, pulling me inside, "I'm so glad you've come. And you, too, Lillian. You're both so sweet to keep me company tonight. You know I've never spent a night alone in my life, and I just couldn't face this one by myself." Tears gathered in her eyes as her composure melted away. "I can't understand why Tonya would want to leave me at this terrible time."

Before I could answer, Tonya, herself, came hurrying down the stairs. She was wearing a spring green pantsuit with a loosely woven turtleneck sweater underneath. Her high heels clattered on the parquet floor of the foyer. Once Tony had re-made himself into a woman, he never missed a chance to dress the part, and I mean dress in the most fashionable way possible. Of course as a young man, he'd come quite close to crossing the line from the fashionable to the overly dramatic. I recalled his white linen suits in the summertime and the velvet cape he wore with such flair in the winter. Of course, his way of dressing only confirmed our suspicions that the boy had tendencies. But we never spoke of them, nor did we ever expect him to act on them. Considering all the possible outcomes, surgical intervention had probably been a good thing.

"I can't thank you enough, Miss Julia," Tonya said. "And you, too, Lillian. I know Mother will be in good hands." She leaned over and kissed Mildred's cheek. "Call me if you hear anything from Daddy. But I'll be back before you turn around."

And off she went without giving her mother a chance to delay her. But for the rest of the evening, Mildred had plenty to say about children who didn't put their parents above all other considerations. She even went so far as to mention the sharpness of a serpent's tooth. Mildred had a way of feeling put upon if anybody's wishes came before hers, so I spent a good deal of time defending Tonya, even though I didn't especially feel that she deserved it.

But as the evening wore on, I began to think that Tonya had made the right decision. Mildred would've taken over every minute of her life if she'd been allowed to. That's what had happened to Horace, and look what had come of it. And, it occurred to me as we ate the dinner that Lillian put together from the condolence dishes, Mildred might easily try the same thing with me. She was not a woman who enjoyed her own company.

Well, I assured myself, that was not going to happen. One night and possibly part of the next day would be my contribution to friendship, then that was it. I had problems of my own to see to, and there was no way I was going to be at Mildred's beck and call, leaving Sam to go and come as he pleased. Or as Helen pleased.

Chapter 15

After several hours of listening to the myriad reasons that Mildred had for complaint, I was more than ready for bed. Lillian had kept herself busy in the kitchen, which Mildred entirely approved of and I envied.

"We need to get to bed," I finally said, interrupting the tenth telling of all that had gone wrong in Mildred's life. "Where do you want us to sleep?"

"I'm putting you in Horace's room," Mildred said with a tired wave toward upstairs. "Ida Lee had already freshened it, since we were expecting him back any minute." She had to stop to dab her eyes.

"And, since Tonya was in such a hurry to leave, she didn't get around to preparing the guest rooms. She said just to put Lillian in her room. I told her that Lillian would be more comfortable in Ida Lee's room over the garage, and that it would be more appropriate, too, but she insisted that both of you be in the house."

I bit my tongue so I wouldn't say anything, but with no thought whatsoever she had offended me and insulted Lillian, who was there out of the goodness of her heart.

"How is Ida Lee anyway?" I asked, a little more sharply than I usually spoke.

"Ida Lee," Mildred said with a great sigh. "She's never been sick a day in her life, and wouldn't you know she'd fall ill when I need her most. It is so inconvenient to have her in the hospital at a time like this."

"But how is she, Mildred?"

"She'll be all right, I'm sure. Tonya visited her this afternoon and checked with the doctor, and he says he thinks she's run down and working too hard. Can you believe that?"

Well, yes, I could, but I said, "I think you

should go see her tomorrow. I'll drive you to the hospital."

"Oh, I just couldn't, not tomorrow anyway. I need to be here in case there's any news from Horace. And, Julia, you know I'm not well. *My* doctor says I have to preserve my strength." Mildred sighed again. "I'll call her tomorrow. I think there's a phone in her room."

I didn't respond, just got up and went toward the kitchen, my insides roiling around and my mind disturbed.

"Lillian," I said, pushing through the door, "I know I don't tell you often enough, but I want you to know how much I appreciate you."

"Well, I 'preciate you, too, but what brought that on?"

"Oh, you know, just . . . well, to tell the truth, Mildred's about to drive me crazy, and I'm ready to get this night over with. And I've made up my mind, we're both going home in the morning. She can just fend for herself tomorrow."

Just then we heard Mildred's voice calling my name from the distant living room, and on top of that, a buzzer sounded on a panel in the kitchen.

"Is that the do'bell?" Lillian asked, as she began to rise from a kitchen chair.

I studied the panel as the buzzer sounded again. "Sit still, Lillian. That's not the door-bell. It's Mildred buzzing us from the living room." I propped my hands on my hips. "If that's not the most demeaning thing I've ever heard of. The idea, buzzing us like we're the hired help."

"I go see what she want," Lillian said, starting around the counter.

"No, you won't. Whatever she wants, she can get it herself. We're not here to wait on her, hand and foot. Just ignore that racket," I said, as the buzzer went off again. "If you'll check the doors back here and turn off the lights, we'll go on upstairs."

I lingered in the kitchen much longer than I'd intended, simply because I refused to be summoned like a handmaiden. Finally, though, we could delay no longer and Lil-lian and I walked through the back hall and into the foyer where we met Mildred.

"Oh, Julia," she said, "I thought you had left me. Didn't you hear my page?"

"Who couldn't? Now, Mildred, we have to get one thing straight: Don't be buzzing me with that thing again. Or Lillian, either."

"Well, I got lonely," she said, looking for-lorn. "You were gone too long."

"I'm going to be gone longer than that if I hear that thing again. Now, we've checked the doors, so let's go on up. Lillian, do you mind getting the lights in the living room? Come on, Mildred, you need to be in bed, and I certainly do."

I almost didn't make it, for Mildred began whining again about Horace and Tonya being gone and how abandoned she felt and how she'd never get to sleep with all the troubles on her mind.

"Take something," I said, nearing my fill of hearing her complaints. "Didn't the doctor leave you a sedative?"

"Oh, I hate taking those things. They make me feel so woozy. Just sit with me a little while, Julia, till I fall asleep."

"I'm not about to," I said, trying to say it lightly but firmly. "Lillian and I both are whipped. We've all had a long day and need our rest. I believe this is your room, Lillian. Sleep well, and you, too, Mildred. See you in the morning."

And I went to the room in the far corner that Mildred had pointed out and closed the door behind me. If she couldn't sleep, she could read a book, because I hadn't signed on to entertain her all night long.

I turned on a lamp and looked around with a twinge of uneasiness at invading Horace's private space. I would've preferred one of the guest rooms, even if I'd had to put sheets on the bed myself. Still, a bed was a bed, and I was ready for this one, even as it occurred to me how far Horace's room was from Mildred's. Her room was in the opposite corner at the head of the stairs, so if Horace ever wanted to visit her he had a long trek to make across the landing.

I couldn't help but wonder how often he made it.

I'll say this for her, though, Mildred, or probably Ida Lee, knew how to make guests feel not only comfortable, but pampered. The room, which overlooked the back garden, was elegantly furnished with a huge canopied bed, draped with beige and brown silk side panels, gilt-framed oil paintings of sleek thoroughbreds on the walls, and mahogany dressers, including a tall, masculine chest-on-chest. Books that I assumed Horace had been reading were on the bedside table and a one-size-fits-all robe on the suede-covered chaise longue. The adjoining bath was equally well appointed with thick towels, Crabtree & Evelyn soaps and shampoo and a Rigaud candle that I didn't dare light.

After undressing for the night, I found myself tempted to rummage through a few drawers and cubbyholes, just to satisfy my curiosity about the kind of man Horace was. But I had too much integrity to engage in snooping. Besides, the room hardly seemed lived in. A swift glance around revealed nothing of a personal nature and I was too sleepy to dig further into such matters.

After raising the back window a couple of inches, I headed for the bed. As tired as I was, it was a sensuous pleasure to crawl into it, pull up the comforter and sink toward sleep. Before I sank too far, though, I had a brief spell of worrying about Lillian, hoping that her room had been as well prepared as mine. I should've checked on it, but it was too late and I was too close to sleep.

The telephone suddenly shrilled beside my head, and I sprang up hardly knowing where I was. Scrambling for it in the dark, I finally found it, my heart racing in fear. Who would call at this time of night? Had they found Horace? Was something wrong at home?

"Julia?" Mildred said, pitifully. "I can't get to sleep."

I was so outraged I could hardly respond, but clearing my throat, I managed to say, "Well, I can, or at least, I did. So what do you want me to do?"

"Could you come sit with me a while? Just till I drop off?"

I wanted to slam the phone down and pull the covers over my head. But I didn't; instead with a great sigh I said, "All right, but just for a little while."

Mumbling to myself, I fumbled in the dark for the robe and wrapped it around myself. Then I stumbled out into the hall where a wall sconce had been left on, giving enough light to get me across the landing to Mildred's door.

Her room was brightly lit, a state of affairs patently unconducive to sleep. No wonder she was sitting up in bed, wide awake and disturbing other people.

"Come sit by me, Julia," she said. "I'm

so sorry to bother you, but every time I close my eyes I begin to imagine what Horace must be suffering. Or even worse, may not be suffering at all." She began crying again, and I had a twinge of pity, thinking of how I would feel if I didn't know where Sam was—which had better be right where I'd left him.

"Now, Mildred," I started as I went around the room clicking off lamps, "you have to turn your mind off. You need to sleep, if for no other reason than to be prepared for whatever tomorrow might bring."

"I know," she said, sniffing bravely. "And I'll try."

Leaving one lamp on, I drew up a chair beside her bed. Sinking down in it, it was all I could do not to put my head back and drop off to sleep. The silence in the room lengthened, broken only by the rustle of bed linens as Mildred adjusted herself. My eyelids began to droop and my head started to nod. Any minute now, I would tiptoe out and regain the bed I'd left.

"Julia, did I ever tell you how I met Horace?"

I stirred and sighed. "No, but . . ."

"Well, it was the year I came out, and

he danced with me at the Governor's Ball in Raleigh. He wasn't my escort, but he was doing the correct thing by dancing with all the debs. We didn't know at the time what was in store for us. Oh, I tell you, that was a wonderful year. So many young men, so many parties and receptions and balls. And clothes, oh, my word, I had the most gorgeous gowns. All bought in New York, of course. Mother was sure I would be engaged by the end of the year, but it didn't happen." Mildred sighed and turned her head back and forth on the pillow. "She was so disappointed, and I felt I'd let her down. But I had callers, plenty of them, too, and not just during my year. They continued to come, but you know, the same ones didn't keep coming back."

"Uh-huh," I managed to say, hoping she'd run down and off.

"But there were one or two, well, one especially. Such a nice young man, well mannered but not very well off, whom Mother seemed to approve of. But he wasn't the only one. I was quite popular, you know. Several went so far as to speak to Father in his study, but then, they all just tapered off."

I didn't respond, since Mildred seemed to be lost in memories of her salad days.

"Well," she said with renewed vigor, "the years passed along, and I was well into my twenties when Father called me into his study. You remember, don't you, Julia, how women weren't expected to know anything about money? And I certainly didn't, nor did Mother. Well, Father was old and frail by that time, and he sat me down day after day and made sure I understood what was what. As I was the only child, I needed to understand my responsibilities. And he told me how protective he'd been of me, fearful, he said, of gold diggers. Well, as it turned out, what he had done was to tell any young man who expressed interest that all my inheritance would be in trusts, locked up tight with no possibility of anyone getting their hands on it. Wasn't that foresighted of him? Because it wasn't true at all, but it was his way of weeding out the fortune-hunters. Which, obviously, they all were since none of them stayed around."

She sighed heavily, then said, "I've

always been grateful to him. But, anyway, Horace came back into my life a year or so after Father died, but I was well prepared by then. I knew what he wanted, but I also knew what I wanted and, with the warnings and instructions left by Father, we negotiated our marriage. And it's worked so well, right up to this point."

I heard her sniff again, then turn over in bed. "He took such good care of me." Mildred's voice began to fade away, then she mumbled, "Daddy, I mean, not Horace. But Horace, too, because he had to . . ." She hiccupped, then let out a soft snore.

I waited, trying to keep my head up, hoping that I'd heard the end of the reminiscences.

Several minutes passed with no word from her, so I began to ease out of the chair. Carefully walking across the thick carpet, I got to the door and looked back. Mildred's mouth was open and she was deep in sleep. Making no sound, I gratefully left the room, closed the door behind me and, in the dim light of the sconce, started across the Oriental rug in the hall. To my left, over the railing of the landing, there was the dark void of the foyer. I paused, suddenly aware of the stillness of the great house and of the fact that I was the only one awake in it. Then I picked up my pace and scurried to the safety of Horace's room in the far corner of the hall.

Chapter 16

Without turning on a light, I made a bee-line for the bed, wanting only to crawl into it and rest my weary head. But as I pulled back the covers and untied my robe, I stiffened and stopped. Something was scraping against the side of the house. Turning carefully toward the open window and listening intently, I heard it again. Dismissing it, though, as the wind blowing the branches of a tree against the side of the house, I began to shrug out of my robe.

Then with a thud of my heart, I stopped

in mid-shrug. There *was* no tree near the house.

Petrified, I stood in the dark room, not knowing whether to run or scream my head off. With a shaking hand, I reached for the telephone, then drew back. If I could hear what was outside, then what was outside could hear what I was doing inside. Maybe it was nothing. A cat, maybe, or a stray dog digging in the boxwoods around the foundation.

Carefully, without a sound, I eased down on the bed and waited. Sleep was far from my mind by this time. Straining to hear and identify the noise, I shivered and stared at the window, trying to get up the nerve to run over and close it.

Lord! I jumped a mile as something thudded against the wall. Then I heard a scratching sound right below the window. I came off the bed in a flash. Somebody or some*thing* was trying to get in.

Flying out into the hall, I ran straight to Lillian's room. Stumbling inside, I crashed against the bed. Shaking her, I whispered hoarsely, "Lillian! Lillian, wake up!"

"What?" She flipped over, stared blearily

at the ceiling, then sat up with a start. "Miz Allen?"

"No, it's me. Get up, hurry. Somebody's trying to break in!"

"Oh, Jesus!" she whispered. "What we gon' do?"

"We'll call the police from Mildred's room. Come on and don't make any noise."

Grabbing her hand, I led her out into the hall. Looking back at the dark room I'd just left, I scurried toward Mildred's room, dragging Lillian with me.

As we entered, I said, "Close the door, Lillian, and stand against it." Hurrying to the bed, I hissed, "Mildred! Mildred, wake up!" I shook her until she rose up in fright, her eyes wide and still red-rimmed.

"Horace? Is he back?"

"I don't know who it is, but get up. Somebody's trying to break in. Where's the phone?"

She flung back the covers and swung herself out of bed, nearly knocking me over in the process. "A portable's on the table. It may not be charged, but we don't need it."

"We have to call 911," I said, rummaging

over and around the magazines, tissues, handkerchiefs and empty glasses on the bedside table. My hands were shaking so badly, I hardly knew what I was doing. "Lord, where is the thing?"

Lillian, still braced against the door, said, "What if they already in?"

My hand closed on the portable phone just as I stepped back and almost tripped over Mildred. She was on her hands and knees, her bottom up in the air, as she reached under the bed.

Straightening up, she pulled out a single-barreled shotgun. "Don't worry, Lillian," she said grimly. "I'll take care of them." Then with a mighty pull on the bed, she hefted herself up, gun in hand.

"Lord, Mildred," I said, stepping back, "put that thing back. You'll kill us all."

"No, I won't, just whoever thinks they can break into my house. I've shot skeet with this little .410 a million times, and I don't mind using it on prowlers. Come on, let's see how they like the taste of bird-shot."

And off she headed, gun in hand and a grim look on her face. She pushed Lillian aside and sailed out into the hall, swinging the shotgun from one side to the other. "Who's here? You're about to get something you don't want."

"Mildred," I pleaded, "wait, wait, don't go out there. I'm calling 911."

Punching in the numbers with a shaking finger, I put the phone to my ear and heard nothing. Clicking it off and on again, I redialed. Not even a dial tone. Slinging the phone down in despair, I hurried after Mildred, grabbing Lillian's arm as I went.

"Stay behind me," I whispered. "I don't want either of us shot."

Mildred crouched in the hall outside her door, swinging the shotgun back and forth. "Where'd you hear them?"

"Outside the back window of Horace's room," I whispered back. "Against the wall. But let's go downstairs. We can sneak out the front door and run to my house."

Mildred squinched up her eyes. "I'm not sneaking anywhere. This is my house and I'm protecting it."

She was a changed woman. An hour or so before, she'd been driving me to distraction with her whining and clinging and helpless moaning. Now all I could see was a heavily armed Amazon in a lavender batiste nightgown with alençon lace inserts.

Charging briskly across the landing and carrying the shotgun with authority, Mildred headed for Horace's room. Lillian and I scurried after her, too frightened to stay behind.

"What she gon' do?" Lillian whispered, clasping a handful of my robe.

"I don't know, but don't get in front of her."

Mildred stopped beside Horace's open door and pressed herself against the wall, the shotgun angled high. I'd seen the same thing on television.

As we edged close behind her, she whispered, "If anybody's in there, I'm firing. So be ready."

"Mildred . . ." I started, but that was as far as I got.

Holding the gun in one hand, she grabbed my arm. "All together now, let's go!"

And she sprang into the dark room, pulling me with her, with Lillian so close behind that she stepped on my foot. The three of us stopped in a crouch, straining to see in the dark.

Lillian suddenly stretched out her arm, pointing at the window. "It's open! They already in!"

I had a brief glimpse of a swaying curtain by the open window, and my heart almost stopped. Then an explosion ripped the air as Mildred pulled the trigger. There was a flash of muzzle fire and the tinkle of shattered glass, and I felt a rain of pulverized plaster floating down. The recoil of the shotgun hurled Mildred into me and me into Lillian, and only the wall kept us all from landing in a pile on the floor.

Stunned and deafened, my mind reeling, I grabbed Lillian whose mouth was open in a scream I couldn't hear. Lillian scrambled against the wall, found a light switch, and the chandelier lit the room in a blaze of light. A haze of smoke and plaster dust hung below the ceiling and the reek of cordite filled the room. I stared in awe at the shattered glass, window frame and wall. Glass was all over the floor, and black smoke dribbled from the valance and one panel of the tattered silk curtains. Mullions dangled from the window and a hole the size of somebody's head gaped in the wall.

I dimly heard Lillian scream, then began to hear her words. "That thing on fire!"

She ran to the bathroom for a wet towel and began beating out the smoldering fire in the curtain.

"Watch out for the glass," I yelled, hoping she could hear me, though I could barely hear myself. "You don't have shoes on."

Mildred peered around. "Did I get anybody?"

"Just the window and half the house," I said. "Mildred, put that gun up. Whoever it was is long gone by now."

"Look out the window, Lillian," she said, "and see if anybody's lying out there."

"Oh, Lord," I moaned, just as somebody started ringing the doorbell and beating on the front door.

Mildred cleared the shotgun, then said, "I better get some more shells."

Dimly, I heard her name being called as the beating and banging continued on the front door. "Wait on the shells," I said, holding her back. "Let's see who that is. We've probably roused the whole neighborhood."

I hurried downstairs, turning on every

light I saw on my way, and yelled through the closed door. "Who is it?"

"Sheriff's department! What's going on in there?"

I unlocked and swung open the door. "Thank goodness!" I cried as a much-too-young sheriff's deputy, looking frantic, stood before me with a huge flashlight in his hand. "Somebody tried to break in! Around the back! That way!" I pointed in the right direction.

The young deputy took off, loping across the porch and jumping over the azalea bushes at the end. I ran back upstairs to warn Mildred to hold her fire. Help had arrived.

Chapter 17

"But who could it have been?" I glanced around at Mildred in the bergère by the fireplace, Lillian on the edge of a straight chair and Deputy Tucker standing in the middle of the living room, asking questions and taking notes.

Through the tall windows, I could see other deputies beating the bushes out on the lawn. Mildred had turned on the floodlights, so it was like daylight out there.

Nobody answered, which was no surprise since we were still suffering from shock, and I was just prattling out loud to ease the strain.

"Mrs. Allen," Deputy Tucker said, "with a nice house like this, you really ought to have a burglar alarm."

"Oh, I do," she said, as I jerked my head up in surprise. "Horace had it put in for me. He's so handy with things like that. We just forgot to turn it on."

Mildred had reverted to her languid Lady of the Manor mode, seemingly unperturbed that the mere flip of a switch could've kept us safe and her wall unscathed.

"Well," he said, jotting a note on his pad, "guess it's a good thing Lieutenant Peavey had me watching the house."

Hardly, I thought, since he'd only shown up after the crisis was over. But why had the lieutenant posted a guard in the first place? Did he know something we didn't? Well, that was highly likely since he was so close-mouthed, nobody knew what he was thinking.

"Mildred," I said, "you need to get somebody over here to repair the damage."

"Oh, I will, in the morning. I doubt anybody'll try breaking in again, not with all the activity out there."

"One more question," Deputy Tucker said, trying to get the interview back on track. "We found a ladder on the ground under the window. Would that be yours?"

"Possibly," Mildred said. "You might check the shed behind the garage, or you can ask Ida Lee. She'll know, but she's in the hospital." After a minute of thought, she went on. "The gardener could've left it, but I can't think why he would. He knows I don't like sloppy work."

"Some ivy was pulled off the wall, too. Did you tell him to do that?"

"Absolutely not." Mildred sat up straight. "It's not the time of year to trim ivy."

"Okay, then let me ask you this. You have a permit for that shotgun?"

"It's a sporting gun, Officer," she said, taking immediate umbrage. "I'm sure I don't need a permit to shoot skeet."

As Deputy Tucker opened his mouth to set her straight, I intervened. "Mildred, you may need a permit to shoot intruders. I'm sure the deputy will help you get one as soon as possible. Then you'll be legal the next time somebody tries to break in."

Deputy Tucker stared at me for a long minute. I gave him a brisk nod, and he turned back to Mildred. "You think you might've hit him?"

"I hope so," she said. "People like that need to be taught a lesson. But since you haven't found anybody on the grounds, I guess I didn't."

"I don't think you did, Mildred," I said. "From where that hole in the wall is, you aimed too high."

She sighed. "I always track too high."

After another few minutes of absorbing this information, Deputy Tucker closed his notepad. "I guess that's it then. We'll check the hospital, see if anybody's come in with gunshot wounds, but looks like we've done all we can do tonight. Lieutenant Peavey may want to talk to you tomorrow—today, I mean, since it's so late."

"Well, I certainly hope he has some news for me," Mildred said. "Lillian, will you see the deputy out? And while you're up, I could use some tea."

I rose and said, "I'll get it. It'll give me something to do. I'm too nervous to sit still."

I went out to the kitchen, turned on all the lights, made sure the back door was locked and put the kettle on. Standing by the stove, I tried to make sense of what had happened. To tell the truth, I was feeling somewhat guilty for having opened that window. That could've been an open invitation to the prowler. Whoever it had been saw an easy way in and jumped, or rather climbed, at the chance.

Thinking back over my actions from the first moment I'd entered the room and readied myself for bed, I suddenly realized that the window had not been locked. I distinctly remembered the sash sliding up so easily that it had taken no effort at all to let in a little fresh air. In fact, the window had gone up so slickly that I'd had to ease it back down a few inches to get it to the right height.

What did that mean? The more I thought about it, the more I thought it had to mean something. After all, there were dozens of windows on the first floor which were much more accessible and so far from the bedrooms that a little noise wouldn't have been heard.

I made tea for the three of us and took a tray into the living room. Depositing the tray on a table beside Mildred, I glanced out of one of the floor-to-ceiling windows. I walked over to it, pretending to look outside. Checking the lock, which was so tight I couldn't move it, I said, "My goodness, they've even got some police dogs out there."

I walked to three other windows, pretending to survey the yard activity while surreptitiously examining the locks. They were all securely closed. "I expect that prowler is long gone," I said, covering my investigation. "They'd have found him if he was still around."

"Come have some tea, Julia," Mildred said. "I'm missing Tonya terribly and just don't want to think about prowlers any more. Except for hoping I peppered him good." She took a sip from her cup, then brightened. "But maybe I did. Maybe he's running or even hiding somewhere while blood from a dozen pellets is leaking out all over the place."

Lillian swallowed hard and pushed her cup away.

But my mind was on something other than an unknown prowler. Ignoring the cup of tea that Mildred had poured for me, I said, "I'll be back in a few minutes. I need to run upstairs."

As Mildred began directing me to the downstairs powder room, I hightailed it across the foyer and up the stairs. Running swiftly across the landing, I went back into Horace's room where the temperature had dropped considerably from all the fresh air that Mildred had let in.

Going to the window on the side wall, I pushed aside the curtains and checked the lock. It was closed tight and wouldn't budge when I tried to open it. Working quickly, I ran my hand along the window frame. Yes, there was the wire for the alarm. Then I went to the back window, stepping carefully so as not to grind glass into the carpet, and did the same thing to that one. No wires!

I stood there for a few seconds, contemplating this turn of events. Why had this one window been unconnected to the alarm system that had the entire house wired up? Had that been Horace's doing? On purpose? And if so, why?

Hearing the doorbell, then voices in the foyer, I retraced my steps, wondering if the deputies had been successful in their search. As I started down the stairs, I saw Lillian talking to Sam. He'd obviously dressed in a hurry, for his pajama top was halfway stuffed into his pants and his feet were sockless. With his hair uncombed, he looked as if he'd jumped out of bed and come running. It did my heart good to see how worried he was. Take that, Helen Stroud.

"Julia!" he said, looking up at me. "What in the world is going on? Something woke me up and when I looked out, all I could see was a line of sheriff's cars. Are you all right?"

I hurried to him, feeling immensely relieved to have his arm around me. "We're all right, but we've had an eventful night, to say the least."

Lillian said, "Somebody come breakin' in an' Miz Allen, she run 'em off with her shotgun."

"Mildred has a shotgun?" Sam's eyebrows went up. "Good Lord, did anybody get hurt?"

"Only the wall," I said, holding on to him, "and the window, but both can be fixed. We're all fine, Sam, a little rattled, maybe, after such a scare."

Lillian frowned. "I'm more rattled than a little. I don't like people come climbin' up a wall an' tryin' to sneak up on people who sleepin' in they beds like they ought to be doin'."

Sam patted her shoulder. "I don't blame you, Lillian, but with all those deputies out there, you're safe now." Turning to me, he said, "How's Mildred?"

"Sam, you'd have to have seen her to believe it. I'll tell you all about it later, but for now, she's back to her old complaining self. Walk in and speak to her."

The minute Sam went into the living room and walked over to her chair, Mildred began telling him about Tonya's leaving and thanking him for letting Lillian and me keep her company. I didn't say anything, but a lot of thoughts went through my mind. For one thing, I couldn't believe that Mildred assumed that Sam had *let* me do anything. Coming from her, who ruled the roost in her own house, the thought was laughable. And a little insulting, if you want to know the truth.

Assuring Sam that we were safe for what was left of the night, I walked into the foyer with him. He wanted to stay with us, and I would've felt safer with him there. But I told him I'd rather he be with Hazel Marie and Lloyd.

"There're deputies all around," I said, "and I'm sure Lieutenant Peavey'll leave someone here the rest of the night. This'll probably be the safest house in town. But, Sam," I went on, lowering my voice, "I've discovered a few things I want to talk to you about. But not here. I'll be home early, so don't go anywhere." And certainly not to Helen's.

Chapter 18

"Charlie Outz, here. Would this be Mrs. Julia Murdoch?"

"It would," I said, about ready to hang up if the caller was selling something. The phone had rung as soon as Lillian and I walked into the kitchen at home that morning. I'd been firm with Mildred, telling her that we had to get Latisha and Lloyd off to school and couldn't console her a minute longer. Lillian had taken a breakfast tray up to her before we left, and, considering the hectic night we'd endured, I felt we had done all that was required. Mildred hadn't liked it, but I couldn't help that.

"Well, Mrs. Murdoch," the hearty voice on the phone continued, "I apologize for calling this early, but you know what kind of bird gets the worm. Thing is, I hear you're interested in that old wreck of a courthouse we got down here."

I frowned and switched my mind away from Mildred. "Yes?"

"Well," he said, seemingly taken aback by my lack of enthusiasm, "some of the commissioners tell me you think it ought to be preserved, and I wanted to talk to you about that. As the mayor . . ."

"Oh, you're the *mayor.* Well, my goodness, why didn't you say so?" I'd gathered who it was long before this, but I wanted him to know that not everybody in town had voted for him. "What can I do for you, Mr. Mayor?"

"Call me Charlie," he said, regaining his heartiness. "I'm a man of the people and I don't stand on formalities."

I did, so I didn't reply.

"Well, see," he went on, "the reason I'm calling is to find out if you have an open mind on the subject. Now everybody knows you're one of the influential people around these parts, and I'd like to get you on the bandwagon to move our little city forward and into the twenty-first century. Listen, Mrs. Murdoch, or Miss Julia as I know your friends call you, and I hope I'm numbered among them, but it's like this, one of the developers, actually the main developer, Arthur Kessler, he's coming into town for a few days, and I'd like for you to meet him."

"Why?"

"Why, so you can get the whole story straight from the horse's mouth. I think if you got to know him, you'd see how fortunate we are to have a man of his caliber wanting to invest in our town. I tell you, if you'd just look at his plans, you'd see what an asset that building will be to our whole community. Why, those condos're going to be the last word in luxury, and they'll draw an influx of wealthy retirees. And you know what that means? It means a higher tax base with no increase in children we'd have to build schools for. Just talk to him and get to know him. He might change your mind about the use of that prime piece of real estate where the old courthouse is."

"Possibly," I said, "but not likely. Still, I'm a fair-minded woman, and I'll certainly listen to what he has to say." In fact, I'd not only listen to what a New Jersey developer had to say, I'd also make sure that he got an earful of what I had to say.

"Well, then, that's good. Nothing like a good heart-to-heart to clear the air. He'll be in late this afternoon, and I want to get you two together real soon."

"We'll see," I said, unwilling to commit myself but anxious to get off the phone and talk to Sam. Whoever heard of phoning so early in the morning anyway? The mayor was certainly eager to smooth the way for new construction on Main Street.

I'd barely hung up when Mildred called to tell me how she couldn't bear to be alone and could I please come back over, just in case Lieutenant Peavey turned up with bad news.

"And, besides, Julia," she went on, "I'm feeling so poorly, it'd be wonderful if Lillian could come, too. There's so much to be done since Ida Lee's not here."

"Mildred," I said, suddenly coming up with the best idea I'd had in ages, "here's what you need to do. I want you to call the Handy Home Helpers and tell the owner that you need Miss Etta Mae Wiggins full time for the next few days. Tell her you need her day and night, even after Tonya gets back, and offer to pay whatever it takes to get her."

"Oh, Julia, I'm not sure I want a stranger in the house."

"Miss Wiggins won't be a stranger long. She's quite capable. Efficient and dependable, too. And, Mildred, she's the one who helped me recover our stolen jewelry, so you already have a connection to her."

"Oh, is that the one? Well, I guess I could see if she's available."

"You do that, and keep upping what you're willing to pay until she is available. Believe me, you won't regret it." And neither would I, since Etta Mae would keep Mildred from pestering me.

"Oh, you're back." Hazel Marie, already dressed for the day in spite of the early hour, pushed through the swinging door from the dining room. "I didn't expect you this early. Hey, Lillian, did you have a good night or did Mildred keep you up to all hours?"

"Just about," I answered, as Lillian's eyes rolled. Since Hazel Marie had apparently slept through the uproar in the neighborhood, we began telling her about our harrowing night.

"An'," Lillian concluded, "you ought to see the hole Miz Allen put in that wall. It like to scare me to death when that gun went off."

Hazel Marie was properly awed at our tale, and she was enthusiastic when I told her about Etta Mae Wiggins. "Oh, we should've thought of her yesterday! She does things like that for a living, and you wouldn't have had to stay over. I tell you, Miss Julia, I don't want you and Lillian staying another night with Mildred. She's dangerous with that gun—who would've believed it? And Tonya can just get right back here and take care of her own mother."

It was certainly gratifying to hear Hazel Marie so concerned for my welfare, and Lillian's, too, of course. And as the rest of the household gathered for breakfast, we had to go over the whole story again and again. We were so taken up with telling it and listening to everybody's comments that we ended up eating in the kitchen, mainly because it was Lillian who enjoyed telling it the most.

Both Lloyd and Latisha were wide-eyed at the thought of Mrs. Allen wielding a shotgun. If it'd been up to me I'd have kept that part of it under wraps. Children don't need to know every little thing that happens.

Latisha was especially entranced, swiveling her head back and forth from one to the other of us as the events of the night were discussed. Finally she said, "I wish just one of y'all would talk, my neck's got a cricket in it from switchin' it around."

Lloyd laughed. "A cricket! You mean a crick in your neck, don't you?"

"I don't know what it is, but I got it."

Lillian came over and rubbed Latisha's neck, telling her to eat her cereal and stop listening to grown folks talking.

As Hazel Marie prepared to take the children to school, I pulled her aside. "Have you talked to Mr. Pickens?"

"I finally got him late last night, and it's just like you said. He can't do anything until he's hired by one of the principals." She frowned, then went on. "That means either Mildred or Tonya, I guess. Anyway, he's got his hands full right now, doing some work for a big insurance company." She looked around, then lowered her voice. "Investigating *fraud*! Don't you think that's an interesting coincidence? I mean, with Richard being accused of the same thing?"

"There may be different kinds of fraud, but I expect they all hinge on money one way or another. But listen, Hazel Marie, there may be more going on than meets the eye. I haven't told anybody all I know about last night—I'll tell Sam, of course— but we really need to talk Mildred into hiring Mr. Pickens." I leaned close and risked telling her my suspicions. "Now, don't tell anybody, Hazel Marie, but I have reason to believe it was Horace trying to break in last night."

Hazel Marie's eyes popped wide open. "*No.* Why?"

Lloyd, burdened with his bookbag, stood by the door jangling the car keys. "We gotta go, Mama. We'll be late."

I whispered to her, "Run on. I'll tell you later."

As they left, with Hazel Marie still on tenterhooks, I went in search of Sam.

Finding him in our bedroom, buttoning up a cardigan, I said, "Sam, I need to talk to you before you head out."

"I need to talk to you, too. Come over here and give me a hug. I declare," he said, wrapping his arms around me, "you gave me a scare last night. When I looked out and saw all the sheriff's cars and lights on all over, I thought my heart would stop. I nearly broke my neck getting there. I thought something had happened to you."

"It was scary for me, too, though I don't know what scared me the most—a prowler halfway up the wall or Mildred swinging that shotgun around. But, listen, Sam, I don't think it was a prowler at all. I think it was Horace breaking into his own house."

Sam pulled back to look down at me. "Really? What makes you think that?"

So I told him about the unlocked and unwired window that was only in Horace's room. "I mean," I went on, "it was the only window I found that was accessible. There could be others, I guess, but I didn't have a chance to check them all. What do you think it means, Sam, if it was him?"

Sam's face was a study in deep thought. "I don't know, Julia, but if it was him, he obviously didn't want Mildred or anybody else to know he was there. And that un-wired window leads me to wonder if he'd used that way in and out before."

"Not without a ladder," I reminded him.

"The rooms in that house have such high ceilings, it'd be a long way to either jump down or climb up without help."

"I don't guess you had time to walk around to the back and check that wall, did you?" I shook my head and he went on. "I may do that today after the deputies leave."

"Why?"

"Well, that ivy could be on lattice or the bricks could be laid to provide footholds. I'd just like to satisfy my curiosity about his possibly going and coming that way. Because I agree with you that it could've been Horace. Who else would know where a ladder was located and which particular window would be unlocked?"

"Oh, my goodness, that scares me even more. That would mean he's hiding out and doesn't want to be found. And, Lord, Sam, what if Mildred had killed him? She'd never in this world get over it."

In his wry way, Sam said, "Neither would he."

I couldn't help but smile, though there was little humor in what had happened or in what could've happened. Still, it lifted my spirits to be attuned to Sam.

"Well, since you're in the mode of giving

free legal advice," I said, as I gave him a little dig about his activities over the weekend, "should I tell anybody else about this? Lieutenant Peavey, in particular. I'm hesitant to tell Mildred. No telling what she'd do if she thought he was alive and climbing the walls." I smiled again. "Literally."

"Let's just keep it to ourselves for a little while. We don't know who it was and we might create more problems by making Horace a suspect. At least for now, he's assumed to be a victim. Let's not make it worse until we know more.

"But, Julia," he went on, "this means I'll have to go see Helen again, and I want you to know about it before I do. And I want you to know that she called me last night, because some deputies showed up and emptied Richard's office there at home. She was frantic, but they were within their rights and there was nothing to be done about it."

My voice was as cold as my heart. "Did you go over there last night?"

He smiled. "No, I stayed right here."

"So why do you need to go this morning?"

"Because the more I thought about what

you said about a connection between Richard and Horace, the more I think it's likely. And if it was Horace climbing the wall last night, what is in his room or in the house that he wants badly enough to sneak in to get it? I want to hold Helen's feet to the fire and see what she really knows."

"You sound like Mr. Pickens, so before you start investigating on your own, I wish you'd get him to help you."

"Don't worry. I'm not doing any real investigating. It's just that after what happened last night when you could've been hurt, I have a personal interest in finding out what's going on."

"Well, all right, but don't stay so long that everybody in town sees your car. I don't need LuAnne running in to tell me what my husband is doing."

Sam put his hand over his heart. "I promise," he said, but he smiled when he said it. "Oh, Julia, I almost forgot. The mayor called last night, too. He wants us, you especially, to meet one of the courthouse developers who's coming in today, and I sort of invited the man to dinner tonight. The mayor has another engagement. I hope you don't mind that I said to send him on. It'll be a chance to check this man out. Besides," he said, pulling me close, "I don't want you meeting some strange man off on your own somewhere."

"Tonight? Why, Sam, when the mayor called this morning, I didn't say anything about any dinner plans. He probably thinks we never talk to each other. But it doesn't matter. Since you've extended the invitation, I'd better get with Lillian to see what we can have. I'll tell you this, though, too much is going on for me to be all that impressed with somebody from New Jersey."

Chapter 19

❧

"Miss Julia! Guess what!"

In spite of trying to catch up on lost sleep, I'd heard the clatter of Hazel Marie's high-heeled mules as soon as she came in the back door. I tracked her as she hurried toward the living room where I was resting my eyes and trying not to worry about what designs Helen might have on Sam.

Blinking blearily and struggling to appear awake, I lifted my head from its resting place on the wing of one of my new Queen Anne chairs. Every time I caught a few winks in the middle of the day, I congratulated myself for getting rid of those hard, uncomfortable Victorian chairs. "I can't guess anything, Hazel Marie. After being up half the night, I'm too sleepy."

"Oh, I'm sorry. Why don't you go lie down for a while?"

"No, all I needed was a little catnap. Now, what's going on?"

"Well, I stopped by Mildred's after I took the children to school, and guess who's there?"

"Etta Mae Wiggins, I hope."

"Oh, poo, you already knew!"

"No, I didn't. I'd urged Mildred to try to get her, but I didn't know she'd succeeded. And thank goodness for it, because she'll keep Mildred off our backs. I just hope Etta Mae can please her. Or, rather, I hope that Etta Mae can stand her."

"It was so good to see her," Hazel Marie said, sitting on the sofa and leaning toward me. "We haven't talked since the two of you got back from Florida. But, listen, you haven't heard the latest."

"About Horace?" I was wide awake by now.

"No, not a word about him. But Tonya called while I was there to see how her mother was and, I guess, to see if there was any news. Anyway, she and Mildred really got into it. And it ended up that Mildred told her about Etta Mae and then told her she could just stay in Charleston for all she cared."

Hazel Marie took her bottom lip in her teeth for a minute, then she said, "It was awful just hearing one side. I can't imagine what Tonya said back to her."

"Well," I said, covering a yawn with my hand. "I hate to say this, but Mildred is a little on the self-centered side, and I expect Tonya has to do everything she can to stand up for herself. Actually, it surprises me that Tonya is still living here. I'd think New York would be the place for her, especially since she used to live there." I did a little lip biting, myself. "Of course, that was when she was Tony, so maybe her friends wouldn't be the same."

"That's probably it. Listen, you won't believe what Latisha said on the way to school. She said she'd about had enough of school and as soon as she finished first grade, that would be it for her."

"You never know what that child will come out with," I said, smiling. "Well, speaking of Lillian, looks like we're having a guest for dinner tonight. Sam invited Arthur Kessler, who's breezing into town for a few days. He's that developer who wants to replace our beautiful Georgian courthouse with a modern high-rise. I can't for the life of me understand why Sam took it upon himself to do that. He knows I'll have to constrain myself and not get into an argument. I wish we had somebody else coming to keep the conversation as pleasant as possible. Will Mr. Pickens be around?"

"Oh, I wish, but he's in Charlotte for a day or two." Hazel Marie's face had a disappointed look, but then she brightened. "I know! Let's invite Mildred and Etta Mae."

I doubted that either of those could add much pleasantness to table talk, what with Mildred's whining and Etta Mae's penchant for raving about roadhouses and Disney World. Yet, they'd fill the silences since, as the hostess, I'd be constrained in saying what I wanted to say to Mr. Kessler.

So I said, "I don't know that Mildred would come, but it would do her good to get out. And I expect Etta Mae would appreciate a break. All right, let's see. There'll be Sam and me, you and Lloyd, Mildred and Etta Mae, and Mr. Kessler. That's an uneven number at the table. Who else could we ask?"

"Well, we could let Lloyd eat in the kitchen," she said, but I shook my head to that. "Then what about LuAnne? She's a single woman, temporarily at least, and she might enjoy getting out on her own. Then there's Helen, who's also a temporary single."

"No," I said a little more sharply than I'd intended. "Even though she's in dire need of friends, Helen has cut me out in every way possible. I'm not giving her a chance to do it again. No, let's stick with LuAnne, and that'll make eight at the table. But that's five women and only three men, counting Lloyd." I thought for a few minutes, then said, "I know. Let's ask the Ledbetters. That adds another woman, but if we get the pastor talking about the state of the church, he'll keep us off the courthouse. And I don't want to get into that with Mr. Kessler, especially at the dinner table."

Hazel Marie got to her feet. "We'd better start calling. It's getting late."

"I don't know what got into Sam to ask that man for tonight," I said, still feeling put upon. "He knows a dinner party takes time to plan."

Hazel Marie laughed. "He was probably thinking of just an extra plate. He wouldn't figure you'd go all out like this."

Yes, I thought, and he wouldn't figure that I'd be worried sick while he was even now visiting Helen again. My stomach tightened at the thought, but I resolutely put it behind me, temporarily at least.

"Let's go talk to Lillian," I said, and headed for the kitchen.

After Lillian got over the shock of hearing that there would be ten for dinner that night, she said, "Somebody got to go to the sto' if we gonna feed that many. What you want me to serve?"

"I don't know. What do you think, Hazel Marie?"

Hazel Marie gazed at the ceiling, a sure sign that she was thinking. "Well, since Mr. Kessler is from up north, I think we should have a typical southern dinner. If he's going to move here and tear up our town, we ought to let him have a taste of what we're like."

"Why, Hazel Marie," I said, as the germ of an idea formed in the back of my mind, "that is inspired thinking. Which typical southern dinner are you thinking of?"

She shrugged, having lost all inspiration. "I don't know. Fried chicken?"

"Watermelon," Lillian said, grinning. "Collard greens. Barbecue ribs. Fried pork chops, maybe."

"Fried pork chops are tempting," I said, "but Pastor Ledbetter's watching his cholesterol. What about shrimp and grits? You don't get any more southern than that."

"That be good," Lillian said, "an' easy to fix. What you want with it?"

"Well, we need something green, so let's have collards as a side dish. That'll give him something to talk about when he goes home. And a fruit cup to start and your good yeast rolls, just to show him we're not entirely in the backwoods. And pecan pie for dessert. Now, Hazel Marie, let's start calling, and do apologize to everybody for being so last-minute. Explain that Mr. Kessler has been unexpectedly foisted on us by the mayor, which is the truth and, believe me, I'm not forgetting it."

The rest of the day was spent scurrying around preparing for our impromptu dinner party. Lillian started on the rolls, since they needed time to rise, and Hazel Marie went to the Winn-Dixie with a long list, while I began setting the table. And all the while, my mind was on Sam, wondering where he was, how long he'd stayed with Helen, what he'd learned from her and why he was getting more and more entangled with her and the case of her missing husband.

After putting the finishing touches on the table, I took my flower snips and went out into the yard, hoping to find enough blooms to make a stab at a centerpiece. I could've called the florist, but I wasn't in the mood to go all out for Mr. Kessler. He'd have to take what we gave him, even if it left a bad taste in his mouth.

As I wandered around the yard, I realized that Hazel Marie's suggestion of giving him a sample of what we were like was flitting around in my mind. As a high-powered developer, he'd assuredly surveyed the area and come up with Abbotsville as the ideal location for his project. If the mayor was right about the plans, Mr. Kessler intended to sink a lot of money in the town. I couldn't think of what had made him pick us off the map, unless he knew something that none of us living here knew.

We had a reasonably mild climate, beautiful mountain views, a lower than average cost of living, neighborly people and, well, maybe that was enough for people unaccustomed to any of it.

I knew there would be few, if any, local buyers of his condominiums, which meant that he intended to attract outsiders to life on our Main Street.

Now, I had nothing against outsiders. They could bring new ideas and cultured tastes and a boost to the economy. I knew that because I was not a native myself, having moved to Abbotsville as Wesley Lloyd's bride some years before and, without boasting, I could say that I'd added immeasurably to the general tone of the town, both socially and economically.

Still, your average outsiders, especially your wealthier ones, tended to think they knew better than the people they came to live among. If I'd heard it once, I'd heard it a dozen times. They were prone to point out that things had been done better where they'd come from. It made us wonder why they'd left.

I found a few bedraggled blossoms in the side yard so I carefully snipped them, hoping they weren't drooping too badly. Then I cut some sprays from a flowering cherry tree, which was about all the color I could find. I'd have to fill in with some greenery and hope for the best. Walking back toward the house, I glanced over at the Family Life Center across the street, that huge brick building erected purely on Pastor Ledbetter's pride, and smiled in remembrance of the image that had once appeared on it. I almost laughed out loud, because that brought to mind something Latisha had said. She'd heard us discussing the Madonna-like apparition that had spread over the bricks and thought we'd had a visitation by a rock star.

I came to a sudden stop beside a hydrangea bush, struck with the possibilities opened up by Hazel Marie's suggestion of giving Mr. Kessler a taste of the South. *Uh-huh,* I thought, *since he seems to have such an appetite for Abbotsville, why don't we give him something to really chew on?*

Chapter 20

∽

No one seemed to have had plans for a Monday evening, as they all accepted our invitation. It had, however, taken some persuasive talking on my part to get Mildred out of her house and into mine. As soon as she walked in the door that evening, she whispered to me, "You're the only one who knows what I'm going through, Julia." And before I could answer, she went on. "But at least you had somebody to bury."

"Oh, Mildred," I said, taken aback at the expression of a tinge of resentment because she didn't. "Let's hope it won't come to that."

"Well, it's all so strange. I'm sure every-body thinks I should be home mourning Horace, not here at a dinner party. But it gets old sitting around waiting for word that never comes."

Etta Mae, who was right by her side, said, "Now, Mrs. Allen, Lieutenant Peavey knows where you are and he'll call if he needs you. Why don't we find you a place to sit so you can see who all's here?" She grinned over her shoulder at me as she maneuvered Mildred toward a chair. "Hey, Miss Julia. How you doing?"

As our eyes met in mutual recall of our Florida adventure, which some might label criminal in nature or as close to it as to not matter, I was glad to see that she'd es-chewed her white uniform in favor of a navy pantsuit. I was fairly sure that Mildred had not approved, but then, Etta Mae prob-ably hadn't asked her opinion. Mildred may have met her match.

As the doorbell rang again, I turned to greet LuAnne and the Ledbetters who walked in with her. Lloyd was right there to take the ladies' coats to the bedroom, and a good thing, too, for Emma Sue side-stepped the pastor as he reached out to help and shed hers into Lloyd's arms. I detected a distinct marital chill in the air.

Sam, undaunted by, or perhaps unaware of, the frigid atmosphere, greeted the pastor and Emma Sue warmly and ushered them into the living room. LuAnne, her color high and her breath rapid, remained expectantly at my side.

"Is he here?" she whispered.

"Leonard?"

"No, Julia, the *developer.* I don't care if I never see Leonard again, but don't tell the pastor I said that. Do you know what he told me?"

I had a pretty good idea, but she didn't give me a chance to respond.

"He told me," she went on, "that I should pray for patience and be ready to welcome Leonard back into the fold as soon as he comes home. That's my duty as a wife, he said, and he told me that divorce is not an option and to not even think of it. Well, I knew he didn't approve of divorce in general, but you'd think he could make an exception occasionally, wouldn't you? So I said, what about adultery, which I'm sure Leonard is committing. Or, trying to commit, but either way the Bible says that's grounds for divorce, but he said that's only allowed, not encouraged, and even then it's only for the spiritually weak. Which I think is crazy, because it takes more strength to divorce than it does to just sit around and let somebody run all over you. And," she said, taking my arm and pulling me close, "he said if we did divorce, neither of us could ever remarry. Don't you think that's going too far? I mean, *I'm* the innocent party here. It's no wonder so many transfer to the Episcopal church."

"I don't know, LuAnne, but Leonard's only been gone two days. It's too soon to be thinking along those lines."

She squinched up her face and whispered, "Not for me, it's not. Is he married?"

"Who?"

"The *developer!* Why do you think I came tonight?"

"Oh, this must be him now," I said, as the doorbell rang. "And all I know is that Mr. Kessler is coming. The mayor didn't mention anybody else."

When Mr. Kessler stepped inside, I introduced myself and LuAnne, who immediately latched onto him. I took his measure

as he spoke, first thanking me pleasantly
enough for my hospitality, then questioning LuAnne on such topics as how long
she'd lived in Abbotsville and how she liked
it. Beaming under his attention, she took
his arm and guided him toward the living
room.

I followed slowly, since all the guests
had arrived, musing all the while over my
first impression of Mr. Kessler. He resem-
bled someone I knew or had seen, but I
couldn't place who it was. He wasn't a tall
man, but neither could he be called short.
In his beautifully cut gray suit, white shirt
and light blue silk tie, his shoulders were
heavy and it was obvious that he was well
fed. Not exactly overweight, just thickset
and solidly built. But well maintained in all
particulars, I gave him that. He had that
sleek, carefully barbered look, with a fair
complexion that I suspected had been
aided by the application of a serum prod-
uct. I'd have to ask Hazel Marie what she
thought. His hair was completely white and
meticulously combed, except for the top of
his head where there was none to comb.
Unobtrusive wire-framed glasses rested
halfway down his nose, so that, with his

head tilted down, he did most of his looking over instead of through them. He had a clipped way of speaking, snapping off each word in an authoritative manner. And even when he merely thanked me for having him, it was as if he was daring me to contradict him.

I wished I could think who he reminded me of. It was somebody I didn't like, I was sure of that. I don't care for aggressive people who feel they have to attack others before they get attacked themselves—which is generally because they're hiding something that needs attacking.

Walking into the living room, I saw that Sam was making sure that everyone was comfortable as he went from one to the other with a few words of welcome. Sam was an easy and thoughtful host, always knowledgeable enough to ask about special projects or interests of each guest. But, given the general tenor of thought and concern pressing in on most of those present, he would have to make a mighty effort, as would I, to keep the party from degenerating into a lament over the possible loss of either a husband or a courthouse.

Lillian came in with a tray of drinks, a fruit punch laced with ginger ale and served in my Waterford cystal. I saw Mr. Kessler take a sip, then look askance at the contents. As his eyes followed Hazel Marie, he took another sip, possibly to confirm the absence of alcohol, and swallowed with a slight curl of his mouth. I smiled to myself, thinking that he'd be further dismayed when he learned there would be no wine with dinner, either. He liked Lillian's hot olive cheese puffs, though, and even stopped her on her way back to the kitchen to ask how she'd made them.

"I jus' th'ow in a little of this an' a little of that," she said, "an' enough cheese to make a dough, then wrap it 'round them olives. Then I cook 'em till they done."

When we went to the table, I placed Mildred at Sam's right and Mr. Kessler at mine. I would have preferred a more amiable guest beside me, but you either do things right or you don't do them at all. I made up for it by placing Etta Mae next to him, in the hope that she'd keep him occupied. Conversationally speaking, of course. Emma Sue was at my left, which earned me glares from LuAnne, who'd wanted to be seated close to Mr. Kessler. But I didn't see it as my responsibility to aid and abet a married woman who was intent on waging a campaign to outdo her delinquent husband.

I placed Lloyd next to Etta Mae, since they enjoyed each other, and Hazel Marie beside him on Sam's left. Pastor Ledbetter and LuAnne filled out the other side. It wasn't the most evenly balanced table, but it was the best I could do, given what, or rather, *who* I had to work with.

Hazel Marie tried valiantly to converse with LuAnne, but she kept getting interrupted by Mildred who wanted not only Sam, but those on either side, to commiserate with her. And, of course, LuAnne was straining to hear anything Mr. Kessler said.

Finally Hazel Marie picked up the condiment dish. "Would anyone care for watermelon rind pickles?" she asked, as she passed the dish to Sam.

Mr. Kessler did not, nor did he much care for the rest of his meal. Oh, he ate the shrimp and took a roll every time the silver bread basket was offered. As for

the grits, he only spread them around on
his plate so that it would look as if he'd
eaten some. I was familiar with that tactic,
since Lloyd also used it when green peas
were served. Lillian frequently found a pile
of them hidden under a lettuce leaf.

As for the collards, well, I pretended not
to hear when he quietly asked Etta Mae
what they were.

"Collard greens," she whispered back.
"They're what helped the South rise
again."

I tried to engage Emma Sue in conversation, but it was a losing proposition. She
mostly sat like stone, her face white and
drawn as she picked at her food. Pastor
Ledbetter, on the other hand, was at his
voluble best, essentially carrying the conversation for the table and eating heartily.
If you ever want to be heartened by the
food you serve, invite a preacher to eat it.
They like any and every thing, and will
make you feel that you're an exceptional
hostess by the enjoyment they exhibit in
consuming it.

"Well, I tell you," he said, as he cleaned
his plate, "that was some fine eating. Lillian is an absolute jewel, Miss Julia, not

another one like her." Then looking across my bedraggled centerpiece at Mr. Kessler, he said, "I hear you're planning to move to our fine town, and if you do, you won't regret it. I've been here for years now, and it's a fine place to live. Of course," he went on with a big smile, "we know it doesn't have the advantages of a big city like Raleigh, but it has its compensations."

At the mention of Raleigh, Emma Sue bowed her head and, in the process of patting her lips with her napkin, did the same to her eyes. Fearing a tearful breakdown, I quickly pressed the bell under the table with my foot to summon Lillian, and met Sam's eyes down the length of the table. His eyebrows went up just a fraction, then Mildred leaned toward him to regain his attention. I had to smile. She had monopolized him throughout the meal, undoubtedly regaling him with the same complaints I'd had to put up with during the Night of the Prowler. Ordinarily, it was a pleasure to have Mildred, since she knew what was expected of a guest, but this night was different. But then, I suppose that any night in which your husband is missing has to be different by any definition.

"It certainly does," Mr. Kessler said, responding to Pastor Ledbetter. "And that's exactly what people who live in metropolitan areas are looking for when they retire. They want a small-town atmosphere with quaint characters who're friendly and community minded. They want to see salt-of-the-earth types when their cars need a lube job. They want to walk down the sidewalk and have people speak to them, and they want repairmen who'll come when they're called."

Yes, and so would I. I couldn't help wondering what fantasyland Mr. Kessler was living in. No one replied to his dream of small-town living, silenced, I supposed, by what he'd apparently seen in Abbotsville that we hadn't.

"One thing I want to do while I'm here," Mr. Kessler went on, "is to meet some of these people, get to know them, learn what they do with their time and how they live their lives. I'll have my staff put some talking points together, so as soon as the sale goes through, we'll be ready to spread the word all over the country about the good life in Abbotsville." He managed a quick, one-sided grin. "You'll all be celebrities by the time I'm through."

The thought of sudden and unwanted fame silenced all of us until Pastor Ledbetter cleared his throat and said, "I hope you won't leave out this community's commitment to the church, although I must say I'm leery of widespread exposure through the media. But I'm sure whatever you do will be tasteful and appropriate."

I wasn't sure it would be, because when it comes to selling something, which in this case would be us, all bets are usually off.

But Lillian distracted us when she came in and efficiently cleared the table, then served generous helpings of her pecan pie, which Mr. Kessler clearly enjoyed. He would've probably accepted another slice if it'd been offered since he'd eaten so little of the main course.

As I rose from the table and indicated that we move to the living room, I mentally sighed with relief. The dinner had gone off well enough. No one had instigated an argument about high-rise condominiums where they weren't wanted, and no one had dissolved into tears in spite of Emma Sue's fragile hold on hers. Of course, Lu-Anne had made no effort to add to the conversation. She'd limited herself to frowning at me, still unhappy with the seating arrangements. And poor Sam had been stuck with Mildred, but, I thought with grim satisfaction, he'd already put himself out for one woman with a missing husband, why not for another?

Actually, though, I'd guess that only two people had truly enjoyed themselves: Pastor Ledbetter who, as I've mentioned before, is easy to please when food is served, and Etta Mae Wiggins who was always thrilled to be included in anything. She'd kept up a constant chatter with Mr. Kessler on one side and with Lloyd on the other, displaying more social ease than I'd previously given her credit for. Mr. Kessler seemed intrigued with her, or if not her, then Hazel Marie. He glanced from one to the other of them often enough for me to notice, though I'm not sure anyone else did. Of course, they were the only women at the table without wedding bands, so that may have been the attraction. I'd have to mention that to LuAnne.

Then as we wended our way back to the living room, Mr. Kessler said, "I'd like to extend my compliments to the cook," and he pushed through the door to the kitchen to speak to Lillian. I almost followed him, but went instead with the rest of the guests. But he had surprised and confounded me by this manifestation of good manners. Especially since he'd eaten so little of what the cook had served.

Chapter 21

❦

Our after-dinner conversation got off on the wrong foot almost as soon as we re-gathered in the living room. As we sat in a loose semicircle around the fireplace, in which Sam had built a small fire to take the chill off the nippy evening, Pastor Led-better took it upon himself to draw out Mr. Kessler.

In the midst of the general conversation, the pastor leaned over and said, "I hear you have big plans for Main Street. It's about time somebody did something with that old courthouse. It's about to fall down."

Wanting to forestall that topic and pretending not to have heard, I jumped in with a question. "Will your wife be joining you, Mr. Kessler?"

LuAnne immediately stopped talking with Emma Sue and turned to hear the answer.

"I'm a widower," Mr. Kessler said. "Unhappily. But call me Arthur."

"I'm sorry to hear that," I replied, then, searching frantically for another subject, went on. "And where in New Jersey do you live?"

"Milford."

I waited a second for further enlightenment, but when it wasn't forthcoming, tried again. "Do you have children?"

"Two daughters. Both grown and married."

By this time, everybody's attention was on him, waiting to learn more. Pleading silently for anyone to help me out, I was relieved when LuAnne finally said, "Oh, children are such a blessing and I know you're proud of yours. I've always regretted not having any, but a single woman is so much better off without them, don't you think?"

My eyes rolled only slightly as she let him know she was available. I declare, what some women won't do to attract a man.

I thought Sam was coming to the rescue when he said, "We have a lot of retirees here from New Jersey. All fine people and an asset to the town."

That perked up Mr. Kessler. "That's exactly the kind we intend to attract. People're tired of congestion and long commutes and hard winters. Like I said, they're looking for better places to live when they retire, places with a low cost of living and where they'll have a sense of community. That's why we think Abbotsville is ideal for our project."

I wanted to ask who the *we* were that he kept referring to, but I preferred staying above and out of any of his plans.

"Well, you're looking at the right place," Pastor Ledbetter said, and we were off and running on the very subject I'd wanted to avoid.

Mildred, roused out of her concentration on her own woes, said, "I hope you'll build something nice, something that will bring in the right kind of people. If you do, I might be interested myself. I don't want to end up rattling around in a big house all by myself."

Etta Mae reached over, patted her hand and whispered something comforting to her. Then she said to Mr. Kessler, "If you're looking for building sites, you ought to look at Delmont. We're only a few miles from here out in the county, and we could sure use some fresh faces. Everywhere I go, I see the same people, I don't care where it is." She laughed. "The ones I see at the hardware store in the mornings pop up again at Ingles in the afternoon, and they're the same ones I see line dancing at the roadhouse that night."

Mr. Kessler gave her long, penetrating look, and I couldn't tell if it was a look of dismay or of interest. Either way, he didn't answer her, just turned his shrewd eyes to Hazel Marie when she said, "Delmont's a nice place. I've always liked it."

"Oh, I like it, too," Etta Mae said. "Especially now. Since Miss Julia gave me the manager's job, I've been able to get some decent people in the trailer park."

Mr. Kessler jumped on that. "You live in a trailer?"

"I sure do," she said, not one bit reluctant to admit to it. "I've got it fixed up real nice with an awning and everything, and now that I don't have to call the cops every night, it suits me fine."

LuAnne's eyes rolled worse than mine ever had. She couldn't imagine living in a trailer, much less announcing it to all and sundry. "My goodness," she murmured.

But Mr. Kessler was definitely interested in Etta Mae. He leaned forward and said to her, "My condos are going to be top of the line, the last word in luxury and there'll be some one, two and three bedroom units, as well as a penthouse. Maybe you'd be interested in moving up."

Etta Mae threw back her curly head and laughed. "Mr. Kessler, a double-wide would be moving up for me."

Hazel Marie quickly said, "But your place is so nice, Etta Mae, even if it is a single-wide."

Mr. Kessler gave Etta Mae another long, almost calculating look. "Call me Arthur," he said.

"Well," Pastor Ledbetter said, "I, for one, think anything would be better than letting that courthouse sit there, deteriorating by the day. But I'll tell you, Arthur, you may have a tough row to hoe getting the commissioners' approval to tear it down. There're some in town who're dead set against it."

Well, there it was, out in the open. Inwardly fuming at the pastor, I bit my lip and remained silent. But it frosted me good that, if he moved to Raleigh, he wouldn't have to live with a monstrosity on Main Street. For Emma Sue's sake, though, I couldn't say a word. But he'd certainly hear from me in the future.

Mr. Kessler gave a quick nod of agreement. "I know there's opposition," he said. "But we expected that, and we'll deal with it. We have the mayor's backing already and almost a majority of the commissioners—only one or two are wavering. They'll come around, though, when they see the plans and hear how it'll mean progress for the whole county."

Mr. Kessler didn't seem to have a doubt in the world that he'd get his way, sooner or later and one way or another. And I didn't doubt that he would, either. You put dollar signs in front of the businessmen on the Board of Commissioners, and you could bet your bottom one that they'd give him whatever he wanted.

And, furthermore, they wouldn't care if more than half the town disagreed with their decision. They'd figure it'd all be forgotten and forgiven by the time the next election rolled around. In fact, they'd run on the increase of the tax base they'd brought to the town.

"Besides," Mr. Kessler went on, "even if we don't get a majority vote, that won't stop us. There's nothing on the books that'll keep an unused courthouse off the market. All that remains to be settled is how much they'll take for it."

And there we had it: It came down to money. I wanted to slap off that arrogant curl of his mouth. He was positive that our commissioners could be bought, either directly or for the supposed good of the town.

So my idea of presenting an alternate plan for the courthouse was dead in the water before I'd even started rowing. There was no way that archives and Boy Scout meeting rooms could compete with luxury condominiums filled with taxpaying property owners.

I'd have to come up with something else, and by the time the guests took their leave, I'd about decided what that something else would be. It was confirmed for me when I went into the kitchen after the last guest had left.

"Lillian," I said, "everything was perfect. You outdid yourself with the shrimp and grits. I think they were tastier than usual."

"Yessum, I spiced 'em up a little. But," she said, frowning, "that Mr. Kessler didn't do much damage to his."

"I noticed. But that was the idea. I didn't want him to think too highly of us."

"Well, you misfigured on that, 'cause he come in here an' say he never have such good yeast rolls and pecan pie. He ast me can I cook roast beef an' steak an' such as that, an' I say I been cookin' such as that all my life."

"Why in the world did he want to know that?"

She took a last swipe of the countertop and looked up at me with a grin. "'Cause he offer me a job."

"A job! Doing what?"

"He say he intend to keep one of them condominiums for hisself, an' he want me to cook for him whenever he come to town. He say he keep on payin' me even when he out of town, an' I never have it so good."

I was stunned and furious in equal measure. The nerve of the man, coming into my home and trying to hire Lillian out from under me. No guest had ever been so rude and underhanded.

Holding on to a chair for support and nearly strangling, I asked, "What did you tell him?"

"I tell him I'm not in the market for another job. I like the one I got."

"Oh, Lillian," I said, relief flooding my soul, "thank you. I don't know what I'd do if you left."

"I don't know what I'd do if I left, either. Can't no other place be like this one. Nobody know what gonna happen next 'round here. It keep me en'ertained all the time."

"I don't know what you mean, but I think it's time you had a raise. I'll see to it at the end of the week."

"Well, I 'preciate it, but you don't have to do that ever'time somebody want to hire me."

"Why? Has somebody else tried to hire you?"

"Yessum, Miz Allen, one time she say Ida Lee need help an' she ast me if I come to work for her."

"Mildred! She asked you?" I had to sit down. "I can't believe a friend would go behind my back. And after all I've done for her, too."

Lillian laughed. "You won't find no friends when it come to money and good cooks. I done learnt that a long time ago."

"I can believe it. But thank you again, Lillian, for being so loyal. You're so much a part of this family that it'd be like losing an arm or a leg if you weren't here. But I'll tell you this," I said with renewed fury, "Mr. Kessler is not going to be around long enough to need either a cook or a condominium. I am going to send that man back where he came from." I got up and stomped toward the hall. "One thing's for sure, if he wants quaint, I'll give him quaint."

Chapter 22

Having heard the telephone ring while talking with Lillian, I wasn't surprised to find Hazel Marie waiting for me in the dining room. No one but Mr. Pickens called so late, a bad habit of his when he was out of town.

"That was J.D," she said, somewhat hesitantly.

"I figured. How is he?"

"Oh, he's fine, but what he called about was to tell me he has to go to San Francisco for an interview. I didn't understand it all, but a big insurance company wants to hire him and put him on a retainer. Or something like that. And, well, he wants me to go with him. Oh, I don't mean really *with* him," she said, her face turning red and her hands waving. "I mean, I'd just go along for the trip. Would that be all right with you?"

"Hazel Marie, you don't have to ask my permission. You do whatever you think is right."

That stopped her for a minute, and I regretted the way I'd expressed myself. I had come to terms some time ago with Mr. Pickens's touchiness on the subject of marriage, and had decided that if Hazel Marie could put up with it, I could, too. Yet, I couldn't seem to keep my opinion of their unblessed union to myself.

So I tried again. "They say San Francisco is lovely. I'm sure you'll enjoy it, and it'll be nice to have Mr. Pickens with you. I'd hate to tackle it by myself."

"Oh, but there's another couple going, too. They're married and they'll join us in Dallas and fly on with us. So that'll make it all right, won't it?"

"Well, of course that puts a different light on it. I know Mr. Pickens wouldn't suggest anything that would compromise you." I didn't know any such thing, but what do you do?

"Well, I just wanted to be sure you wouldn't mind looking after Lloyd while I'm gone. It'll only be three or four days."

"You know I don't mind," I said, since that child was the very reason I'd come to terms with her open-ended connection to Mr. Pickens. If he ever got it in his head to propose marriage, which Hazel Marie would jump at, they'd move into a home of their own and take Lloyd with them. I've learned that you can put up with a lot of less than optimal situations in order to keep something important.

"You go on and have a good time," I told her. "We'll be fine."

"Oh, good," she said, "I've never been to San Francisco and I can't wait to see it. J.D.'s driving back from Charlotte tonight and he'll pick me up in the morning. We'll fly out from Asheville around ten. Oh, I am so excited. I don't know what to take, but I better go pack something."

"Wait a minute, Hazel Marie. What about Horace Allen? If Mr. Pickens is going to be gone, how can Mildred hire him?"

"Well, that's just it. She hasn't done a

thing and neither has Tonya. I talked to both of them, gave them his cell phone number and everything, and he says they haven't been in touch. So, this insurance thing is such a big opportunity, he can't afford to sit around and wait for them."

"Well, I declare," I said, wondering at the disinterest of both Mildred and Tonya in putting a tried and true private investigator on Horace's case. I think if my husband were missing, I'd have everybody and his brother out looking for him.

At least, that's what I'd do if I couldn't find Sam. I'd have to think long and hard if Wesley Lloyd had ever taken off.

As Hazel Marie ran upstairs to pack for another getaway with Mr. Pickens, I put the unseemliness of it out of my mind. But it took an act of will to do it. They'd been in Mexico together, but since I wasn't supposed to know he'd joined her there, that was easy enough to overlook. This time, though, they were being flat-out open about their plans, even to the point of Mr. Pickens coming to the house to pick her up. I declare, when you close your eyes to one seemingly innocent expedition, you start yourself on a slippery slope. And don't tell me about a married couple going along. I knew how much chaperoning they would do.

Well, I thought with a sigh, *at least Mr. Pickens is as true and faithful to Hazel Marie as any husband, and more so than many.* Just look at all the well-married absent ones at the present time.

But, as I stood there in the dining room, I realized that Hazel Marie's unexpected flight to San Francisco would put a crimp in my own plans. I had no other option but to rethink the idea that had been forming in my mind and come up with some adjustments.

"Sam," I said, walking into the living room where he was moving chairs back to their original places. "You won't believe what that Mr. Kessler is up to."

"You mean," he said, relocating a side table, "besides the courthouse?"

"That's bad enough," I said with a flip of my hand. "But what really runs all over me is the fact that he tried to hire Lillian right from under us. That's why he went to the kitchen to compliment the cook." I pursed my mouth with the thought of it. "But it wasn't compliments he was offering, it was a job."

"I wouldn't worry about that. Lillian's not going anywhere."

"Well, that's true," I said, sinking onto the sofa. "She said she wouldn't. But he is really stirring up trouble and I don't want him around."

"Not much you can do about that." Sam took a seat beside me and put his arm around my shoulders. Then with a raised eyebrow, he asked, "Is there?"

I gave him a sidewise glance. "Well, you never know." Then, settling down to another subject, I said, "Listen, Sam, Hazel Marie's taking off with Mr. Pickens in the morning, which means he won't be here to help look for Horace, although it seems Mildred is not interested in him doing it anyway. So if she's not worried about her own husband, I'm not, either." I took Sam's free hand and stroked it. "And that leads me to the other abandoned wife. What did Helen have to say this morning?"

"Well, she's in pretty much of a state, I'll tell you that. There's not been one word from Richard or about him. And the longer he's gone, the more suspect he becomes. FBI agents came while I was there and took every paper, file and folder they could find." He sighed. "It's a good thing I was there when they came. At least I could assure Helen that they had the authority to do it. But she was almost catatonic by the time they left—just sitting there staring into space. I'd almost rather deal with hysterics than that."

I looked away as my mouth tightened. "I don't know why you have to deal with either one. Where is the lawyer you advised her to get? That's who ought to be helping her."

"She hasn't gotten around to it yet. And I'm not sure she's capable of doing anything unless I'm there to get her moving."

"Sam!" I said, turning to stare at him. "Helen Stroud is the most capable woman in town! She can do anything she turns her mind to, so don't be fooled by that helpless act. She needs a lawyer, and she doesn't need you hanging around holding her hand."

Sam pulled me to him. "I don't hold her hand and, to put your mind at rest, I stood over her while she made a call to Stenson over in Asheville. She has an appointment with him tomorrow afternoon, so my dealings with the Stroud case are about over."

"You hope," I said darkly, unable to let go of my suspicions. Helen was too reliant on him and he was too trusting for my peace of mind. "Well, enough of that. What did you think of Mr. Kessler— 'call me Arthur'?"

Sam smiled as he ran his hand up and down my arm. "I think he's going to get that courthouse torn down and get his building up. He'll intimidate the commissioners and promise them the moon and get what he wants. Did you know that Tom Wilkey is already on his payroll?"

That got my attention. "He *is?* For what?"

"For carpet, tile and all the other floor covering—every inch that'll go in the condominiums. Now, wait, I expect he's not officially on the payroll, but Kessler has him figuring square feet to give him an estimate of what will be needed. With, I expect, the assumption that it'll all be bought from Wilkey's Carpet and Tile."

"That's not right! How can Tom Wilkey be objective when he stands to make money if it goes through? He ought to excuse himself."

"Recuse, Julia. But you're right, he should. And I expect he will, or he'll have to, when the newspaper puts the arrangement on the front page. Which is what's going to happen in a day or two."

"Well, good. Tom has gotten my last vote. I declare, Sam, seems like you can't trust anybody. But, you know, there's something else going on. I don't doubt for a minute that Mr. Kessler knew exactly what he was doing when he asked Tom for an estimate. He *knew* he was a commissioner."

"Sure, he did. And I wonder who else he's gotten to."

"Now that's a scary thought. The man is a snake, Sam. He's going around corrupting people who're normally as honest as the day is long." I ran my hand across my brow. "*What* am I saying? If they can be bought, they're not honest in the first place. How can they live with themselves?"

"People rationalize, Julia. And justify. It's human nature, I guess." Sam hugged me close. "Which doesn't say much for human nature, does it?"

I nestled closer. "No, and Mr. Kessler's playing on it for all he's worth." By this time, Sam's hand was running up and down my back. "But he may be headed for a fall. Somebody, sometime, may just take him down a peg or two."

"That'd be nice," Sam said against my ear. "But Arthur Kessler's not on my mind right now."

Chapter 23

When Mr. Pickens arrived the following morning to collect Hazel Marie, it was as if their cross-country trip was no more unusual than an evening out. And, to my consternation, I realized that we were all conspiring to overlook the fact that the two of them would be spending three or four days—and nights—together. You'd think he would've shown some shame.

But not him. He came in, greeted us all, then joined us at the breakfast table, perfectly at ease with himself. Hazel Marie, of course, couldn't sit still long enough to eat a thing. She was up and down constantly, remembering first one thing and another that she needed to pack, kissing Lloyd good-bye three times, reminding me that her cell phone would be on if we needed her—although what she could do thirty-thousand feet in the air, I didn't know—and telling Lillian that she'd already changed her bed linens.

And all the while, Mr. Pickens sat at the table, seemingly oblivious to her excitement and my disapproval. Probably he was accustomed to both and no longer took notice. While I got Lloyd off to school, Mr. Pickens accepted breakfast from Lillian and talked with Sam as if this were just another morning when old friends met.

"What's the latest on the missing?" Mr. Pickens asked.

Sam smiled wryly and shook his head. "Not a thing. The two of them have disappeared. At least as far as I know. The sheriffs may know something, but they're not giving anything out. The talk around town is that Stroud had reason to take off, but nobody knows what's up with Horace Allen." Sam glanced over at me and winked. "Given his wife, he may've had a different reason."

"Hazel Marie said there might be some connection between them. A paper they found?"

Sam nodded. "Yeah, found it in Allen's car, but that doesn't necessarily prove anything. I'd hate to have my car searched and have conclusions drawn from what was found."

Mr. Pickens laughed. "Ain't that the truth."

"Helen Stroud said," Sam said, as I strained to hear what Helen had said, "that Richard was putting together a real estate investment venture. She doesn't know any more than that, but apparently he'd put a lot of his investors' money into it. Or that's what he told them he was doing."

While pouring another cup of coffee at the counter, I nodded at Lillian. That's what Richard had told me he was doing. It had all seemed aboveboard at the time and maybe it was, if that money had ever gotten into real estate. And if it hadn't, where was it now? Then, standing at the counter and looking out the window at the back-yard, I thought, *real estate?* Interesting that Richard had been planning such a venture at the same time one was being planned for Main Street.

"Lillian," Mr. Pickens said, turning in his chair, "would you tell Hazel Marie I'm gonna leave her if she doesn't come on? Or the plane's gonna leave both of us."

But about that time, we heard the thump of a suitcase being hauled down the stairs. Mr. Pickens got up to help, and I heard him tell her that they weren't staying a month.

Hazel Marie held the kitchen door for him as he struggled with the largest suitcase she owned. "But I have to be prepared," she said, her face showing the excitement she felt. "And besides, you don't know what all I'm not taking."

In the flurry of getting them off, I saw Sam preparing to leave as well. As he pulled on a jacket, I realized for the first time that he was wearing a suit and tie, which was not his usual attire for a morning of research.

"You have a meeting today?" I asked, as he came to give me a good-bye kiss.

"I promised Helen I'd go with her to see her lawyer," he said, then held up a hand as I started to protest. "Just for the first meeting. We'll leave around noon, for a one o'clock appointment. I told you, didn't I?"

"I must've forgotten," I said stiffly and endured his kiss, but he didn't seem to notice.

As the back door closed behind him, I turned to see Lillian's raised eyebrows. She quickly looked down at the skillet she was scrubbing.

"Don't say anything," I said, but thinking that if she'd noticed something amiss, then I wasn't too far off the mark myself. "He's just being his usual helpful self, although some help can be carried too far."

"I don't say anything," she said. "Nobody need to worry 'bout Mr. Sam." She was giving the skillet a scrubbing like it'd never had. "Though I can't say the same 'bout no halfway widder woman."

"That's exactly what I told him. But . . ." I was interrupted by the front doorbell. "Who can that be?"

"Hey, Miss Julia," Etta Mae Wiggins said with a big smile on her face. "Is Hazel Marie home?"

"Why, no, Miss Wiggins, I mean Etta Mae. But won't you come in?" It was my nature to address people formally for as long as possible to avoid any misunderstanding as to an assumed friendship. Yet I'd come close to hurting Miss Wiggins's, I mean, Etta Mae's, feelings by seeming to hold her at arm's length. So I addressed her as Etta Mae, but continued to think of her as Miss Wiggins. I occasionally got mixed up as to whether I was speaking or thinking.

"I don't want to put you out," she said, stepping inside. "But if she'll be back soon, maybe I can wait for her. I wanted to see if she'd like to go to lunch."

"She won't be back for a few days, but do have a seat." I indicated the sofa. "She just left for San Francisco with Mr. Pickens. A married couple is going along, too."

"San Francisco! Oh, that lucky duck. Well," she said, laughing at herself, "that is so cool, but I guess she can't go to lunch, can she?"

"No, and that's too bad. I'm sure she'll be sorry she missed you. But how is it you're free? Did Mildred give you the day off?"

"I wish! No, she let me go. Her daughter's

back and her maid is out of the hospital, so she said she wouldn't need me anymore. So here I am, footloose and fancy-free for a couple of days."

"My goodness. Does that mean you're out of work and won't get paid? I'm surprised that Mildred would be so inconsiderate."

"No'm, she's not. She paid Lurline—that's the owner of Handy Home Helpers—for the full week up front. So I'll get my salary whether I'm working or not. I mean, Lurline could find me something else to do, but I thought what the heck, I could use a few days off. But since Hazel Marie's not here, I'll probably just go to the library and get something to read. Or maybe I'll clean my single-wide. Do something to fill the time."

"Well, Etta Mae," I said, recalling her considerable help in another time of trouble, "since you are free, I may have a better way to fill your time. If you're open to a suggestion."

"Oh, you know me. I'm open to most anything. What you got in mind?"

"Well," I said somewhat hesitantly since I didn't know how she'd take it. "Did you get the impression last night that Mr. Kessler was showing some interest in you?"

"Oh, yeah," she said, laughing. "I nearly always get some of that. It doesn't mean anything in the long run."

"Well, I'm hoping it does. You see, it's like this." And I proceeded to explain to her my idea of dissuading Mr. Kessler from destroying a piece of our history and putting us on the path of progress with an influx of condominium owners.

"Wow," she said, her eyes big. "You think it'll work?"

"I don't know, but it's all I can come up with. From what he said last night, he's planning to sell his condos by promoting our town as the ideal place to live. If we could show him a different side from what he's seen, well, he might change his mind."

"You mean, like, show him the dangerous curves on the mountain and the county dump and the paving company on the edge of town? Things like that?"

"I'd certainly include them, but I was thinking more of just driving him around and introducing him to some of our more outstanding citizens."

She frowned. "Seems like that'd make him want to come here even more."

"I'm using the word *outstanding* advisedly." I smiled. "But not untruthfully. I'm thinking of people like Brother Vernon Puckett, for instance, and Thurlow Jones, Dixon Hightower and the like. And he really ought to meet Lieutenant Peavey, who may be an excellent sheriff's deputy but cannot by any stretch of the imagination be considered an attraction."

"Oh, I get it! You want to show him the kind of good neighbors those city folks will be getting. Listen," she said, leaning forward, her eyes sparkling, "if that's the case, you ought to put my granny at the top of the list."

"Good idea. In fact, I'd like to show him Delmont, because, see, I don't care if he builds an eight-story monstrosity, just so it's where I don't have to look at it. Main Street is just not the place for it, especially since he'll have to destroy that beautiful courthouse with its Corinthian columns and gilded dome with a justice statue on top to make room for it. And since it's inappropriate for me to be escorting him around by myself, I'm going to need a companion. I was counting on Hazel Marie, but now I can't. You're an able substitute, though, and we've worked well together in the past. Would you be up for it?"

She laughed and slapped her knee. "You better believe! What do we do first?"

"Well, first, I should call Mayor Outz and find out what's been planned for Mr. Kessler. Then we'll know how much time he'll have for us."

"Mr. Mayor?" I said when I was finally put through to him. "This is Julia Murdoch, and I'm calling to let you know how much we enjoyed Mr. Kessler's company last night." Etta Mae made a face, and I had to turn away to keep from laughing. "And, also, to ask how long he'll be in town and if he'll have any free time to let us acquaint him with the town."

"Why, Miss Julia," Mayor Outz said, just oozing sincerity, "what a pleasure to hear from you, and let me extend my thanks for entertaining him so royally in your home. I knew you'd like him. Everybody does, and it'd be more help than I can say if you'd take him off my hands for a few days. He won't be here any longer than that, but I'll tell you the truth, I'm about to suffocate in paperwork. Working on the budget, you know, and I can't just ignore that to pal around with whoever decides to drop in. But we don't want to lose Arthur Kessler, do we? No, ma'am, we don't. We want him to feel at home here and welcome and wanted. So, if you see it as your civic duty to show him around and introduce him to some of our fine citizens, why, I'll dance at your wedding."

"No need for that. Just tell me where I can get in touch with him and leave the rest to me."

With Mr. Kessler's cell phone number in hand, I hung up the phone and smiled triumphantly at Etta Mae. "He's staying at the Mary Grace Haddington House, but he's probably already at the courthouse. The mayor is happy to turn him over to us."

"Call him," Etta Mae urged. "Let's call him now, before he gets busy with something else. But wait. Where're we going to take him first? We ought to have a plan of some kind."

"I'm thinking," I said, my eyes squinched up with the thought, "that Vernon Puckett would be a good one to start with. Did you see that article about him in the paper a couple of weeks ago? He's started a new church just half a block up from the courthouse, right on Main Street. It's where the Quality Furniture Store used to be, and it's been empty for a long time. I think their quality ran out."

"I didn't know Brother Vern was back in town."

"He's in and out all the time, doing first one thing and another, but nothing for very long."

"That's the truth," Etta Mae agreed. "Last I heard, he was holding tent meetings and printing tracts. Or was it preaching on TV?"

"All of the above, and anything he can think of. He's Hazel Marie's uncle, you know, and a thorn in my flesh for years. I almost hate to renew the acquaintance, but if anything can turn Mr. Kessler off, I'd think it'd be having a storefront church as a neighbor."

"I guess," Etta Mae said, a thoughtful look on her face. "Of course, we don't know what kind of preaching Mr. Kessler likes. He might be one of those Holy Rollers like Brother Vern."

"I doubt it. Mr. Kessler strikes me as somebody who wants to hear a sermon with three topics and an amen. If he wants to hear any at all."

Etta Mae fiddled with her pocketbook strap. "I don't know how you feel about it, and I hate to admit it, but Brother Vern's preaching doesn't do much for me. I mean," she hurried to add, "I know he's a man of God and I shouldn't criticize, but I'd just as soon listen to a different kind of preacher." She glanced up at me. "That's just my opinion. I hope I haven't offended you."

"Offended me! Listen, Etta Mae, Brother Vern is a self-proclaimed preacher. He's never been to seminary or anything. And if he was the only preacher available to me, I'd stay home and read the Bible. You haven't offended me. I'm of the opinion that he ought to be banned from the pulpit, which, come to think of it, I think he has been. At least, from some of the churches around here. Why do you think he's had to start a church of his own? Because he can't find anywhere else that'd let him in, that's why. No, don't you worry about offending me where he's concerned. He's given me enough trouble over the years."

Etta Mae gave me a relieved smile. "Okay. I just have a hard time dealing with preachers in general."

"You and me, both. Now," I said, picking up the phone again, "I'm going to call Mr. Kessler and invite him to a guided tour of the town."

Chapter 24

❦

"Here we are, Arthur." I brought the three of us to a stop in front of the double doors of the Quality Furniture Store. We'd walked along the sidewalk from the courthouse, where Etta Mae and I had met Mr. Kessler. He'd spent the morning there with a representative of a demolition company getting an estimate of what it would take to bring down the building. He'd seemed pleased when I'd called and suggested that he join us so we could introduce him to some of the townspeople. Then, in his assumption that I'd be interested in the destruction of the courthouse, he mentioned the word *implosion*. I nearly dropped the phone.

"Just ignore the furniture store sign," I said, motioning Etta Mae closer. She had a tendency to hang back, as I had learned when she helped me chase crooks in Florida. But when a monumental surprise is needed, why, she could come roaring to the rescue. "Now, Arthur, as far as I know, this is the newest church in town. You'll find that Abbotsville is a hotbed of churches. They spring up overnight, seems like. That's because we're a very religious community, and Brother Vernon Puckett is as religious as they come. Why, I can't tell you how many different spiritual avenues he's been down. And, since his new church is only a hop and a skip from the courthouse, I'm sure it'll be an added attraction for anybody looking to buy a condo."

Mr. Kessler's eyes darted from the storefront to Etta Mae and back to me. He wasn't sure I was serious, and of course I wasn't. But I wanted him to think I found nothing unusual in the display of Bibles, tracts, devotional books and plaques spread out in windows that had once featured chrome dinette sets and plush La-Z-Boy recliners.

"Let's go in," I said, pushing the door open and setting off a tinkling bell. "I called Brother Vern, so he's expecting us."

Well, even I had to stop and catch my breath when we stepped inside. The furniture company had occupied a huge space, much larger than Brother Vern's fledgling church needed. He, or somebody, had attached a metal pole that spanned the width of the building about a third of the way back. A navy blue curtain hung from the pole, effectively hiding the back of the building and creating a more intimate meeting area. A large white banner was draped across the curtain. I had to blink twice at the words, GOD HAS RICHES UNTOLD WAITING FOR YOU, that were stenciled on it. Metal folding chairs, about six rows of them flanking a center aisle, substituted for pews. An oak pulpit with a microphone stood at the front, and an upright piano was catty-corner to the left of it, facing the congregational chairs. A chrome-decorated drum set was beside the piano. I counted two more stand-alone microphones nearby. Maybe Mr. Kessler's condo owners wouldn't have to leave home to hear the services.

"Welcome! Welcome!" Brother Vern swished aside the navy curtain and came rushing toward us, his ruddy face beaming. He hadn't changed much since the last time I'd seen him, except for a few added pounds and considerably darker hair. He was a patriotic sight in a navy double-knit suit that didn't wrinkle except where he did, a white shirt and a bright red tie. I had to avert my eyes at his footwear. He was fashionably correct, since Easter had already come and gone, but to my mind it would always be too early for white patent-leather loafers.

He greeted me, nodded briefly at Etta Mae, but his attention was clearly focused on the man with us.

"Brother Vern, this is Mr. Arthur Kessler," I said, beginning the introductions. "It looks as if he might be your neighbor, so I thought the two of you should meet."

Brother Vern clasped Mr. Kessler's hand in both of his and shook it as his broad welcoming smile gave way to a look of deep piety, consisting of a deep frown and a heavenward glance under half-closed eyes.

"Brother Kessler," he said, still pumping

his hand. "The Lord be praised. I can tell you're a man of prayer. It's just comin' off you in waves, Brother, and I can tell because I'm a man of prayer, too. It takes one to know one, don't it? But you folks have a seat. Pull up one of these metal chairs, but be careful how you sit. They're a little rickety, 'cause they were donated by the Good Shepherd Funeral Home when they updated. You don't look a gift horse in the mouth, though, do you? You won't find anybody that appreciates a gift like we do here at the Hallelujah House."

Mr. Kessler retrieved his hand and began to back toward the door. "We can't stay. Mrs. Murdoch and Etta Mae are showing me the town, and I have to get back to finish my survey of the courthouse."

"Oh, well, I don't want to hold you up." Brother Vern edged closer and put his hand on Mr. Kessler's shoulder. "A busy man like you has all kinds of business to tend to. But let me just say that I am looking forward to seeing that fine building of yours rise up from the ashes. And as soon as the lobby's finished, I'll put a tract rack in it so the people there will have ready access to the Word of God. And, of course, a schedule of our meeting times. I tell you, Brother, I'm lookin' forward to our membership rolls expanding a hundredfold when you get all them new people moved in. Right now, since we're so new and all, the nub of our membership come from the Rescue Mission or they walk in off the street. We could use some new blood and, listen," he said, moving closer and lowering his voice in a confiding manner, "the people you bring in will want to hear my message. It's human nature to want prosperity and wealth, 'specially if you don't have neither one. But, you know what's a fact? Them that has always wants more. And I know where to get it. Our Lord owns the cattle on a thousand hills and ever'thing else. Now, nobody wants a herd of cattle these days, but that's just a symbol for what God wants to give away, and all we have to do is ask.

"And I'll tell you something else," Brother Vern continued, holding Arthur's upper arm. "You heard of them twelve-step programs? Well, I got a four-step program. Number One, Trust God, because you can't get nowhere without trust. Number Two, Invest in God, because, just like in a bank, you can't make interest if you don't invest your capital. And Number Three, Ask God, because he wants to hear what you want so he can supply it. And Number Four, Wait on God, because he's sittin' up there ready to shower you with all good things. But all in his own good time, you have to remember that and not go buying cars and condos and takin' vacations on credit."

Mr. Kessler had a slightly desperate look on his face. He glanced at his watch, then at me. "I do believe we need to be going. Good to meet you, Reverend Puckett. I wish you success in your endeavors." And he turned and headed for the door with Brother Vern right behind him.

"Oh, don't you worry about me," he said, his broad smile restored to its former glory. "You just tell them city folk that this is one place where the Word of God is preached. To their benefit, don't forget that!"

By this time, Mr. Kessler was out on the sidewalk, while Brother Vern hung on to the door, still talking. "And if anybody needs any spiritual help, teachin' or preachin' or prayin', anytime of the day or night, why, I'm right here ready to minister to one an' all." He started to close the door, but was struck with another thought. Leaning out again, he called, "Oh, Brother Kessler, a God-thing just hit me in the head! You gonna need a chaplain. That would be a fine thing to offer prospective buyers. Tell 'em it's one of the amenities you're offering. A Condo Chaplain, what do you think of that?"

But Mr. Kessler was making tracks down the sidewalk and didn't reply. Etta Mae and I had to nudge Brother Vern aside to get ourselves out and hurry after him.

Puffing a little as I reached Mr. Kessler's side, I said, "Isn't it inspiring to hear such enthusiasm? Brother Vern is always in the forefront of the newest trends. He was one of the first preachers around here to move from radio to television preaching. And now, here he is, all taken up with what I think is called wealth theology, which ought to interest you, Arthur. But I will admit, Brother Vern can get carried away at times. His heart's in the right place though. He's just an example of how willing our people are to go the extra mile to be good neighbors."

Mr. Kessler came to a halt on the sidewalk as we reached the courthouse. "Fences make good neighbors, and I might have to put one up." He swung around and glared at me. "Was he serious? Does he think he'll have the run of my building?"

"Oh, I imagine he does," I said placidly. "We're real friendly around here. Aren't we, Etta Mae?"

"Yes, ma'am, we are," she said. "Why, we don't hardly ever lock our doors. The only time we do is when Dixon Hightower gets one of his prowling fits. Why," she went on with a laugh, "I remember when ladies used to hang their wash out to dry and Dixon would go from yard to yard, taking whatever he wanted. Sears had a big run on dryers after that."

"Who's Dixon Hightower?" Mr. Kessler demanded.

"Oh," I said with a careless wave of my hand, "he's one of our young men who's never entirely grown up. He's harmless and really a sweet boy. There're just certain things he can't resist taking when he sees them. It used to be little, shiny things— anything from a piece of tinfoil to a silver teaspoon. Now, though, he seems to have moved on to the soft and silky."

"Yeah," Etta Mae said, "the last time he went on a spree, they found seventy-two pairs of ladies' underpants stuffed in his closet. The cops had a time trying to figure out who they all belonged to, especially when some ladies wouldn't own up to the bigger sizes."

I hadn't planned to mention to Mr. Kessler the nature of Dixon's objects of interest, but I was happy enough for Etta Mae to do so. Forewarned is forearmed, in case Mr. Kessler was accustomed to silk boxers.

"Don't worry about Dixon," I said. "You're a widower and your daughters live somewhere else, so he won't be a bother to you. You might never even see him."

"Unless," Etta Mae said with a laugh, "you're planning to string clotheslines on the grounds."

"That'll be the day," Mr. Kessler mumbled and stomped off. Then he wheeled around. "I appreciate you ladies taking time to show me around. But I'd be interested in meeting some of the natives and seeing the more cultural aspects of the town. Could we do that next time?"

"Oh, culture!" I said. "Why, we're loaded with culture, Arthur. Etta Mae and I will try to trim the list down to a manageable size, then we'll get an early start tomorrow and hit the high spots."

I took Etta Mae's arm and turned her toward the sidewalk. "He wants to meet some *natives,*" I whispered fiercely. "What's he going to do, take pictures for *National Geographic*? Or make tapes to amuse his sophisticated clientele? I tell you, Etta Mae, the man thinks we're a different species." I stopped suddenly and glared in his direction. "Curiosities. That's what he thinks we are. And you know what? I believe there're a few odd specimens here and there we can show him."

Chapter 25

❦

We left Mr. Kessler to map out the ruin and destruction of a town landmark and walked down the side street toward the Not-So-Old Market where I'd parked my car. The sidewalk was cluttered with cast-off furniture, plastic toys and what can only be described as unmitigated junk, all for resale.

"Etta Mae," I said, as she slowed to look at the merchandise, "think culture."

"I'm trying, but I don't know what it is exactly."

"Listen, it's a fine line we have to walk. We want to show him the worst while pretending it's the best, but when we don't even have the worst, what do we do? I mean, Abbotsville is too small for a concert hall or an arts center or a museum or anything like that." Taking her arm, I went on, "Let's cross the street here."

When we were settled in the car, I turned on the ignition to roll down the windows but didn't start the engine. "Let's think about this for a minute. We need a plan, a schedule or something. Today's visit with Brother Vern was too much spur of the moment, although I think it went well, don't you? When the mayor called back to tell me it would be a good time to show Mr. Kessler Main Street since he'd be downtown anyway, I just grabbed the opportunity and called on you. But, I'll tell you this, Mayor Outz is not going to be running this show. You wouldn't believe how eager he is to sell the courthouse. There's nothing objective at all about his position, so he'd undermine us before we can undermine him, if we give him half a chance."

Etta Mae frowned as she twisted her mouth in thought. "What I don't understand is why the mayor is so worried about Mr. Kessler. I didn't think there was any question that he would buy the courthouse if the commissioners approve it."

"Oh, I think you're right about that. Arthur Kessler wants that property, but Charlie Outz is your typical politician trying to make sure there's no slip betwixt cup and lip."

"Ma'am?"

"What I'm saying is, the mayor is holding his breath between now and next Tuesday when the commissioners will vote on selling the courthouse down the river. He wants to ensure Mr. Kessler's interest and, at the same time, I have no doubt he's working the commissioners to get their votes. The thing is, Etta Mae," I said, turning to her, "we could aim our campaign at the county commissioners and try to get them to vote against it, but I don't trust a one of them. They could swear on a stack of Bibles, but when it came down to it, who knows what they'd do. So my plan is to aim at disengaging Mr. Kessler's interest in buying it. That way, it won't matter how easily swayed the members are. They can vote to sell it all they want, but if there's no buyer, why, it won't matter."

"So we have till next Tuesday?"

I nodded. "Yes, a week from now. And Arthur Kessler will be here until then, making his plans, suborning commissioners with promises of buying locally and making sure there're dollar signs in everybody's eyes. And when he gets their votes, he's free to tear down the courthouse and put up anything he wants. You know, Etta Mae, the town doesn't have any restrictions on what an owner can do with his property. Once he gets that site, Arthur Kessler can throw up the worst-looking building in the world. Why, he could put up a pool hall or a bowling alley, if he wanted to." I sighed and tapped my fingers on the steering wheel. "We missed our chance several years ago when some of us wanted to have Main Street designated a historic district. It didn't go anywhere because some of the downtown merchants didn't want anybody telling them what they could and could not do, and the courthouse, itself, got us bogged down, too. Some of us thought it should count as an antique, but it's a little less than a hundred years old. At least, that was the argument, which I never thought should have applied. Anyway," I said, cranking the car, "we might as well go on home."

Driving slowly along the streets toward my house, I returned to the subject. "Did you know that the mayor wanted me to have Mr. Kessler as a houseguest?"

"Really?"

I nodded, leaning forward to check for oncoming traffic at Pine Street. "Yes, that's how I learned that the town is paying his expenses. Charlie Outz said the town would pay a per diem if I'd put him up. I told him 'No, thank you, I don't take in paying customers.' He probably wanted me to have him for nothing, but I didn't offer. So they ended up putting him at the Mary Grace Haddington House. In their best room, too, the only one with an adjoining bath. No telling how much it costs. And," I went on, stomping on the gas, "Arthur Kessler is a millionaire many times over. Why in the world should a town that can't afford to build adequate schools pay that man's room and board? It beats all I ever heard. And Arthur Kessler accepts it as his due."

"That's bad," she said. "You'd think, if they had to do it at all, they'd put him at the Days Inn out on the interstate. That's ever so nice, and you can get a room for around forty dollars a night. Thirty-nine ninety-five, I think, in the off-season. I'd take that over a room in somebody's house any day."

Wondering how she knew the cost of a motel room, I pulled into my driveway without asking for clarification, not really wanting to know. Etta Mae's new red Camry was parked at the curb. I started to compliment her on it, then reconsidered. The less said about how she had been able to get it, the better.

"Let's sit here a minute, Etta Mae," I said, as I switched off the engine. "We need to come up with something cultural, and the only thing I can think of is my book club. What do you think of that?"

"No offense, but not much."

"Good!" I smiled at her. "That means it won't impress Mr. Kessler, either. The only problem is, it doesn't meet for another two weeks. Of course, with Helen Stroud, who's our president, being a recluse these days, it might be longer than that." I thought for a minute, then said, "I guess I could see if everybody else wanted to have an extra meeting at my house and have you and Mr. Kessler as guests."

"Um, well, what do you do at a book club?"

"Oh, we all read the same book beforehand and then discuss it. Don't worry about it, as a guest you wouldn't be expected to contribute anything. Unless you wanted to, of course. This year we're not reading any current books, just some good, old ones. The next one on our list is *The Great Gatsby.* I'll loan you my copy if we decide to meet early. It's short, so it won't take long." I gathered my pocketbook and opened the car door. "Come to think of it, though, I haven't quite finished it myself. Got hung up on that green light on the pier, for one thing. It's got to be a symbol of something, but I can't figure out what. Come on in, Etta Mae, we can plan better inside."

As we walked toward the back door, the family's usual entrance, I realized how easily Etta Mae seemed to fit in. I hadn't even considered taking her in the front door.

"Hey, Miss Etta Mae," Lillian said, smiling as she always did whenever Etta Mae showed up. "Miss Julia, Mrs. Allen say for you to call her when you get home."

I put my pocketbook on the counter and asked, "Is it news about Horace?"

"She don't say what it is. Y'all want some coffee?"

"That'd be nice. I'll call Mildred in a little while. Have a seat, Etta Mae. We'll sit here in the kitchen, if you don't mind. As you see, I'm treating you like family."

Etta Mae was pleased at that. She pulled out a chair and sat down. "It sure is nice not to have to be somewhere every hour of the day. I don't know when I've had the time just to do whatever comes along."

"All right," I said, sitting across from her, "we need to think culture. What else can we show Mr. Kessler?"

Lillian stopped in midpour, the coffeepot suspended over the cups. "What you mean, culture?"

"Well, I don't know. I've always considered myself a cultured person, but I'm not sure why. We're assuming that Mr. Kessler is referring to art and music and plays and the like, of which there's a complete lack in Abbotsville, except for the senior play at the high school. They put that on a couple of weeks ago, so that's out."

Etta Mae sat up with a sudden light in her eyes. "But won't that work? I mean, if Abbotsville doesn't have any culture, won't that do what we want?"

"It could," I said, musing over the possibilities. "But I think it'd have more impact if we could show him something that he thought *we* thought was culture, but it's really not. See, I want him to meet people who don't think like he does. He's so wrapped up in showcasing this quaint little town with all its warm and welcoming neighbors. He intends for that to be a big selling point to prospective buyers of his condos. So I want him to meet some of the people who'll be their neighbors."

Lillian put a plate of brownies on the table. "Y'all could have a party an' let him meet people that way."

"Well, we could," I said with little enthusiasm. Then, struck with another thought, I said, "I know! Why don't we have a soiree?"

"Okay, but what's a soiree?" Etta Mae asked.

"It's just a party, but *soiree* will sound more cultural to Mr. Kessler. Let's make it an afternoon affair and everybody can dress up in garden hats and filmy dresses and such. What do you think?"

"I don't think I have anything filmy. Or a hat, either."

I waved my hand. "Hazel Marie'll have something you can wear. Now, how about this? Why don't we have some entertainment to make it a little special? That would really make it a cultural affair. You know, like a musical afternoon."

Lillian shook her head. "I think you gettin' ahead of yo'self. Who you know can entertain with any kind of music?"

That stopped me, because if there was one area in which I was sadly lacking, it was in musical aesthetics. But Etta Mae had the answer.

"Tina Doland!" she said. "She's the soloist at First Baptist, and I heard her one time at their Christmas concert. Sent shivers all down my back."

"Because she was good or because she was terrible?"

"Um, well, she sounded kinda high and churchified, I guess. Real different from Faith Hill, anyway."

"Well, I declare," I said, not exactly sure

who Faith Hill was. "I didn't know Tina could sing, but that brings up another problem. We don't have a piano, which she would surely need. Lillian, remember when I wanted Lloyd to take piano lessons and almost bought a baby grand?"

"Yessum, an' I 'member you don't have enough room for one of them things an' you was about to build a music room onto the house 'til Lloyd, he say he want to play the drums instead, which take up a lot of room, too, but not as much as a piano."

"Lord, yes, I was thrilled when he wanted to be in the band, but who would've thought he'd want a drum set? Anyway, it turned out that he had to take piano lessons, anyway, but not so many as to make it worth adding on to the house. Well," I said, deflating slightly, "I guess that takes care of our musical afternoon."

"Miz Allen," Lillian said, "she got a big piano in her living room. Maybe she have yo' party there."

"So she does!" I jumped up and headed for the phone. "And it's just what she needs to get her mind off Horace. I'll call her right now."

Lillian started shaking her head again.

"You better hope she don't have to have Mr. Horace's casket in the living room same time as yo' party. Miss Tina be singin' a different tune then."

Chapter 26

"Mildred?" I said when Ida Lee got her to the telephone. "I'm glad to hear how well Ida Lee sounds. I hope there're no lingering effects from her hospital stay."

"No," Mildred said with a long-suffering sigh. "The doctor said all she needs is rest and good nutrition, of all things. I told Ida Lee it would've been so much easier on me if she'd had an actual disease that could have been treated and cured. Instead, she has to have some nebulous condition that'll take months to correct. But I missed seeing you today, Julia. The reason I called is to remind you that Horace is still missing and to tell you how hurt I am that everybody seems to have forgotten me."

"You mean to tell me that Lieutenant Peavey and all those deputies he's got out looking still haven't come up with anything? Mildred, that is the strangest thing. No wonder you're feeling neglected. Hasn't he told you anything?"

"Well, yes, he came around early this morning and, I'li tell you, Julia, that man needs some training in compassion and empathy. He just flat out told me that they now consider Horace a missing person, not a victim of a car wreck. And then," she stopped to take a rasping breath, "he had the nerve to ask if I was sure I hadn't heard from him. And the worst thing of all, he said they were calling off the search party because they believe Horace disappeared of his own volition."

"Oh, my word."

"Yes, and I had to go back to bed for the entire morning. But, you know, the more I think about it, the more I wonder if Lieutenant Peavey isn't right. If Horace was having financial problems, which he always was, and if I refused any more advances, which I did, then the poor man had no recourse but to disappear. Except he certainly didn't give any thought to me when he did it. Here, I've been worried sick about him, spending these wretched days with my mind filled with all the terrible things that could've happened, only to learn that he just took off and left without any concern for what I would suffer. So, I decided that I'm not going to ruin my health by mourning a man who's probably sunning himself on a South Sea island somewhere."

A South Sea island? Those words rang a bell, but she didn't give me time to pursue them.

"So," Mildred went on, "I got up about noon, determined to take a new lease on life. And to make the point, I put on the new coral silk dress with matching sweater I ordered from Neiman Marcus. The sweater has gold embroidery on it."

The thought of all that coral silk made me shudder because Mildred was a big-boned woman with a thyroid condition. I put the thought aside and said, "I'm so glad to hear it, Mildred. I've been worried about you, and I think you're right to take care of yourself and look to your own well-being. But let me tell you what's been going on while you were in mourning." And I started in telling her about Arthur Kessler and the courthouse and the mayor and the county commissioners, but I stopped short of revealing my plans to undermine them all. "Now, I know that you expressed some interest in buying one of those condominiums, but, Mildred, I hope you'll reconsider. For one thing, have you ever been downtown on a Saturday night? You wouldn't believe the racket all those souped-up trucks and cars make as they cruise Main Street. And during the summer they have street dances every week and parades for every holiday. They'd be right outside your windows, and you wouldn't have a minute's peace, living down there. And have you noticed all the men who hang around downtown looking for handouts? You wouldn't like it, Mildred, and consider this, there could be other condominiums built by other people in a more congenial area. You're accustomed to peace and quiet, and believe me, a serene atmosphere is the last thing you'd get in Arthur Kessler's courthouse replacement."

She was quiet for a few seconds, then said, "I hadn't thought of that. And you're right, I do have to have my peace and quiet. It's my nerves, you know. I'm glad you reminded me, Julia, because that decides it. I wouldn't buy one of his condominiums for anything."

"Well, see, Mildred, we want to fix it so nobody will buy one. In fact, we don't even want the thing built. That courthouse is an architectural treasure and some of us are trying to save it."

"Oh, that sounds like a good cause. How much do you need?"

"No, I'm not looking for donations, at least not yet. What I want to know is how would you feel about helping me discourage Mr. Kessler? You see, he wants to know how cultural we are, so I'm thinking of having a musical soiree—something tasteful yet boring. Since your house is so much better suited for such things, would you mind being the hostess? I mean, now that you're out of mourning."

"Well, why not?" she said with a gaiety that made me wonder at her state of mind. "I'm not one to sit around moping about a husband who's flown the coop of his own

volition. Let him go, I say. And good riddance, too."

"My goodness, Mildred, you sound just
like LuAnne. That's exactly what she said
about Leonard."

"Don't bring LuAnne Conover up to me!
Our situations are not at all the same. She
ran her husband off herself. Julia, that
woman talks all the time. I'm surprised he
stood it as long as he did, and I wouldn't
be surprised if he never comes back. But
wait a minute," she went on, "I don't get it.
How would a musical soiree discourage
Mr. Kessler from putting up his building?"

Well, that was the question, wasn't it?
I'd hoped I wouldn't have to explain it to
her, because you never knew how much
she took in or how much would end up
spread around town. I always watched
what I said around Mildred for fear it would
come back at me. She had a good heart,
though, so I tried not to hold it against
her.

"Well, it's like this," I started, choosing
my words carefully. "The mayor asked me
to show Mr. Kessler around town, which
I'm doing with Miss Wiggins's help. And
Mr. Kessler wants to see what Abbotsville

has to offer, culturally speaking. I was at my wit's end until I thought of you and Tonya. You two are the most cultured of all of us—so well traveled and all of that. And Tonya has lived in New York and seen all the plays and concerts, so I'm hoping your cultural experiences will sort of rub off on the rest of us." I stopped for a minute, then added, "Besides, you have a piano."

I rubbed my forehead, thinking that was the weakest excuse for an explanation I'd ever given anybody. "And," I went on, "I guess I want to show Mr. Kessler that we small-town southerners are sort of a closed society. We're not going to welcome with open arms any incursion of retired outsiders, no matter how wealthy they happen to be. That's not exactly true, of course, but he has this idea of using us as a selling point to upscale buyers. Which, I don't mind telling you, I heartily resent."

"Well, put that way, I do, too. I'm not interested in being put on display. And you know something else, Julia? Those people'll come in here and be so high and mighty we won't be able to stand them. Yes, let's do have a soiree, and I'll make it so grand that his condo owners will be too intimidated to want to join us. Upscale, my foot. I'll show him upscale!"

"Well, good," I said, hoping I'd explained enough. "But, Mildred, we don't want him to think we're too grand. He'll put us in a brochure or something. Now as for who to invite, I thought the book club and the garden club. And some from our Sunday school class. Of course there'll be a lot of overlap, but it can't be helped. We'll just have an intimate gathering of good friends to hear entertainment by Tina Doland, who I'm hoping can't sing too well. We'll invite Mr. Kessler and try to bore him to death."

"For goodness' sakes, Julia, you're thinking too small. Let's have a big group, the more the merrier, I always say. You know the garden club wanted to put my house on the tour this year, but I just wasn't up to it then. But I am now. I'm going to open my house to anybody who wants to come. Put an invitation in the newspaper and everything."

I backed away from the telephone, frowning at it, then pressed it close. "Are you sure you want to do that? No telling who you'll get."

"Let 'em come! Let 'em all come, I don't

care. Listen, Julia, everybody in this town knows about Horace and what he's done to me, and I want them to know that I'm not sitting here grieving my life away. What better way to do that than to have a big blowout? And I know you want to have a dainty little garden party type of thing, but since it's at my house, I'm going to have a pig pickin'. I'll have Robert dig a pit in the backyard, so he can smoke that pig all night and half the day. We'll set up tents and tables around the pool so people can eat outside. We'll have beer and soft drinks and a bluegrass band. That'll be fun, won't it?"

I was stunned. Mildred Allen, the grandest lady in town, wanted to have a pig pickin'? But then again, I thought to myself, how perfect would it be to present Mr. Kessler with a whole roasted pig as our idea of a cultural feast?

"And listen, Julia," Mildred went on before I could say anything, "if you want to have something more sedate inside the house, you can. People can just wander back and forth between Tina Doland and the Crooked River Boys until they reach their particular comfort level. I tell you, this will be a party to end all parties, and not one soul in this town is going to think that Horace Allen has stabbed me in the heart."

I was finally able to get off the phone after we decided on a date for the party and after she told me she'd have Ida Lee telephone a few personal invitations. Even there, of course, my idea of a pseudo-grand social occasion began its downward spiral. We should've had engraved invitations sent out at least three weeks ahead of time. But as far as Mr. Kessler would know, our party had been planned for weeks and wouldn't be at all a last-minute affair thrown together for his benefit.

Of course, it was turning out to be more for Mildred's benefit than for Mr. Kessler's. If she wanted to have a musical-soiree-cum-pig-pickin', though, who was I to complain? It would certainly give Mr. Kessler a taste of Abbotsville culture, although it might come more in the form of culture shock than anything else.

I couldn't have been better pleased if I had planned it all myself.

Chapter 27

〜⊙〜

"Well, Sam?" I sat down beside him on the sofa after supper and after Lillian had left and after Lloyd had gone upstairs with homework on his mind. I had been anticipating this time alone with Sam all day, in spite of the fact that I'd had a gracious plenty of other things to occupy my mind. During the afternoon Etta Mae and I had made our plans for the soiree, engaged Tina Doland to make a special appearance and, being pleased with the prospect of what we were doing, laughed whenever we looked at each other. Etta Mae had been elated when I told her about

Mildred's pig-pickin' plans, but Lillian had shaken her head, saying over and over, "Y'all done lost yo' mind." Lillian was more set in her ways and determined to do things in the appropriate manner than I ever was.

All along, though, the niggling thought of Sam and Helen driving to Asheville together stayed in the back of my mind. Where were they, what were they doing and when would they stop doing it? I kept reminding myself that I had married an affable and obliging man and had no one to blame but myself when those virtues were put to use in the service of somebody else. In contrast, Wesley Lloyd Springer, my late first husband, would never have gone out of his way to be helpful to anybody, and I'd thought the less of him for it. Of course, if I'd thought any lesser of him, I wouldn't have thought of him at all.

But that was neither here nor there as far as my current situation was concerned. I was ready for Sam's amiability on Helen Stroud's behalf to come to a screeching halt.

"Well?" I said again.

Sam folded the newspaper and turned

toward me. He smiled and said, "Well what?"

"You know what. How did the afternoon go? Did Helen meet with that lawyer? What all happened?"

He picked up my hand and threaded our fingers together. "It was a long afternoon of hand-holding. Metaphorically only, I assure you." He squeezed my hand. "To tell you the truth, Julia, I might've made a mistake in the beginning by offering my help. I felt sorry for Helen because none of Richard's problems were of her making, and I thought a little support from a friend would be appreciated. But she may be becoming too dependent on me."

I could've told him that two days ago, but all I said was, "Didn't she like that lawyer?"

"I don't think she knows what she likes. He gave her good advice, pretty much what I'd already told her, but it's as if she's lost all sense of herself. You know, I'd always thought Helen was a strong woman, capable and independent-minded. But she's not, at least not in this situation. It surprises me how clingy and helpless she seems to be."

"That surprises me, too. I guess Richard was her foundation and now that he's apparently out of the picture, or will be if he goes to prison, she has to have somebody else to lean on. And it looks like that's you, Sam, but I have to tell you that I am not comfortable with her making you his substitute."

Sam's forehead wrinkled and he leaned his head back against the sofa. "Neither am I, Julia. For one thing, it's not good for her."

I snatched my hand out of his. "For *her!* It's not good for you, first of all, and second of all, it's not good for me. I don't like it that you're always in her company and I don't like the way you jump whenever she calls. In fact, I don't like anything about it, and I think you ought to put a stop to it. She's got a lawyer now. Let her lean on him."

"I may be in too deep," Sam said. "I'm not sure how to get out of it."

"Well, I'll tell you how. You can just be too busy. You can have other appointments. You can be doing something with me. There're all kinds of ways to get out of being at her beck and call. And I'll tell you something else, though I doubt it'll matter to you, but people are beginning to notice and to talk. So just think about the position you put me in anytime you feel the urge to run to her aid."

Sam cocked an eyebrow at me, a smile beginning at the corner of his mouth. "And what about my position when somebody says that you're running around town with Arthur Kessler?"

"That's different! And just *who* is carrying tales about me?"

"I'm teasing you, Julia."

"Well," I said, somewhat mollified, "I'm only doing it for the good of the town and you know it. The idea of thinking I feel sorry for that man the way you feel sorry for Helen, there's just no comparison at all. I don't even like him. In fact, I'm trying to get rid of him, while you, well, you just keep encouraging Helen."

"Not anymore though. She has a lawyer now to look after her interests, so I can bow out. Why don't you get her involved in the soiree? She's a good organizer and maybe what she needs is something else to think about."

"Well, I would, if she'd answer her

phone. I've left I don't know how many messages and she never returns my calls. But I'll write her a note. That way, she can't say I didn't try." I scrooched up close to him, pleased and reassured that he'd had enough of Helen and her problems. "What she really needs, Sam, is to take a few lessons from Mildred and, I guess, LuAnne, too. Both of them are saying good-bye and good riddance to their husbands, although I'm not sure they really mean it. But still, they're taking hold and going about their business instead of falling to pieces like Helen's doing."

"Lot of husbands missing, aren't there?"

"There sure are. But I'll tell you this, Sam Murdoch, if you decide to take off I might just come after you."

"You might, huh?" Sam grinned and put his arm around me. "To bring me back or to beat me to death?"

"It depends on how I'm feeling at the time." I leaned my head against his chest and listened to the strong beat of his heart. "The way I feel now, I'd bring you back."

He rubbed his face against my hair and

pulled me closer. "Tell you what, let's not waste that feeling."

I got up the next morning wondering why I'd ever worried about Helen alienating Sam's affections. I didn't have a thing to worry about with that man, no matter how much she depended on him. So, bright and early, I called Mr. Kessler to see if he was free to visit a few people around town. He seemed eager enough and asked specifically to meet some natives of the area. The way he said it put me off, because it sounded as if he expected to view a bunch of aborigines in their native habitat. And if that's what he wanted, I could certainly give it to him.

I called Etta Mae immediately afterwards. "Etta Mae, would your grandmother be up to having visitors this morning? Mr. Kessler wants to meet some natives."

She giggled, and it so early, too. "Sure, she'd love to see him. But I have to tell you, my granny is not too with it these days. She's as sweet as she can be and I love her to death, but she says exactly what she thinks when she thinks it."

"That's perfectly all right. But, Etta Mae, I

don't want her to think that we're putting her on display or making fun of her in any way. And I don't want you thinking it, either."

"Oh, I don't. If he wants to meet a native, she's certainly one and no different from a dozen others I could name. She was born and raised in this county, and the only time I can remember her leaving was when I took her to the beach a few years ago. It was the first time she'd seen the ocean and all she said was, 'That's more water than anybody needs. Let's go home."

I asked Etta Mae to drive my car since she knew the county better than I did, so Mr. Kessler sat up front with her and I was relegated to the back seat. On our way to Hattie Wiggins's house, Etta Mae began to prepare Mr. Kessler for what he'd see.

"My granny still lives in the house she came to as a bride, some, oh, I don't know, maybe sixty-five years ago. My great-granddaddy Wiggins built it, but it's been added onto several times so it's kinda crookedy. She has an electric range I helped her buy, but she still uses her wood stove half the time. And one time when we were having a heat wave, I went by and she had the refrigerator door standing wide open. She said she didn't much like how it took up so much room, but it was hard to beat when it came to cooling down the kitchen." Etta Mae laughed. "I have to warn you, Mr. Kessler, she's a pistol."

Mr. Kessler settled back in his seat and smiled complacently. "Sounds like the salt of the earth."

We traveled a few more miles with little being said, while I thought to myself that Mr. Kessler was not the easiest person in the world to converse with.

But after a while he half turned toward the back seat and said, "And how is Hazel Marie? I haven't seen her lately."

"She's away," I said. "Out in San Francisco seeing the sights. She'll be back in time for the soiree."

"She's your daughter, isn't she?"

I saw Etta Mae's eyes snap up to the rearview mirror to glance at me, as I tried to think how to best explain Hazel Marie. But then I wondered why explain at all. The unusual relationship between Hazel Marie and me could be another nail in Mr. Kessler's coffin.

"No," I said blandly, as if the relationship was perfectly normal, "Hazel Marie is my first husband's almost second wife, and Lloyd is their child."

Mr. Kessler's head whipped around, a look of astonishment on his face. "What?"

"It was one of those, you know," I said with a wave of my hand, "off-the-books arrangements."

"And she lives with you?"

"Oh, yes. Ever since Mr. Springer passed, we've been the best of friends. We have so much in common, you know."

Etta Mae glanced again in the rearview mirror and I could see her eyes sparkling. I hoped she wouldn't laugh out loud and spoil the moment.

Mr. Kessler apparently mulled over my answer for a few minutes, then he said, "If you don't mind me saying, that sounds a little polygamous."

I'd thought the same thing myself, especially when I'd first learned of Wesley Lloyd's extracurricular activities. But my purpose now was to make Mr. Kessler think we were a bunch of ingrown and inbred unsophisticates, unlikely to be thought of as your ideal neighbors. "Well, not exactly," I responded, "because Mr. Springer didn't actually marry her before he passed. And, you know, it takes all kinds. People around here learn to make do with what they have. I decided I wanted to help raise that child, so it made sense to pool our resources and raise him together."

Another few minutes elapsed while Mr. Kessler thought about this, but he couldn't leave it alone. "And you all get along?"

"Like a house afire. When we're all together, you won't find a happier bunch of people. Why, there's Mr. Pickens, who's at our house more often than not. He's Hazel Marie's steady boyfriend, although I think he's a little more than that, but we don't talk about it. I've been trying to get them legal for the longest time, since I think there's a law in this state against cohabitation, but Hazel Marie didn't get caught when she was doing the same thing with Mr. Springer so she's not worried about it now."

Etta Mae ran the car off the road, spraying gravel everywhere, and had to swing it back on.

"And," I went on, "there's Lillian and Latisha, who's her great-granddaughter.

They're at our house half the time, and I'll tell you this, whoever happened to hire Lillian if she ever left me would have to take Latisha, too. Lillian would never go where that child wasn't welcome. They're both part of our family. That's the way we do things in the South. At least in this part of the South."

Mr. Kessler didn't have another word to say, but Etta Mae broke the silence as we passed a brick ranch house perched on a rise to the left of the road. "That's Boyce and Betty Sue's house. Boyce is Granny's last living son and he tries to look after her." Etta Mae laughed. "When she'll let him. Right now, she's mad as thunder because they put in an above-ground swimming pool. Says it's a waste of money since there's a perfectly good pond down in the pasture for whoever wants to strip in public."

Etta Mae slowed as dust billowed up around the car, then she turned down a rutted drive toward her granny's house.

Chapter 28

⁕❦⁕

"It sure needs scraping," Etta Mae said, spinning the wheel as my car, bought for the Florida trip and now turned into an off-road vehicle, lurched along the ruts of the long dirt drive. "Boyce is supposed to keep up Granny's place. At least that's the arrangement." Etta Mae's voice took on an edge. "He lets things go too long."

Granny Wiggins's house sat a goodly way from the gravel road, squatting beneath a cluster of huge oak trees in the middle of what looked to be an acre or two of grass and weeds. A sagging fence enclosed a pen near the barn, and chickens wandered around the yard, scratching out a living.

As we approached, I could see a garden laid out in rows along the side of the house, and behind that several tilted outbuildings in bad need of paint, as was the house. Corn stalks were about a foot high in the garden and stakes for bean runners were already set out. The house took my attention as Etta Mae pulled the car under one of the trees and switched off the motor. We sat for a few minutes looking around at the display on the front porch. Clay pots, plastic pots, Maxwell House coffee cans and Crisco lard cans filled with ferns and geraniums and begonias lined the railing and the steps.

"Your grandmother certainly has a green thumb," I said, for lack of any other comment to make.

"She sure does," Etta Mae agreed. "She takes cuttings everywhere she goes. I caught her snipping a few at Home Depot one time, and nearly died. I thought they'd arrest her for shoplifting or something. She'd even brought some damp paper towels to wrap them in. Which showed prior intent, I guess. But she crammed them in her pocketbook and walked out of there, telling me to stop worrying because the plants needed thinning anyway." Etta Mae couldn't help smiling at the memory. "The cuttings all rooted, too. You're probably looking at some of them now. Well, let's go in before she wonders what we're doing."

As we opened the car doors and began to step out, I was struck by the lack of grass up close to the house. Too shady, I supposed, noticing the raked lines in the hard-packed dirt under the trees and around the front steps. But beyond the house site, green pastureland rolled away on all sides, broken occasionally by clusters of trees in the distance. Far away and surrounding the valley were the Blue Ridge mountains with a few white clouds scuttling over them.

The three of us stood for a minute enjoying the scenery and the warm breeze ruffling through the trees. An old tire swing hanging from a limb swayed to and fro.

"We live in a beautiful part of the country," I murmured, then regretted calling Mr. Kessler's attention to the fact.

He stood, eyes narrowed, gazing off in the distance, then slowly turned in each direction, surveying the prospect. "How much of this does your family own?" he asked Etta Mae.

"I'm not sure," she said. "Granny has about a hundred acres, I guess. My great-granddaddy staked out this whole valley, but, well, hard times came and she's down to this."

Before he could respond, the screen door banged open and a tiny white-haired woman came barreling out onto the porch, her face squinched up like she was getting ready to run us off. Her hair was up in a bun, except for what was flying around her face, and a pair of glasses sat crooked on her nose. She had on a pink housedress dotted with blue flowers and a white apron over that. Tennis shoes, huge and clunky in comparison to her skinny legs, were on her feet with thick stockings rolled down around her ankles. She came to a stop at the edge of the porch and put her hands on her hips, staring down at us and looking for all the world like a hen ruffling her feathers.

"Whoever you are," she yelled from over the railing, "I don't want any."

"Granny," Etta Mae said, "it's me. I brought some friends to see you."

Granny squinted down at her, then broke into a beaming smile that revealed a too-perfect set of teeth. "Why, Etta Mae, honey, come on up here and give me a hug. And bring your friends, too, but don't expect me to hug any strangers."

That was fine with me, since I didn't care for such familiarity. Mr. Kessler followed me up onto the porch, but he seemed just a bit hesitant about doing it.

Etta Mae introduced Mr. Kessler and started to introduce me, but Granny broke in. "Why, I know you. Old man Springer was the tightest human ever lived when he ran that bank. He kept trying to buy my place out here for the longest, but I wouldn't sell it. Not to him, not to nobody."

"I'm married to Sam Murdoch now," I said. "Mr. Springer's been gone for some time."

"Good for you!" she said, cackling. "I'd say that was a move up, wouldn't you? But y'all set down. Take a load off. We could set in the front room, but there's a nice breeze out here. I'll have to apologize for the way the yard looks." She suddenly swung around and grasped Etta Mae's arm. "Etta Mae, you got to talk to Boyce and tell him to start down by the road when he brings that Toro riding mower over here. I don't want him running that thing up around the house at the crack of dawn. I can't hear a word Diane Sawyer says for all the racket that thing makes."

"I'll tell him, Granny," Etta Mae said soothingly. "But you know he wants to do it before it gets too hot, and he does have to be at work early."

"Work! Ha! That boy don't do a thing at work but hang on the counter and ring up the cash register. And before I turn around, that Betty Sue's over here, snooping and prying in everything in the house." She turned back to us. "Set down! Set down! It's been a age since I had comp'ny. Park it in this rocking chair, Mr. Whatever-your-name-is. And Mrs. Springer, take that swing over there."

Mr. Kessler mumbled, "Kessler," at the same time I said, "Murdoch," but she didn't catch either one.

Granny plopped herself down in another rocking chair, her legs spraddled out because they barely reached the floor. "Well, this sure is nice," she said, smiling at us. "I knew I was going to have comp'ny sometime today. My nose's been itching all morning and it never fails that somebody'll show up. Remember that, Etta Mae? 'My nose itches. I smell peaches. Here comes a man with a hole in his britches.'" She leaned toward Mr. Kessler. "Guess that don't mean you, though, does it?" Then she sat back in the chair and pushed off with the toe of her foot to set it rocking. "Not with that fancy suit, it don't."

Before anybody could say anything, she suddenly sprang to her feet. "What am I thinking of! You folks're hungry and me just a-settin' here. I got a good pound cake on hand, just made it last week. And some Fig Newtons not even open yet. I'll be back in a minute, just make yourselves at home."

Etta Mae grabbed her arm. "Wait, Granny, we don't need anything. We came to visit with you. Mr. Kessler wants to talk to you because you've lived here so long. Sit down, now, and let's just talk."

Granny did, but she eyed Mr. Kessler suspiciously, and I didn't blame her. He'd been noticeably quiet, although to give him credit, he'd hardly had a chance to say anything.

"You work for the newspaper?" Granny demanded. "Or you one of them college professors wantin' to put me on tape?"

"Ah, no," he said, clearing his throat, "neither one. I . . ."

"Well, good. I've had a bellyful of people stickin' a tape recorder in my face, wantin' me to put down history before I kick the bucket."

Mr. Kessler gathered himself and began again. "I assure you, Mrs. Wiggins, it's nothing like that. I'm getting ready to develop some property . . ."

"Not this property, you're not. Etta Mae, I told you and I'll tell anybody else that I'm not selling. Why'd you bring a land-hungry *developer* out here?"

She said *developer* the way I thought it.

"No, Mrs. Wiggins," Mr. Kessler said before Etta Mae could reassure her. "I'm not interested in your property, although it's a fine place." He glanced quickly at me, hoping, I expect, for a little help, but this was his problem, not mine.

"My property is downtown," he went on, although I wanted to correct him on that. It wasn't his yet. He leaned toward Granny and laid on what little charm he had. "I just wanted to meet a native of Abbot County, somebody who's seen this area grow from a farming community to an up-and-coming retirement area."

"It's growed enough, if you ask me," she said, giving him a sideways look. "But do what you want downtown. I got no business down there anyhow. But you can leave the farms and orchards and mountain ridges alone. You folks come in here and first thing you know there's stores everywhere you look. If it's not a McDonald's, it's a Hardee's. Don't nobody cook at home anymore, not with a hamburger here and a hamburger there. Every time Betty Sue takes me to Delmont to the Winn-Dixie something's closed down and two more's took its place. I can't find my way around anymore, and I'm tired of it."

Mr. Kessler opened his mouth, then closed it again. He didn't know where to go from there.

But Granny took up the slack. She jerked straight up in her chair and said, "I tell you what, though, you put one of them chain Dollar Stores in Delmont and you'll be doing a good thing. We got a halfway one already, but Betty Sue took me to a real one over in Abbotsville and I like that place. Etta Mae, you ought to give it your business. You can go in there lookin' any way you want. You don't have to dress up or anything, not like when you go to Wal-Mart or something."

Mr. Kessler leaned back in his rocking chair and sighed. He fidgeted a little and looked longingly at the car.

Etta Mae finally got Granny to talk about the old days, drawing her out about how cows used to wander along the wide dirt track that was now Main Street in Abbotsville, and how once the Abbot County sheriff had the bright idea of using the volunteer fire department to hose down Main Street after a winter storm had piled up huge drifts of snow.

"Why," she cackled, "it didn't even get up to twenty degrees that whole blessed day, and that stuff froze over like nobody's business. Ended up with a solid layer of ice from one end of Main Street to the other, as any fool shoulda knowed would happen. Couldn't nobody, man nor beast, walk on it for a week." She sat back placidly and said, "What else you want to know?"

"Well, uh," Mr. Kessler said, "how long have you lived here?"

"Since the day I married Mr. Wiggins. I come here as a bride and I'll stay here till they carry me out, feet first. Ain't nobody gonna move me out before that. This place's been bought and paid for many times over, if you want my opinion, what with taxes going up and up. Etta Mae helps me with that, 'cause I'll tell you something, Mister, them Social Security checks ain't hardly worth spit in a bucket." Granny rocked a few seconds, then went on. "'Course I'm plenty glad to get 'em."

"Now, Granny," Etta Mae said, "Boyce helps, too."

"Huh!" Granny said, dismissing Boyce with a wave of her hand.

By this time Mr. Kessler began to get restless and I could tell he'd about had enough of viewing the natives. I gathered my pocketbook and suggested we let Mrs. Wiggins get on with her day. He was immediately on his feet, thanking her for her time and for the hospitality. Etta Mae hugged her again and spoke softly to her, promising to come back soon for a longer visit.

"You do that, honey," Granny said. "Anytime you want to. The door's always open."

She stood watching us from the porch as we got into the car, Mr. Kessler taking the front seat again, which I thought was ungentlemanly of him as I crawled into the back. Etta Mae started the engine and began to back around to head out, waving to Granny one last time.

Mr. Kessler, craning his neck to look back over the fields, said, "You and your uncle going to inherit this place?"

"I guess," she said. "We're all that's left anyway."

The car dipped and swayed on the dirt track, then scratched off when we reached the gravel road.

"I'll give you a bit of advice," Mr. Kessler said. "One of you ought to get a power of attorney before your grandmother loses her mind completely. That way, you can put her place on the market and get her into a nice retirement home where she'll be taken care of. And," he said, reaching into his breast pocket and holding out a card, "when you do, call me. I've been looking for some land for a golf course. I'll make you a good offer."

Etta Mae slammed on the brakes, bringing the car to a standstill in the middle of the road. She gripped the steering wheel with both hands, her shoulders hunched over, as she stared straight ahead. I saw her breathe deeply a couple of times in an effort to control herself. It didn't work too well.

Ignoring the card he still held out, she turned to glare at him through narrowed eyes. In a voice tight with anger, she said, "I want you to know I was raised to respect my elders and to treat others as I want to be treated, but I'll tell you here and now, my granny is not going to a retirement home. Not as long as I'm around. If I'd known what you were after, I'd have never brought you out here, so you can get it off your mind. Her home is not for sale." She mashed down on the gas and the car moved off with a rattle of gravel against the underside.

Mr. Kessler smiled. "No offense intended, but keep it in mind. You never know when you might need to sell it." He crossed his arms over his chest and turned his head to watch the scenery out the window. Probably, I thought, calculating the worth of every plot of ground we passed.

I caught Etta Mae's flashing eyes in the rearview mirror and if I'd ever thought her heart wasn't in my plan to fix Mr. Kessler's little red wagon, I didn't think so any longer.

Chapter 29

❧

The drive back to Abbotsville was marked by a heavy silence which Mr. Kessler seemed perfectly at ease to let lengthen. Etta Mae, however, drove hunched over the wheel, her breath coming in short snatches as if it was all she could do to hold herself in check. She didn't ask Mr. Kessler where he wanted to go; she just pulled to the curb at the courthouse and waited for him to get out.

He had the temerity to behave as if nothing was wrong and the grace to thank us for the outing. Then he said that he looked forward to any other expedition we wanted to make. Etta Mae didn't glance his way, just revved the motor to hurry him on.

Hesitant to step into the middle, I nonetheless said, "There's someone else I'd like you to meet, Mr. Kessler, if you're available later today. Mr. Jones is a member of one of Abbotsville's finest families, and I think you'd enjoy meeting him. The two of you might find a lot in common."

We made arrangements to meet around three o'clock, and he closed the door and walked away.

Before I could commiserate with Etta Mae, she snatched up the card he'd left on the seat. "Look at this! Just look at it!" Her hand shook as she flapped it in front of me. "Does he think I'm going to change my mind? I'll show him!" She tore the card into little pieces and threw them out the window. "If they charge me with littering, he's getting the bill."

Then she leaned her head against the steering wheel and laughed. "Lord, I don't know when anything has flown all over me like that. I could've wrenched his head off, and I still might."

"I don't blame you," I said, feeling some shame that I hadn't stepped in to put him in his place. "I couldn't believe he would be so crass as to suggest you move your granny out of her home like that. The man has no sensitivity at all. And I'll tell you this, Etta Mae, we've got to get rid of him before he buys up the whole county."

She lifted her head. "Just tell me what to do."

I sat back in the seat as the car continued to idle at the curb. "I'm thinking," I said. Then looking at the courthouse grounds and the shops and stores across the street, I went on. "Just look at this town, Etta Mae. It could be a picture postcard. It is absolutely beautiful, so clean and neat with flower boxes and garden benches and Bradford pear trees lining the street. There's hardly another town like it. And it's filled with just the kind of good and decent people that Mr. Kessler wants to use as advertisements so he can make a killing. He'll exploit this town and eventually turn it into the very thing that all his new people are running away from." I stopped and bit my lip, thinking about what I'd just said. "I'm as progressive as the next person, don't you know. If it's done right. And I'm not against new people moving in. But we have something special here, and I resent being used by Mr. Kessler for our own eventual destruction. As far as I can see, Etta Mae, the two of us are the only ones standing in his way. And I firmly believe he'll run right over us if he figures out what we're doing. Unfortunately, our plan to introduce him to your grandmother sort of backfired on us. All we did was show him a prime piece of real estate, and the upshot of that was to put it in his head to get it away from her."

"She won't sell. And he'd better not bring up the subject to me again."

"What about your uncle?"

"Oh, Lord." She leaned her head against the steering wheel again. "Boyce would sell in a minute if he could." She looked out between the spokes of the steering wheel. "If he gets it in his mind that Granny's losing hers, I guess he could petition for power of attorney, couldn't he? Oh, me," she moaned, "what am I going to do? He's closer kin than I am, so I wouldn't have a thing to say about it."

I leaned up on the front seat. "You need to get her to a good lawyer and fix it so he can't. She needs a will and she needs to put you in charge. I'd do that as soon as possible if I were you. Before Mr. Kessler gets to your uncle."

"You're right and I will. But, man," she said with a sad laugh, "I hate to bring all that up to Granny. She'll have my hide."

"It's for her own good. Now let's go eat. I'm about to cave in and Lillian'll be wondering where we are."

As soon as we walked in the door, Lillian looked up and said, "'Bout time you got here. This soup 'bout simmered down to nothing. But 'fore you set down, Miss Julia, Pastor Ledbetter say he got to talk to you. He want you to call him soon as you get home."

"Well, they Lord, what could he want? Etta Mae, have a seat at the table and let me call him." As I dialed his office at the church across the street, I kept mumbling to myself. "I know he's going to want me to do something, and I don't need another thing to be worried with. He can just get somebody else. I've done my turn and then some."

But he didn't ask me to lead this or chair that, all he wanted was to talk to me, "as soon as you can come over," he said. It was apparent to me that he was agitated over something, and since I'd made it my business lately to steer clear of him, I didn't think he could be upset over something I'd done.

"Let me get a bite of lunch," I told him, "then I'll run over. But I have an appointment at three o'clock, so we'll have to be finished before that."

After we ate, I left Etta Mae to rest at my house until it was time to pick up Mr. Kessler. As I went out the door, she and Lillian were lingering companionably at the table while they discussed the merits of thick, fluffy biscuits over thin, crispy ones.

Pastor Ledbetter came out of his office and into the Fellowship Hall to meet me as soon as he heard the back door close. That showed how anxious he was, for he usually sat in his office until Norma announced a visitor. But Norma was apparently still at lunch, because her desk in the outer office was empty, and I was grateful for it. Norma Cantrell felt it her duty to poke her nose into everybody's business, declaring that it was her job to keep the pastor from being bothered with trifling matters. The woman set my teeth on edge.

Pastor Ledbetter led me into the inner office, closed the door behind us and stood until I was seated in one of the damask wing chairs in front of his desk.

As he sat down in his executive chair and looked across the desk at me, I had a sinking feeling. The grim look on his face told me that I was in for a counseling session. It crossed my mind to go ahead and ask forgiveness for what I'd done and for what I'd left undone, whichever was on his mind. Except he wasn't the one I should've been speaking to.

Nonetheless, I prepared myself for the onslaught, sitting stiffly in the chair with my back straight, my feet together and my hands clasped on the pocketbook in my lap. "I hope you're well, Pastor."

"Thank you, I am," he said abruptly as if he had to get the amenities out of the way. Then, steepling his fingers, he went on. "Miss Julia, I am deeply disturbed over the troubled marriages of some of our most influential members. I'm sure you know who I'm talking about since they're all close friends of yours. I've made it a point to counsel each one of these women, prayed with and for them, and yet I don't see any movement toward reconciliation. And, from what I hear, you've had a hand in their refusal to listen to reason." He paused to let that sink in, then he went on. "It seems to me that you'd want to be giving these women more constructive advice, given the success of your current marriage."

Well, at least he didn't want me to take on another job in Sunday school or vacation Bible school or the Women of the Church or some other organization suitable for women.

"If my current marriage is a success," I said in response to his last comment, "it's because it's a good one for a change. But let me understand, I assume that you're speaking of Mildred Allen, Helen Stroud and LuAnne Conover, is that right?"

He nodded. "Yes, I've spoken with all three, and they seem to be absolutely unbending in their determination to throw over the traces of their marriages. Against, I might add, all admonition of Scripture and my own counsel."

I sat forward in surprise. "Even Helen?" *Sam hadn't told me that.*

"She's more adamant than the others, if that's possible. Now, Miss Julia, you mustn't think that I'm revealing any confidences from my counseling sessions. I asked each one if I could discuss the problem with you, mainly because they all mentioned you in one way or another."

"Oh, yes? And just how did I become a topic?"

He waved his hand as if it were of no concern. "They mentioned they'd spoken to you and that you'd given them suggestions they intended to follow. You apparently have a great deal of influence over them, which is why I felt compelled to speak with you and urge you to amend your advice so these marriages can be saved and strengthened, instead of torn apart."

"Well," I said, "I must correct one thing. I have spoken with Mildred and LuAnne because they came to me, but I haven't had one word with Helen. She is completely out of touch with anyone. Except Sam, but that'll soon stop, since she has a lawyer now."

The pastor hunkered over his desk and gazed at me. "Now, see, that's what I'm talking about. As soon as you get lawyers involved, the next thing you know it's divorce court, which is the very thing a Christian woman ought to avoid. Miss Julia, it seems you and I are offering contradictory advice, which can only create confusion. Since these women rely so heavily on you, I want to make sure we're on the same page. It's the family that we should be focusing on. Our duty, Miss Julia, is to support and sustain Christian marriages, not to urge or even tolerate breakups and divorces. What those women need is encouragement to bear up under trying circumstances, to be faithful in sickness and in health, whether rich or poor." He leaned back and proclaimed, "A woman who would give up on her husband at the least little thing is not much of a wife."

"And," I said, my back getting straighter and stiffer, "a man who would take off at the drop of a hat is not much of a husband. Listen, Pastor, it's the husbands you should be going after. You will notice that all these wives are at home, right where they should be. They're not the ones who left, it's the husbands who've walked out, snuck off, committed fraud and embezzled money or whatever each one of them has done." I gave a sharp nod of my head for emphasis, then went on. "Are you saying that you want me to urge my friends to just sit at home and wait patiently for their wandering husbands to return? And then take them back as if nothing has happened?"

He nodded complacently. "And kill the fatted calf, as it were. Yes, Miss Julia, that's what marriage is all about. It's not a matter of cut and run at the least little stumble. We all make mistakes, and sooner or later Horace and Leonard and Richard will need their wives by their sides. You know what it says in the Book of Ruth. There's even a hymn that's often used at weddings: 'Entreat me not to leave thee; whither thou goest, I will go, and whither thou lodgest, I will lodge.' I just read that passage to Emma Sue last night."

I couldn't resist the opening he gave me. "That is a beautiful passage and a worthwhile sentiment, I grant you. But, Pastor," I said, raising my voice, "Ruth was speaking to her *mother-in-law*! Not to her husband and, in fact, that mother-in-law went on to help her find a new husband. I'm surprised Emma Sue didn't straighten

you out about that. She knows her Bible."
And so did I, as I had just so satisfactorily
proven.

He didn't like it, but he couldn't refute
anything I'd said. "Well, all Scripture is written for our admonition and . . ."

"Not if it's taken out of context, it's not."

"I think we may be off the subject," he
said after a long, less than friendly gaze. "I
just wanted to talk to you about encouraging these wives to be faithful to their vows
so that their marriages will remain intact."

"How do you do that when your husband is off who-knows-where? Horace Allen has let Mildred think he's dead on a
mountainside, and Leonard Conover is off
looking for himself, and Richard Stroud
is somewhere counting other people's
money. I'll tell you this, Pastor, I wouldn't
put up with it, and I cannot urge my friends
to do something I wouldn't do."

"But, Miss Julia," he said, almost smugly,
"you did put up with it. Look how you remained faithful to Mr. Springer all those
years when he was, well, not being very
faithful to you. I admired you for that and
often held you up as an example of a virtuous wife."

That flew all over me, but I ground my teeth and held on. "Don't admire me too much, because if I'd known what he was doing I wouldn't have put up with it. And, since you've brought it up, let me just say that I still resent the fact that you and half the town knew what he was up to and nobody had the gumption to tell me."

"No," he said, shaking his head, "it wasn't my place to make trouble."

"Make *trouble*! I'll tell you who was making trouble. It was Wesley Lloyd Springer, that's who. And did you talk to him? Did you go to him and quote Scripture and tell him to honor his marriage vows? No, you did not. You let him go on doing whatever he wanted and making a fool of me. And that brings me to another question: Would you be urging the husbands to hold on to their marriages if it'd been the wives who'd taken off? I seriously doubt it, don't you?"

"Well, of course I would. But I think we're off the track again. I just think that it's incumbent on all of us to help keep marriages together as much as we can."

"That'd be fine if we could find the other halves of those marriages. It's a little hard to keep anything intact if you have only one of a pair. Pastor, look, I appreciate what you're trying to do, but I can't in good conscience urge a friend to do what I wouldn't do. As far as I'm concerned, when a man wants to leave, there's not much a wife can do but accept it and go on. And it's the going on with strength and grace that I'm urging my friends to do."

Pastor Ledbetter sighed deeply. "It looks as if we don't see eye to eye on this matter."

"Apparently not."

"Well," he said, moving some papers over to indicate the discussion was at an end, "I must say that I'm disappointed, but as for me and my house, we will serve the Lord wherever and however he leads."

Not if it means moving to Raleigh, I thought but didn't say. Emma Sue had about had her fill of decisions being made for her, but he'd find that out when he learned that Emma Sue had been asking my advice, too.

He picked up one sheet of paper, studied it intently and said, "I hope that things are well with you and Sam."

I stood to indicate I'd gotten the message that the meeting was over. "Thank you, things are fine. And if they're ever not, why then, Sam knows how I feel about straying husbands. Nothing will come as a surprise to him. Good day, Pastor, it was good to visit with you."

I left then, mulling over what we'd discussed, pleased with myself for stating and holding my position, and possibly making him rethink his.

I was halfway home before it hit me. What did he mean by hoping all was well with Sam and me? *Did he know something I didn't?*

Chapter 30

Etta Mae and I drove over to the Mary Grace Haddington House that afternoon to pick up Mr. Kessler, but I'd had to talk her into it. She'd been simmering while I was busy straightening out the pastor, and by the time I got home she was ready to pack it in. She announced that she couldn't take any more of the man's arrogance and started begging off.

"Etta Mae," I'd said, "you can't leave me in the lurch like this. I don't want to be seen tooling around town by myself with him, day in and day out. You know how people talk. Besides, he's hard to talk to, and three make better conversation than two. You have to help me."

"Well," she said, reluctantly giving in, "I guess I can do it for you. But if he mentions Granny's farm one more time, I won't be responsible."

I smiled. "And I won't hold you responsible. Let's go."

We were both lost in our own thoughts as we drove down Main Street toward the end of the business district where a few large, nineteenth-century houses remained in various states of disrepair. Of course, the Mary Grace Haddington House stood out like a jewel since the Websters had bought it and remodeled it from top to bottom, turning it into a bed and breakfast temptingly advertised in *Southern Living*. Ed and Lila Webster were from somewhere in Alabama, and how they ended up in Abbotsville, I'm sure I don't know. I can't even imagine the money it had taken to convert that old Queen Anne mansion into a modern inn, nor how they'd come to have that much for such a purpose in the first place. Still, they were lovely people, even with an unknown background, and the inn was perfect for out-of-town guests that you didn't want underfoot all day, even if it only served breakfast.

Mr. Kessler was waiting for us on the porch. As Etta Mae approached the curb, I saw him walking back and forth, ignoring the rocking chairs arrayed for the viewing pleasure of the inn's guests. Apparently, rocking and watching cars go by was one of the amenities offered by the Websters. But Mr. Kessler was a man of action, too eager to buy and sell and get on with things to spend time in such a wasteful manner.

He came striding down the walk toward the car, his summer-weight wool suit buttoned, his shoes shined, his tie knotted to perfection, looking as if he were about to chair a meeting. I wondered if the man ever gave it a rest.

As he took his accustomed place in the front seat beside Etta Mae, he greeted us in his typical abrupt, northern fashion, mentioning that he was looking forward to meeting Mr. Jones, whom I'd earlier described as a mover and shaker in Abbotsville. I responded with as much warmth as I could muster, which wasn't much since it still grated on me that he continued to accept the front seat as his due, completely oblivi-

ous to my own good manners in leaving it
vacant for him. Any southern gentleman
would've at least offered to sit in the back.

Etta Mae nodded a greeting, then con-
centrated on her driving. I can't say that
we have a traffic problem in Abbotsville,
but when the schools let out, as they were
now doing, it does pick up considerably.
All those mothers in vans and SUVs, don't
you know, and high schoolers whipping
their tiny cars in and out are enough to put
your nerves on edge.

And my nerves were edgy enough already. I was still reeling from the pastor's
implication that all might not be well with
Sam and me. He might've meant nothing
at all by what he said. Then again, he'd
been put out with me, which was par for
the course in our dealings with each other,
so there may have been a world of harm-
ful intent behind his words. Preachers are
human, too, and not above giving a little
tit for tat now and then. I'm sure I don't
blame them, for I'd hate to have to put up
with the complaints and criticisms of your
typical church members. Still and all, it's
most unattractive for a man of God to get
personal.

When Etta Mae maneuvered us out of the traffic jams around the schools and turned onto Woodrow Wilson Drive, which paralleled Polk but ran farther west, I pointed out to Mr. Kessler that we were now in the historic district of the town.

"Many of the early families had estates in this area," I said. "But, of course, over time the town inched out this way and people began to sell off parcels for others to build on. It's still mostly residential, except for a few groceries and convenience stores here and there." I sat forward on the edge of the seat to look out the front. "Turn left here, Etta Mae."

Thurlow Jones's street was lined with huge oaks and it was like driving through a tunnel as their branches formed a canopy overhead. Most of the houses sat far back from the street with mature, well-kept plantings in the front.

"This is it." I pointed to the right, where a large, brick house almost covered in ivy sat by itself in the middle of a block, surrounded by a crumbling brick wall. Overgrown hollies and straggling nandinas lined the inside of the wall and spread out to hang over the sidewalk. Several large magnolia trees dotted the yard and, peeking through the wrought iron gate that led to the walkway, I could see weeds everywhere.

The gate at the driveway was open, so Etta Mae pulled in and came to a stop. No one had a word to say as we took in the scene before us. The house retained remnants of its former architectural beauty, but now a shutter hung askew from a missing hinge, and a feeler of ivy had snaked through the hole in an upstairs window. The lawn, if you could call it that, was so overgrown that I could hardly make out the front walk. The place looked abandoned, but that's the way Thurlow Jones kept it.

Mr. Kessler peered around, his eyebrows raised. "This is it?"

"Now, Mr. Kessler," I said, leaning forward on the seat, "don't be put off by what you see. Thurlow is a fine man from a fine family of judges and state senators, and he was educated at Washington and Lee. He's generous to a fault and highly thought of in the community."

I didn't mention that our thoughts ran along the lines of *eccentric, odd duck* and *crazy as a loon.* I also didn't mention that he was the last of a long line of strange people, which did not exclude the judges and state senators, several of whom had ended up either in jail or in mental institutions. Somehow, though, the family had held on to their wealth, for Thurlow was known to be loaded. As well he should be since he never spent any of it. Well, to be fair, he was generous with his donations and contributions. He just chose to donate and contribute to the oddest causes.

I opened the car door and prepared to step out, then noticed that Mr. Kessler remained in his seat. "He's expecting us, Mr. Kessler."

"Let's forgo this visit," he said. "My time's valuable, and I'm pushed as it is."

"Oh, no," I said, opening his door. "You must meet Thurlow. If you want anything done in this town, you have to know him. Why, he's behind every progressive step we take, and I'll tell you something else. He has the county commissioners in his back pocket."

Mr. Kessler frowned and cocked an eye at me, interested but not quite believing. "Is that so?"

"Yes, indeed. Don't let the state of his home fool you. He's a man who doesn't believe in putting up a front—a man of the people who does his work behind the scenes. He's the pride of Abbot County, and I can't tell you how much everybody respects and admires him."

"Well," Mr. Kessler said, stepping from the car and smoothing his suit coat as he looked around. "That puts a different light on it. Some of our greatest entrepreneurs were a little out of sync with the common run. I like to think I'm one of them myself. Frankly, Mrs. Murdoch, I admire a man who doesn't flaunt who he is and what he has. I'm looking forward to meeting him."

Etta Mae lagged behind us as we tromped through the weeds to the front door. I motioned to her to hurry along, but she still had a sulky look on her face and only caught up with us as I rang the doorbell.

The door sprang open while I still had my finger on the bell. Thurlow stood there before us, squinting out from the dark interior. "No need to keep mashing it," he said. "It don't work just like everything else around here. Except me. I'm still running

just fine. So, Lady Springer, is it? Oh, forgive my terrible lapse of manners. It's
Madam Murdoch now. Come on in here,
woman, and let me get a good look at
you."

He reached for my arm, but I sidled
away, smiling as if I wasn't about to smack
him. Thurlow had grown smaller since I'd
last seen him, or perhaps more stooped.
And if his house and yard looked as if
they needed sprucing up, they were nothing compared to him. He wore a stained
wool shirt—Pendleton, by the looks of it—
and baggy pants that may have once
helped make up a suit of clothes. His hair
was a little grayer and, like his lawn,
needed mowing. A glint of white whiskers
spread across his face, and the glasses
perched on his nose were smudged with
who-knew-what.

"Thurlow," I said, "I've brought Arthur
Kessler to meet you, and of course you
know Miss Etta Mae Wiggins. I hope you
were expecting us since I called to let
you know we were coming."

He ignored Mr. Kessler as he squinted
intently at Etta Mae. "Well, that's a sight
for sore eyes."

Since he hadn't invited us in, I attempted to nudge him a little. "I hope we're not disturbing you."

"Oh, hell, no. What else I got to do except have afternoon tea. Do come in, ladies and," he glanced at Mr. Kessler, "whoever you are."

We followed him across the dark hall filled with huge pieces of furniture into a front room just like it. Tall glass-fronted bookcases lined the walls, while hard, Victorian sofas and rump-sprung Lawson chairs sat in no particular order around the room. Newspapers had been thrown to the floor and left where they'd fallen, and a few books were open and facedown on almost every table.

"Well, have a seat if you can find one," Thurlow said, which was about as gracious as he ever got. "And just go on and tell me what you want. I ain't got time for chitchat, nor the heart for it either, since you broke it marrying Sam Murdoch."

"Oh, Thurlow," I said, sitting gingerly on a blue velvet hard-as-a-rock sofa, "you know that's not true."

His eyes glinted behind his filthy glasses. "Well, I tried to catch you but you ran too fast for me. I'll say this, though, you brought in a mighty nice substitute today." Thurlow switched around suddenly to look Etta Mae up and down. "What'd you say your name was, girl?"

"Etta Mae Wiggins," she said, pulling herself up as tall as she could manage. "And proud of it."

"Ah, yes. I know your family. Bunch of backwood heathens, if you ask me. But I'm sure you've come up in the world. You look like it anyhow. Set yourself down and be sure to swing your legs thisaway." He cackled like a fool. "I need a little spurt of adrenaline every now and then."

Etta Mae's face flushed red, so I quickly stepped in. "Behave yourself, Thurlow. Etta Mae, ignore him. He likes to shock people, but," I said, reminding her of our purpose in coming, "that's just his way and we love him for it, don't we? Now, Thurlow, Mr. Kessler, here, is a man of parts who's come to Abbotsville to move us into the twenty-first century since we seem to be lagging a little behind. I knew you'd want to meet him and I've assured him that you're the man to know if he wants to get anything done in this town. And what he wants to do is build luxury condominiums down on Main Street. Won't that be nice?"

"Do tell." Thurlow turned what might have been an appraising eye in Mr. Kessler's direction. "Luxury condominiums, huh? I might just buy me one or two. Maybe move in myself. This place," he said, flinging out an arm to include everything, "is too much for me. Hard to keep up, even if I wanted to. What size condos you building?"

Mr. Kessler had perched himself stiffly on the edge of a straight chair, and he sat there looking like he'd rather be anyplace than where he was. But, thinking Thurlow had influence, he leaned forward to state his case. "As soon as I get the county's approval of the sale, I'll put up an eight-story building that'll be the crown jewel of my company and this town. I'll call it the Crowne—spelled with an *e*—Plaza, and it'll outshine anything in this part of the state. You'll be proud to have had a part in it, Mr. Jones. But to be specific, the one-bedroom units will start around half a million. The others go up from there. Then there'll be the penthouses for a couple of select buyers."

I enjoyed watching Mr. Kessler walk a

fine line between trying to impress this influential quaint character and trying to hide his own feelings of superiority. Mr. Kessler's throwaway tone implied that, even though he might need a little local help to get them built, his condos would be beyond Thurlow Jones's capacity to purchase. But if he meant to intimidate, it didn't work.

Thurlow nodded as if it were exactly what he'd expected. "You get 'em built and I'll think about it. I got a cousin needs looking after. He's in a home now, but they about to kick him out. I could put him in one of your condos and hire a man to watch him. Just tell the neighbors to lock up. He does like to drop in at odd hours." Thurlow slapped his knee and cackled gleefully. "Come to think of it, Kessler, you might be an answer to prayer for that boy. Well, he's not much of a boy anymore. Pushing sixty or so by now. He's my burden, but I sure don't want him around here, messing things up. You just put me down for one of them two-bedroomers, and I'll think about a bigger one for me. But not on the same floor, oh, hell, no, don't do that."

Mr. Kessler looked as if he'd eaten

something that disagreed with him. "Well, I don't think . . ."

"You don't want to think, you want to sell. And I'll tell you this, you're some sales-man. You just walked in here, and you got at least one and maybe two sold. And you did it . . ." Thurlow leaned over and snapped his fingers in Mr. Kessler's face, "just like that."

Chapter 31

I gathered my pocketbook and began to rise, ready to bring the visit to an end. Mr. Kessler was immediately on his feet and Etta Mae began to edge toward the door. Thurlow had given his usual outrageous performance, as I had counted on, so there was no reason to linger. I couldn't help but smile at the thought of Brother Vern preaching in the new lobby and Thurlow and his cousin wandering the halls of Mr. Kessler's building. So far everything was working as I'd hoped.

Thurlow hopped up from his chair, telling us not to hurry, he didn't have anything else to do and we could stay as long as we wanted. He scurried around me and walked up behind Etta Mae. I saw him put one hand on the small of her back as if he were guiding her across the hall. He gestured toward the door with his other hand, perhaps to distract her. Then before I could get to him, the hand on Etta Mae's back began to slip downward.

She jumped to the side. "Touch it, and I'll slap you cross-eyed."

"Ooh," Thurlow said, laughing and holding his hands up to prove his innocence. "Ain't she feisty!"

I hurried Etta Mae out before she made good on her threat, thanking Thurlow as I went and then having to wait in the car as Mr. Kessler seemed unable to get away from Thurlow who was wagging a finger in his face. Etta Mae continued to fume for a few minutes, but began to calm down when I told her of my own run-ins with Thurlow.

We were still smiling when Mr. Kessler finally got into the car and closed the door. "Well," he said, "he's certainly one of a kind. I expect you don't have many like him."

"Oh," I said airily, "he's pretty typical of

your average businessman in these parts. Sharp and independent-minded under all that foolishness he carries on with." I sat back, feeling fairly pleased with the way the visit had gone. Then, as a thought struck, I leaned forward. "Why, Mr. Kessler, I just thought of something. Thurlow's the very reason you can even think of putting up a skyscraper on Main Street."

"I can't imagine why," he said, with just a tinge of sarcasm.

"Well, some of us, I mean, a group of so-called liberal do-gooders wanted the county to pass some zoning restrictions. Thurlow rose up in protest, threatening to sue the town and the county and everybody involved. Said if a man couldn't do what he wanted with his own property, we might as well be living in Russia."

There was a stretch of silence until Mr. Kessler asked, "What happened to the zoning?"

"Oh, it didn't pass. Obviously, since you're right before replacing that wreck of a courthouse with a new and modern edifice. And just think," I said, reaching up to pat his shoulder, "you have Thurlow to thank for it, and you've as good as sold two units to him. Who knows, you might end up doing a lot of business together, especially since you won't have any zoning restrictions to worry about. The county's wide open, Mr. Kessler, thanks to Thurlow and a few more like him."

As Etta Mae drove us back toward town, there was another stretch of silence as my words hung in the air.

Then Mr. Kessler, in that authoritative manner of his, said, "As a developer, I'm a strong supporter of open-use zoning. A man ought to be able to do what he wants with what he owns. That's the American way. But it cuts both ways. Once a man owns something, he can put in his own restrictions, and I see that the Crowne Plaza will have to institute a few, specifically concerning who can buy in and who can't."

I sat back and let that bit of hypocrisy hang in the air. It was a settled fact that Mr. Kessler's attitude toward property rights depended on whose ox was being gored.

That evening as I joined Lloyd and Sam in the dining room, I started right in telling them how well I thought things were going.

"Mr. Kessler was really put off after we went to see Thurlow Jones," I said, walking to my place. "And when Granny Wiggins got through with him, well, I think he's seeing a different side of this town."

Sam pulled out my chair, then rested a hand on my shoulder. "I hate to tell you this, Julia, but the word is out. It looks like the commissioners have pulled a fast one."

I shook out my napkin, as he took his place at the head of the table. "What've they done now?"

"They've voted to sell the courthouse."

"Oh, no," I cried, nearly springing off the chair. "They can't do that! Sam, when did this happen?"

"Last night, apparently," he told me. "They held a called meeting with no public notice, which may've been illegal. A few of us are getting together tonight to see what we can do about it. I'm afraid we're too late though."

"Can the commissioners do that?" My hands were shaking, I was so angry and upset. "And not even wait till Tuesday at their regular meeting? Do they have the authority to just sell it out from under us? It belongs to the taxpayers. Don't we have a voice in this?"

"Well, we can protest, which we'll do. And try to get a ruling from the state to slow it down or have a bill introduced to stop it. But it'll take time, and from the looks of it, Kessler is ready to move."

Lloyd spoke up then. "Somebody said at school today that they're already bringing in bulldozers."

"You mean *today*?" I demanded. "Sam, do you know about that?"

Sam nodded. "Afraid so, Julia. I drove by this afternoon and they're unloading heavy equipment at the back of the courthouse in the parking lot. They'll probably start with the annex."

"Oh, Lord," I said, leaning my head against my hand, "they were doing it at the exact same time that Etta Mae and I thought we were making progress." I glared at Sam. "Arthur Kessler knew about this all along, didn't he? Oh, Sam, the courthouse could be a pile of bricks by tomorrow. And we haven't even had the soiree yet, which was going to change his mind about developing anything in this town. What are we going to do, Sam? What *can* we do?"

"I'm sorry, Julia." Sam gave me a tender look down the length of the table. "I hate to see it go, too. But once they start, there's no going back. I heard that they're bringing in a crane with a wrecking ball sometime this week. One swing of that thing, and it's over."

I didn't know whether to put my head down and cry or just scream it off in frustration. "I will get back at every one of those commissioners if it's the last thing I ever do." I adjusted my salad plate and tried to reconcentrate my mind, aware now of the child sitting across from me, taking it all in. "Lloyd, I don't mean to be vowing revenge exactly. It's just that there are consequences to every action, sometimes good consequences and sometimes bad. I intend to see that this action has bad consequences for all concerned. Although," I said, wiping my eyes with my napkin, "it'll be too late for that beautiful, historic courthouse."

"Here, Julia," Sam said, passing the bread basket, "you need to eat something. Have a roll."

"I don't think I can. I'm just devastated about this."

He patted my hand again and looked

sympathetically at me. But I didn't need sympathy; I needed help. But, as usual, it would be left to me to come up with something. The rest of the meal proceeded quietly enough, although interrupted by my having to sniff now and then. My mind was working, though, considering, then discarding one idea after another, until gradually a few ideas stuck.

As Sam moved his chair back before standing, I reached out to detain him. "Sam, since the weather's so nice, why don't you take a day or two and go on a motorcycle ride? You've let that machine sit in the garage too long, and it'd do you good to get out a little. Go up on the parkway or somewhere and take in the sights."

Lloyd's eyes popped wide. "Can I go?"

Sam laughed and patted the boy's shoulder. "I'm trying to organize a protest. I can't take off now. But it's a good idea. Maybe when Pickens gets back, we'll go."

I didn't want him to wait for Mr. Pickens. I wanted him out of the house today and for a few more to come.

He leaned over and kissed me. "Don't let it get you down, sweetheart. I'll let you know what we come up with tonight."

I had little confidence that anything could be done, so when he left, I propped my elbows on either side of my plate and buried my face in my hands. "I can't think what to do, Lloyd," I said. "It is all such a shame. Worse than that, it's an outrage. And I've been working so hard to show Mr. Kessler that we aren't the kind of people he'd want to live next to."

Lloyd said, "Maybe he doesn't believe you."

I raised my head to look at him. "You think?"

"Yessum, I bet he's figured out what you're doing. He may even like the town better because of all the interesting characters you've been showing him."

"Oh, my." I sat up straight, wondering if I'd done myself in while thinking I was doing Mr. Kessler in.

"What I mean is," Lloyd went on, "he probably figures that you and Etta Mae kinda stand for what's normal in the town. You, 'specially. He knows you're not the type of person to run around with Brother Vern or Mr. Jones, and he's met some of your friends at the dinner party. That's who he'll figure are the regular people in town."

"Lloyd," I said, wonder filling my words, "you are the smartest boy alive. You're absolutely right. You have given me a whole lot to think about."

"I have?" He grinned, delighted that he'd helped. "When you decide what to do, let me help."

"Well, I'll tell you about it."

"Etta Mae?" I said as soon as she answered her phone. I'd run to the bedroom and closed the door as soon as Lloyd went to his room. "Have you heard? Well, get over here as early as you can in the morning. We have things to do."

Hanging up and dialing again, I could hardly wait for LuAnne to answer. "LuAnne, has Leonard come home yet?"

"No, and he better not. I've had it with him."

"Good," I said, cringing a little as Pastor Ledbetter's cautionary counsel resounded in my mind. "I just wanted to tell you that I'm pretty sure Arthur Kessler is interested in you."

"He *is*? What did he say?"

"Oh, just that you're an attractive woman. And he asked if you were seeing anybody."

Lord, forgive me for lying, but remember it's for a good cause.

"He *did?* What did you tell him?"

"I don't have time to talk right now, Lu-Anne. I just wanted to let you know, so you can let him know you're interested the next time you see him. And to warn you. I think he's a little shy. You might need to make it kind of obvious, if you know what I mean. I've got to go now."

"Wait, Julia . . ."

But I hung up, unable to get myself in any deeper. I'd have to be on my knees for a good, long session by the time this week was over.

Chapter 32

"Can you believe this!" Etta Mae waved the newspaper at me as soon as I opened the door the next morning. I couldn't miss the bold headlines. "That low-down sneaking Arthur Kessler! All this time that we've been driving him around, he *knew* he was starting demolition today!"

"That's exactly what I told Sam," I said, leading the way to the kitchen. "Now, Etta Mae, I have something in mind that'll buy us a little time. But I need your help. I'm about to call Mildred and give her a list, and here's yours. You can use Hazel Marie's phone. It's on a separate line."

"I better fix y'all something to eat," Lillian said. "You not gonna get much when you in jail."

"For goodness' sakes, Lillian, we're not going to jail." I said, paying no attention to her head shaking and eye rolling.

"What is it?" Etta Mae asked, studying the list I'd handed her.

"It's every service station and convenience store in the county and several outside. I mean, that's your list. I'm giving Mildred one, and I'll have one. We're going to call them all and tell them not to sell any gasoline for that bulldozer."

Etta Mae frowned and screwed up her mouth. "Track hoe," she said, still studying the list, "and it uses diesel. Sorry, Miss Julia, but this won't work. They'll buy from a distributor, not from one of these places."

"Well, my word, I spent half the morning going through the Yellow Pages for nothing."

"No problem. There's only one oil distributor in Abbot County and maybe three in Buncombe. I'll call them. What'll I tell them?"

"Tell them that we're in the process of

getting an injunction against Arthur Kessler and they're not to deliver any diesel fuel to the Abbot County courthouse anytime soon. Tell them if they're called to the site, they're to be too busy and I'll make up whatever they lose in the process."

"Are we?"

"Are we what?"

"Getting an injunction?"

"What's that?" Lillian asked.

"Oh," I said, too busy thinking to give either one an answer, "I'm not sure, but Sam's working on it. But what we have to do is stop that machine before it does any damage."

"I hate to tell you this," Etta Mae said, "but I drove by the courthouse on my way here, and it's already running. And a front-end loader, too. They're uprooting the trees in the back and breaking up the pavement in the parking lot. Big chunks of it, too. They've got dump trucks and flatbeds and I don't know what all. They mean business, Miss Julia, and they're going all out to get it done."

"Oh, my Lord," I said, getting more agitated by the minute. "Those things're running amuck. Etta Mae, let's take some lawn chairs down there and sit in the parking lot. They'll have to stop then."

"My Jesus, Miss Julia!" Lillian cried. "You can't do that. That 'quipment run all over you."

"No, it won't. We'll call the newspaper and the Asheville television station and create a stir. I'll tell you this, Etta Mae, and you, too, Lillian, I've never had much use for protesters who throw themselves in front of progress, but I am ready to strap some chains on. One way or another, we've got to stop those machines."

"They'd just pick us up and move us out," Etta Mae said, "but I know something that could slow them down."

"What? I'm ready for anything."

"Sand. Or dirt. A coupla handsful of dirt in the fuel tanks. That'd put them out of commission for a few days until they could clean them out or bring in more." She paused and thought for a minute. "And every time they brought in a new piece, we'd have to sneak down there and gum up the works again. Pretty soon they'd have night guards, so I don't know how long we could go without getting caught."

"Y'all goin' to jail," Lillian said, wringing a dishcloth in her hands. "I know you, Miss Julia. You jus' bound to do something you ought not do, an' you gonna get caught and end up in the jailhouse."

"It's a worthy cause, Lillian. Besides, I don't aim to get caught. All right, Etta Mae, we'll let them have their fun today, but tonight, well, we shall see, won't we?"

When Etta Mae left, with instructions to take a nap in preparation for our foray that night, Lillian continued with her dire warnings of arrest and incarceration.

"What you gonna tell Mr. Sam?" she demanded. "What he gonna say when you go outta here in the dead of night and sneak around th'owin' dirt in people's gas tanks?"

Well, that was the question, wasn't it? I was certainly facing a moral dilemma since I had somewhat promised Sam never to get into a dangerous situation again. After he'd pieced together some of the riskier aspects of my expedition with Etta Mae in Florida, he'd said, "Julia, please promise you won't endanger yourself that way again. My poor heart couldn't stand it."

And I'd promised. So, as I now saw it, I had to leave those machines alone and think of something else. Sam's peace of mind meant the world to me.

"He's not going to know," I told Lillian, "because I've changed my mind. I'll just go with Etta Mae and be back in less than an hour. He won't know a thing about it. He's a sound sleeper."

"Uh-huh," she said, her mouth pinched up so tight she could hardly speak. "An' I 'spect he not sleep so sound when that phone ring sayin' you on the way to the Atlanta pen."

"Oh, Lillian, we're not going to the Atlanta pen. It wouldn't be a *federal* crime, you know. And if we do get caught, which I don't intend to be, they'll keep us an hour or so until Binkie and Sam can come bail us out. It's nothing to worry about."

"Well, I am gonna worry 'cause I already am. You jus' . . ."

The ringing of the telephone interrupted her, which was just as well, since I'd heard enough. I snatched it up and answered it.

"Arthur Kessler here," Arthur Kessler said. "Thought you might like to come down to the courthouse and watch the action. You saw the paper this morning, didn't you?"

It was all I could do to keep a level tone in my answer. "Why, yes, I did. And I was surprised to read that the commissioners met in secret and voted to give you the go-ahead."

He chuckled! I'd never been exactly sure what a chuckle was until one came out of his mouth. "Well, you know," he said in that smug way of his, "sometimes you have to make an end run to get around those who would hold you back. Perfectly legal, though, but if anybody tries to stop us, well, that old courthouse'll be gone before you know it."

My teeth were ground together so tight, I could hardly get the words out. "You certainly know how to get your way, I'll give you that."

While he went on chortling over his end run, I was thinking hard. What Lloyd had said about Mr. Kessler knowing that Etta Mae, Mildred, LuAnne, possibly Emma Sue and, certainly, I represented the majority of Abbot County residents had stuck in my mind. We were the "salt-of-the-earth" types, not the likes of Brother Vern, Granny

Wiggins and Thurlow Jones, that he would use to attract buyers of the units in the Crowne Plaza. I'd already started disabusing him of that idea by setting LuAnne on him, but that would take time to bear fruit. So if the courthouse was going to be saved, we didn't have time to waste because Arthur Kessler had been ahead of us every step of the way. He'd come to town expecting to deal with a bunch of country hicks—nice enough, but gullible and easily manipulated—and so far, that's exactly what we'd proven to be.

So he could pat himself on the back all he wanted for having pulled a fast one, but that just gave me free rein to pull a stunt or two myself. There'd be no trouble with my conscience after this.

When he paused for my response, I gave him one. "I would like to see what's going on," I told him, "but my car's acting up a little. Would you mind coming to pick me up?"

He assured me that he wouldn't mind at all. His rental car had been sitting idle too long, since Etta Mae and I had been doing all the chauffeuring.

As soon as I hung up, Lillian asked, "What's wrong with yo' car?"

"Nothing's wrong with it. I just wanted him over here."

She eyed me suspiciously. "What for?"

"I'm going to show him that woman's image on the Family Life Center across the street."

"They's not no woman on that building. You tole me that when I was seein' her. You tole me it was just some kinda something oozin' outta them new bricks an' it jus' look like a woman's face. And it's a lady, not a woman. 'Sides, it all washed off now an' don't nobody see nothin' no more."

"I know that and you know that. But Arthur Kessler doesn't. It's called acting, Lillian, play like, pretend, whatever you want to call it, but that man's going to have to rethink what this town is like before I'm through with him."

I spent the fifteen minutes before Mr. Kessler's rental car pulled to the curb getting myself in the right frame of mind. I would have to pretend to be excited about the destruction he was wreaking, while at the same time trying to undermine his idea of Abbotsville as the ideal spot for the development that nobody wanted but him and a few short-sighted commissioners. Well, and Mildred and Thurlow, too, which had rocked me back on my heels. Who would've thought they'd be interested in what amounted to high-rise apartments in the middle of town with less space to heat and no yard to care for?

But, I thought, as the glimmer of an idea wiggled its way into my mind, if that's the case, I happened to own a block or two at the end of Main Street with nothing on them that would ever be missed—certainly no historic buildings. With two, possibly three, units as good as sold—I mean, both Mildred and Thurlow were friends of mine—putting up my own condominiums would catch a wave of the future and, on top of that, be a smart investment. I determined to talk to Binkie about it just as soon as I disabused Mr. Kessler of the same idea.

So out I pranced to meet him, plastering a welcoming smile on my face.

"So this is the day," I said, shaking his hand since he had shown enough courtesy to step out of the car at my approach. "The one you've been looking forward to, the day the destruction begins."

"Oh, I don't look at it as a day of destruction. It's a day of new beginnings. The crown jewel of my company will rise up on that spot and finally," he stopped and gave a little laugh, "and finally, my partners will see that I was right all along."

"Oh? I'm not sure I knew you had partners."

With a condescending smile, he set me straight. "In a monumental undertaking like this, you always have partners. You didn't think I'd put my assets into it, did you?"

"Well, I don't know much about high finance." Which wasn't exactly true, but I don't tell every Tom, Dick and Harry my business.

"It's called spreading the risk. And I'll have to say," he stopped to give that smug little laugh again, "my partners have taken a few risks, but they knew that going in. It'll all straighten out, though, when the Crowne Plaza is ready for occupancy."

I couldn't believe it, but he actually rubbed his hands together. It was all I could do not to take one of mine and smack him to kingdom come. Instead, I let my eyes wander to the Family Life Building—another monstrosity perpetrated on us Presbyterians who had to pay for it and on me who had to live across the street from it.

"Oh, look!" I cried, pointing to the tall brick wall facing us.

"What?" Mr. Kessler turned in that direction.

"She's back! See her, Arthur? She doesn't show herself to just anybody. You must be special to her."

"What? Who? I don't see anything."

"Right there on the wall! See, see the shawl over her head, and look at her eyes. They're so soulful. You can just make out her features. Oh, this is a blessed day! I've seen her many times in the past, but she appears less and less frequently—only when something momentous is about to happen. It must have to do with you, Arthur."

Mr. Kessler's head was stretched forward out of his collar, his eyes squinched up as he stared at the wall. "What are you talking about? I don't see anything."

"You don't? Why, she's right there, big as life. Well, somewhat bigger, given the size of the wall. Well, I declare, it must be me she's aiming at. She's very selective, you know. Not everybody can see her, just certain ones. The elect, I guess." Then I cringed, fearing I'd given myself away by using a Presbyterian concept in a Catholic context. But being theologically ignorant, Mr. Kessler let it sail right past. He kept on gazing first at me, then the wall, with a look of confusion on his face.

"You sure you see something on that wall?" he asked.

"As sure as I'm standing here. Oh, she is so beautiful, but of course the Holy Mother would be, wouldn't she?"

"The Holy Mother?" Arthur Kessler gave me his full attention, pulling his head back and looking down his nose at me. "I think you're seeing things."

"I certainly am," I said, "and honored to be able to. If I could kneel and get back up again, I'd do it right here on this blessed sidewalk."

Then, thinking in for a penny, in for a pound, I crossed myself. I got it a little off-kilter since I'd forgotten to practice. But for better or worse, I made the sign of the cross going from nose to navel and arm to arm, which was as good as your average

Presbyterian could do and Mr. Kessler didn't know the difference.

"Maybe you better stay home," he said. "Too much excitement's not good for you."

"Why, how thoughtful of you, Arthur. And, yes, I think I shall stay home. I need some meditation time after being given this sighting. It may be that the lady has a message for us, and if so, I'll pass it along. It may have to do with you, since you were here when she appeared."

"You do that," he said, and abruptly opened the car door and slid inside.

I stood with my hands clasped in prayer, my eyes turned heavenward, as he sped off. Then I smiled and went inside.

Chapter 33

Lillian looked up from whatever she was doing at the sink as I trudged back into the kitchen. "I thought you goin' to watch 'em wreck the courthouse."

I flopped down in a chair at the table and put my head in my hands. Smiling tiredly, I said, "The lady on the wall told me not to."

Water sloshed in the sink as Lillian dropped a head of lettuce. "What you say?"

"Oh, I'm just teasing. The lady didn't say a word. How could she? I didn't even see her, but Arthur Kessler thought I did. So he wasn't all that eager to take me down there." I laughed a little, as much as I could manage under the circumstances. "He suggested I stay home and rest, which means, I hope, that I did a good acting job. Maybe I qualify now as one of his quaint characters."

Lillian turned back to the sink and started pulling apart lettuce leaves, mumbling, "You one of them, all right."

I rubbed my hands across my face, feeling more and more sick at heart. "None of it's going to work, Lillian. Even Sam admits it's too late. I've just got to face it. We can fill machinery with dirt every night that rolls around, and they'll still get it running. And I can pretend to be half-crazy, along with the likes of Thurlow Jones, and it won't stop him. That man is bound and determined to destroy our history and put up a monument to himself." I sighed and rubbed my eyes. "Reminds me of Pastor Ledbetter, and you see how far I got trying to stop him. That Family Life Building stares me in the face every time I step outside."

Lillian went to the refrigerator and took out a pitcher of lemonade. Without a word, she poured two glasses and brought them to the table. Then, sitting across from me, she said, "Can't nobody get what they want all the time. Maybe you oughtta put something else in yo' mind 'stead of this."

"Well, what . . . ?" The ringing of the telephone cut me off, so I walked over and answered it.

"Julia?"

At the sound of her voice, I had to sit back down. "Helen?"

"Of course it is," she said, as if she hadn't been out of touch for days on end. "I guess you know they're tearing down the courthouse."

"Yes, I know it, and I've been knowing it. And trying to do something to stop it, too, with mighty little help from anybody else, I might add."

"Well, you should've called me. I would've helped, because I've been trying to organize a historic association to preserve our heritage for the longest time. I'm surprised you didn't let me know what was going on."

This was a new Helen Stroud. Never had she spoken to me or to anybody else in such a snippy way for as long as I'd known her. But then, I'd never known her to lean on somebody else's husband as she'd been doing, either.

So I came right back at her. "I tried to let you know, Helen, but when you don't answer your door or return anybody's calls, what am I supposed to do? Camp out on your doorstep?"

"You could've e-mailed me. Did you think of that?"

Well, no, I hadn't, since Lloyd would've had to have done it for me. "No, Helen, I didn't. I figured you didn't want to hear from me. Besides," I said, wanting her to know I wasn't totally out of the loop, "Sam told me of his visits with you, so I knew how you were doing."

"Well," she said, "well, we need to do something about the courthouse."

"I've been trying, but everything I come up with is either a criminal act or a crazy one. If you have any ideas, I'm open to them."

"You probably don't know this, but I've done a lot of research on the courthouse, because I thought it was the obvious place to base the historic association. And come to find out, that building's about the third one on the site. The original one burned around the time of the Civil War, and the second was so poorly constructed that it was torn down in the early twenties, and that's when the one we have now was built. Right before the Great Depression, which in hindsight was good timing. Anyway, it has no great historic value, but I'd still like to see it saved."

"No great historic value? I didn't know that."

"No, and in fact, it's about to fall down by itself. It has some termite damage and the foundation's settling. It would cost a mint to restore. Frankly, tearing it down is probably for the best, but it breaks my heart to say it, because the building is an architectural jewel."

"Well, my goodness, maybe I should've done a little research myself. But like you say, it is a beautiful building and I hate to see it go."

"Well, the county's waited too long to do anything, and, really, Julia, nobody's been all that interested. Which is just a shame."

That flew all over me, because who had been working her fingers to the bone to discourage Arthur Kessler from his destructive course, and who had been closed off in her own house without a word to anyone? Except to my husband?

"I've been interested, Helen, but I'm at my wit's end. I don't know what else to do at this point," I said, ready to end this conversation. "Because you're right. If we'd started earlier, gotten better organized, maybe the courthouse could've been saved. As it is, though, I guess we'll have to live with the wreckage." I took a deep breath and the plunge. "Speaking of which, how is Richard? Have you heard from him?"

"That's something I can't discuss, Julia, on my lawyer's advice. And I'm surprised you'd ask."

The question I wanted to ask was: *Which* lawyer? But I didn't. Instead I said, "You shouldn't be surprised. Everybody who invested with him is interested, and I'm one of them."

"Oh," she said in a strangled kind of way, making me feel ashamed of myself. Still, I saw no reason to pretend that Richard Stroud's actions hadn't affected me.

"Well, be that as it may," I went on, "it looks as if Arthur Kessler is getting his way, in spite of how we feel. But when you have all the money in the world you can do whatever you want, regardless."

"Yes," she said, clearing her throat, "from what's going on down there today, it looks like we've lost that battle. But, uh, Julia, as a matter of curiosity, where does Mr. Kessler's money come from?"

"I really don't know," I told her. "He speaks of his company, whatever that is, and implies that he's done a lot of developing in other places. He sort of brags about this new building being the crown jewel of his company—that's what he's going to name it—the Crowne, with an e, Plaza. To give it an English flavor, I guess." I paused, then went on. "Come to think of it, though, he's mentioned partners a few times and laughed about them taking all the risks. So either he has a lot of money not being used or he doesn't have any and has to use other people's. It'd be interesting to find out which it is, wouldn't it?"

"I guess so, but it wouldn't matter. Either way, I expect that courthouse is coming down. But, Julia, there is something that ought to be and can be saved, something that does have historic value."

"What?"

"The figure of Lady Justice on top of the dome. From what I've found out, it was made in France in the late 1800s and shipped over here for the building that was put up after the original burned. It was a gift to the town from the family of a certain Andrew Milsap, who'd moved here to recuperate from tuberculosis around 1885. He died, but the family was grateful to the town, I guess, for making his last days comfortable. Anyway, the figure was saved when the second courthouse was razed and put on the dome of the new one. I mean, the one that's now the old one, since we now have another new one."

"Well, I say," I said. "I didn't know that. Well, Helen, there's no reason in the world we can't save that statue. Surely Arthur Kessler won't deny us that. I'll speak to him about it right away."

After hanging up the phone, I turned to Lillian. "Well, if that doesn't beat all. That was Helen Stroud, and she as good as told me that I've been spinning my wheels all this time for nothing."

"Huh. Nothin' new 'bout that. What she say Mr. Stroud doin' with all them other people's money?"

"She wouldn't talk about it. Some lawyer told her not to, and she wouldn't even say that she had nothing to do with what Richard did. Not that I think she did, but I wish she'd come right out and say it. It'd make me feel better, if nothing else."

"You want a sam'ich? It about lunchtime."

"Not yet, thank you. It's still a little early, and I need to go see Mr. Kessler."

"What for? I thought you had enough of him this morning, or him enough of you, one."

"Well, that's true of both of us, I expect. But, if I can't save the whole building, I can save an important part of it. Where's my pocketbook?"

I picked my way through the spectators who lined the side street as they watched the parking lot being gouged and broken up. As I drew closer, a thrill ran through me at the sight of a line of protesters held back by sawhorses and yellow tape. It did me good to know that I wasn't the only outraged soul in town. A few sheriff's deputies, looking somewhat embarrassed by the duty, strolled in front of the objectors who, other than bobbing their signs up and down, were a well-mannered lot.

I glanced at some of the signs as I threaded through the crowd. Several read: SAVE OUR COURTHOUSE, others: PRESERVATION NOT RUINATION, and more than a few: DEVELOPER, GO HOME. A low chant of "Don't tear it down" began and gained in strength as a huge crane with a wrecking ball dangling high above it was unloaded on the far side.

I gathered, as I sidled through the onlookers, that that's what they were waiting for—to see the ball make its first mortal hit on the courthouse. I tried not to think about it, just moved on through, searching for Arthur Kessler, the architect of destruction.

I finally spotted him, standing with his hands in his pockets, surveying with a satisfied look on his face what was being done on his authority. A few commissioners stood behind him, watching just as raptly, as slabs of concrete were wrenched from the parking lot and diesel motors growled and a worker began to climb up into the cab of the crane. I wouldn't have shown my face if I'd been a member of the county commission.

"Mr. Kessler? I mean, Arthur?" I tapped him on the shoulder, fearing he couldn't hear me for all the noise.

He jerked around with a menacing frown on his face. Then, seeing me, it quickly turned into a pleased-with-himself smile. "Decided to come watch the excitement, huh?"

"Not really," I said, although I had to practically lean against him to be heard. "I want to ask you something. See that figure up on the dome?" I pointed above one of the huge trees still standing and beyond the tip of the crane. "See how she's holding out scales in one hand and a sword in the other? And she's blindfolded? That's because she represents justice, balancing truth and lies on her scales and cutting through all the lawyerly obfuscation with her sword. It's an image of Lady Justice and it has an important history that ought to be preserved. Could you tell them to be careful of it and not ruin it? It would be a lovely gesture if you'd donate it to the county. I mean, since you're planning to wreck it, anyway."

He threw his head back, shading his eyes with his hand against the glare of the midday sun. "You mean, way up there on the top?"

As I nodded, he looked back at me. "Mrs. Murdoch, there's not a way in the world to save that thing. Not without a lot of extra time and money it would take to send somebody up there to get it. Sorry, it'll have to come down with the dome and the rest of the building. But, sure, you can have it," he said with a careless shrug, "if it survives."

"But, Arthur . . ."

"We better step back," he said, drawing me with him. "They're about to tackle the annex." And sure enough, the crane cranked up to a deafening roar and began to turn slowly on its tracks toward the addition on the back of the courthouse.

As I opened my mouth to argue some more, he glanced at me with one of his know-it-all smirks. "I think you've got images and figures or whatever on the brain. Seeing something on a blank wall this morning, and now worrying about something sticking up on the dome. You're a nice lady, Mrs. Murdoch, but you need something else to occupy your mind. I don't have time for this."

I turned on my heel without a word and parted the crowd before me as I walked away from there, my face flaming and my head held high. *A nice lady,* I thought to myself, *I'll show him nice.*

As I reached my car, I heard the crash of the wrecking ball, then the splintering of wood and the clattering of bricks as the first blow against the annex was struck.

Chapter 34

You never know what the weather's going to be in the spring of the year. I'd worn a sweater the day before, but this day had heated up to an immoderate degree. By the time I walked to the car, which was not parked in the shade, I was about to melt. I put the windows down while waiting for the air conditioner to cool the interior. And waiting to cool myself down, too. Arthur Kessler had shown his true colors in his total disregard for the preservation of the past. Even though that past included a termite-riddled building. There was such a thing as the Orkin man, you know.

But Mr. Kessler had no concept of the value of tradition or history or what was important to other people. Just tear down and rip out whatever was in his way—that's all that mattered to him. I would've gnashed my teeth if I'd thought it would do any good.

"Ma'am?"

I jerked back from the window as a face suddenly appeared next to mine. "What! Who are you?"

"Andy Jordan. *Abbotsville Times.* We're running a special edition on the courthouse, and I'm doing a front-page article featuring local comments. Would you care to comment on what's happening here?"

"I certainly would. Get in the car, young man, and I'll give you a comment."

He hopped to it, running around the front of the car and sliding into the passenger seat. He'd replaced the windbreaker I'd first seen him in with a T-shirt that had seen better days, but he still wore his Panthers ball cap.

He clicked his Bic pen and held a stenographer's pad at the ready. "Okay, let's have it."

"First of all," I said, more than ready to

pour it out, "I am heartsick that the commissioners voted to turn a developer loose on what belongs to every taxpayer in this county. Arthur Kessler has no sense of history nor does he have any concept of the architectural value of that building, even if it is on its last legs. They don't build them the way they used to anymore, and I'm speaking aesthetically, not structurally. I'm sure that whatever he puts up in the place of the courthouse will be a modern eyesore—stark, sterile and tasteless."

Scribbling fast, Andy Jordan said, "Can I quote you on that?"

"You certainly may." I took a minute to collect my thoughts. "And another thing, I asked him as courteously as I knew how— appealed to his civic responsibility, you might say—to at least save the figure of Lady Justice on the dome, and he as good as told me to go jump in the lake. Too expensive, he said. Too time-consuming, he said. Well, what's the hurry, I'd like to know. That figure or statue or whatever it is up there was a gift from a grieving family to the town, and it was made in France more than a hundred years ago. If the building itself is beyond repair, as I've been told but which I'm not sure I believe, that figure certainly is not. It ought to be saved and placed somewhere to remind us all of what justice is, even though I haven't seen much of it lately. And furthermore . . ."

"Hold on. Let me get that down." He bent over his pad, writing furiously, his tongue sticking out of his mouth.

"Well, hurry up," I said, my concerns boiling up and overflowing. "I don't have all day. Now, as I was saying, I may be wrong—you can look it up somewhere—but that figure represents the centuries-old idea of fairness in the law and the blindness of true justice as far as the status of litigants is concerned. Or something like that. She is blindfolded, you know. Oh, and another thing, Lloyd was just reading about this the other day . . ."

"Who's Lloyd?"

"My . . . just put the son of a friend. Anyway, he was studying this in Civics or History or something. The ancient Greeks, when they established the rule of law in Athens, well, they put up a statue to Athena, the goddess of wisdom, to remind them of the rule of law and of the right way to do things. And that's important in this day and age, too, when everybody and his brother think that the law is something to get around and loophole out of. The people of Abbotsville need a reminder as much as anybody, and the figure of Lady Justice would serve the purpose admirably. She stands for something important and shouldn't be relegated to the county dump, which is already full. But that's another subject." I glanced over at him. "Did you get all that?"

"Boy, did I ever."

"You might add that Mr. Kessler not only does not appreciate history, he doesn't know it, either." I cringed as the air was rent by another crash of the wrecking ball. The car shuddered from the thud of falling bricks. I could hear the gasping awe of the crowd of onlookers and wondered if they were enjoying the spectacle or lamenting it. "I'll tell you this, young man," I went on, filled with grief at the loss and anger at the futility of my efforts to run Mr. Kessler out of town. "It is a crying shame what that man is doing to us. He is ruining our skyline forever. Who wants to see an upended box of condos instead of that gilded dome? I, for one, do not." I paused to wipe my eyes, overcome with the unfairness of it all. "Did you get that?"

"Oh, yeah. Anything else?"

"No, that's about it. Well, you might mention that there's to be a barbecue soiree at Mrs. Horace Allen's house this Saturday afternoon. Mr. Kessler will be there because he wants an opportunity to meet the people of Abbotsville. So anybody who would like to tell him how they feel about replacing a piece of history with an influx of new residents is welcome to drop by and speak their mind."

"Oh, boy. Me, too?"

"Absolutely. Bring your pad and Bic, too."

"Okay, I'll do it. Now, if I can get your full name and address. Your age, too."

"I am Mrs. Julia Springer Murdoch and I live on Polk Street. That's enough for the paper, because I don't want any uninvited drop-ins at my house. As for my age, you're old enough to know better than to ask. Now, I've got to get home." And I rolled up the windows and revved the motor.

"Yes, ma'am. Thanks, thanks a lot for this." He opened the door and stepped out, talking to himself as he went. "My editor's gonna love this. Man, oh, man."

My feet and my spirits were dragging as I walked into the house. I felt as low as the courthouse soon would be. The annex was just a pile of bricks and shattered joists by now, and there was nothing I could do about it.

"Well, Lillian," I said, putting my pocketbook on the counter with a great sigh, "the annex was all but gone when I left, and they're starting on the courthouse itself tomorrow."

"You better move that," she said with a nod at my pocketbook. "I'm rolling out dough here." She sprinkled flour on a pastry cloth and smoothed the rolling pin over it.

"So you are." I picked up the pocketbook and put it on the table, earning a frown from her. But I was too dispirited to care. "What kind of pie are you making?"

"Choc'late, for a change. None of that fruit looked too good at the produce stand this mornin'." She lifted a round of pastry and fitted it into a Pyrex pie plate. "Lord he'p us," she suddenly exclaimed. "You never did get no lunch, did you? 'Less you eat downtown, which I hope you did."

"I've lost my appetite," I said, sitting at

the table and propping my head on my hand. "Oh, Lillian, I am just heartsick at what's going on down there."

"Well, you better get over it. Lloyd be home here any minute now, an' he don't need to see you mopin' 'round 'bout something nobody can change, once it done." She walked over to the stove and stirred the chocolate mixture in a saucepan. "What you need to do is put all that behind you, and think up something you still can do something about."

"You're right about that," I said, a tiny ray of hope stirring in the back of my mind. "Only thing is, I don't know if it can be done."

Footsteps and the sound of the screen door opening made me sit up straight and put a smile on my face. "Hey, Miss Julia," Lloyd said as he entered the kitchen. "Hey, Miss Lillian. Something sure smells good." He let his heavily laden bookbag slide off his shoulders onto the floor, then grinned at me. "I'll take it upstairs soon as I have a snack. I'm about to starve. You wouldn't believe what the lunchroom served today."

"Set down then," Lillian said, smiling at

the boy, as she removed the saucepan from the stove. "I got cheese and crackers and some grapes for you. You, too, Miss Julia. You gonna cave in, you don't eat something."

She joined Lloyd and me at the table, bringing with her two cups of coffee and a glass of milk for Lloyd. "Now don't y'all ruin yo' supper. No need to be cookin' all day if everybody jus' pick at it."

I nibbled at the cheese and crackers, my mind churning away. Finally, I said, "Wonder how hard it'd be to get up on that dome?"

Lillian frowned. "What dome?"

"The one on the courthouse, of course. Mr. Kessler is bound and determined to destroy everything in his path, but that statue on the dome is worth some little effort to save. And I'll tell you this," I said, my spirits reviving with a spurt of adrenaline, "if it can be saved, it ought to be. Just because Arthur Kessler won't get it down in one piece, doesn't mean I can't."

"You better not be thinkin' what I think you thinkin'," Lillian said, glaring at me.

"Of course not," I said, waving my hand, but I probably was. "I know for a fact that the dome was cleaned and regilded some years ago, so that means somebody had to go up there to do it. All I have to do is find out who it was and send him back up again. This time with a wrench or a saw instead of a scrub bucket."

Lillian frowned even deeper. "I don't like the sound of that. You fixin' to get somebody to steal something don't b'long to you, an' you get in trouble an' whoever you get will be in the same turmoil, too."

"No, no, Lillian, that statue is mine. Mr. Kessler gave it to me as plain as day. He said if it survived the destruction of the building, I could have it. He didn't say a word about how or when it survives. All I have to do is find somebody who knows how to get up to it."

Chapter 35

❧

"I know," Lloyd said, brushing cracker crumbs off his shirt.

"You do? Who?"

"Mr. Poochie Dunn. We saw him on the dome that time our class toured the court-house. Well, not on the dome exactly, but way up there on that little walkway around it. Miss Spenser got real mad at us 'cause we wanted to watch him instead of a trial. She made us write a paper on justice in America, which I didn't think was fair."

"Poochie Dunn," I said, letting the name roll off my tongue. "I didn't know he was still alive."

"Oh, he alive all right," Lillian said. "Not even a ole man yet, though he look it. He mos'ly wander 'round the streets, not turnin' his hand to a lick of work."

"Well, I'm about to give him a job." And I got up and opened a drawer, looking for the telephone book.

I ended up calling Etta Mae first, mainly because Poochie Dunn wasn't listed, at least under that name, and because I needed her help to find him.

"Sorry to wake you," I told her since she sounded as if she'd been taking the nap I'd recommended. "But plans have changed and our focus is redirected."

"Ma'am?"

"I was just down at the courthouse, and it'll be a pile of rubble by this time tomorrow, the way they're going. Now, Etta Mae, there's still something that can be salvaged from this swath of destruction Arthur Kessler's bent on making. If we hurry. So, here's the question: Do you know how to get in touch with Poochie Dunn?"

"Poochie Dunn? Why?"

"Because I want that statue and he's the only one who can get it for me."

"What statue?"

"Oh, Etta Mae, you know. The statue of Lady Justice up on the dome. Mr. Kessler's not making one effort to preserve it, but he said I could have it if it survives the demolition. Well, I have no intention of taking a chance with that wrecking ball pounding away at everything. We've got to get our hands on that statue tonight, and Poochie's the one to do it."

Lloyd's eyes popped and Lillian yelped behind me. "Tonight! You not gonna do no such a thing."

I waved my hand to quiet Lillian, while listening to Etta Mae's response.

"Well, okay, I guess," she said. "Poochie's not always clicking on all cylinders, you know. Maybe that's why he's willing to climb that high. Nobody else would do it, that's for sure. He lives in a boarding house across from the old depot on the street that goes out to the lumberyard. You know the one I'm talking about?"

"I'm not sure. Will you go with me?"

"Sure," she said, sounding wide awake by this time. "And if we don't find him there, why, we can just drive up and down Main Street. He wanders around a lot."

We arranged for her to come by for me in

an hour, a delay that didn't set well with me but I had to accept it. She needed time for a shower and a change of clothes, as well as time for the drive from Delmont. And for several layers of makeup, if I knew her.

"I can't just sit around doing nothing," I said, hanging up the phone and turning back to Lloyd and Lillian. "I am so agitated I'm about to jump out of my skin." My head jerked up at the sound of a car pulling in the drive. "Oh, there's Sam. He's a little early today. Now, you two, not a word to him about this. He has enough on his plate without adding Poochie Dunn to it."

Lillian shook her head. "Well, he oughtta be told what you up to."

"I'll tell him, don't worry," I said, hurrying to the door to meet him. "But in my own good time."

"Uh-huh," she said, opening the oven door to check on the roast, "an' I know when that'll be. If it up to you, Mr. Sam won't know a thing till you get whatever you thinkin' 'bout doin' already done."

I ignored her, pointed my finger at Lloyd and said, "Not a word now." He grinned, and I opened the door to my sweet, trusting husband.

As always when I saw his eyes light up, my heart lit up, too. "Julia," he said, and in front of everybody he put his arms around me and kissed me good. I didn't deserve him, but I was glad I had him. So there, Helen Stroud and all the other women who would snatch him up in a minute if I ever let my guard down.

I disentangled myself, slightly embarrassed, but pleased by such an ardent display of affection. "My goodness, what a nice welcome. But come sit down and tell us what's going on downtown."

He took a seat across from Lloyd, spoke to him and shook his hand in greeting, pleasing me with his gentlemanly attention to the boy. Then he looked up at me. "Well, sweetheart, the courthouse is as good as gone. I'm sorry, since I know you wanted to save it."

"We still have a little time," I said. "I was there about midday, and they were just tearing down the annex. Maybe something will happen before they get to the main building."

He shook his head. "No, I was just down there, and the last thing they did before quitting was put a hole in the back of the courthouse. Right through the courtroom where I've tried hundreds of cases."

"Oh, my goodness," I said, my hand against my chest. "Why did they do that?"

"To get a jump on tomorrow, I guess, and also to make sure nobody'll have second thoughts. The commissioners have been getting complaints all day, to say nothing of all the protesters marching up and down the street. They might've realized how unpopular they've become and put a stop-work order on the demolition. Too late now, though." He sighed and rose from his chair. "Lloyd, let me change clothes and we'll go look through the rubble before supper. We'll be scavengers and see if we can find us a nice souvenir. You want to go, Julia?"

"I think not. I couldn't stand seeing it. But see if you can find a brick with a date on it, or something like that."

Lloyd, saying he needed to change out of his school clothes, followed Sam out of the kitchen.

I turned to Lillian and whispered fiercely, "You see? You see what kind of man Arthur Kessler is? He will be the ruination of this town if we let him. Oh, my," I said, running my fingers through my hair, as a new thought struck me. "With Sam in and out, I better change plans with Etta Mae. And with Mildred, too. I'm not about to honor that man with a soiree, barbecued or otherwise, now that he's actually struck a blow at the heart of this town."

With Lillian rolling her eyes and mumbling under her breath, I called Etta Mae again.

"I'm just about to leave," she told me. "I'll be by to get you in about twenty minutes."

"Something's come up, Etta Mae, so you'll have to find Poochie by yourself. Sam's home and I don't want him to know what we're doing, and I have to run over to Mildred's and try to put a stop-work order on the soiree. I don't want Mr. Kessler to think we're celebrating him or anything he's done or plans to do."

Etta Mae wasn't too thrilled about going on a Poochie hunt by herself, but I finally talked her into it. When she realized that she would be on her own, she asked, "What'll I do with him when I find him?"

"Well, I don't know. If you think we can

depend on him to show up, have him meet us at the courthouse about one o'clock."

"In the *morning*?"

"That's the best time, Etta Mae. Sam'll be good asleep, and nobody'll be on Main Street. Tell Poochie what we want so he'll bring the right tools and whatever he needs to climb that thing. He'll know. He's done it a dozen times. Just be sure he'll be there, and I want him sober as a judge. It's only fitting, given where we'll be.

"Oh, and Etta Mae," I went on, "don't come to the house. We don't want to disturb anybody's sleep. I'll meet you around the corner on Jefferson a little before one. And, listen, when you talk to Poochie, make sure he knows that I'll make it worth his while."

I hung up the phone, feeling more than a little anxious about leaving such an important part of my plans in somebody else's hands.

"Jus' th'owin' money 'round like a crazy woman," Lillian said, plunking a skillet down on the stove. "Mr. Poochie ain't nobody to be climbin' no courthouses with."

"Oh, I'm not climbing anything, Lillian.

My goodness, no." I laughed at the thought. "Besides I'm afraid of heights, but I'm going to be there to be sure Poochie does. And be there to take care of that statue when he gets it down." I frowned as I thought of the intricacies of moving an art object. "I'm wondering how heavy it is, and how he'll manage to disengage it and hold on to it at the same time. But surely he knows what he's doing. Well, I'm not going to worry about that. He's done it before, so he can do it again. My worry is where we're going to put it once we get it. Be thinking about that, Lillian. I'm going to run over to Mildred's and tell her to call off the soiree."

"No way in the world, Julia," Mildred said in no uncertain terms. She settled herself more firmly in the wicker chair on the side porch where we were sitting. "Why, we've already dug a pit in the backyard and everything. I have a whole pig on order to be delivered tomorrow. It needs to cook all night and all day, you know. And everybody I know's been invited, and Tina Doland's been over here every day practicing on my Steinway. No, it's too late to call it off. Besides, it's taken my mind off Horace, and I want people to know that I'm not sitting around grieving like an abandoned woman."

"Well," I said, stirring a breeze against my face with one of Mildred's lovely fans. The porch was a pleasant, shady place but it was that still, muggy time of day when the temperature soars. "Well, you're not going to feel abandoned, come Saturday. You might as well know that I gave an interview to a newspaper reporter this morning and kind of mentioned you were having a barbecue. And that everybody was invited."

She stared at me for a minute, then reached for a little silver bell on a side table and tinkled it to summon Ida Lee.

"Well," I said, somewhat defensively, "that's what you said."

Before she could answer, Ida Lee appeared with a tray of glasses and a pitcher of lemonade. She handed each of us a glass, then started to leave.

"Ida Lee," Mildred said, "Tell Robert to dig another pit behind the pool house and please order another pig from the meat man. Looks like we're going to have a crowd to feed."

When Ida Lee left, I said, "Mildred, I'm sorry. I shouldn't have issued a blanket invitation in your name. I overstepped, but you know I'll help with the expense."

Mildred heaved herself out of the wicker chair, taking the green and white striped cushion with her. Brushing it off her backside and walking to the edge of the porch, she said, "No, you won't. It's my party, and actually, I'm glad. I only hope that Horace hears what a good time I'm having. Wherever he is." She sniffed in a ladylike manner and leaned over to look closely at a peony bloom. "Bless his heart, I hope he hears about it because he's always urging me to become more community-minded. He'll be so pleased. I'm just sorry that he'll miss it." Flicking ants off the bloom, she added, "These bushes need spraying."

I nodded in response and kept fanning, unable to come up with anything suitable to say. There was a lot I could've said though. What in the world was the woman thinking, feeling sorry for Horace? After all he'd put her through and was continuing to put her through? He was still among the missing, wasn't he? I say, bless his heart.

Changing the subject, I asked, "How is

LuAnne doing? Have you heard from her lately?"

"My Lord," she said, straightening up and waddling back to her chair, "that woman is about to drive me crazy. Lu-Anne's always been more talk than action, but now she's over here every day, wanting to help do this, wanting to change that or whatever pops into her head. 'What can I do?' she asks a dozen times a day. 'Why don't we do such-and-such? Let's do it this way.' And on and on. You know how she flits around anyway, but with this soiree, well, I've never seen her so excited about anything. I don't know what's gotten into her." Mildred took a long drink of lemonade, then went on. "I finally asked her what her problem was. And do you know, she actually thinks Arthur Kessler is interested in her. I didn't say anything, but I don't know where in the world she got that idea."

I did, but silence seemed the safest course.

By the time I was back home, Sam and Lloyd had returned from their search of the rubble behind the courthouse. Lloyd had found a a short rod of steel which he was convinced had come from a jail cell in the annex. They were both covered in brick dust up to their knees, so supper had to wait while they showered and changed, while I listened to Lillian grumbling about her roast getting as tough as shoe leather.

After she served supper and left for the day, Lloyd went to his room to text some messages or send e-mail or do something having to do with electronics, while Sam and I sat in the living room reading magazines. The television was on, but after the news, which Sam never missed, it was turned down too low to bother either of us.

I turned the pages of a *Time* magazine, but my mind was elsewhere—specifically, on the night's business that lay before me. Would Poochie show up? Could I entice him to climb to the top of the dome? Could he get the statue off and then down?

The first order of business, though, was to get Sam in bed and sound asleep. I heard Lloyd walking around upstairs and was relieved when he called down to wish us good night. That, I thought, would be-stir Sam, but he kept reading something in the *National Geographic,* a magazine he'd become attached to ever since, he'd told me, as a boy he'd discovered pictures of naked natives in it. By now, though, I assumed he'd had his fill and was reading instead of looking.

Becoming more edgy and irritated, I flipped through the pages of the *Time* issue that I'd been trying to read. Hearing a low rumble of thunder off in the distance, I looked up. "Is that thunder?"

"I hope so," Sam said without raising his head. "We could use some rain."

Well, I couldn't. At least not tonight. All I could do was pray that it would hold off until morning. But it was one more thing that was urging me to get down to the courthouse and get our business done.

"I declare, Sam," I said, snapping through one page after another, "there're more ads than articles in this thing. And the lead article is on the brain, of all things. I thought this was supposed to be a news magazine. I'm tired of seeing something on health or exercise or how to lose weight or some other such thing every week that rolls around. If I wanted to read such as that, I'd buy a medical magazine, not a *Time.* I don't know what those editors are thinking, do you?"

"Uh-uh," he said, continuing to read without showing one sign of sleepiness.

"Well," I said, slapping down the magazine and standing up, "I'm going to bed."

That got his attention. He looked up at me over his glasses, his eyebrows raised. "Really?"

"I'm on my way," I said, walking toward the bedroom.

Down went the *National Geographic* and up off the sofa he came. "I'm right behind you," he said.

Chapter 36

It was all I could do to stay awake, especially with Sam sleeping soundly beside me. *Finally,* I thought, as the clock on the bedside table flipped to twelve-thirty. I carefully eased out of bed and, with a last glance at Sam, walked barefoot out of the room and down the hall.

I felt my way through the living room and then the dining room, both lit dimly by the streetlight on the corner, and slipped into the kitchen. Thunder, sounding closer, rumbled again as it had been doing off and on through the night.

Lord, I thought, please don't let it rain,

but if it has to, I could do without a storm. Blindly, I ran my hands along the wall, avoiding chairs, fearing to make the least noise, since I didn't dare turn on a light. As I reached the pantry door at last, I eased it open, slid inside and closed it behind me. Switching on a light, I pulled out a dress, underclothes and shoes from behind a ten-pound sack of Martha White flour where I'd hidden them earlier.

I dressed hurriedly, wishing briefly for the green, cropped, polyester pants I'd bought in Florida but thrown out once I was back in Abbotsville. That's the problem with keeping a neat clothes closet. Just as soon as you get rid of something you think you'll never wear again, you'll wish you had it back. As it was, though, a print housedress and my clunky gardening shoes would have to do, especially since I'd only be giving a pep talk to Poochie to start him up and a payment when he came down with the statue. It wasn't as if I'd be doing anything active like ransacking an SUV.

When I was dressed, I switched off the light and opened the door into the kitchen. I had to stand there a minute or so until my eyes adjusted to the dark. Thunder, still some ways off, rolled around, and I waited and listened to see if it had wakened anybody.

Tiptoeing to the back door, I unlocked and opened it, cringing with each click of the lock. As soon as I stepped out on the back stoop, I felt the soft, steady fall of rain. *So much for prayer,* I thought, and slipped back inside. It took ages for me to slide steathily back through the kitchen, the dining room and the hall to the coat closet. I found Hazel Marie's yellow rain slicker—with hood, I might add—and my umbrella. Just as I backed out of the closet, I had a second thought. Hanging my umbrella back on the hook, I felt around for Sam's old bumbershoot, thinking I might need something more serviceable than a little fold-up number. Four people, if they were friendly, could huddle under the bumbershoot.

I tightened the hood around my face as I stepped off the back stoop and onto the drive to the sidewalk. It was all I could do to open the huge umbrella, but after struggling with it a few minutes it provided a welcome shelter. I hurried past the house and around the corner toward the place on Jefferson Street I'd told Etta Mae to wait. I'd not dared crank up my car. Sam or Lloyd, one, would've heard and raised a hue and cry about hijackers or something.

It was a strange experience to be walking the lonely streets of Abbotsville on a dark and rainy night all by myself. The rain wasn't heavy, but it tapped steadily on top of the heavy canvas of the bumbershoot. The glow from the streetlights wavered in the downfall as I looked around for Etta Mae, parked somewhere along the silent street.

Although feeling fairly dry and cozy under the canopy, I was beginning to worry that we'd missed connections. My feet were getting wet, and I'd about had enough of walking in the rain. But a car door opened ahead of me, and Etta Mae stuck her head out.

"Miss Julia!" she said in a loud whisper. "Is that you?"

"Why, yes, it is, and thank goodness you're here. I'm about to drown."

"Hurry and get in," she said, closing her door and leaning over to open the one on the passenger side.

It took me innumerable minutes to maneuver myself into her low-slung car and to manhandle the huge umbrella in with me. At last, I was inside with the door closed and the dripping bumbershoot sticking up between my knees.

"Is that a tent?" Etta Mae asked.

"Just about. Where's Poochie?"

"He's meeting us on the side street on the other side of the courthouse. He needed his truck for all his equipment."

"I just hope he's there," I said, wiping my face with a wadded-up Kleenex that Hazel Marie had left in a pocket. "Lord, I wish this was a rainy night in Georgia or any place besides here."

Etta Mae giggled as she cranked the car and drove to the corner to turn toward the courthouse. I looked back, but no lights had come on in my house. So far, so good.

I jerked in surprise and possibly emitted a little shriek—I'm pretty sure Etta Mae did—as lightning lit up the world.

"My word!" I gasped. "How close was that?"

"Not very. Listen, six one-thousand, seven one-thousand, eight . . . , nine . . . "

She paused, then said, "Hear the thunder? It's miles away and headed south. I checked the weather station before I left."

"That's reassuring. Be sure and tell Poochie, too. I expect he'll be glad to hear it."

As our destination was barely six blocks from my house, Etta Mae was soon easing down the street that ran along the side of the courthouse. She pulled in behind a pickup truck that gave off a dull, black glint from the streetlight. I could tell, even in the dark, that the truck had seen better days a long time ago. The bed of the truck was piled high with what looked like junk of one kind or another. I could make out bedsprings and something that looked like slats sticking up over the cab, not to mention a barrel or two and a paint-smeared canvas drop cloth hanging out over the muddy tailgate.

The door of the cab opened as Etta Mae parked and switched off our lights. Hunched over against the rain with his hands in his pockets, Poochie Dunn ambled over to her window.

She rolled it down and said, "Hey, Poochie. Crawl in the back seat."

He slid inside, along with a sharp, wet

dog odor, leaned back against the seat and grinned. "I changed my mind. I ain't goin' up there."

"Well, for goodness' sake, Poochie," I said, twisting around to look at him. He was a small man, not much bigger than Lloyd in my estimation. From what I could see, he was wearing a pair of striped coveralls and some kind of ball cap, and though the light wasn't good, I do believe he had a number of teeth missing.

That announcement along with his complacent grin about undid me. "Why'd you get us out on a night like this if you weren't planning to do it? We could all be in bed instead of skulking around, acting like sneak thieves or something."

"I was plannin' on doin' it, but I ain't goin' up in no storm. Uh-uh, not me." I don't know how he did it, but he could talk and grin at the same time and he kept proving it. "That thing up there's nothin' but a lighnin' rod. My granddaddy tole me to stay on the ground when it storms, and he knowed, 'cause that's where he watched for enemy planes."

Etta Mae turned to look at him. "*Recently?*"

"Naw," Poochie said, shaking his head. "He was a air-raid warden in Dubya-Dubya Two."

"Oh." Etta Mae nodded, then flinched as another lightning flash lit up the town, followed by a roll of thunder.

"It's still a long way off," I said, then with exasperation heavy in my voice went on. "Poochie, do you know me?"

"Yes, ma'am. Etta Mae tole me, but I knowed you before that. You brung my mommy a ham for Christmas one year, an' I don't never forget a kindness."

That set me back a minute, for I didn't remember anything about that particular charitable act. Which just goes to show how careful you have to be. People remember, for good or bad, what you easily forget.

But it was all for the good on this particular night. "Well, now I need you to do me a kindness. I want that statue up there in the worst way, and you're the only man in town with the know-how and the *courage* to go up and get it. How's your mother, by the way?"

"She died."

"Oh, well, I'm sorry, but listen. You could

already be up there instead of sitting here talking. Just tell me what it'd take to encourage you and you've got it."

He shook his head, still smiling. "Too dangerous."

"Poochie, I'm begging you. They're going to bring that building down *tomorrow,* and just shatter that beautiful statue."

"It don't look so good up close."

"Well, of course not, being exposed to the weather for all these years. But it's worth preserving, and we have to get it down tonight. You're our only hope."

"Uh-uh," he said, shaking his head but still smiling. "They put a big hole in the back wall today. The whole shebang could come down with me on it."

I turned back to the front and stared out the windshield, my mouth tight with frustration. "What would it take to get you to at least try?"

He was silent for so long that I had to turn back to see what he was doing. He was smiling. "A new used truck."

My heart lifted. "You got it! Etta Mae, did you hear that? He's going to do it."

Etta Mae frowned. "You sure it's not dangerous?"

"Of course it's dangerous," I said, almost euphoric at the thought of having what I wanted. "But Poochie knows what to do."

"I mean the lightning."

"Why, Etta Mae, you're the one who said it was miles away. See, there's another flash, but it wasn't nearly as bright as the other one. Now, Poochie, how long will it take? We'll sit right here until you're back down with the statue. We won't leave you, be assured of that."

"No'm, I have to have some help," he said, opening the car door. "It's gonna take me, you and her to get my ladder up there."

Etta Mae and I stared at each other, her eyes as big as mine felt. We hadn't bargained for this.

Chapter 37

I hope to goodness I never have to struggle with two made-to-order, wet and slippery wrought-iron ladders with minds of their own ever again in my life. What I'd thought were slats turned out to be two twenty-foot-long extensions, both curved to fit over the dome. And, if I understood it right, the plan was to attach one curved piece of the ladder to the bottom of the dome, then Poochie would climb it while Etta Mae and I lifted the other piece up to him. He would then fit it into the sockets on the first piece, allowing him to climb to the top of the dome and, thus, to the foot

of the statue. Or something like that. I didn't
see it as necessary that I understand the
logistics of his getting there. I just wanted
him there.

Poochie strapped a tool belt around his
waist, looped a coil of rope over his head
and across his shoulders, then stuck a few
mechanical odds and ends in the pockets
of his coveralls. After gearing himself up,
he pulled the two ladder lengths out of the
truck bed with enough clanking and scraping to wake the whole town. Cringing, I
looked around to see if we'd alerted anybody, then opened the bumbershoot to
hide under. I'd already tightened the hood
around my face, so I doubted anybody
would recognize me. And I also wanted to
protect my hair from what had now become
a thick drizzle since it was unlikely that
Velma could fit me in for another set before
the soiree.

After aligning the two pieces of the ladder side by side, Poochie took the front
end and Etta Mae the back. I walked in
the middle, bearing as much of the weight
as I could one-handedly. It was all I could
do to manage that much, what with holding on to the umbrella with my other hand,

especially when a gust or two of wind assailed us. We climbed the steps from the street to the level of the courthouse and across the lawn to the steps leading to a side door.

"Put 'er down," Poochie said, leaning the ladder against his thigh. "I got to find the right key."

"For goodness' sake, Poochie," I hissed. "There's not a thing in there. Everything's been moved to the new courthouse. It couldn't be locked."

"Vandals," he said. I rolled my eyes. The building would be torn down in less than twenty-four hours. Who cared if it got vandalized?

After fiddling around with a ring of keys, he opened the huge door, and Etta Mae, who'd been taking a breather, lifted her end and followed him inside.

The wide hall that had courtrooms and offices leading off it was dimly lit by streetlights gleaming through the gaping hole in the back wall, courtesy of Arthur Kessler's last-minute wrecking fit. Another gust of wind blew through the hole, lifting and swirling papers that had been left strewn around the floor.

"I don't know," Poochie said, shaking his head. "She may not be steady enough to hold us."

"Oh, it's fine," I said, encouraging him. "This floor's like the Rock of Gibraltar. How're you getting up there, Poochie? I thought you'd climb the outside."

"Uh-uh," he said as he turned and led us down a narrow hall to an interior door. "They's stairs up to the cupola." He said *cup*ola, as in a cup of coffee.

And we began to climb up one narrow flight, turning, then on up another flight. It wasn't easy maneuvering the curved ladder pieces around the turns, and several times I got scraped against the wall. But the bumbershoot was now folded and I was able to manage fairly well. Etta Mae didn't have much to say, just kept her end of the ladder extensions lifted as she followed in Poochie's wake. She was puffing and straining every step of the way, though, and as we climbed into the exteme heights of the building, I began to worry about her stamina.

"Here's where it gets tricky," Poochie said as he stopped at the head of the last flight of stairs which had led us into the dark, musty-smelling attic.

Etta Mae stopped, too, and let the ladder lean against the wall. "If it gets any trickier," she said, gasping for breath, "I'm done for."

I wanted to spur her on, but had to wait while another roll of thunder, much nearer, rumbled overhead. I shivered as we heard the wind whistling through the hole far below us. We all looked at each other as the building creaked and groaned around us. It was all I could do to encourage myself, much less Etta Mae, to keep on.

"You're doing fine, Etta Mae," I said. "Don't give out on us now. So, Poochie, where do we go from here?"

"Up," he said, lifting his end and leading us across the creaking floor. Dust was stirred up by our footsteps, and Etta Mae sneezed, almost dropping her end.

"Hold on," Poochie said, stopping again beside a wall. "I gotta get that hatch up there open. When I get up where the colyums are, y'all lift up the ladder and I'll pull it through." And up some rungs on the wall he scampered, pushing up a door in the ceiling and disappearing from view.

"I don't like this, Miss Julia," Etta Mae whispered. "This whole thing's going to come down with us in it."

"We're almost there, Etta Mae. Keep your spirits up. Poochie knows this building better than anybody, and he wouldn't be doing this if he thought it'd come down."

"He's thinking new pickup," she mumbled.

Poochie's head appeared above us. "Lift 'em up," he called down. "Then y'all come on up."

After heaving the heavy ladder pieces up through the trap door and having my hood scraped off during the process—just ruining my hairdo—Etta Mae and I began to climb the rungs, the bumbershoot hung on my shoulder. What an interesting experience! Terrifying, too, I might add, and I couldn't have done it without Etta Mae melded to me, occasionally giving me a lift from below.

As I crawled out onto the floor of the cupola on my hands and knees, the wind swirled my dress tail over my head. Lord, we were out in the open, ninety-something feet in the air with only a ring of columns to keep us from being blown off. Afraid to stand up, I scooted over, bumping into the ladder that took up most of the space, so Etta Mae could gain access.

"Oh, my Lord," she said, looking around in awe. "You could see for miles up here if it wasn't so dark." Her hand clamped down on my ankle. "Miss Julia, I want to go home. I don't like heights."

"Me, either, but we're too close to quit now. What's next, Poochie?"

He stuck a finger straight up at another trapdoor near the edge of the cupola's roof. "Up there." Then he leaned one of the ladder extensions against a column. "When I get up, lift me up that other 'un, then y'all climb up and we'll pull this'n up after you."

A blaze of lightning lit Etta Mae's frightened face, and when a gust of wind came close behind it, I said, "Well, listen, Poochie, we'll hand up the ladder, but if it's all the same to you, we'll just wait right here."

"No'm. I got to have help puttin' the ladder together once it's on the dome. Don't be skeered. They's a little walkway 'round the dome with a ledge on it. You won't fall off if you don't look down. 'Sides, I can't manage by myself."

I wished I'd known that before engaging him, but it was neither here nor there at the moment. I'll not go into how we got up on the parapet that surrounded the dome. Suffice it to say that it was similar to our first trapdoor experience, with the added indignity of having my dress tail blown up around my head. A good thing that I'd left the bumbershoot on the floor of the cupola or I might've sailed off over Abbotsville like Mary Poppins.

I'd never been so scared in my life when we gained the open-air parapet, and Etta Mae was equally petrified. Having come so far, I had a sudden fear that Poochie would tell us we had to go higher. I could see myself inching up that rounded dome, then suddenly slithering down it.

While Etta Mae and I crouched below the parapet, Poochie busied himself with anchoring the first extension of the ladder to the foot of the dome. He moved around easily and confidently, as if there were no danger of hurtling off into space.

I reached up and tugged at his shirt

sleeve. "Poochie, I hope to goodness you'll go the rest of the way by yourself. You won't need us up there, will you?"

He grinned, shook the ladder to test its stability and said, "No'm, y'all just stay right here. Up there's no place for wimmen."

I would've rolled my eyes if they'd been in their sockets, for it was no place for women where we were. "How're you going to manage?" I managed to ask, just as lightning lit up the sky again.

"Oh, I'll just put this rope around 'er, unbolt the base, and swing 'er down to you. She ain't heavy, so you won't have no trouble."

Not heavy? I thought statues were made of marble or granite or something. But I had no time to think of that, for Poochie commenced to climb the first extension. When he got almost to the top of it, clinging halfway up the dome, he called down. "Hand me up the other'n, and don't drop it."

"Etta Mae," I said, hovering as close to the dome as I could, "get a grip now. We're almost through. Help me get this part of the ladder up to him."

She was hugging the dome, her arms spread wide embracing it for all she was

worth. Looking up at me with the most pitiful expression on her face, she whimpered,
"I'm scared to death."

"I am, too. But just one more heave of
this thing, and that'll be it. We can rest
while he gets the statue loose." The wind
whistled around the dome, swirling the tail
of my dress every which way. I tucked it
between my knees and bent to lift the top
end of the ladder extension.

Etta Mae was a good and brave girl. As
scared as she was, she helped me get the
rest of the ladder to Poochie, then we
crouched down on the parapet, huddling
close together as the wind whipped around
and the building groaned below us.

"I hope he's got what he needs," I said,
leaning close to Etta Mae's ear. "A lug
wrench or whatever it takes to loosen the
statue."

Etta Mae started trembling and shiver-
ing, scaring me into thinking she was going into convulsions. From the altitude, you
know. Then I realized she was laughing.
"Not a lug wrench," she managed to say.
"That's for tires. Maybe a crescent wrench,
I don't know."

A gust of wind blew rain sideways across

the dome, so I pulled the hood tighter around my face, doing what I could to save my set. Having left Sam's big umbrella in the cupola, I now wondered why I'd wrestled with the thing that far not to have it when we needed it.

"Awright down there!" Poochie's voice was thin and hard to make out, but I slid up against the dome and came to my feet, holding on for dear life. "I'm a-comin' down. Reach up and get this thing."

"He's got it, Etta Mae! Look lively." I glanced up to see the shadowy figure of the statue dangling above my head as Poochie lowered it by a rope. It swayed in the wind, clanking against the dome. "Come on, Etta Mae, help me. It might be heavier than he said."

I reached up and grasped Lady Justice's feet just as she whirled around in the wind, hitting me in the head with the scales she held out in one hand. I saw stars for a minute, then thanked the Lord that I was still on the parapet and that it hadn't been the sword in her other hand that had gotten me.

Etta Mae leaned into me, reaching for the statue, and as Poochie played out the rope, we lowered it to the floor of the parapet. "My Lord, Etta Mae," I said, "it's not heavy at all. Look, it's barely as tall as I am, and as light as a feather." I gave the statue a rap with my fist and got a dull tink in response.

"Why, it's tin!" Etta Mae said, running her hand over the figure. "That's all it is. Two pieces of molded tin welded together with nothing inside. Miss Julia, we've risked our lives for a tin can."

"Well," I said, wondering why the French would've used such a common material, "it's a well-crafted tin can. What's this stuff on it?" Some kind of coating was flaking off the figure and I had to wipe my hand on my dress.

"Comin' down," Poochie called, just as something pinged against the dome. Then kept on pinging.

"What's that?" Etta Mae cried, clinging to me as I clung to Lady Justice. "Oh, my Lord, is it hail?"

"Hey!" Poochie yelled above us, as another salvo of pings sprinkled the dome. "*Aye God,* it's the Germans! They're dive-bombin' us!"

Etta Mae dropped to the floor of the

parapet, pulling me and Lady Justice with her. We crouched below the ledge as another barrage sprayed the dome.

Poochie slid down the ladder and sprawled out below the ledge, covering his head with his arms. Cursing the Germans up one side and down the other, he slithered through the trapdoor and dropped to the floor of the cupola.

"Go, Etta Mae," I said, pushing her toward the opening. "We've got to get off this thing."

"Somebody's shooting at us," she wailed, scrambling for the trapdoor.

"Well, it's not the Germans," I muttered, crawling after her while dragging the tin statue with me. "Oh, Lord, Etta Mae, how're we going to get this thing through the trapdoor? Her arms're so spread out, we'll never get her through."

Etta Mae's feet were dangling through the trapdoor, but there were no rungs and both ladder extensions were still on the dome. She leaned over and yelled, "Poochie! Where are you? How do we get down?"

When he didn't answer, we looked at each other with the awful realization that

he'd left us stranded in space with somebody shooting at us and burdened with a tin
statue that wouldn't fit through the only exit
available.

"Hold on, Miss Julia," Etta Mae said, as
she proved her mettle again. "I'm going to
drop down, then you dangle the statue over
the ledge and I'll grab it and pull it through
the columns. Then you drop through and
I'll catch you." And down she went, falling
to the floor of the cupola.

I looked through the trapdoor, fearing to
see her crumpled up on the floor. "Are you
all right? Etta Mae, are you hurt?"

"I'm fine," she yelled back. "Dangle it
down. I'll get it. Hurry, before they start
shooting again."

Reloading, I thought, thankful for the re-
spite. I quickly dragged the statue up onto
the ledge, grasped the rope that was still
tied around it and shoved it over the side.
Leaning over as far as I dared, I let Lady
Justice dangle in the air. Just then, a spray
of bullets laced across the columns of the
cupola. Etta Mae screamed and I felt the
tug of a hit on Lady Justice as she swayed
at the end of the rope.

"Get her, Etta Mae! Hurry!" Then she

did. Lady Justice was ripped from my hand, and I heard her clank against the columns as Etta Mae yelled, "I got her! I got her!"

I ducked down below the ledge again, but not before catching sight of a stocky figure on the front lawn raising a rifle to his shoulder. I gasped with recognition, and then with outrage.

I *knew* that figure!

Chapter 38

❧

Pulling myself up just enough to clasp the ledge with both hands and peer over it like Kilroy, I yelled, *"Vernon Puckett! Cut that out!"*

My words echoed and bounced around the rooftops of the buildings surrounding the courthouse. I watched as Brother Vern's head swiveled from one side to the other, searching for the source of the instructions he'd received. Before he could react, a blast of lightning lit up the square, throwing Brother Vern, the courthouse lawn and all the shops across the street into bright relief. Almost immediately, thunder boomed and rolled from one end of the world to another. Brother Vern stood transfixed, awed and terrified by the cosmic display. Then he dropped the rifle and fell to his knees, his arms spread wide and his head thrown back as he gazed heavenward.

I couldn't believe it, but his tremulous voice floated up to me, "What wouldst thou have me do, Lord?"

Not one to let an opportunity pass, I mustered a little more authority and yelled at the top of my voice, *"Throw that gun away and get out of here!"*

And that's what he did. He scrambled to his feet, picked up the rifle by the muzzle and slung it across the courthouse lawn. It went sailing into the bushes, just as sirens and red flashes started up from the sheriff's office a few blocks away. Brother Vern turned on his heel and hightailed it across the side street, disappearing behind the A-One Appliance Shop, on his way to the former Quality Furniture Store, now the anointed Hallelujah House.

I could've felt sorry for him if he hadn't always been a thorn in my flesh, and if he hadn't put our lives in jeopardy by peppering bullets all over the place. But I did have a few misgivings, knowing that Brother Vern would have to adjust his entire theological stance after hearing the Lord speak in a woman's voice.

But misgivings aside, my next task was to get down to the ground before the law got there. Lord, I'd hate to be taken into custody by Sergeant Coleman Bates, to say nothing of being sniffed out and mauled by Deputy Max Von Rippen of the K-9 Corps. I'd be listed in the sheriff's report in the *Abbotsville Times,* making me the number one topic of the garden club from now till doomsday.

"Hurry, Miss Julia!" Etta Mae called up through the trapdoor. "Drop down. I'll catch you."

I was only too happy to, although if I'd thought long and hard about broken hips and ankles and wrenched backs, I might've still been clinging to the parapet. But Etta Mae clasped my lower limbs as I hung from the edge of the trapdoor and helped lower me down. Or, more accurately, she broke my fall.

We ended up sprawled together on the floor of the cupola, ripping off my hood in the process, but with, as far as I could tell, no lasting injury. Etta Mae was a little slow getting up, but that was probably because I'd landed on top of her.

"Hurry, Etta Mae," I said, grabbing Lady Justice and dragging her to the opening in the floor of the cupola. "You get down on the rungs and I'll push her through to you."

With the rack lights from the patrol cars bouncing back from the low clouds and the sirens screaming ever closer, I mentally blasted Brother Vern again. The idea! Discharging a firearm within the city limits! He knew better than that, and all he'd done was create a ruckus and slow down our confiscation of a relic doomed for the trash heap.

As Etta Mae stood on the rungs of the interior wall of the courthouse, I dumped Lady Justice, feet first, through the hole of the trapdoor.

"Oh, my Lord," I said, ready to cry in frustration when she went so far and no farther. Her outstretched arms, one holding scales and the other a sword, would not go through. "She's stuck, Etta Mae. What're we going to do?"

There was a minute's silence from below, then, "Bend her."

"Bend her?"

"Yes, she's only tin, so bend her arms and we'll straighten her out later."

So I did. I untied the rope and scrunched both arms of the figure close to her body, thanking the French for their foresight, and pushed her on through. Then I switched myself around and climbed down after her. From then on, it was clear sailing. Down the narrow, twisting staircases we went, hauling Lady Justice with us until we reached the main floor of the courthouse.

Etta Mae trotted out smartly once we were off the stairs. Whispering over her shoulder, she said, "Wonder why somebody was shooting at us?"

"He just wanted to scare us. Probably thought we were vandals."

"I guess he got that right," she said with a giggle, as she stopped at the side door that Poochie, in his headlong flight, had left wide open.

"No, Etta Mae," I said, "we're just getting what was given to us. That's not vandalism by any stretch of the imagination. Now hurry on out."

So far, so good, I thought. But cars screeching to a halt in front of the courthouse made my anxiety soar, and I took a stronger grip on Lady Justice's feet and pushed Etta Mae, who had her head, onward and outward.

Etta Mae moaned. "We're gonna be arrested!"

"No, we aren't," I whispered, pushing her on. "They won't see us. They're looking for a gunman on Main Street, so let's get her in the car before they change their minds."

We slipped out the side door into a sudden downpour, absolutely ruining my hair but delaying any nosy deputies on the prowl for a gun-wielding suspect.

We dashed across the lawn to Etta Mae's car, Lady Justice with folded arms bouncing along with us. "Poochie's still here!" Etta Mae said in a loud whisper. "There's his truck and, thank goodness, because this thing won't fit in my car."

She was right. I stopped on the sidewalk, quickly surveyed the situation and came to the same conclusion. The only way the statue would fit in her small car would be to fold her up like a letter and stuff her in, a desecration I would not be a party to.

I ran to the back of Poochie's truck, hauling Etta Mae and Lady Justice with me. "Where is Poochie?" I said. "We need some help."

Etta Mae stood the statue upright and said, "Hold her while I get up in the truck. Then I'll haul her in."

As she crawled into the truck bed, I got my first good look at our prize. *My Lord, she was bare-breasted.* Well, half bare-breasted in the Roman toga sort of way. *Those French,* I thought, wondering what else a close inspection would uncover.

"Lift her up," Etta Mae whispered, as she leaned over the tailgate. "Quick, before those deputies get here."

I did, and between us we slid the statue over the tailgate and into the truck bed. Etta Mae slung the drop cloth over it, covering our prize from prying eyes. "Where is that Poochie?" she asked, hopping lightly down.

I didn't have to answer for the truck's motor started up, spurring me to dash to the cab. Knocking on the cracked window, I called in a loud whisper, "Poochie! Open up. I want to talk to you."

He rolled the window down, smiled and said, "I ain't never goin' up there again."

"Well, me, either, you can count on that," I said, wiping the water and my dripping hair from my face. "But I want to know why you took off without us. We could've still been stranded up there."

Still smiling, he shook his head. "I don't never hang around when they's shootin' goin' on."

I would've rolled my eyes if they hadn't been too tired, so I just said, "Listen, now, the statue won't fit in our car, so we put it in your truck bed and I want you to leave it there. Keep it covered and don't tell anybody anything about this night's business. Go on home now before those deputies get around here."

"What about my ladder? Y'all just left it, didn't you?"

I just stared at him, then I said, "Yes, we did. It was all we could do to get ourselves down, what with being left by ourselves and getting shot at, too."

"Weren't nothing but BBs. They won't do more'n nick you, 'less they hit a eye. You can get blinded that way."

"It was a BB gun? My land, I thought we'd be killed. But we can't talk all night, Poochie. We have to get out of here. Those deputies'll be on us any minute."

"What about my new used truck?"

I started to tell him that it had just gained a few years of previous use owing to his desertion from the rooftop, but I refrained. He was now the caretaker of what we'd expended so much effort to get, and I needed to keep him happy.

"Tomorrow," I said, then thinking of the time, "or rather, later today. I'll come by in a few hours to get the statue, and we'll go truck shopping." I looked up across the courthouse lawn and saw the strong beams of official flashlights sweeping the shrubbery and the tops of the trees. "You take care of her, you hear? And don't go anywhere until I come to get her. Now, go."

He put the truck in gear and pulled onto the street, while I dashed to Etta Mae's idling car. Holding the door closed, once I was in the passenger street, not wanting to slam it, I said, "Let's go, Etta Mae. I don't want to be questioned about any of this night's events."

"I'm with you," she said fervently, easing

the car without turning on the headlights down the street and whipping it around the corner. Sighing with relief once we were out of sight of the courthouse, she switched on the lights and headed toward my house. "Although," she said with a shaky titter, "there've been times when I wished I wasn't."

Chapter 39

❧

If I say I was slow getting out of bed the next morning, I wouldn't be exaggerating. Glancing at the bedside clock as I struggled upright, I was amazed at the lateness of the hour. Lloyd would already be in his first period class—thank goodness for Lillian and Sam who'd gotten him off while letting me sleep in. Of course I'd have to come up with some explanation for lingering in bed, so having had a restless night would have to do. It was all I could think of, plus it had a certain ring of truth about it.

But I tell you, it was a wonder that I was able to crawl out and straighten up, what with all the creaking joints and aching muscles. I'd used parts of my anatomy the night before that hadn't been called on in more years than I cared to think about. And they were letting me know that I wasn't as young as I once was.

And, Lord, when I glanced in the bathroom mirror, I thought I'd faint. I looked like the wreck of the Hesperus after sleeping on wet hair. I'd tried to towel it dry when I changed clothes in the pantry the night before, but let me tell you, it was a frightful sight first thing in the morning.

I called Velma before leaving the bedroom and begged her to take me. "I'm in dire need," I told her. "I've got to have some help."

"I can fit you in if you get here in fifteen minutes," she said. "I'm booked solid the rest of the day and tomorrow, too, right up to the time of the soiree. Then I'm closing up and going myself."

"I'm on my way." I hung up, grabbed a scarf to cover my head and dashed through the dining room and kitchen and out the back door, telling Sam and Lillian that hair had top priority and I'd be back soon. With Lillian calling after me that I needed breakfast, I got in the car and sped toward Velma's Kut and Kurl. As I crossed Main Street, I heard and felt the thud and crash of the day's first onslaught of the wrecking ball against the court-house several blocks away. I gripped the steering wheel and gritted my teeth, feel-ing the loss of something that couldn't be replaced. What made it even worse was knowing that Arthur Kessler would be watching with that satisfied smirk on his face.

Finally under the dryer, I had time to think over the night's escapade and try to plan the day's activities. And also to take a little nap, my head hanging askew as hot air dried my rolled hair.

One thing I can say for Velma, she's fast even though she talks a blue streak. While she combed and backcombed my hair, I heard all about last night's shooting on Main Street.

"Those boys," she said, referring to the sheriff's deputies, "looked all over creation and they never did find out who was doin' it. I mean, they spread out all over the place, rattling doors and lookin' in alleys and I don't know what all. It's the strangest thing, is all I can say. Who you reckon would do such a thing?"

"I'm sure I don't know," I said. "Spray it real good, Velma, if you will. It has to last through the soiree tomorrow and church on Sunday."

When I got back home, feeling and looking 100 percent better, Sam was sitting in the living room reading the paper. He looked up as soon as I walked in, Lillian right behind me with coffee and toast and predictions of wasting away to nothing if I didn't eat something.

"Well, Julia," Sam said, putting aside the paper and smiling at me, "you flew out of here with hardly a word this morning. Is everything all right?"

"It is now," I said, sitting beside him and patting my hair. "I just slept wrong and had to get to Velma's before she filled up. You know how important hair is. A messy head can just ruin your whole outlook."

"I've noticed that myself," he said, his eyes twinkling, as he stood up. "Well, I just wanted to be sure you were okay. Oh, and by the way, a bunch of us're going to help Robert barbecue the pigs tonight, so I expect it'll be an all-night affair."

"You'll enjoy that. Who all's going to be there?"

"Whoever drops by, I guess. We'll help feed the fires, tell a few tall tales and think we're having a good time."

"Um-hmm," I said, drinking coffee and wondering what they'd be drinking throughout the night.

Sam leaned down and gave me a kiss. "If you don't have anything for me to do, I think I'll wander down to the courthouse and watch it come down. I expect the protesters will be out in force as well."

"I should hope so. In fact, I hope they'll run Arthur Kessler out of town, but I guess that's too much to expect. And it's too late now anyway. Too late yesterday even, what with him putting that hole in the back wall."

He turned back, giving me a raised eyebrow. "I told you about that, didn't I?"

"Yes, you did," I said, my heart jumping for fear that I'd mentioned something I shouldn't have known. "Remember, you said it was the last thing he did yesterday before quitting time."

"Oh, right." He headed for the hall closet, opened the door, then called to me. "Julia, where's my old bumbershoot? They're predicting more thunderstorms this afternoon."

My eyes popped open as I pictured the umbrella lying on the floor of the cupola where I'd left it. Putting my cup carefully on its saucer, I said, "It should be in the closet. That's where it always is."

I heard him rummaging around in the closet, mumbling to himself. "Well, it's not here," he said, then stuck his head into the living room. "I guess my hair will just get ruined."

"Oh, you," I laughed, thanking the Lord again for such a sweet-natured, unsuspecting and trusting man. Wesley Lloyd Springer would've been fuming and stomping around half the day. Then he would've told me for the thousandth time that everything had its place and everything ought to stay in its place. As if it were my fault that he couldn't find what he wanted.

But not Sam. Sam simply chose one of the other umbrellas in the closet and went on his way. Of course, this time it *was* my fault that his bumbershoot was not in its place, but that's not the point.

As soon as the house fell silent, except for Lillian singing "Beulah Land" in the kitchen, I called Etta Mae.

"Etta Mae? How're you feeling this morning?"

She yawned. "Is it morning already?"

"Yes, and we have to figure out how to get that statue from Poochie and what to do with it when we get it. You have any ideas?"

"Well," she said, as I heard the rustle of bed covers, "my car's out. If it wouldn't fit last night, it won't fit today. You think we could lay it down in the back seat of your car?"

"I think we can. It's only about five feet tall, so it ought to fit. But what's worrying me is what we'll do with it then."

"Um, well, I kinda thought you already had that figured out."

"Not exactly. I was too intent on just getting it and thought I'd worry about what to do with it when we got it. The thing is, Etta Mae," I said, unburdening myself on her, "I can't bring it here. Sam would have a fit if he knew what we did last night. And so would Lillian. They're so protective, you know. So I'd as soon you don't mention what we did."

"Um, well, are you just going to hide her? I mean, like forever?"

"Oh, no. I want everybody to know that Lady Justice has been saved from destruction, and I want her put somewhere permanent so everybody can see her. Maybe the garden club could sponsor her, donate her to the town or something like that. I haven't figured it out yet."

"You mean like a garden ornament or something?"

"Well, that's a possibility, I guess. I'll have to give it some thought."

Etta Mae gave it a little thought of her own for a second or two, then she said, "I'm not sure you have a lot of time to think. Poochie's not the most reliable soul, you know, so I wouldn't leave it with him too long. He could sell it for scrap metal if it'd bring anything."

"Oh, my word, don't say that. Etta Mae, we have to do something to relieve him of that temptation, and that means getting it out of his hands as soon as we can. The thing is, though, we can't let anybody know that I had anything to do with getting her. They'd tell Sam, sure as the world, and I'd have a hard time explaining to him."

"If that's the case, then," she said, "I think we can trust Poochie to keep her overnight. Then he can bring her to the soiree tomorrow. You know, like he was the one who got her down. By himself, I mean."

"Oh, good," I said, "I'll gladly let him take all the credit for saving her. But just to be on the safe side, Etta Mae, you talk to him and tell him that getting a new used pickup is dependent on having that statue—in one piece, mind you—at Mildred's tomorrow afternoon. Tell him I've already started calling the used car lots to be sure he'll have a good selection. Tell him he'll be driving that new vehicle first thing Monday morning."

"I think you promised him today."

"I know I did, but if he got it today we might never see him or Lady Justice again. You know how he is. Remind him that I'm an old woman who's stove up today from all the exertions he put us through last night."

"That'll do it," she said, "especially when

he sees what shape I'm in. My back's killing me."

Ah, I thought with some satisfaction as I hung up the phone, it's not just age that gets you.

Chapter 40

⚜

Even putting the phone in its cradle set up an aching protest from my arm to my neck, and I began to wonder how I was going to manage the rest of the day. I could hardly rise from a chair, much less achieve an upright posture to walk across the room. Contemplating a short nap or a long soak in a hot tub of water to recuperate, I wasn't sure I'd ever be able to get out of either one.

I didn't have to decide between them, though, for a clamor at the front door took my attention. Somebody was both ringing the bell and knocking, setting up a din that sent me flying to answer it. I met Lillian on her way to do the same.

"Law," she said, her eyes wide, "who makin' all that racket?"

We reached the door at the same time, opened it and stood aside as LuAnne Conover sailed in, all atwitter.

"Julia," she said, her hands fluttering with excitement, "you won't believe what's happened!" She grabbed my arm and practically dragged me into the living room. "Come sit down. I've got to tell you . . . Oh, hey, Lillian. You'll excuse us, won't you?"

Lillian mumbled, "Yes, ma'am," and left for the kitchen, her dignity undisturbed. If it'd been me, my eyes would've rolled right up inside my head, but Lillian had better manners than most people, including me on occasion.

"What is it, LuAnne?" I asked, as visions of some catastrophe sprang to mind. "Has something happened at the courthouse? Sam's down there. Don't tell me there's been an accident?" All I could picture was a wall of bricks, timbers and nails falling askew and burying the crowd of spectators, Sam among them.

"No, no," she said, her hands flying every

which way. "Nothing like that. No, this is good! In fact, it couldn't be better. At least, I think so, but it really puts me on the spot, and I need some advice."

"Well," I said, mentally wiping my brow in relief, "thank goodness for that. Now, what kind of spot are you in?"

She leaned close, her eyes dancing with delight, her color high and her voice low and intense. "Leonard called."

"He did? Why, that's wonderful, LuAnne. He wants to come home?"

"Not yet, he doesn't," she said with some satisfaction. "Oh, you'll never guess." She actually hugged herself.

"Well, I probably won't. So why don't you tell me."

"He wants to take me to the soiree tomorrow. Don't you just *love* it? I mean, like a date. It's like he wants to start over again and, you know, court me."

"He actually asked for a date?" I could hardly believe it of the staid and unimaginative Leonard Conover. To tell the truth, I had a hard time picturing him in a courting frame of mind under any circumstances. But she knew him better than I did, so I took her word for it.

"Well, no, not in so many words," she admitted, "but he said he didn't want to go to the soiree by himself, and since he knew I'd be going, we ought to go together. But that's the way he is, Julia. You have to read between the lines, and I know he wants to date me. So what am I going to do?"

"Why," I said, "I guess you go with him, if that's what you want to do. I mean, it looks as if he's making the first move and that's what you wanted, isn't it?"

"I did, but now that I have another opportunity, I really don't know what I want." She had calmed down by this time, and had her hands clasped in her lap. "You know what just frosts me? All this time I've been patiently waiting for Leonard to come to his senses and now that he has, it's at the absolutely worst time in the world."

"I don't understand. Why?"

"Don't be dense, Julia. You know why." She leaned over and hissed. "*Arthur!* That's why. He's expecting me to be his date at the soiree. You told me so yourself."

"Oh," I said, recalling my rash words of a few days before, and with the recall, feeling thoroughly ashamed of myself for misleading a friend. My only excuse was my desperate effort to make Arthur Kessler change his mind about our town and its inhabitants. Which hadn't worked anyway, as the demolition of the courthouse proved.

"Well, LuAnne," I said, trying to decrease her expectations, "if Arthur hasn't called and asked you—*specifically,* that is—then I wouldn't burn any bridges. A bird in the hand and all that, you know. And, after all, you are still married to Leonard."

"Oh, that," she said, waving her hand to brush aside that little snag. "He left me, which in some cultures is as good as a divorce. And don't shake your head at me. I know it's not in ours, but, Julia, when have I ever had a chance like this? I mean, *Arthur Kessler*! A man of the world and a man of means and he's interested in *me*! I owe it to myself to give him a chance. Every time I think about what it could mean, my heart just starts racing."

"Well, I don't . . ."

"Stop right there, Julia. I don't want or need cold water thrown right at this minute. Let me enjoy having two desirable men panting after me. My goodness," she said, fanning her face with her hand, "I feel like a girl again."

"All right, no cold water," I said, although I couldn't help but think that she was not only feeling like a girl, but acting like one as well. "But do remember that Arthur hasn't declared himself, so don't count on him."

"I don't intend to. No, what I'm going to do is play one against the other. I'm not committing to either one. They can both dance to my tune, for a change. Listen, Julia, I *know* men. And I know that they want what they think they can't have and that's why I'm not going with either one. I'll make my choice when we're all there." She pushed her hair back and settled into the sofa with a look of satisfaction on her face. "Now, what should I wear?"

"I'm not sure, LuAnne, I guess it depends on whether you're going to the tea inside Mildred's house or to the barbecue outside. I would think that each one calls for a different look."

"Well, I'm going to both, depending on where Arthur and Leonard are. I mean, I may have to switch back and forth. So what do you think? A nice pantsuit, maybe?"

Before I could respond, she went on.
"Oh, I know. I'll wear my full-cut black
pants. The ones that look like a long skirt
when you stand still. And I have a see-
through organdy top to go with them."

"See-through?"

"Oh, Julia, it has a camisole underneath.
Don't be so quick to think the worst." She
jumped to her feet, smoothed her dress
and started for the door. "I've got to go. So
many things to do, you know. I'm having
my hair done and my nails, which'll take
the rest of the day. Then I have to get a
good night's sleep, so I'll be at my best
tomorrow. Thank you, Julia, for your help.
You're always so encouraging."

I didn't think I'd been all that helpful, but
all I could do was wish her well and wish I
hadn't had a hand in what was sure to be
a delusion. A delusion where Arthur Kessler was concerned surely and maybe
even where Leonard was, too.

I followed her to the door, but before
she left, she turned quickly and said, "Oh,
I almost forgot. I passed Mildred's house
on my way here, and there was a car
parked across the street and down a little
ways. Whoever was in it ducked down just

as I went by so I didn't get a good look. But, Julia, it looked just like Horace, so if it was, I don't guess he's dead. But what could he be doing, just sitting there without going in? It's all very strange, if you ask me. Well, I have to run. See you tomorrow." And off she went without a care in the world, much less any interest in the possibility that Horace Allen may have risen, alive and well, from the wreckage of his car.

Horace Allen, I thought as I closed the door and turned back to the living room. Had it been him? I could've shaken LuAnne for being so taken up with her own affairs that she hadn't stopped to make sure. And if it had been him, why was he sitting outside his own home, just watching and waiting? Of course, I could understand that it would take a lot of getting ready and girding oneself in preparation for facing Mildred's wrath, but he couldn't sit out there all day. Or could he?

There was only one thing to do. "Lillian," I called. "I'm going to walk down to Mildred's. I'll be back in a little while."

As soon as I was out of sight of my house, I crossed the street and strolled innocently down the sidewalk toward Mildred's. I passed the brick wall of the Family Life Center, refusing to even look at it, especially since Pastor Ledbetter was running another Retire-the-Debt campaign, and proceeded on until I was almost past the magnolia trees in Mildred's yard. As nonchalantly as I could, I leaned over and looked into each car that was parked along the street. There wasn't that many, but I regretted not asking LuAnne what kind of car she'd supposedly seen Horace in. Not that she would've known, but a color would've been helpful.

Finally, I glimpsed the sliver of a head barely sticking up in the driver's seat of the next-to-last car on the block. Before approaching, I glanced across the street, noting the crepe myrtles and tall azaleas at the edge of Mildred's yard, obscuring the car from the sight of anyone in the house.

I padded softly up to the passenger side, bent down to peer through the open window and said, "Horace?"

"What!" He jumped a mile, sparks from his cigarette spraying across his none-too-clean shirt as he beat at them with his

other hand. "Good Lord, you scared me to death!"

"Not any more than you've scared everybody else." I opened the door and slid inside. "Mind if I sit a while? Horace, where in the world have you been? Don't you know that Mildred has been frantic and that the whole town's been mourning you, thinking you were dead? You should've seen the flowers and food they brought. What happened to you?"

He shook his head. "You don't want to know."

"Well, of course, I do. Everybody does, especially Mildred, so you might as well get your story straight."

His mouth turned down and big tears welled up in his eyes as he slumped farther in the seat. "I'm ruined, that's the truth of it. She'll never forgive me."

I looked him over. He looked ruined, for I'd never seen him in any state but the most well dressed and put together of any man in our set. In fact, he'd seemingly prided himself on his made-to-order suits—bespoken, he called them—which made the most of his slim and lanky frame.

But now, a rip in his pants leg revealed a white length of leg, dried mud spotted his shirt, his arms and hands were red and scratched and he could've used a haircut as well as a good scrubbing. He was no longer Mildred's dashing attendant, quick to satisfy her every whim, but a pitiful remnant sitting there feeling sorry for himself.

"Well," I said sternly, unwilling to commiserate with him since I have little sympathy for grown men who cry over fixes they've gotten themselves into. "You're not helping matters by sitting out here, bemoaning the situation. You need to pull yourself together and see about getting some medical attention, for one thing. You don't look so good. Where'd you get this car anyway?" It was a far cry from the one he'd left wrecked on the mountainside. When it was in its original condition, I mean.

"Borrowed it."

"Well, I wish you'd borrowed some clothes while you were at it. Mildred's not going to recognize you."

"I tried to get some clothes the other night," he said, wiping a tear from one eye, "but Mildred tried to kill me."

"Was that *you*? It was you who was

climbing up the side of the house? My word, Horace, why didn't you just ring the doorbell? What possessed you to try to sneak in that way?"

"I couldn't face her," he said, while I noted that he couldn't face me either and I'd never lifted a gun. He sat there, slumped over, his eyes on his lap, unable or unwilling to look up.

"You need to come to some conclusion here, Horace. You need help and sitting in a car all day is not going to get it. And what're you going to do if a deputy sees you? They're looking all over creation for you as it is, and, believe me, you don't want to get crossways of Lieutenant Peavey." I shuddered at the thought, not wishing Lieutenant Peavey on my worst enemy. "Besides, you know I'm going to tell Mildred I saw you. I can't let her go on thinking you're among the dead or missing forever."

"She doesn't care." Then he lifted his head to stare at me with eyes full of hurt and maybe a little anger. "She's having a party tomorrow. A *big* party! I'd hardly be cold in my grave, if I was in one."

"Well, my goodness, Horace," I said,

thinking fast, "she's only doing it because you wanted her to be more community-minded. She's doing it for you, in your memory, so to speak." I didn't mention that she was also doing it to show the town that she could rise above being forsaken by an errant husband. "Now, why don't you go on in and throw yourself on her mercy? Think of all those nice, clean clothes hanging in your closet."

"I've lost a lot of her money," he mumbled so low that I had to ask him to repeat it. Then a little stronger and with a hint of self-justification, he went on. "It was Richard's fault. It was supposed to be such a sure thing." He took a deep, ragged breath. "It's all gone now, and Mildred will never forgive me. She always said I didn't know how to handle money and, boy howdy, I've proved her right. I guess the only thing I can do is just go on in and face the music." He swatted his hand across a muddy splotch on his shirt, which did no good, then opened the door and shambled off across the street.

And I just sat there, too stunned to hinder him. He'd said *Richard*? Richard Stroud?

Chapter 41

❧

I lingered beside Horace's borrowed car vacillating between going home and knocking on Mildred's door to see what kind of reception Horace was getting. Discretion prevailed, though, and I turned toward home. I had no desire to be within wounding distance if Mildred dove under her bed after that shotgun again.

But I nearly jumped out of my skin when a motorcycle one street over backfired, then roared off toward town. I declare, I'd been in so many near-combat situations lately that I was beginning to suffer from one of those stress syndromes.

I forgot about that, though, and picked up my pace when I saw a familiar car parked at the curb in front of my house. Hurrying through the kitchen door, I was greeted by a hubbub of welcoming smiles and hugs and kisses, some of which I could've done without. Hazel Marie and Mr. Pickens were home.

"Oh, Miss Julia," Hazel Marie said, her eyes shining with the wonder of it all, "you should've been with us. San Francisco was beautiful. The Golden Gate Bridge! The fog! The hills and the streetcars! I've never seen anything like it. You would love it. Oh, and I've got pictures. I took pictures of everything. I can't wait to show you."

"And I can't wait to see them. You look wonderful, Hazel Marie." And she did. Like a million dollars, in fact, which probably wasn't too far off the mark. Whatever she and Mr. Pickens had been up to, it had done wonders for her complexion.

And speaking of whom, there he stood, one hand on a chair back, smiling complacently at Hazel Marie's excitement.

"Well, Mr. Pickens," I said, "thank you for getting her back safely. I hope you had a good time, too."

Lillian broke in then, telling us to sit down, she was slicing a caramel cake.

"I wouldn't turn that down," Mr. Pickens said, then to me, "Yes, I had a good time and a successful one, too."

"Oh, that's the best thing," Hazel Marie said, pulling out a chair. "That insurance company hired him! He's on retainer, which means he can work for them and for himself, and he'll be making a mint! I'm so proud."

"Hardly a mint," Mr. Pickens said with a deprecating shrug. But I could tell he was pleased with himself, probably for more than just getting hired. "Lillian, I've been missing your cooking."

"Oh!" Hazel Marie hopped up from her chair. "Lloyd'll be home any minute and I've got to get his presents out of the suit-case. I'll be right back."

"Latisha comin' with him," Lillian said. "I hope that's all right."

"Oh, good. I've got presents for her, too. For everybody, in fact."

Lillian put the rest of the cake slices on the table, then followed her out. "She have them clothes strung all over the place, I don't go right behind her."

"Well, Mr. Pickens," I said, picking up my fork and taking advantage of one of the few times I had him alone. "I guess now that you have regular employment, you'll be making an honest woman of Hazel Marie."

He glanced up over a forkful of cake halfway to his mouth, then put it down. "I've been thinking about that."

"Don't think too long, especially if you're sitting there trying to think up some other delaying tactic. May I remind you that your last excuse of not wanting to live off Lloyd's money from his father didn't hold much water with me. That's commendable of you, but it's plain that you're prospering now and it's time to take the next step." I gave a sharp nod of my head for punctuation. "And if you don't know what that step is, I can certainly tell you."

"My goodness," he said, close to laughing at me, "you're a little testy today. She may not have me. Have you thought of that?"

I snorted, but somewhat delicately, at the thought and waved my hand. Before I could finish my response, Lloyd and Latisha came through the door. Bookbags hit the floor and Lloyd said, "Last day of school! Hallelujah!" Then he saw Mr. Pickens and his face lit up. "Mama's home? Where is she? Hey, J.D. Where's Mama?"

Mr. Pickens stood up, offered his hand to the boy, then drew him close in a hug. "She's upstairs unpacking a few presents. Well, actually, we had to buy another suitcase to bring them all home." Lloyd started for the stairs, calling his mother, but Mr. Pickens said, "Wait, she's bringing down some surprises."

"She better hurry," Lloyd said, beside himself with excitement. "I can't wait to see her."

Mr. Pickens laughed, then squatted down in front of Latisha. "Hey, little girl. Remember me?"

She ducked her beribboned head, smiled and gave him a flirtatious glance. "Maybe."

Mr. Pickens clutched at his heart. "You've cut me to the quick, forgetting me like that. Get up here and have some cake. Maybe it'll improve your memory."

Latisha giggled. "I don't forget you. I jus' don't want you to know it."

Mr. Pickens's eyebrows shot up as he looked at me. "They learn early, don't they?"

When Hazel Marie and Lillian came back down, their arms were loaded with bags and boxes. After hugging and carrying on over Lloyd, Hazel Marie began handing out the gifts she'd brought. I'd never in my life seen so many T-shirts and miniature bridges and other odds and ends that constituted mementos of San Francisco.

"And this is for you," she said, handing a small box to Latisha.

The child opened it and pulled out a trinket that made her eyes light up. Then she asked, "What is it?"

"It's a snow globe," Hazel Marie said. "See, you turn it over and snow falls on the Golden Gate Bridge."

"Look at that, Great-Granny," Latisha said, holding it out to Lillian. "I got me a little bridge inside a ball."

As we all sat around the table, eating cake and talking over and around each other, Hazel Marie couldn't keep her hands from Lloyd. She hugged him time and again, patted his hand, looked him over and, in general, displayed how much she'd missed him. Her obvious and ardent love of the child—hers and my first husband's child, I might add—was the major redeeming factor in my ability to overlook what she'd done to get him. And then, gradually, her sweet nature and guileless heart endeared her to me for herself alone. I just wished she'd tamp down her attachment to Mr. Pickens long enough to rope him in. A cool head in such matters can be much more effective than an overheated heart.

Mr. Pickens, himself, broke into my reverie. "Where's Sam?"

"Downtown, I guess, watching the desecration and destruction of our courthouse. He may even be protesting."

"Oh," Hazel Marie said, "are they really tearing it down?"

"Yes, they are," I said. "Courtesy of Mr. Arthur Kessler. And I don't think I'll ever get over it, in spite of the fact that Sam tells me the courthouse isn't worth saving. But as far as I'm concerned, being old and decrepit is no reason to put anything out of its misery." Seeing the merriment in Mr. Pickens's eyes, I quickly added, "I am not speaking personally, Mr. Pickens."

"Didn't enter my mind," he said with a straight face. "So what else has happened since we've been gone?"

"Horace Allen's home."

"What!" Hazel Marie exclaimed, as Lillian's mouth dropped open. "When? Where was he all this time?"

"I have no idea," I said. "I just saw him go into the house a few minutes ago. For all I know, he may be back out again, depending on Mildred's mood at the moment."

After we'd discussed all the possible reasons for Horace's mysterious absence, none of which were satisfactory, I told them of the barbecue soiree that would be held the following afternoon. "Everybody's invited, and you'll have your choice of an inside tea with finger sandwiches and entertainment by Tina Doland or a pig pickin' in the yard with music by the Crooked River Boys."

With a straight face, Mr. Pickens said, "I know which one I'm going to. I love finger sandwiches."

Latisha, who'd been ignoring the conversation going on around her in favor of creating a snowstorm inside her globe, suddenly looked up. "Me, too," she said. "Can I go? I wanta hear that woman sing, if that's what she's gonna do. I might could help her out."

Lillian said, "Hush, chile."

"Of course you may go," I said. "You and your great-granny both. And from what I hear, Miss Tina could use some help. Now, Mr. Pickens," I went on, turning to him, "you're probably too tired from the rigors of your trip, but I understand that there's to be an all-night party around the barbecue pits tonight. No finger sandwiches, but Sam'll be there and you might enjoy it."

After finishing the cake and hearing about the highlights of the trip—several times, in fact—everybody began to disperse into various parts of the house. Mr. Pickens left to check in at his office and to prepare for the men's party that night.

"Miss Julia?" Lillian said, as we cleared the table. "Mr. Horace really come back home?"

"I saw him, Lillian, and talked with him, but I didn't get much information. Just that he's been involved in some way with Richard Stroud and he's lost a lot of Mildred's money. He was afraid to face her, and it must've taken every bit of his courage to get out of the car and go in. He was so pitiful-looking that I almost felt sorry for him. In spite of the fact that he brought it all on himself." I leaned closer. "But, listen, it was him who tried to break into the house the night we were there. He wanted to get some clean clothes. Have you ever heard the like? All that trouble, plus getting shot at, just for a change of clothes." I shook my head at the wonder of it. "Of course, he was always particular about the way he looked."

Chapter 42

⁓❦⁓

Sam crawled into bed sometime before sunup that night, reeking of wood smoke and other unsavory odors. If sleeping far up into the morning was any indication, he'd thoroughly enjoyed himself in Mildred's backyard.

When I later commented on his late rising, he said that he'd needed his beauty sleep. "I have to be fresh for the real party this afternoon." Then he yawned widely and shook his head. "My social life is about to do me in."

The rest of us had been up early, scurrying back and forth between our house and Mildred's, as Lillian and Hazel Marie helped Ida Lee set up for the indoor and outdoor parties. Lloyd was outside entertaining Latisha and, as I fixed toast and coffee for Sam, I took the opportunity to have a quiet chat. I'd already told him of seeing Horace sitting in a car trying to get up the nerve to enter his own home, but I wanted to know what happened when he did.

"Let's hear it, Sam," I said, sitting beside him at the table, "was Horace there last night?"

"If he was, he didn't come out. For all any of us knew, he's still among the missing." He bit into the toast and chewed a while. "Come to think of it, Mildred didn't put in an appearance either. Not that I expected her to, but we were in her yard."

"Well, with Horace showing up like that, she probably had too much on her mind to extend a formal welcome. Who all was there?"

"People came and went all night." He laughed. "I should've went long before I did. I'd feel a lot better now. James was there all night, helping Robert baste the pigs and feed the fires, and Ledbetter stopped by for a few minutes. Not looking too good, either, now that I think about it. He seemed sort of subdued or downcast about something, not his usual outgoing self."

I nodded, thinking that the pastor was probably having trouble at home, but I didn't want to get into that. "Who else?"

"Well, Pickens was there for an hour or two, fairly late, around midnight or so. And Coleman came by with several other deputies when their shift ended. That's a pretty wild bunch when they're off duty, but," he quickly added, "not Coleman. Binkie and the baby have sure quieted him down. And that Delmont deputy, Bobby Lee something-or-other, came with his guitar. He can really play that thing. Has a good voice, too. Guess who else showed up with a musical instrument?"

"Who?"

"Thurlow." Sam laughed at the memory. "He brought an old fiddle, and when he finally got on the same page as Bobby Lee, they sounded pretty good. I'll have to admit, though, it was mostly us old geezers who stayed the night, and probably all paying for it this morning."

"I wish you'd found out more about

Horace," I said, and since I wasn't eating, propped my elbows on the table. "We don't even know if he was in the house or if Mildred had sent him packing."

"Well, nobody seemed to know he'd come back at all, so I didn't bring it up. I expect we'll find out this afternoon. He'll either show or he won't."

"I guess so. I'm just surprised that Mildred hasn't called. Well, anyway, I have to get myself prepared to see Arthur. I don't know why we're even having this party, since it was supposed to deter him from doing what he's already done. I declare, Sam, I wish that man had never heard of Abbotsville, or us of him."

"That's another thing, Julia. Don't go downtown for the next few days. The courthouse is nothing but a pile of rubble, and you don't want to see it. At least wait till they clear it off."

I nodded agreement, wondering how I would be able to muster up any courtesy at all to Arthur Kessler after what he'd done. Standards have to be maintained, of course, but sometimes I'd much prefer letting somebody have it with both barrels. So to speak.

"Oh," Sam said, as he poured another cup of coffee, "did you ever know Poochie Dunn?"

"No," I said, jolted by the sudden change of subject. "I mean, yes, vaguely. Why?"

"He dropped in for a little while last night. I don't know when I last saw him, but he hasn't changed a bit. All he could talk about was the new truck he's getting. Apparently it's a toss-up between a Dodge Ram and Ford F150, either of which he's always wanted." Sam smiled. "Beats me where he's getting the money. He's never held a job more than a week at a time."

"Well, I think he works odd jobs, so maybe he's been saving up." I wanted an end to the discussion of Poochie Dunn, since it was clear that he'd not divulged a word about our rescue operation. Now, if he'd just make it to the soiree with an intact statue and continue to hold his peace, all would be well.

After a few minutes, during which I hoped thoughts of Poochie Dunn were fading from Sam's interest, I said, "Sam, what do you think Horace meant when he said his present predicament was all Richard Stroud's fault?"

"From what you said he said, it sounds as if they'd gone into something that required them both to put up a good deal of money—Horace getting his part from Mildred and Richard getting his from his clients. I'm just speculating here, but that sheet of paper they found in Horace's car and what he said to you yesterday indicate some kind of connection."

"What could it have been?" I mused.

"Beats me, but whatever it was apparently didn't pan out or they wouldn't have gone on the run. Talk about your irony," Sam said with a lift of his eyebrows. "Maybe somebody scammed them, just as they'd run scams to get the money in the first place."

"Sounds more like justice to me," I said, "at least as far as Richard and Horace are concerned. It's no justice at all for those people who've had their money stolen." My mouth tightened. "They'll probably never get a cent of it back."

"I expect you're right," Sam said, nodding in agreement. "But speaking of Richard, I wonder if Helen's heard from him, now that Horace has turned up."

"Why don't you call and ask her?" I watched closely to see if he'd been waiting for just that suggestion. It was, however, as far as I was willing to go. "I wouldn't go over there if I were you. Richard may be coming out of the woodwork, too, and you might run into him."

"No, I think I'll leave that alone," he said, warming my heart. Not that I begrudged his offering a helping hand to a friend, you understand. It was just that Helen seemed to need more than the hand I was willing to lend her.

"Well, Julia," Sam said, standing and picking up his plates to take to the sink, "I think I'll walk over and see if Robert needs some help this morning. I expect everybody's cleared out and left it with him."

After a quick kiss, Sam left while I continued to sit, thinking and wondering about Horace and Richard and what they could've been up to. And wondering, too, if Lieutenant Peavey had been informed that the lost, at least one of them, had been found.

"Miss Julia," Lillian said as she came through the swinging door into the kitchen, "that smoke from them pig pits is gettin' all through the house. Everything we got gonna smell like hick'ry-smoke pork roast from now on. They oughtta done them pigs out in the sticks somewhere."

"I thought the same thing myself. I'd be surprised if Mildred hasn't broken some ordinance or something, but nothing would do than to dig those pits in her yard. I mean, she has the biggest yard in town, but still."

"Yessum, an' I 'spect she have them things dug as far from her house as Robert could get 'em."

"Yes, and they're probably closer to ours than to hers. Well, let's close the windows and turn on the air conditioner. It's going to be up in the eighties later today anyway."

I walked back to the bedroom, trying to decide what to wear to a social event the likes of which had never been seen in Abbotsville before. There was no precedent that set the appropriate attire for such polar opposite entertainments. And I certainly didn't intend to confine myself to one or the other. Nor did I think that anyone would. Hazel Marie was going to wear some kind of flowing pants outfit that she said was suitable for both a tea party and a pig pickin'. It had taken her some while to come up with that compromise, though, because she'd really wanted to wear a camisole and jeans.

"If I'm overdressed," she'd said, putting the jeans back into the closet, "I'll just run home and change." Then she'd said, "Miss Julia, this is when you absolutely need a pantsuit, but since I know you won't get one, here's what you have to wear." And she'd reached into her closet and pulled out a long skirt that looked like a patchwork quilt or Joseph's many-colored coat or some such, it was so garish. "It's silk," she said, "so it's not heavy, and all you have to do is pick out one of the colors and match a top to it."

Since it was either that or a church or house dress, I decided to wear it and hope I wouldn't be the only one in an ankle-length dress.

I was standing by the bed, considering several tops, when the phone rang. I answered it and heard, "Julia, it's Helen. Is Sam around?"

My hand tightened on the receiver. "Why, no, Helen, he's out at the moment, and I'm not sure when he'll be back. May I give him a message?"

"Could you track him down for me? Now

that I've made up my mind, I really need to speak with him."

"I wouldn't know where to start, and we're all busy here helping Mildred get ready for her big do. As soon as I see him, though, I'll tell him you called."

There was a long moment of silence, then I heard a clear sob as she said, "Lieutenant Peavey and some government agent just left. They've been after me and after me, Julia, convinced that I know where Richard is. And now that Horace has come home, they've started in on me again. Would you believe they wanted to confiscate my *passport*? And I don't even *have* a passport."

"Well, my goodness, Helen, do they think you'll leave the country?"

"I guess they do. There's been somebody sitting in a car watching my house every day since Richard's been gone. I think they either suspect or know that Richard is out of the country. And if he is, you know what that means, don't you?"

"He doesn't want to get caught?"

"Well, yes, but what it really means is that he's not coming home, and the only way to make them believe that I'm innocent is to divorce him. And that's what I'm going to do. I can't live like this any longer, and I want Sam to recommend a good divorce lawyer."

"I thought you already had a lawyer in Asheville."

"I do, but he doesn't do divorces, and I'd trust Sam's recommendation over his any day."

Well, so would I, so I couldn't fault her for that. But I didn't know how I felt about having Helen running around town, free as a bird after a divorce.

"I'll tell him," I responded. "But, Helen, have you heard anything more about Horace? I know he got home yesterday, but I don't know any more than that. Not even how Mildred's handling it."

"I haven't talked to her. All I know is what I gathered from the questions they asked me this morning. And," she said with a considerable tightness in her voice, "it sounded as if Horace has put whatever they were up to all on Richard. He used only Mildred's money, so apparently he has only her to answer to, whereas Richard . . . Well, I guess you know about that."

I wanted to say, *You better believe I do,*

since he did it with some of mine, but I didn't. All I said was, "What do they think Richard did with the money?"

"Absconded with it, Julia!" she said, more sharply than I was accustomed to being spoken to. "Why else are they turning my life upside down, as if I helped him do it?"

"I know that, Helen. Everybody in town knows that. It's obvious that Horace wasn't in on everything or he'd have stayed gone, too. I meant, what did Horace *think* they were going to do with it?"

"I don't have any idea. Some kind of real estate venture is all I know, and I don't know that for sure. Julia," she went on with a catch in her voice, "I've got to go. It's all too much for me."

I felt a stirring of pity for a woman I might have recently misjudged. She had been a steadfast and trusted friend for many years, and now in her hour of need I had turned my back on her. Not without some reason, of course, but I'd been known to be wrong on occasion.

"Helen," I said, "why don't Sam and I pick you up and you go to the party with us? I promise you that no one will say an unkind word to you, because one of us will be by your side the whole time. And this might be a good time for you to show the town that you are free of Richard and of anything he's done. And, also, it would give you a chance to get Horace alone and find out what he knows. If Mildred has let him stay, that is."

She cried for a minute or so, then said, "Thank you, Julia, but I just can't. I can't face anybody until this is settled and everybody knows that I'm in the dark as much as they are. And a divorce is the only way to do that."

She was probably right, although, divorced or not, it'd be a long time before she'd be able to buy anything without somebody suspecting she was using their money to do it.

"Well, if you change your mind," I said, "just give me a call. I'll tell Sam to call you, but it may be tonight after the party or tomorrow."

"That's all right," she said, sounding resigned to not getting started on her divorce right this minute, it being Saturday and all. "Just whenever he can. Oh, and, Julia, do one thing for me, if you will. Don't say anything to Pastor Ledbetter about this. He'd be after me worse than Lieutenant Peavey, telling me how I'm sinning if I divorce Richard. As if Richard hasn't sinned against me ten times over."

"Don't worry about that," I assured her. "I know how he feels about divorce, especially if it's a wife who wants one, and I'd be the last person to give him an opportunity to start in on it again. I've heard all I want to hear on that subject."

Chapter 43

By late afternoon, cars began to arrive at Mildred's and line both sides of Polk Street and Jefferson, too. Families with skipping children, dating couples walking arm in arm and groups of teenagers streamed down the sidewalk toward Mildred's house.

Inside our house, we were all busy getting ready. Lillian had come from Mildred's to dress Latisha, having brought her party dress from home that morning. She had the child dressed in a pink, hand-smocked dress with a big bow in the back and layers of petticoats underneath.

"You mind yo' manners now," Lillian said

as she tied the last tiny pink bow in Latisha's hair. "An' I want you to keep this new dress clean."

I'd walked in just as she said it. "That's wishful thinking, Lillian. Children will be running all over the place, getting covered with dirt."

"Not me," Latisha said. "I already know what I'm gonna do. I'm goin' swimmin' in that big ole swimmin' pool that lady's got."

"No, you not!" Lillian said, clasping both Latisha's arms and making her look her in the eye. "You stay away from that swimmin' pool, you hear me? Miss Julia," Lillian went on, worry lining her face, "what if somebody fall in that thing?"

Latisha piped up. "I'm not gonna *fall* in, I'm gonna *jump* in, right in the middle of it."

"Oh, my," I said, suddenly as concerned as Lillian. "I wonder if anybody's thought about the pool. Surely Mildred's had it covered or the gate locked or something. Every child there will be fascinated with it."

"All taken care of," Hazel Marie said, breezing into the kitchen and bringing with her a whiff of Joy perfume. "Mildred's got two lifeguards on duty. Red Cross trained and everything."

With that worry taken care of, we began to make our way to the site of the parties. As was everybody else in town, it seemed. People were milling around the front door, while others headed straight for the back of the house where chairs and tables had been scattered around under the oak trees that shaded the yard. Dotted here and there were #2 washtubs filled with ice and cold drinks, there for the taking, and many were doing just that. I caught a glimpse of a large, striped tent with a wooden dance floor set up across from the poolhouse and heard the Crooked River Boys beginning to warm up.

Lillian grabbed Latisha's arm as the child started to dash off. "You come back here. You got to say hello to yo' hostess 'fore you go runnin' off."

"Walk with me, Latisha," Lloyd said, holding out his hand. "Let's go in the house first. You wanted to hear that lady sing, didn't you?"

"Oh, yeah. I forgot about her." And she walked docilely beside him as we waited our turn to get inside.

It was a relief to walk into the air-conditioned house, since the short walk had us all sweltering. Mildred, in a long, flowing caftan and her signature diamond brooch, stood by the door, greeting her guests.

I knew I was glowing from perspiration, but she was glowing from something else entirely. "Julia," she said, drawing me close, "you'll never guess. Horace is home!"

Quickly grasping that he had not told her that I'd had an earlier sighting than she, I said, "Why, that's wonderful, Mildred. Where was he all that time?"

"It doesn't matter," she said, almost purring with happiness. "All that matters is that he's home again. The poor darling was scared to death that I'd be mad with him. That's why he stayed away so long. But he's home now, and I'm so happy. We'll have a real celebration now."

I murmured something in response, but all I could think was that Horace had worked his charms on her again. If it'd been me, I would've wanted to know where he'd been and why he'd been there. I couldn't think of a single explanation that would justify the misery he'd put her through, and as far as I could see, his un-explained absence and subsequent return created more cause for interrogation than celebration.

Feeling pushed from behind as others edged inside, I thought of the celebrated return of the prodigal son that Pastor Ledbetter had referred to in our most recent talk. He must have made the same point to Mildred, which, from her obviously warm reception of Horace, she'd taken to heart. In this instance, though, it was a case of the return of the prodigal husband celebrated with a fatted pig or two instead of a calf.

As we moved deeper into the foyer, Hazel Marie kept twisting around to see if Mr. Pickens was there. "He said he'd meet me here, but I'll bet he's outside."

"He probably is, and Sam, too," I said, thinking that I'd soon be headed that way myself. I needed to locate Etta Mae so we could both be on the lookout for Poochie Dunn before he found those tubs in the backyard. Mildred was a faithful Presbyterian, but she could be wishy-washy on the subject of temperance and I knew that some of those tubs would be holding more than ice-cold Cokes and Grape Nehis.

I came to a dead stop in the doorway of the living room as Tina Doland, standing beside the piano, strained for more high notes than her voice was able to hit with any accuracy. Several people were sitting around listening attentively, some with frowns on their faces, but all I could do was admire her flower-spattered chiffon gown for a minute and turn around to leave. It was always a wonder to me why any solo-ist would choose "People" to sing in public.

Latisha lingered in the doorway, seem-ingly entranced with Tina's efforts. Then she turned to Lillian. "Great-Granny, that lady need help."

Lloyd doubled over in a laughing fit, and it was all I could do to keep a straight face. Hazel Marie said, "Maybe we should go out back."

"Good idea," I said, and started winding my way through the crowded foyer toward the large sunroom off the kitchen, the oth-ers following close behind. Passing the dining room, I glanced at the heavily laden table, surrounded by guests who were fill-ing plates from the trays and epergnes and chafing dishes displayed upon it. Flo-ral arrangements on the table, the sideboard and the hall tables reminded me of the usual elegance of all Mildred's entertainments. And partaking of all that food and elegance was none other than Brother Vernon Puckett reaching across the table for two ham biscuits to pile on top of an already full plate. I quickly turned away, not wanting to catch his eye. I might've felt inclined to issue another divine instruction and really upset his apple cart.

"We stoppin' off here," Lillian said, keeping a grip on Latisha's arm and pushing through to the back hall that led to the kitchen. "Ida Lee countin' on me to help out."

"Well, not me," Latisha said.

"Yes, ma'am, you, too," Lillian told her. "I want you where my eye on you every minute."

I delayed her with a hand on her arm. "Don't stay in the kitchen all evening, Lillian. This party's for everybody and that includes you."

The first person I saw as we went into the sunroom was Horace. He was holding court with a number of ladies from the garden club and the book club. I declare, he was a changed man from the last time I'd seen him. In fact, he'd reverted to his former dapper self, as if his absence from home had never occurred nor had a load of birdshot ever been aimed in his direction. He was wearing a pair of white trousers with white buck shoes, a navy blazer with brass buttons and, would you believe, an ascot. He stood casually talking with one or the other of the women around him, one hand in his pocket and the other gesturing with a cigarette in an onyx holder. He had quickly and easily assumed his former social position, thereby assuring that no one would ask any uncomfortable questions. He was back home with apparently no recriminations or penalties, which would've made me ill if I'd thought about it long enough.

But after speaking with Mildred and seeing the joy in her eyes, I had little wonder that Horace was pleased with himself and with his ability to satisfy any lingering concerns that she might have. I just shook my head and tightened my mouth. People ought to be held accountable for what they do, else they'll just keep doing it.

But that's her problem, I thought to myself and went straight on through the sunroom and out onto the back lawn. There must have been a couple of hundred or more people milling about, some sitting in chairs nursing cold cans of something while others walked from one group to another, talking and laughing together. Young people and children were swimming and jumping into the pool, shouting, "Watch this!" and "Look out!" The Crooked River Boys were strumming and sawing away under the tent, sweat streaming down their faces, while Robert and James and a number of men, Sam and Coleman among them, lifted the pigs out of the pits and carried them to the oilcloth-covered tables. As Robert took a cleaver and a huge fork to begin chopping the roasted meat, guests swarmed around the tables, ready to dig in.

The sinking sun blazed long rays through the trees and across the lawn, as the sultry air filled with the aroma of roast pork and the sound of hungry people. I stood on the wide steps of the patio, sweeping my gaze across the hordes, looking for Etta Mae and the first sight of Poochie Dunn. I wanted to catch him as soon as he arrived to remind him that silence is golden, and in this case, automotively imperative.

"There's J.D.," Hazel Marie said, pointing toward a group standing around a washtub. "You want us to fix you a plate, Miss Julia?"

"Not yet, thank you. You run on, I'll wait for Sam." As she left, I turned to Lloyd, who seemed unable to decide whether to eat, swim or just wander around to see who all was there. "Lloyd, I want you to help me find Etta Mae, if you will. I need to talk with her, so if you see her, tell her to find me."

"I'll go look for her now," he said, his decision of what to do first made.

I stepped away from the house and began walking across the lawn, speaking to first one and the other as I went. There were any number of people I didn't know, perhaps some who'd come from surrounding towns. Blanket invitations as Mildred had issued seemed to have brought them out in droves. I didn't linger with any of them, but it was easy enough to learn the general topic of conversation—the destruction of the courthouse. Everywhere, people were talking about the loss and murmuring against Arthur Kessler.

My eye was taken by one or two single

men who were overdressed for the occasion and who seemed to be observers rather than participants. Gray suits and ties do tend to stand out at a pig pickin', and I wondered if they were some of the agents investigating Richard Stroud. *How nice,* I thought, *that they could enjoy our town's hospitality, but how strange if they thought he'd show up here.*

Then, almost walking up on several of the county commissioners talking together in a tight group, I veered in the other direction, surprised that they had the nerve to show their faces. I noticed with some satisfaction that other people were avoiding them as well. They were an isolated group at the party, and so they would be on election day, too, if I was any judge of the general atmosphere.

Hearing my name called, I turned to see Emma Sue Ledbetter tiptoeing across the thick grass as quickly as her high heels would permit.

"My goodness," she said as she came near, "every time I put a foot down in this grass, I mire up to my ankles. I may just take these things off and go barefooted. How are you, Julia?"

I thought I'd been doing fairly well until I saw her. For the first time since I'd known her, she was in a revealing frock. A sundress with no straps at all and with a hem above her knees. The only redeeming feature was a filmy stole across her shoulders, the ends of which she clasped modestly over her fronts.

I tried not to stare or to express my shock. "I'm fine, Emma Sue. How are you? You look . . . lovely."

"Do you like it? It's the first dress I haven't made myself in years. Just bought it right off the rack, but to tell the truth, I'm a little nervous about it." She reached under the stole, grasped the top of the bodice and jerked it up. "It keeps sliding down on me."

"Well, it's perfect for the occasion. So summery and, ah, cool-looking."

"Oh, you don't have to pretend with me, Julia," she said as her eyes became suspiciously red-rimmed. "I know it's inappropriate for a pastor's wife, but that's why I wanted it. I don't plan to be a ministerial adjunct all that much longer."

Chapter 44

"Emma Sue," I said, a note of concern in my voice, "what have you done?"

"Oh, don't worry, Julia," she said, with a delicate sniff. "I haven't lost my mind. I've just put my foot down, that's all."

That didn't reassure me, as I recalled a certain Poker Run motorcycle race in which she'd also put her foot down, her defiance of Pastor Ledbetter's wishes nearly giving him a stroke.

"Look over there," she went on, pointing across the lawn where the pastor sat alone almost hidden by the drooping limbs of a crepe myrtle. "See him? He's over there, sulking like a two-year-old because he's not getting his way. Whenever my feelings are hurt, he tells me how unattractive it is to mope around. But that's exactly what he's doing, and it *is* unattractive. I've told him so, too."

Not wanting to get in the middle of a marital disagreement, I carefully asked, "Would this be about his call to Raleigh?"

"Well, what else?" she said blithely, trying to act as if she didn't care. But a certain frantic look in her eyes betrayed her. "Julia, I told him. Listen to what I said and see if you don't agree. I reminded him of the advice he always gives to seminary students. He tells them that whenever a minister thinks he's received a call, but his wife hasn't, then the minister can be sure that the call is not from God. And I told him that *I've* had absolutely no communication from anybody." Her eyes darted from one side to the other. "Don't you think that would be enough to make him at least think twice about going to Raleigh?"

"Yes, I would, Emma Sue. Especially since you're so adamant on the subject."

"He's not seen adamant yet," she said

with renewed determination. "If he's so bound and determined to pick up lock, stock and barrel and move across the state, then that's just what he can do. I'm staying here. I told him that, too."

"Oh, Emma Sue, you can't mean you're divorcing him!"

"Of course not, Julia. You know we don't believe in divorce. But there's more than one way to skin a cat. I'm just not going to live with him. He can go to Raleigh if he wants to, but I'm staying here in my own house." Her eyes narrowed as she lowered her voice. "Then we'll see how bad that new church wants him when he shows up without a wife."

"Well," I said, hardly knowing what to say, "I've heard of couples who live apart but never divorce, so I guess it could work."

"It'll have to because that's what I'm going to do. And, Julia, when you look at it, it'll be perfect. I'll stay in our house here, and when he's ready to retire, he can move back. Thank goodness we bought our house and didn't accept a church-owned manse. And we did it that way, Julia, only because Larry said we'd stay on in Abbotsville after he retired. So all I'm doing is holding him to his word." She jerked her bodice up again. "Don't you think?"

"Well, yes, but I can't imagine that he's happy about it."

"Oh, he's not, believe me. He's so used to making all the decisions that he's just miserable now." She sidled closer to me and whispered, "Julia, do you think the church would hire me? I mean, pay me a salary to keep doing what I'm doing?"

"Lord, Emma Sue, if we paid you for what you do in that church, we couldn't afford you." Emma Sue taught Sunday school, organized activities for the youth, led the Bible study in our circle, worked in the kitchen when we had covered dish suppers, fed and put up guest preachers, visited newcomers, the sick and the bereaved, held a minor office in the Presbytery, set up vacation Bible school for the little ones and held an open house every Christmas for the entire membership.

"I wouldn't ask for much," she said wistfully. "Just enough to tide me over. Keeping two households will be expensive."

"The only thing I see wrong with it is if Pastor Ledbetter leaves, we'll have to call another preacher. And if that preacher has a wife, which he's bound to have or we wouldn't call him, then that wife would be expected to take your place. I'm not sure the deacons would be willing to pay you for what they could get free from her."

"They'd better not count on that," she said. "Things have changed since we came along. The young wives today already have jobs or professions. They're not so willing to be unpaid help in a two-for-one deal."

"I'm sure you're right, and more power to them," I said. "But I'll tell you what, Emma Sue. If you want to apply for the job you're already doing, I'll write a supporting letter for you. And Sam will speak for you, too, I'm sure. He admires you so much."

"He does?" Tears welled up in her eyes, surprising me for being so late in coming. Emma Sue was known for crying at the least little thing.

"Everybody does. You may feel unappreciated, but you're not. We all know what you do, and I, for one, think that the pastor is foolish if he goes off and leaves you."

As I searched my pocketbook for a Kleenex to hand to her, I felt an obtrusive presence beside me. "Good evening, ladies," Arthur Kessler said, glancing briefly at us, then sweeping his gaze across the milling crowd. He removed a folded handkerchief from his ecru linen jacket and mopped his forehead. He'd dressed for his idea of a southern soiree and was now suffering from it. I saw the tail of the tie he'd removed sticking out of a pocket. "Lovely evening for a wingding, isn't it?"

"It's hardly a *wingding*," I said coolly, as Emma Sue clutched her stole closer and turned aside to blot her eyes.

"Well, whatever you call it," he said, not the least abashed. "I'm always interested in local customs, so this is a treat for me."

Uh-huh, I thought, *you've come to observe the natives.* And went on to realize that even if he hadn't already torn down the courthouse, our soiree wouldn't have deterred him one iota. All my efforts had been of no use, and here I was, stuck at a hot, sweaty and futile pig pickin' that ordinarily I would never have attended at all.

Mr. Kessler's eyes flicked my way. "You know what goes on in this town, Mrs. Murdoch. So I have a question for you."

"I'll be happy to answer it if I can," I said coolly, offended at the implication, "but I assure you that there are any number of things that go on, of which I know nothing."

"Be that as it may," he replied with a wave of his hand. "Have you heard anything about what happened to my statue?"

I stood very still. "What statue?"

"*My* statue. The one on the courthouse dome. That *was* on the dome, that is. It wasn't there yesterday morning when I got on site. I reported the theft to the police as soon as I saw it was gone."

"*Theft?* Why, why, Arthur," I said, swallowing hard to keep from strangling, "you said you didn't want it. You said the town could have it if it survived the demolition."

"It didn't have a chance to survive anything. Somebody climbed up there during the night and stole it. They took something that belongs to me. That's pure theft in my book."

"But, Arthur, how can it be?" My heart was fluttering in my chest at this turn of events. "You wouldn't have it anyway since you were willing to let it be destroyed when the building came down."

"But," he said, rounding on me, "whoever took it didn't know that, did they?"

"Well, no, I guess not." Poochie certainly hadn't.

"If you hear anything, you let me know. I don't want anybody in this town thinking they can steal from me and get away with it."

"I certainly will," I murmured, wondering how I could politely but quickly move away. Then wondered why I thought it had to be done politely.

I was saved by LuAnne Conover who came bustling up to us. "There you are!" she chirped, her eyes lighting up at the sight of Mr. Kessler. Then she came to an abrupt stop, her eyes popping out at Emma Sue. "Oh!" they both gasped, staring at their identical sundresses.

"Well!" LuAnne said, attempting to laugh it off. "I guess we both went to Dillard's, didn't we?"

Emma Sue's face turned red and tears flowed copiously. "I'm so sorry, LuAnne. If I'd known, I never would've bought it."

"Don't be silly," LuAnne said, a bit

sharply. "No one will even notice." She was wrong. Whispers would seep throughout the female contingent at the soiree, and every one of them would have to look to see for themselves. "It looks much better on you," LuAnne said in an attempt at graciousness. Of course, with her well-rounded and slightly plump little figure she could afford to be kind. She had enough to keep her bodice up without hiking it up every time she took a breath.

"Oh, Arthur," LuAnne said, turning her full attention on him, although he had turned away to survey the crowd. "It's so good to see you. I've been looking forward to this so much. It's such a lovely evening, perfect weather and everything, and everybody's in such a party mood. I'm glad you're here to enjoy it with us."

"Very interesting," he said, as if he were making an anthropological observation. He barely looked at her, his head continuing to turn from side to side, as if he were searching for someone or maybe something. Like a missing statue.

But maybe it was Leonard he was keeping an eye out for, and as I looked past LuAnne's bare shoulder, I saw Leonard lumbering through the crowd, his eyes boring in on her. LuAnne glanced back, aware, I assumed, that he was on her trail. She hooked her arm through Mr. Kessler's and said, "Let's get closer to the music, Arthur. Who knows? We might decide to dance a little."

My eyes rolled back just the least little bit as they moved away. LuAnne could go overboard on occasion, and this looked to be one of them. I saw Leonard change course and continue to follow the wife he'd discarded and now wanted back. At the same time, I caught a glimpse of Granny Wiggins over by the tent, tapping her foot in time to the music. I stretched a little to see if Etta Mae was near her—we really needed to talk now—but all I saw was Thurlow Jones doing a buck dance, so I quit looking.

"Oh, Julia," Emma Sue said, giving in to a quiet crying fit, "I'm so embarrassed."

"I am, too," I said, seeing LuAnne give Mr. Kessler a slight bump with her hip. "Oh, you mean the dress. Don't let it concern you, Emma Sue. It happens all the time, especially at large gatherings. Nobody'll think a thing about it."

We both knew that was untrue, but what are good manners, except a lot of pretense? You compliment the hostess when you can hardly get her food down your throat and when you think her home has had the worst decorating job in town and when you know you've never seen a tackier outfit on anybody. You save up what you really think for when you get home.

"I think I'll go inside," Emma Sue said. "Maybe no one will notice if LuAnne stays out here. Besides, Tina's going to sing "Ah, Sweet Mystery of Life," and I want to hear that."

Well, Lord, I didn't, so I said, "I'll just mingle out here a while and wait for Sam to get through helping Robert. Come find us, Emma Sue, when you're ready, and eat with us."

She gave me a grateful, but teary, smile and moved toward the house. I moved out to continue my reconnaissance of the yard, edging around and peering into clusters of people, speaking but not stopping, as I searched for Etta Mae and Poochie Dunn. One thing was certain, there would be no great and wonderful unveiling of

Lady Justice at the soiree. She had to stay under wraps for the foreseeable future or one or more of us would end up in jail. And with Arthur Kessler so determined to catch a thief, even the Atlanta pen wasn't out of the question.

Chapter 45

~◦⊙◦~

As I slipped along the outer edge of the lawn toward the heavily planted area that hid the tool shed and the potting shed, Japanese lanterns hanging from the trees begin to twinkle all across the yard. Dusk had crept upon us and, instead of subduing the merriment, the fall of darkness seemed to increase it. And the crowd had increased as well. I began to despair of ever finding either Etta Mae or Poochie until we were all three rounded up and shackled together.

"Hey! Miss Julia!"

I turned to see Etta Mae wiggling her

way through the crowd, a big frown on her face but not much on the rest of her. Sundresses must've been the fashion choice for this event, for she had on the skimpiest one yet. Tight and short and black, her dress and what it revealed had eyes following her as she made her way to me. One thing, though, her dress had straps, but they were so tiny and thin that I would've never depended on them for heavy-duty work. Regardless of her dress, though, I was relieved of half my burden of worry to see her.

"Oh, Etta Mae," I said with relief. "I've been looking all over for you. Have you seen Poochie?"

"No, but I've seen Arthur Kessler." Her face darkened and her eyes squinched up, glinting with fire. "From a distance, which is where he better stay. I'm watching him like a hawk, and if he even looks at Granny, I'm gonna have his hide. You know what he did?"

"Yes, I do. But I didn't know you did."

"Granny told me. She said he drove out to see her this morning and tried to talk her into selling the farm. Can you believe that? And after I told him to leave her alone.

When I picked her up for the party, she was so upset she could hardly talk, her hands were just shaking. He told her she was too old to keep the place up, and it was already so run down it wasn't worth anything. He said it was dangerous for her to be living alone and she'd be better off in a rest home. And, on top of that, he offered her a hundred thousand dollars and I *know* it's worth more than that."

"Really! I can't believe he'd be so crass." I paused and thought about it. "Well, yes, I can, too. But listen, Etta Mae, that's not all he's done. He's gone back on his word after telling me plain as day that the town could have that statue. Now he's claiming that it's been stolen and he's reported it to the police."

Etta Mae's eyes bugged out. "You don't mean it!"

"I do, indeed. I just saw him and he is livid. We've got to find Poochie and get that thing hidden. And warn him not to say a word. Lord, Etta Mae, I don't want to be arrested for theft. Well, for anything, really. You think we ought to give it back?"

"No way!" Etta Mae said with an emphatic shake of her head. "You know he won't take care of it. He'll destroy it just to prove he can do whatever he wants. And to keep us from having it, which he'll do since he thinks we're thieves."

"My feeling exactly. So what should we do?"

"I'll tell you what I'd *like* to do." Etta Mae laughed a little, but there was little humor in it. "I'd like to do what Granny did. She took a broom to him and ran him off. And I," she declared with a great heave of her bosom, "*I* am ready to take him *down*."

"First things first, Etta Mae," I said, trying to divert all that ferocity into more productive avenues now that we were in agreement to keep the statue out of Mr. Kessler's destructive hands. "We have to find Poochie, take possession of the statue and get it hidden. And keep it hidden for as long as it takes, which is as long as Arthur's in town. One of these days, he'll be gone and we can bring it out. Then Poochie can take credit for saving it. But we have to find him first."

"He should've been here by now, though I guess it's a good thing he hasn't already come prancing in carrying that statue. With Mr. Kessler on the warpath, there'd be you-know-what to pay." She stretched up on her tiptoes to scan the crowd for Poochie. "He won't just not show up. He's counting on that new truck."

"New used, Etta Mae. Let's not give him any ideas. But what'll we do if he doesn't come?"

She twisted her mouth, giving it some thought. "I guess I'm more concerned with what we'll do if he *does*. I mean, where're we going to hide it tonight?"

"I'm thinking Mildred's potting shed. It's off the beaten path and she doesn't use it anymore. Come on, I'll show you." I took her arm and led her onto a narrow, winding path behind a row of hemlocks that lined the far edge of Mildred's lawn. We eased farther away from the festivities and into the dark. Brushing aside honeysuckle tendrils and making one last turn, we emerged onto a small clearing. Right in front of us was a miniature house almost covered with ivy. Carriage lamps, flickering with gaslight, were on each side of the door.

"Mildred doesn't do much potting," I whispered. "She had this built when she first joined the garden club, then sort of lost interest in dirt."

"It's so cute," Etta Mae said. "It looks like a dollhouse."

"Well, cute or not, let's just hope it's not locked. And not stacked full of manure and fertilizer, either."

The sounds of revelry had diminished behind us, muffled by the dense growth we'd pushed through. The little house was so secluded that I felt I had to whisper, even though the party seemed far away. It was the perfect place to hide Lady Justice until her final destination could be determined. And that, as long as Arthur was around, could be a long time coming.

"Try the door, Etta Mae," I said, looking around to be sure we were alone. "I'll keep a lookout."

She walked over and turned the doorknob, giving the door a push. It opened about an inch and stuck. "It's open, but it won't open. All the way, I mean."

I joined her and leaned my shoulder against the door. "At least it's not locked. Let's push together."

Well, we got it open, but it wasn't easy, reassuring me that the shed was not often used. There was just enough light for us to make out the work benches along two

walls with old pots and the occasional garden implement scattered on them. And
sure enough, under the benches were bags
of foul-smelling organic material stored for
future use.

"This is perfect, Etta Mae," I said. "We
can lay her on those bags under the bench,
and nobody'll be the wiser. If Poochie ever
shows up. Maybe we'd better go look for
him again."

Etta Mae followed me outside, saying, "I
want to check on Granny, too, though I
guess I ought to be more worried about
Mr. Kessler. No telling what she'll do if he
mentions selling again."

"Surely he has more sense than to ac-
cost her here. Let's take a few more minutes to look for Poochie. I can't rest until
that statue is out of his hands and hidden
away. And it has to be done tonight, because I can't have him showing up at my
house tomorrow and dumping it on me."

As we looked for the return path, she
said, "Now tell me again why we're doing
this?"

"Why, Etta Mae, all three of us are in
danger of going to jail. According to Arthur,
we're thieves. I don't want an arrest on my

record, or on yours, either, and he's furious enough to push it as far as he can. He'd take great pleasure in seeing whoever has the statue behind bars. And I've just been elected president of the Lila Mae Harding Sunday School. Can you imagine?" I paused as a shudder ran across my shoulders at the thought. "And you wouldn't believe the uproar it would cause if Sam and Lillian and Hazel Marie knew what I'd been up to. And Lloyd, too, to say nothing of Mr. Pickens. Just think about it. Climbing up to the highest point in Abbot County and being shot at comes close to being the most unlikely thing I've ever done. If it got out, I'd be bandied around town as having lost all sense of decorum and perspective. Besides," I went on, "I sort of promised Sam I'd never endanger life and limb again, which as you know I went right ahead and did, and, according to that Indian giver, Arthur Kessler, I've become a thief in the process."

"Oh," she said, ducking under a branch. Then she came to a halt. "Wait, I have an idea. Why don't we walk toward Jefferson Street before we go back to the party and see if Poochie's truck is there?"

I immediately swerved to the right and took off down a wider path, wondering why I hadn't thought of it myself. "We should've done this in the first place. There's a gate in Mildred's brick wall somewhere down here. It's where Robert has supplies unloaded."

We found the gate and slipped through it onto the sidewalk behind the house, seeing lines of guest cars parked on both sides of the street just as they were on Polk. Once we were free of the bushes and trees in the yard, I could see more clearly by the streetlights at each end of the block and a few house lights across the street.

"Walk down that way, Etta Mae," I said, "and see if you see his truck. I'll go this way and we'll meet on the other side of the street."

She nodded and left. I set off, too, grateful for the tall brick wall at the back of Mildred's property. No one at the soiree would be able to see me. Nonetheless, I hurried past, looking intently for a listing and rusted-out pickup that was Lady Justice's temporary chariot.

Crossing the street at the corner and

heading for the middle of the block, I saw Etta Mae running toward me. "He's here," she panted as we met. "He parked down at the end on a yellow line. He got the instructions wrong and thought he was supposed to wait in the truck." She grinned. "He says he's about to starve to death, smelling that barbecue and not being able to have any."

"Well, he can hold his horses a while longer," I said, striking off with her. "We could've already been through with it if he'd done what he was told."

And wouldn't you know, there he was, grinning as he leaned against the side of his truck, waiting for us. No telling who had seen him, either, since he'd parked directly under a streetlight.

"I was about to give up on you," he said, pushing himself upright. "And go on and get myself some of that barbecue."

"We were waiting on you," I said sharply, "but never mind that now. Let's get the statue out and under cover as quickly as we can. Poochie, you get up in the bed and hand her down."

He hopped up and spent some nerve-racking time fiddling with something. When my patience had about worn thin, he lifted the statue and slid it over the tailgate. Etta Mae and I grabbed hold and brought her down, completely wrapped in the drop cloth.

"My word," I said, marveling at Poochie's sense of modesty. "I didn't expect her to be in a shroud, but that's very sensitive of you, Poochie. Are you sure she's in this thing?"

"That's her, all right. You meet anybody, they won't know what you got."

Yes, I thought, *they'll just think we're moving a body,* but I said, "Come on, Etta Mae, grab your end and let's get going. Poochie, you can go on and eat, but not a word to anybody, you hear? I'll get with you on Monday to look at trucks."

"Oh, I'll jus' go on with you," he said with that inane smile. "I ain't in that big of a hurry."

"Well, listen, Poochie, there's been a change of plans. At first we were going to let you take all the credit for saving the statue since it was all your doing from start to finish."

"It was?"

"Yes, I mean, no, but we wanted you to

be the hero. But now we have a big problem. Mr. Kessler is saying that we stole the
statue, but he doesn't know it was us. So
we not only have to hide this thing, we
can't let anyone know that we know anything about it. You understand?"

"Sure," he said around what appeared
to be an uncomprehending smile. "Just
make out like I don't know nothing."

"That's it, exactly. Now let's get this thing
hidden."

Looking both ways and seeing no one, I
lifted the head end of the statue and pulled
Etta Mae across Jefferson and through
the gate into the yard, Poochie right behind us. Ducking under some hemlock
branches and noting how dark it was along
the path, I hurried toward the potting shed.

As I rounded a curve in the path, enter-
ing the small clearing in front of the shed, I
saw the flare of a match or the flash of
some kind of light inside. I came to an
abrupt halt.

Etta Mae didn't and Lady Justice almost
shot through my grasp.

"Hold up, Etta Mae," I whispered. "There's
somebody in the shed." I crouched down
and felt her do the same.

"Who is it?" she whispered back.

"I don't know. Two people, I think."

Poochie duckwalked up close. "I bet it's somebody doin' what they ought not be doin'," he said with a soft laugh.

The last thing I wanted was to come up on a pair of secret lovers. What other people do is no business of mine, except now that we were so close, it would be interesting to know who they were.

"Sh-h-h, let's get out of sight." I began to creep toward a clump of boxwoods near the shed, drawing the statue and Etta Mae along with me. "Maybe they'll leave in a few minutes."

They didn't. They kept talking and, as we huddled together beside the shed, Etta Mae started flipping the statue over. Before I knew it, she had the four of us—me, Poochie, herself and Lady Justice— covered with the heavy drop cloth.

"Camouflage," she whispered.

Lord, it was hot under there, and smelly, too. No telling where that canvas had been, or Poochie, either. Then, glancing sharply at Etta Mae, even though I couldn't see her, my mouth opened in surprise. I recognized one of the voices.

Arthur Kessler was laying down the law to somebody, although his voice was hushed and I could only pick up a few words. ". . . you responsible," he said. "You brought me in, and now I need . . . for the next payment . . . minimum down to demolish . . ."

Another voice, pleading, almost whining, whispered back, "It wasn't me . . . . He brought me in, too."

"I don't care. What do you think's . . . that pile of bricks? You get Stroud back here any way you can, or I'm going to . . ."

"But, Arthur . . ."

I clamped my hand over my mouth to muffle a gasp. It was Horace Allen who was doing the pleading. And being threatened, too. Their footsteps shuffled on the floor of the shed and more whispered words drifted out as they headed for the open door.

I clamped down on Etta Mae's arm and scrooched lower under the drop cloth.

The whispering men stepped outside and stopped. I could've reached out and touched one of them. But I didn't. I tried to make myself smaller, sensing the tension between them.

"Listen, Arthur," Horace said, barely above a whisper, "he's got the money. Mine, too, remember, and nobody knows where he is, much less me. How am I supposed to find him?"

"You get this and you get it good," Arthur Kessler said. "I've put the last cent I'm putting into this venture, and as far as I'm concerned what's left of the courthouse can just sit there. The county can repossess it. I didn't sign on to be investigated by the FBI. I'm getting out." I heard him move away, then, as if turning back, he said, "And one more thing. Nobody knows that you and Stroud were backing me, and it better stay that way. So you keep your mouth shut."

"But, Arthur, it's me that'll be left holding the bag. If you leave and they don't find Stroud, what'll I do?"

"That's your problem. The whole town's crazy, anyway."

"Wait. Wait, don't leave," Horace said, trying to whisper but not quite making it. "What're you going to do?"

There was a moment of silence when it seemed that Mr. Kessler wasn't going to answer. Then he said with an immoderate tone of self-assurance. "First, I'm getting some investors I can trust, not that it's any of your business. Then I'm putting in a golf course on some county property I've found. You and Stroud can take care of your-selves."

Etta Mae's hand dug into my shoulder so tightly that I almost yelped. "Granny's farm!" she hissed.

We heard the swish of branches as one or the other of them strode off toward the soiree. I heard Horace's voice recede as he followed, pleading, "But, Arthur," one more time, but I could find no compassion in my heart for him. I flung off the canvas camouflage and rose from our hiding place, filled with an outrage like I'd never felt before. My strategy had worked, all right—Arthur was fed up with the town and was scrapping plans for a high-rise—but a lot of good it was doing me. There he went, blithely walking away from the mess he'd created on Main Street. He would be gone, as I'd wanted, but so was our historic court-house. It was a bitter pill to swallow, and I was nearly choking on it. But my outrage was nothing like Etta Mae's. I could sense the fury building up in her as she sprang to her feet and started after them.

"Wait, Etta Mae," I said, stumbling after her. "Let's hide this thing first, then we'll get him. He won't get away."

She barely slowed down. "You better believe he won't."

I took off down the path behind her, calling back over my shoulder, "Take care of the statue, Poochie." My heart was pounding as I slipped between the bushes that crowded the path, anxious to catch Etta Mae before she publicly flew into Arthur Kessler. He'd wanted to see the natives in their natural habitat, but, believe me, when one of our natives gets up a head of steam, he'd see a lot more than he wanted. Just read the police reports in the *Abbotsville Times*.

Chapter 46

❧

Etta Mae slung branches and vines right and left as she did her best to run down the path. I had no trouble keeping up with her since she was somewhat hobbled by the tight dress she was wearing. As we neared the party, the sounds of laughter and bright voices and the Crooked River Boys playing "Country Roads" got louder. Etta Mae stopped where the path opened onto the lawn and, eyes blazing, surveyed the crowd.

I popped out beside her on the edge of the broad lawn, lit up now with candles on the table, lanterns in the trees and a lot of strategically placed landscape lights. People were swarming all over the grounds, and I had to stretch and strain, trying to find Arthur Kessler.

"Hold on, Etta Mae," I said, panting heavily. "Let's report him to somebody. Maybe to the commissioners or the FBI, if we can find them, but to somebody who'll stop him before he defaults on the courthouse and leaves town."

"I'm not studying the courthouse right now," she said, her ample bosom heaving with built-up anger. "I'm studying that sorry, underhanded idiot who thinks he can put Granny in a home and a golf course on her place. I'm gonna fix him good."

I was doing a little heaving, too, from my exertions on the path. "No, Etta Mae, don't do that," I said, fearing she'd end up in jail for public brawling before they got around to booking her for theft. "Let's go find the commissioners and tell them he's the mastermind who inveigled two prominent businessmen to steal and who was given permission to destroy an Abbot County landmark before paying in full and who's now about to slip out of town, leaving us with the ruins. They'll stop him."

"Look!" she suddenly screeched. "Look at that!" She ignored my effort to calm her down, pointing a rigid finger at a spot near the tent where a mass of people were dancing.

I craned my neck to see what she was looking at. "What?"

"Arthur Kessler and *Boyce*! They're talking!" And she hiked up her skirt which, short as it was, didn't have far to go, and took off running, her bare limbs twinkling in the dusk. "I'm putting a stop to that right now!"

"Wait, Etta Mae!" I called, but she didn't have waiting in mind. So I hiked up my long skirt an inch or so and plunged into the crowd after her. We drew more than a little attention as we threaded our way through clumps of people, many of whom stopped midbite to watch us pass.

Etta Mae came to a puffing stop right between Boyce and Arthur Kessler. She had to wait a minute to catch her breath, but then she lit into her uncle.

"Boyce Wiggins!" she said. "What do you think you're doing? I'll fight you tooth and nail before I let you sell Granny's place. Don't you know Arthur Kessler's a *devel-*

oper? Don't you know what he's done down on Main Street, which, if you don't know it, he's planning to run out on? You want him leaving a mess like that next door to you? And if you think you're putting Granny in a home, you better think again because she's staying right where she is. And you!" she screamed, rounding on Mr. Kessler, "I told you once and I'm not telling you again! Granny's not selling! You hear me? Nobody's selling anything to you in this town."

I had stopped a little behind her by this time, having been somewhat hindered by a lack of stamina. Noticing the amazed faces that I'd passed, turning first toward the Wiggins scene, then back to me and beyond, I looked back, too. There was Poochie, Lady Justice bouncing under his arm, the drop cloth snagged on her sword and trailing along behind him.

"Dad blame it!" Poochie said, tripping on the canvas and catching himself before he fell. "What you want me to do with this thing? I got to eat sometime or 'nother."

"Poochie, for goodness' sake!" I said, turning him back. "I told you to hide it. Get it out of here before Mr. Kessler sees it."

But it was too late. Mr. Kessler had seen it and he was plowing through the crowd, ignoring Etta Mae as he pushed people aside right and left.

Etta Mae whirled away from Boyce and took out after Mr. Kessler, screeching, "You get back here! I'm not through with you!"

But Mr. Kessler had his eyes on the prize. He ran up, snatched the statue from Poochie and clasped it to his bosom. "This is mine! Where'd you get it?"

"Off the dome," Poochie said, snatching it back. "Where you think?"

"You stole it!" Mr. Kessler yelled, scrabbling and reaching for the statue as Poochie held on, evading each grab.

I was screaming, "Wait, wait!" as spectators edged in closer.

Etta Mae popped through, took Mr. Kessler by the arm, none too gently, and whirled him around. At the sight of her blazing eyes, he raised his hands to ward her off.

"Nobody stole anything," she screamed, "except you! That statue belongs to the town because you didn't pay a red cent for it." She turned, aware now of the crowd eagerly listening. "You know where he was

getting the money to put up his luxury condominiums? From Assured Estate Planners, that's where. *Your* money!" Murmurs
swept through the crowd, and Etta Mae
got up a fresh head of steam. "And now,
he thinks he can run my granny off her
place and put her in a *rest home* just so he
can ruin something else!"

Figuring now was as good a time as
any, I stepped up. "And see this?" I pointed
to the statue. "Stand her up, Poochie. This
is all that's left of our beautiful courthouse."
I glared at Arthur Kessler. "It's because of
you that it's standing here on the ground
instead of way up in the sky where it belongs. You gave it to us, and we're keeping
it. And now you're trying to take off and
not even clean up after yourself."

"He better not take off!" a loud voice
called out from the crowd. "My wrecking
crew's not been paid. I'll slap a lien on him
so fast he won't know what hit him."

"Wait your turn," I snapped, then faced
Mr. Kessler again. "I, for one, don't care if
your Crowne Plaza never gets built. I hope
it doesn't. But there's a pile of rubble to be
removed and a gazebo to be replaced and
landscaping to be reinstalled. And you're

going to do it. The garden club beautified those grounds once, and we're not going to do it again."

"I should say not," Mildred bellowed. And a number of other garden club members added their agreement.

Mr. Kessler's head twisted from side to side, but he was surrounded by Abbotsvillians who didn't take too kindly to developers who quit before the job was done.

But that didn't stop him from trying to talk his way around them. "No problem," he said, drawing himself up as he glanced around at the crowd. "We'll work something out. I just need a little time to get my investors in line."

"Investors!" I yelled, stung almost beyond words. "You know who his investors were? You, me and everybody else who gave money to Richard Stroud. It was *our* money that destroyed the courthouse, and it was going to be *our* money that built a monstrosity on Main Street." I could hardly speak I was so mad and so dizzy from turning back and forth, addressing first the crowd and then Mr. Kessler. "But Richard Stroud had other plans, didn't he? He left you with a problem, and now you want to leave us with one. Well, we won't stand for it."

An elbow suddenly pushed me aside as Granny Wiggins wiggled out of the crowd and stomped up to Mr. Kessler. "You come in here wantin' to buy me out? Well, I got news for you, Buster. You might could pull the wool over the eyes of these city folks," she said, swinging her arm around at the crowd, "but you don't fool me. My advice is for you to get a shovel and start movin' that mess you made."

People began to push in closer, threatening mayhem as angry shouts rose from several directions. Coleman and Mr. Pickens stepped up, and just in time, too. "What's the problem?" Coleman asked, standing foursquare in front of Mr. Kessler. Mr. Pickens stood beside him, and between those two forces of law and order, Mr. Kessler was going to have to answer for his deeds.

Eager to reestablish themselves in the town's favor, several commissioners began demanding to know what he planned to do. Coleman was a sworn law officer, but Mr. Pickens, being privately employed, didn't have the authority of the sheriff. But at the sudden appearance of two of the previously unidentified gentlemen, they both stepped aside.

I heard the gray-suited men mention Richard Stroud's name to Mr. Kessler, then they each took an elbow and began to move him out. I had no doubt he was in for a night of intense questioning as a person of interest in the case. They might've wanted Richard Stroud, but I expect they could make do with Arthur Kessler. As they turned him away, somebody lobbed a half-eaten barbecued rib over my head. It landed on Arthur's shoulder and made a nasty stain on his fine linen jacket. I think Thurlow did it. I wouldn't put it past him.

Watching as Arthur Kessler protested his innocence, repeating over and over to the stone-faced men on each side that he was a victim of Richard Stroud's machinations as much as anybody, I just shook my head. *Good riddance to bad rubbish,* I thought, and wished the same applied to a certain block on Main Street.

"Hey, Miss Julia," Poochie said, all of a sudden standing right behind me. "What you want me to do with this thing? I'm tired of luggin' it around."

"Put it down, Poochie," I said, "for goodness' sake. And quit following me."

With Mr. Kessler now in safe hands, the crowd immediately turned its attention to the flaking and folded statue that had followed me all over the yard. Poochie, looking proud and smiling importantly in the spotlight, had her standing up with his arm around her.

"This," I said, sweeping my hand toward the statue, "is what's left of our courthouse."

"Yeah," Etta Mae chimed in, "and you wouldn't even have that if it wasn't for Mi . . . me and Poochie Dunn. But mostly Poochie."

I'll tell you the truth, Lady Justice made a mighty poor showing, even in the soft glow of Japanese lanterns. Both arms were still folded from the time we'd shoved her through the trapdoor. The scales she held were wrapped across the hilt of her sword, and as Poochie swung her around for everybody to see, the sword caught on Granny Wiggins's dress, lifting it up above her knees.

She jumped back, swatting at it and tugging her dress down. "Get that thing away from me!"

"It's okay, Granny," Etta Mae said. "It's okay. Keep it still, Poochie, and help me straighten out the arms."

With no base to rest on, Lady Justice kept tilting over, but Poochie held her while Etta Mae and I pulled her arms away from her body in a semblance of her original position. But not without a lot of flaking off and not without a constant inclination to topple over sideways.

"I'll fix that," Poochie said. He took the sword and straightened it enough for the tip to enter the ground and hold her up. He stepped back to admire the result. There she stood, her scales held aloft but the rest of her listing to the side, like an old woman leaning on a cane.

People began to push closer, examining and admiring the listing, flaking statue. Then Latisha's shrill little voice piped up. "Great-Granny, that lady's just about nekkid."

"Oh, my goodness," Emma Sue Ledbetter said, as she pulled the stole from her shoulders and draped it across Lady Justice, hiding the one bare breast. "There. Now she's decent." And, with a hike of her slipping sundress, she melted back into the crowd.

"Julia," Sam said, coming up behind me and putting a strong arm around my waist. "I think we need to talk."

Before I could answer, Etta Mae popped up beside him, "Oh, Mr. Sam," she said, her eyes shining, "isn't it wonderful what Poochie did! He got her down for us. It was Miss Julia's idea, but Poochie got 'er done. I mean, down. We just watched from the sidelines."

"That's right," I said, looking Sam right in the eye, for Etta Mae had said not one word of untruth. "We owe Poochie a debt of gratitude."

"And a new . . ." he started, but Etta Mae turned him on his heel and, with her hands on his back, marched him off into the crowd.

Mildred pushed her way into the circle surrounding the statue, then stopped in admiration. "My goodness, it's Lady Justice right here on my lawn. How appropriate. Now she can rule over the festivities."

"Why, Mildred," I said, "that's a grand idea. We can say that justice has prevailed, can't we?" Then remembering the loss of our courthouse and, at the same time, catching sight of Horace, standing palely—having witnessed Arthur's comeuppance—but safely, behind her, I added. "Generally speaking, that is."

Chapter 47

Loretta Tillman, who was the society editor for the *Abbotsville Times* back when it had a society page, would've written up the soiree in her column and ended it with the words, "and a good time was had by all." But that's not my way. Oh, we had a good time for the rest of the evening—I even danced several numbers with Sam even though he was about asleep on his feet from staying up all night. Dancing is not exactly my cup of tea, but it was better than standing around listening to the speculations about Arthur Kessler's arrest or detention or whatever it was. He'd probably

get off scot-free, according to Sam, because, unlike Richard, he'd not stolen anything and, in fact, had been left holding
the bag like so many others of us.

But contrary to Loretta's generalized
endings, I like to know the details and I
expect you do, too, or you wouldn't have
gotten this far. So here they are.

LuAnne was not only mortified, but *hurt,*
at Arthur's shameful departure in the care
of federal agents. "He fooled me, Julia,"
she told me later. "He led me on, making
me believe he was so cosmopolitan and
so sophisticated. And all along, he was
nothing but a crook." Then she got a mushy
look on her face. "Well, like I always say,
home is where the heart is, and one in the
hand is worth two in the bush. And now
that Leonard's home, and happy to be
there, mind you, it's all worked out for the
best. Still," she said longingly, "it was fun
while it lasted."

Mildred and Horace have settled back
into their former roles: She demands and
he hops to. She tells anyone who'll listen
that she's forgiven him for throwing her

money away and for making her plan a funeral that never came about, but every now and then she laments, in a joking way, the loss of her shooting skills. "I used to be a crack shot," she's said on more than one occasion. "I really need to practice more." Horace always jumps up and offers a pillow for her back or some other helpful ministration. I think they're happy together. Well, *she's* happy. I don't know about him, but he's still around catering to her every wish.

Helen Stroud divorced Richard so fast it must've made his head swim. I guess he didn't care, though, because the word around town is that he's on a South Sea island somewhere, having never been brought to justice. But I'm a firm believer that your sins will find you out, and sooner or later he'll get his.

After the dust settled, Helen had lost her lovely home to help reimburse those who'd lost more than that. She ended up in a small condominium—not built by Arthur Kessler, I assure you—and continues in all her offices because we keep electing her. I'm happy to report also that her strength of character has reasserted itself and she's come to understand that my husband has more important business to tend to than hers. We're still friends, but I keep a close watch on them both.

I still laugh when I recall what Latisha said when Poochie first stood Lady Justice up in Mildred's yard. Everybody had pushed in close to see and touch the statue, although she did look strange with her arms bent the way they were. Latisha took a good, hard look at her and said, "Why that woman got her arms wrapped around like that? She cold?"

And speaking of Lady Justice, the garden club has bitten the bullet and made plans for a town park on the site of the old courthouse—just as soon as all the lawsuits are settled and Mr. Kessler is forced to remove the remains. We'll have our gazebo back and all the plantings, which will be laid out along formal pathways with benches to provide rest for the weary. Lady Justice will be the focal point of the park, although Greg Rogers, the landscape designer we engaged, almost disengaged us because a certain contingent kept insisting on a burbling fountain as the centerpiece, relegating Lady Justice to a lesser spot. You can imagine how that went over with me, after what I'd gone through to get her. But the plan is fixed now, drawn and voted on, awaiting only the clearing of the rubble. I'm pleased with it, so you know how the design turned out.

Then we had another problem with Lavinia Markham, who got exercised over the statue's indecent exposure of one breast. "It's just stuck out there," she said, "for everybody to see, and I, for one, think it gives the wrong impression of our town. Why, who knows? It could encourage massage parlors and tattoo artists and all sorts of unsavory things."

Emma Sue thought we should keep a scarf draped over the offending shoulder, but was voted down when somebody remarked that it would resemble a wet T-shirt contest whenever it rained.

Finally, some of the garden club members volunteered to keep a garland of flowers or greenery—depending on the season—around the statue's neck and arrange it artfully enough to prevent shock

and overstimulation in any close observers.

And continuing to speak of Lady Justice, when Brother Vern heard that she is
to be installed in the center of the park,
half a block from the Hallelujah House, he
was fit to be tied. He showed up at a Board
of Commissioners meeting, took the microphone and proceeded to rant for thirty
minutes about the audacity of putting up a
false idol in our midst. "How am I gonna
preach the word of God," he'd bellowed,
"with that heathen woman holdin' forth on
the courthouse grounds?" Of course, she'd
been holding forth *above* the courthouse
grounds for a hundred years or more,
which hadn't seemed to bother him. He
had to be restrained from going another
half an hour.

After the meeting, as he stormed out
still full of righteous indignation and threatening to sue the county for sponsoring a
pagan religion, I'd walked alongside him
for a ways.

"Brother Vern," I'd said softly so as not
to be overheard, "if you look closely at that

statue, you'll notice a tiny hole in her left shoulder. It's hardly noticeable because she's so flaky, but it can be pointed out. It's just about the size of a BB shot, and you know they're still looking for whoever discharged a firearm in the city. If I were you, I'd get over this concern about paganism in the park and concentrate on what you heard from on high."

I thought he'd burst wide open, he was so filled with outrage and sudden understanding. After he got his mouth closed, he turned on his heel and stalked off. We didn't hear another word on the subject from him, but he's still preaching and occasionally casting a few aspersions at people who pretend to speak for the Lord. I don't let it worry me, but if Lady Justice ever comes up missing, I'll know where to look.

Pastor Ledbetter still rules the roost across the street. Oh, he went to Raleigh, as I understand it, and met with the session of that new church. From what Emma Sue told me, he laid bare his soul, telling them of the burden of having a suddenly unsubmissive wife who was suffering through the change of life—which was the wrong tack to take since Emma Sue was long past that, as anybody who could count would know. Apparently he expected them to take pity and welcome his solitary self with the open arms of fellowship. That didn't happen. His brothers in Christ went into a closed meeting, then retracted their call, telling him, as he'd often told us, that any man who couldn't control his own family had no business running a church. So he's back home, and still expostulating from our pulpit. He recently gave a series of sermons on woman's place in God's plan for the world, but I didn't listen. He'd given those sermons several times before, so you'd think he'd have learned better by now. I think the latest series was aimed specifically at Emma Sue, but she was probably tired of hearing it, too. I know on at least one Sunday when we were streaming out of the church, she handed me a list of possible candidates for the offices of the Women of the Church in the next election. "I know I shouldn't have done this during the sermon," she whispered, "but I thought I'd better jot them down while they were on my mind."

I should say something about Etta Mae Wiggins. That young woman has proven herself a worthy companion in so many ways, and I'm ashamed of myself for thinking so little of her in the past. One can't help how one was raised, but the virtues of dependability and courage and willingness to help can outweigh one's lack of social graces. Besides, social graces can be learned, whereas one either has integrity or one doesn't. And she does.

Mayor Outz has been hinting around for the park to be named for him—he suggested a plaque at the foot of Lady Justice with his name on it—but I'm putting a stop to that. In the first place, it doesn't need a name. The courthouse park is what we're already calling it, and that's the way it'll stay. And in the second place, if it's named for anybody, it should be called the Etta Mae Wiggins Park or the Poochie Dunn Park, but there's no way I could publicly justify either one without giving away my own participation. I've said a dozen times in Sam's hearing—I'd never tell him a direct story—that I don't know exactly how or why Poochie took it on himself to rescue that statue.

And Sam? Well, Sam is the same, thank goodness. I'm not a person who likes change, especially in a husband. If you start out with one who's kind and considerate and even-tempered and who doesn't demand an accounting of what you do every minute of the day, you have every right to expect him to stay that way. And that's Sam, straight up and down.

I must admit, though, that on occasion he'll give me a long, thoughtful look. But only when that statue is brought up in conversation, which I try to do as infrequently as possible.

Oh, I forgot to mention that Poochie got his truck. He settled on a red 2003 Ford Ranger 4X4, loaded with an extended cab—whatever all that means. The price was a little steeper than I'd had in mind to pay, but Poochie proved to be a bit sharper than we'd given him credit for. When I'd tried to steer him to something more in line

with my thinking, he'd given me that innocent smile and asked, "You ever tell Mr.
Sam how you climb up on that dome?"

I turned him right around, saying, "Let's
not look any further, Poochie. I think that
Ford Ranger is the truck for you."

So he's happy and so am I, now that
he's out of my hair, and I intend to devote
myself from now on to easing any concerns that Sam might have. A virtuous
woman is more precious than rubies, you
know, and being virtuous in all my works
is what I aim for. Just as long as nobody
steals from me like Richard Stroud did or
causes an upheaval of the town like Arthur
Kessler did or shoots at me like . . . Well,
there are times when even a decorous and
retiring woman has to take on the whole
town, if need be, and use all the faculties
at her disposal to see that justice does indeed prevail.